M. L. WHITE

Shifter Prophecy

First published by White Wolf Publishing LLC 2025

Copyright © 2025 by M. L. White

All rights reserved. No part of this publication may be reproduced, stored or transmitted in any form or by any means, electronic, mechanical, photocopying, recording, scanning, or otherwise without written permission from the publisher. It is illegal to copy this book, post it to a website, or distribute it by any other means without permission.

This novel is entirely a work of fiction. The names, characters and incidents portrayed in it are the work of the author's imagination. Any resemblance to actual persons, living or dead, events or localities is entirely coincidental.

M. L. White asserts the moral right to be identified as the author of this work.

M. L. White has no responsibility for the persistence or accuracy of URLs for external or third-party Internet Websites referred to in this publication and does not guarantee that any content on such Websites is, or will remain, accurate or appropriate.

Designations used by companies to distinguish their products are often claimed as trademarks. All brand names and product names used in this book and on its cover are trade names, service marks, trademarks and registered trademarks of their respective owners. The publishers and the book are not associated with any product or vendor mentioned in this book. None of the companies referenced within the book have endorsed the book.

Second edition

ISBN (paperback): 9798899713323
ISBN (hardcover): 9798899715051

Cover art by SeventhStar Art

This book was professionally typeset on Reedsy.
Find out more at reedsy.com

To my sister Hannah,
For all the love and support
and late night book discussions.
Thank you for everything!
- M

Contents

Shanely	1
Bastian	18
Shanely	29
Shanely	52
Shanely	59
Bastian	67
Shanely	74
Bastian	93
Shanely	98
Bastian	106
Shanely	112
Bastian	119
Shanely	126
Shanely	132
Bastian	143
Bastian	153
Shanely	174
Shanely	198
Shanely	216
Shanely	225
Shanely	231
Shanely	243
Shanely	252
Bastian	271
Shanely	277
Series Order	284

Bonus Chapter	286
Bonus Chapter	293
About the Author	303

Shanely

"Mommy! It's time to go!" Aerith, my fearless four year old, shouted by the back door. I quickly threw my hair back into a ponytail before grabbing my shoes.

"I'm coming, sweet pea. Daddy won't leave without us!" I said with a chuckle. Aerith was too excited though to even pay attention.

She looked just like me with bouncing reddish-brown curly hair and grayish eyes. Sadly, Aerith's eyes were just like Peter's. I was hoping I would have passed on my family's trademark green eyes, but it just didn't happen. Aerith still wasn't showing any signs of being a shifter yet which surprised us all. She still smelled like a human too which was disappointing. I wanted her to carry nothing from her biological father over, but Bastian kept insisting we give it more time. I really hoped she'd end up with a wolf or bear. She was my cuddler though and loved to climb up in my lap just to be close.

Having a daughter was the best thing I could of ever done and I was excited to have a little one with Bastian. A mini him would be perfect and I had been thinking about it a lot lately. We've been so busy these last few years that we haven't had the chance to even discuss babies. Plus with all the warnings I had been having, it probably wouldn't be the best time anyways. Patrick, thankfully, moved away shortly after I gave birth to Aerith for some training exercise. I honestly wasn't sure what it was for, nor did I care. Without him here, I got a few peaceful and quiet years being warning free, which was amazing because they hit me like a ton of bricks every time I got one. Sadly, my Uncle heard Patrick was set to return at the end of summer though, so I would have to be careful again. I was dreading the day I had to see Patrick and his stupid smug smile.

I refused to think anymore about it though as today was going to be a good day. We had plans to find my mate for lunch. Bastian had become the official Head to the enforcers for the McCoy Pack, and he ran the training program my Uncles started long ago. Between that and the machine shop he and his brothers ran together, he was really busy. I made sure we always came to the lodge on the days he was here, so we'd get more time together. I followed a bouncing Aerith down the path towards the lodge. She was carefree and oblivious to the world around her, and I loved seeing her free spirit. I also noticed she was running barefoot again. It gave me hope there was some shifter in her after all, if she needed to feel close to the earth and the forest like we did.

I watched her run and play as we made our way to my mate. I couldn't be happier with the life I made for Aerith here in Diablo. Aerith was growing up with the family I always wanted and it made my heart burst with joy that I could give her what I always wished for. She really did have it all. Elijah, Cade, and Caleb were the best uncles to her. Honestly, it was like she had four very different Dads.

Caleb was the worrier and always made sure she was safe and doing alright. Elijah read to her constantly and was the best at getting her to sleep. Cade was the goofball. They were constantly playing or running around getting into mischief. She seemed to get her ornery side from him too, but Bastian was her safety net. Her comfort. If she was scared or hurt, she'd run past them to Bastian every time. Honestly, whenever Bastian came into the room she'd leave whoever she was with to go to him. She's even ditched me to run to her daddy, and while I feigned sadness, my heart honestly melted every time she did. Bastian took the role of fatherhood rather well, like he was destined to be a Dad, despite having a horrible father himself. Aerith was smitten with her Daddy and never once questioned if he really was her biological Dad. He was hers even if not by blood. No one but my immediate circle knew the truth about Aerith's father. It was safer to keep it a secret, and I never wanted to make Bastian feel less than what he was. He was her

Dad and that's all that mattered.

I couldn't forget her Aunt Bay either, who dotes on her constantly, and is always buying her things. I saw the price tags, and it wasn't cheap either! I honestly didn't know where the money was coming from since she was cut off from her father along with her brothers. The only thing I knew they all had left was their trust funds, which couldn't be touched until they were 25, which she wasn't yet. Bay simply waves me off whenever I say anything about it, and I didn't want to offend her or seem ungrateful. Bay and I were becoming closer, and she truly felt like my sister and not just sister-in-law. I loved having girlfriends that I could vent to or shop with. I never really had that before. Between Bay and Alana, I felt like I had close friends with people who really wanted to be my friend too.

The lodge soon came into view, and I scanned the area looking for my mate. As well as meeting my handsome mate for lunch, I also wanted to meet with my Uncle again to try and figure out more about this Tiger King. We haven't heard anything since the two bounty hunters mentioned him wanting me after Derek attacked me in Dead Man's Hollow. None in our pack had ever gone missing either, so we didn't even know there was a bounty on wolves by the mysterious man. So far all my Uncle knew was he was fierce, and had a large streak of tigers southwest of us. My Uncle Cain always kept his distance since tigers were known to be unpredictable and temperamental, but that was the extent of our knowledge and I wanted to know more.

Honestly, I felt like we should know more but I wasn't the Alpha so it wasn't my call. I was definitely okay not having that weighty responsibility, but it made me nervous not knowing what to expect from the Tiger King. No one really even knew what he looked like, and Bastian would never let me ask other shifters about him. He said it was better to keep to our own and leave it be. The Tiger King has never come after us for killing his bounty hunters, and Bastian didn't want to rock the boat so to speak. Which I understood but I felt like I was always looking over my shoulder waiting for his retaliation. I didn't like that feeling.

Now that Aerith wasn't a baby anymore I was ready to start getting more involved with the pack's politics, and what better way to start than to learn about this new possible threat. I wanted to be prepared just in case we ever had to deal with him.

I was lost in my own head when my phone rang, startling me from my thoughts. I answered, "Hello?"

Silence.

I looked back at my phone and all it said was unknown.

I tried speaking again, "Hello?"

I decided to just hang up when no one responded. *Weird*, I thought to myself as I rolled my eyes and shoved my phone back in my pocket. Before I could even begin to worry about it, Aerith bolted to the left all excited.

"Daddy!"

My mate turned and gave us both a big smile, waving hi as we got closer. Bastian had around five wolves still in their human form running laps around the lodge. I assumed they were Bastian's new enforcer recruits, and I watched them make their way around. As we approached the group I noticed my mate looked a little tired today, and I wondered if he stopped by his machine shop before coming here. Sometimes I think he has too much on his plate but he never complains. Ever since Derek's attack, Bastian's shifted his workload to work here at the lodge more than the machine shop, but he still has to go sometimes. Cade and Elijah need help sharing everything, but I wished Bastian didn't do so much all the time. He needed sleep too.

And I *needed* him.

"There are my two favorite girls!"

I had to admit despite looking tired, he looked really good today. He still sported his black fade and short beard like always, and today he was wearing black basketball shorts and a gray sleeveless shirt. Top it all off with a backwards hat, and it was enough to make me weak in the knees.

He picked Aerith up before giving me a kiss.

"We've been apart too long. I was getting anxious," I said as I leaned into him. I watched the group of guys make their way around from the back of the lodge.

"Me too. I don't like being away from you guys," he replied as the group of young men slowed their pace to meet us.

"Hi!" Aerith waved at them all. All the boys smiled and waved, despite being out of breath, which was saying something for a wolf.

"Working them a bit hard, are we?" I asked.

He smiled. "They can handle it."

We all turned to look at the driveway hearing a car coming down the lane. We could hear it long before we could see it although Bastian had a leg up on everyone with his sense of sight. He had spectacular vision and could see way farther than most wolves. He and his brothers were unique as they each split a different sense between them. Bastian had better sight while Cade could hear the best, and Elijah had the better nose. It made their names known among shifters for their tracking skills, and the boys used their skills wisely. The triplets shared a lot of unique abilities.

"Are we expecting anyone?" I asked. He simply shrugged, setting Aerith down. My mate inhaled deeply but didn't give any indication he sensed any danger.

"Aerith. Go play with the guys for a minute, alright?" I told her, and she bounded off to tackle the boys. I had to give it to them. The young enforcers jumped right in to play with her even though they all looked exhausted. It made me appreciate the pack even more.

I heard Bastian swear under his breath pulling my attention to him. He gently pushed me behind him, and I leaned to the left to sneak a peek around his shoulders.

A police car came into view, and I wondered what in the world they were doing here. Bastian was tense, and I tried to see who was driving. I wasn't a full wolf yet, so my shifter abilities were spotty at best unless I was in my bear's form. I had no idea who it was.

Bastian gritted his teeth as his eyes flashed gold. The car came to a stop as Bastian began to push me towards the lodge. *He must be able to see through the tint,* I thought to myself. He muttered to me, "This wasn't scheduled, Shanely. Go inside now. It's not Calvin..."

The car door slammed shut as Patrick stepped out of the vehicle, cutting Bastian off. He wasn't supposed to be back until later this summer, yet here he was in pack lands with my daughter and I well within sight. *Great,* I thought to myself frustrated.

I glanced up at Bastian, and his eyes glossed over slightly. I could hear his hive message through the mind-link requesting anyone near the lodge to make their way to us. Stay out of sight, but nearby. My eyes went to Aerith, who was busy playing, and I gripped my mate's hand. She had left the boys and was rolling around in the grass chasing something. I loved how carefree she was. Aerith was completely oblivious to everything around her, and I hoped she stayed that way.

Another officer stepped out of the vehicle and joined Patrick in front.

"Bastian," Patrick said with a nod.

Bastian studied him for a moment as the other officer shifted on his feet. He looked new, and I didn't recognize him from the normal cops in this town. The new trainees Bastian had been working with could sense a shift in our moods. They stood up alert now, while two stepped closer to Aerith.

"Didn't realize you'd be back so soon, Patrick. What can I do for you, Officers?" Bastian asked with more control than I expected to hear out of him. Patrick's presence just struck a nerve with Bastian, and his wolf was *always* aggressive when he was around.

"Yeah well... I had completed most of my training, and since we had something big come up around here they decided to send me home early. We're on the lookout for a group of individuals that have been running an illegal fighting ring here in town. We've managed to break up a few, and we've arrested some, but we haven't been able to find who's starting them. However, last night we managed to catch a photo by a security camera before the last bust. We've never seen masks like these at the rings before, and I'm wondering if it's the ring leaders," Patrick replied. His fellow officer handed Bastian a photo.

I stepped over slightly to look with Bastian. The photo was dark, and there were at least four people bolting from what looked like a side door in a back alley. All wore animal masks and black hoodies, but the one in front looked very familiar. That one had curly hair and a wolf mask.

"Shanely? It's been a long time, hasn't it? How are you doing, hun?" Patrick asked casually. He stepped forward some, giving me a sly smile. It made my skin crawl the way he looked at me, and I could feel Bastian's anger rise towards the cop. Bastian stuck his arm around me, and I merely nodded my head. I was afraid to trigger another warning by speaking.

"I see you stayed married to a Fenrir then?" Patrick asked, looking at the ring on my finger. "Shame, really."

"That's enough," Bastian interrupted, pulling Patrick's gaze from me.

"Careful, Fenrir. Remember who's the officer now," he snapped back.

Our bond had grown much stronger over the years we've been together, and I could now feel Bastian's emotions when we were close. Right now, it was nothing but rage, and I gripped his arm trying to calm him. I didn't dare step away for fear of him shifting in front of these two. My mate had a massive amount of self-control, but Patrick seemed to bring out the worst in him, and right now he needed me.

"Then remember who's wife you're speaking to," Bastian snapped back.

Patrick smirked. "Oh, I know full well who I'm talking to."

Bastian started moving forward, but I held his arm, refusing to let him take another step. Aerith came bounding up then holding a small flower in her hand. "Mommy! Look what I found!"

Patrick's eyes drifted to her as Bastian picked her up and handed her off to one of the recruits. Aerith looked confused at first, but thankfully got distracted pretty quickly. Patrick's eyes shifted to her and then back to me.

"Aerith, go with Brody. He's going for ice cream in the kitchen, and I know he said he'd share," Bastian replied quietly, and she beamed. Brody played along and ushered her inside.

"This your kid?" Patrick asked, and I narrowed my eyes.

"Yup, but she's none of your business, Patrick," I replied in a snarky tone. I knew I shouldn't speak, but I was so ready for them to just leave.

"Such hostility! Makes me wonder what I ever did to piss you two off?" he smirked, and Bastian was moving forward again.

I halted my mate before asking, "Is there anything else, Officer?"

"We're just making our rounds and passing out that photo," the other officer replied. "We're letting everyone know that these illegal fights *will* be stopped and anyone involved will be arrested. We'll be making random stops around town until those four especially are caught."

"No one living here on McCoy land participates in fights like these. We keep to our own," Bastian practically snarled.

"Oh, we *all* know how you like to keep to yourselves, but still we get to check," Patrick said, smirking. "It's funny how those in that photo all wear animal masks though, don'tcha think?"

"That doesn't mean anything, Officer. Looks to me like they're just masks," Bastian said sarcastically. I eyed Patrick carefully. *What was he getting at?*

"Oh, I think it's a key piece of evidence actually. Especially that wolf mask, but don't worry Fenrir. We'll be back another time. Oh, and Shanely?" Patrick said, and my gaze drifted to him. "She's a cute kid. Doesn't seem to look like Bastian though, especially with those pale eyes. You have a good day, Shanely. See ya around, Fenrir."

He winked at me before getting back in the car.

Bastian was fuming mad as he watched them drive away, but all I could think was how odd that conversation was. *What was the point of coming here other than to get under my husband's skin? And why come all the way up the mountain to our land if the fights are happening around town?*

I left Bastian to direct the new recruits as he was in full enforcer mode now and bolted inside to the kitchen. True to *his* word, Brody had given Aerith the entire tub of chocolate ice cream. She was covered in it but wore the biggest smile on her face.

"I swear I didn't know she'd eat that much that fast!" Brody stammered but quickly shook with laughter. The tub was half gone.

"Okay, little one! Time to be done," I said, chuckling at the defeated look on her face. "Let's clean you up, little wolf."

Brody tossed the tub back in the freezer as he asked, "Everything go alright?"

He eyed me a bit when I nodded, but I didn't really know what to say. The whole encounter was just odd. As I reached into the drawer for a rag to wipe her face off, a sharp pain hit the side of my head, and I gasped. Suddenly, my eyes rolled to the back of my head as I fell into darkness.

SHANELY

***

"Shanely? Come out, come out, wherever you are," a creepy voice whispered. My eyes fluttered open, adjusting to the dark room I was in. Most of the furniture were covered with sheets, and everything smelled musty and was full of dust and cobwebs. I stayed quiet as a mouse behind the grand piano, my heart thundering in my chest. The only light in the room came from the occasional lightening from the storm outside. Thunder boomed throughout the house, and I held my breath, waiting to hear that voice again. Heavy footsteps sounded from the other side of the door, and I knew I didn't have long to think of my next move. My belly ached again, and I stifled a scream, holding onto my swollen belly.

I was in labor.

I could hear the shuffling of feet draw closer, so I quietly moved to the other side of the room and listened in against the door. I needed to find Aerith and leave this place. I carefully turned the door handle and peeked into the hall. It was quiet, and I waited for a bit just to make sure. I slipped out of the room not bothering to close the door behind me. I tried to carefully walk down the hardwood floors without stepping on a spot that would creak.

"Shanely, we talked about this! You promised me you weren't going to run away again, and I promised not to touch you until you delivered. If you don't hold up your end of our deal then neither will I," Patrick's voice bellowed this time and panic swept through me.

Patrick took me, I thought to myself as movement sounded behind me. I turned, finding him in the room I just left, and I made my feet move faster.

I quietly tried to open Aerith's door, but it was locked. I swore as I looked for the key that always hung next to the frame, but it was missing. Another contraction hit, and I struggled to breathe.

Patrick's large shadow filled the doorway I left opened, and I quietly stepped into the next room instead. I locked the door behind me and went straight to the window. It was windy and raining hard because of the storm, but there was nowhere else for me to go. I looked to my right and found a small ledge between this room and Aerith's. I looked down and groaned. We were on the top floor, and the ground below looked so far away. I tried not to focus on that as I opened my window. It was now or never.

I carefully swung my leg over and stepped out onto the small ledge below. My body shook with fear as I made sure I had my footing before bringing my other leg over. Once outside, I clung to the window frame. My heart thundered in my chest as another icy wind passed by me. Aerith's window wasn't super far away, I told myself as I took a deep breath. I gripped the small ledge above my head, making sure to move slowly so I wouldn't slip and moved my feet. The wind howled, and the thunder startled me, but I kept going.

I managed to reach her window and found her sleeping soundly on the bed. She had no idea what was going on around her. The window squeaked loudly as I pushed it up, and Aerith sat up in bed abruptly, her eyes wide, and looking ready to scream. I quickly put my hand to my lips, hoping she could see me as I stepped inside. She ran to me, and I wrapped my arms around her.

"Mommy!"

"Shh, baby. Don't make a sound, okay? We're leaving tonight, but Patrick's still in the house. We need to make our way to the garage so we can..."

I quickly covered her mouth as I heard footsteps outside her door. We stilled as keys jiggled the handle on the door. He was coming in! I screamed inside my head as I quickly looked around the room. We needed to hide, and I quickly scooped her up when I found a spot. I carried her to the closet and buried us inside as the main door opened. Another contraction hit again, and I bit my hand, trying not to make a sound.

"Shanely?"

I could barely see Patrick through the slots in the closet doors. He carefully moved to the bed, ripping the covers off. He swore before noticing the window. He walked out of my line of sight, shutting the window before leaving the room entirely.

I breathed a sigh of relief and waited a few more moments. It was quiet, minus the storm, and I carefully opened the closet door. The hall was quiet too, and the two of us made it to the grand staircase in no time. I tried to stay within the shadows and listen carefully. I tried to do everything my husband taught me. If only this stupid bracelet wasn't on then I could use my shifter abilities.

We carefully made it down the stairs before another contraction hit, and I had to lean against the railing this time. I was running out of time.

"Hello, Shanely," Patrick said from behind us, and I turned, only to have him grab me by my throat. Aerith screamed as he squeezed tighter. I clawed at his hand, but he only tightened his grip. Patrick's wicked smile was quickly blurring as my lungs begged for oxygen again. I wasn't hurting him, I thought as I clawed him again. He was unmoving.

"I see why you're trying to run now. Is my child ready to meet his Daddy?"

I glared at him, and in one last ditch effort to escape, I slapped his face. My nails cut him surprisingly deep, and he dropped me. I coughed, gasping for air as I grabbed Aerith and bolted from the room.

Patrick called me every name in the book as he rushed towards me. We barely made it to the kitchen before Patrick tackled us to the ground. I tried to fight back as he flipped me over and straddled me. I saw stars when his fist connected to my face. I struggled to stay awake and turned towards my daughter. Aerith had run under the table, bawling with her hands covering her face. My heart snapped in two, and Patrick gripped my face, forcing me to look at him again.

"You made a mistake doing that. It's time you learned your place."

* * *

"Whoa! I got you, babe."

Bastian had his arms wrapped around me as he waited for me to get my bearings. I shut my eyes tight, waiting for the room to stop spinning, and for my legs to work again. The fear I felt in my warning lingered, and I was breathing heavy trying to calm myself. My head felt awful when I finally opened my eyes though.

Brody was holding Aerith, his eyes wide with fear. He stammered, "I don't know what happened, Bastian. She was fine one moment, and the next thing I knew her eyes were rolling, and she just dropped."

"It's okay, Brody. You did the right thing by calling me. Shanely? Are you okay?" he asked me.

I slowly nodded my head, processing the new warning I just received. It had been three blissful years without a warning, and the first time I see Patrick, I get one. *It couldn't be a coincidence.*

"Did you see it too?" I asked, and Bastian nodded grimly.

"You seem to share them with me now," he replied.

"Did you recognize anything this time?"

He shook his head no, and I sighed.

"Neither did I."

"It's okay, my love. It's not going to happen," he stated firmly.

"They're consistent, Bastian. How are we going to prevent this?" I asked.

"Well staying away from Patrick is a good start. You've been warning free since he's been gone."

"But he's back now, and it sounds like he's going to use this fighting ring as an excuse to keep annoying us. I can't always avoid him, Bastian."

"We'll figure this out, Shanely, but I promise you it's not happening, okay? There is no way Patrick will *ever* get his hands on you. If I need to kill him, then I will. I'll do anything to keep you safe."

"Killing him will only start a war, and you know it," I replied, giving him a pointed look.

"Only if we're caught," he snapped back with a devilish grin. "Now I need to check back in with the guys and find your Uncle. Will you be good here for a bit?"

I nodded, and he kissed my forehead. He hauled me to my feet, making sure I was steady before giving Aerith a kiss goodbye too.

"Stay here, love," my mate told me before heading back outside.

I gave him a smile before I turned back to Brody, who still had a sticky Aerith in his arms. "Thanks for watching her Brody and for bringing her in here."

"Anything for the pack," he replied before handing her back to me. She gave him a cheesy smile as he ruffled her hair before heading back to his group with Bastian. I was grateful to the pack. They all were there for one another always, and I loved that Aerith would grow up with everyone around. I was thankful he thought quick on his feet too. I didn't know I'd have another episode like that again. *I guess I need to be more careful from now on.*

I sighed and sat Aerith back down on the counter to clean her face. She squirmed around, but soon I could see her adorable face again. The door opened, and to my dismay Emma walked in. I wanted to groan out loud, but I didn't want to start anything with her again. Why she stayed behind instead of fleeing with her father and the rest of her family baffled me. She somehow passed Octavia's lie test though, so my Uncle allowed her to stay on probation. She was not to communicate with her family at all, and Uncle Cain's been monitoring her like a hawk over the years. Emma's followed the rules for the most part, but something wasn't right. Unless she's hoping to sway Bastian's heart somehow and defy fates, I can't think of another reason why she'd stay here, other than to make my life a nightmare.

I wish she'd just find a mate and go away. Her long blonde hair swayed around her hips, and she wore the smallest pair of shorts I'm sure she owned. She was thinner than I was and loved to rub it in my face. I usually rolled my eyes, knowing my curves came from carrying Aerith, but it was honestly starting to weigh on me.

"Well, there's the mixer! I see Bastian's all in a tizzy. Did you cause trouble again, Shanely?" she snidely asked, leaning on the counter across from us. I double checked Aerith's face, but she was clean and itching to get down.

"Nope. I'm sure he's just annoyed by all the skimpy outfits you wear around the pack. It's really not appropriate, ya know? I'm sure whoever ends up being your mate won't like knowing that this is how you tend to look around other males."

Emma bristled at my words, and I almost felt bad. *Almost.* She yanked open the fridge door, taking out a water bottle in a huff before snarling back at me.

"I'd be careful, Shanely. Bastian may not be looking right now, but he's still a guy. You keep putting on weight, and soon he's gonna start looking."

I glared at her as she swayed her hips right out of the room. I wanted so badly to put her in her place, but Aerith was right here, and I wasn't normally an aggressive person. I wasn't the Alpha Female either, so I can't banish her, even though that's all I wanted to do right now. I inhaled deeply to calm myself before I turned back to Aerith. I tried to remind myself that what Emma said wasn't true. After years of abuse from Peter saying the same things about my weight, I struggled with my self-worth. Hearing it from Emma wasn't helping either because I was already nervous about the weight I've gained from having Aerith. Bastian always told me he was thrilled with it, saying I was finally at a healthy normal weight and that it made his wolf feel more at ease, but I wasn't sure. I never wanted to give him a reason to not find me attractive.

"Mommy, why is that lady so mean?" Aerith asked me.

I frowned, hating she was picking up on Emma's behavior. It wasn't how pack mates treated one another, but I guess she did need to learn that not everyone would treat her right. What I wanted to teach her was not to let others control how she felt or especially how she viewed herself. I spent a lifetime struggling with insecurities over how other people viewed me, so it was hard to be certain that I was doing a good job teaching my daughter to do the opposite.

"Emma is a very sad person, and when people are sad they sometimes want to make others feel sad too. She's just jealous, and we need to ignore her."

"Why doesn't she just find something that makes her happy then?"

"I don't know, honey. Sometimes people just need to figure things out for themselves, but let's not worry about her, baby. We can't let her ruin our day, now can we?"

She smiled up at me as my sister Bay and best friend Alana walked in the front door. Bay still had her bouncy, kinky curly hair as usual, but today it was tucked up into a ponytail, where Alana had cut her hair short earlier this year. It was a gorgeous long bob, and they both had on running gear. *Must of had a nice jog on the trails this morning,* I thought to myself.

"Hey, little wolf!"

"Hi, Auntie Bay!" Aerith shouted as she jumped from the counter into her Aunt's arms. "Hi, Auntie Alana!"

"Hi, baby!" Alana greeted her. "So what's got Bastian in a such a mood?"

I groaned. "Officer Patrick was here."

Her eyes grew big. "He was here?!"

"Why was he here? When did he even get back?" Bay questioned, holding Aerith on her hip.

"I have no idea when he got back, but he was called home early from training because of all the illegal fights that have been going on in town."

Bay's eyes grew wide as she stammered, "Interesting... Well let me watch Aerith for you! I'm sure you have lots to discuss with my brother!"

She swiftly took off in the other direction, and it only confirmed my suspicion.

"Freeze!" I shouted. Alana looked nervously between us.

"Maybe I should watch Aerith?" Alana offered, taking her from Bay before heading outside.

I stared Bay down. I knew she normally avoided my gaze out of respect for my supposed title, but there was more to it today.

"How long?"

"How long what?"

So she was going to play dumb now? I thought to myself as I rolled my eyes at her.

"How long have you been fighting?" I whispered angrily, hoping no one else would hear. I snuck a glance towards the main doors and the back offices. Thankfully, we were alone for now.

"I have no idea what you're talking about."

"Really? Because Officer Patrick had a pretty little picture of you in a wolf's mask! What, did you think I wouldn't be able to recognize you?"

She sighed, leaning back on the counter. "Fine, you win. I've been fighting on and off for the last year."

"A year?!"

"Shh! Look yes, about a year, but the ring's been really tight lipped and low-key. It's only blown up in the last few months because of the new owners, but I'm being careful. I promise! Besides... The fights that douche bag is breaking up are just the human rings, and I've stopped doing those. They must have caught my picture when I went to watch one."

"It's not just about you, Bay! Don't you get it. Patrick showed up on pack lands unannounced! I had another warning because of it, and he saw Aerith. What if he decides to poke around more? We could all be in danger if he shows up randomly and sees one of us shift. It isn't worth it!" I cried out in frustration.

"Look, I didn't mean for it to come to pack lands, but I'm good at what I do, Shanely. I love boxing and cage fighting. It's literally all I have left of my old life. I've worked really hard for Mor'du, and I don't want to lose it. I'm sorry," she replied as she made her way out the kitchen.

"You have to stop. They're on a man hunt now. They have your picture! Patrick is going to keep coming around now, and we can't risk the pack," I said, following closely behind her.

She gave me a sad look. "Shanely, I can't now. I'm already committed to a certain amount of fights. With these new guys it would be safer for me to keep fighting than to try and back out of our deal."

"What did you do?" I asked as worried filled my heart.

"Just leave it alone, Shanely. Please for everyone's sake just pretend you don't know. Everything has been calming down around here since Derek. I mean look at you! Bastian's even been letting you out of his sight lately and that's saying something. If you tell him anything about this then you can kiss your freedom goodbye."

"Bay, this isn't about my freedom. It's about making sure everyone's safe. Patrick is the Division even if he doesn't know it right now. Whatever deal you made, undo it. Just tell them you'll pay them or something. Negotiate for something else," I demanded, putting my hand on my hip.

She raised an eyebrow at me. "Becoming an Alpha female, are we?"

"In this matter, yes. Quit the fights now before they discover who or what you are."

The front door opened and in walked my mate. His heavy steps stomped throughout the house, and I already knew he was looking for me. I stole a glance as he made his way over and sighed. *He definitely wasn't happy.*

Bay must have picked up on it too because she merely spat out the word *fine* before bolting from the door. I shook my head. *I was going to have to watch her.*

Bastian immediately buried his face in the crook of my neck, inhaling deeply as he wrapped his arms around me.

"Whoa, what's going on now?" I asked as I rubbed his back, trying to relieve some of the tension building.

Bastian groaned. "Your Uncle is not happy about Patrick's early return. We're reaching out to the bear clan to let them know what's up and to see if they've heard anything about these fights. Which means another late meeting with the enforcers, which turns into a late night at the machine shop."

"Ah, so a night away from us then? You've had a lot of work come your way lately. You should hire someone to help you guys with your rush jobs. Maybe one of the new enforcers needs a trade?" I offered.

He pulled back from me before gently rubbing my cheek. "That's not a bad idea actually. I'll ask them at the meeting tonight. We've just been slammed these last few weeks with these big jobs, but I'm tired of being away from you guys, especially now that Patrick's back."

"I know, baby. How's your wolf? Does he need calming?" I asked.

"You have no idea," Bastian groaned as he rested his head back on my shoulder. I giggled softly.

"Well, you have two choices here. One, we could go for a run, seeing how Alana has Aerith or we could go home to an empty house for a nap. Your pick," I said.

He perked up at that. With a wolfish grin, he threw me over his shoulders and started jogging to the front door.

"Bastian!" I giggled as we swiftly made our way down the steps to the trail leading home. Some of the pack smiled at us, while a few gave us an odd look, but I couldn't stop giggling as I squirmed in my husband's arms.

"You said my choice, right? Well I believe there's a third option," he replied before swatting my butt. I squealed again, making him chuckle. We disappeared into the woods and away from the lodge.

Bastian

A few weeks passed by since Patrick came back to town. God, he was a thorn in my side. He was constantly looking for information concerning the fight ring, but none of us were involved! I don't understand why he thought we were in the first place, and a person wearing an animal mask wasn't valid enough information to start throwing accusations around.

I grilled Bay shortly after the first time Patrick showed up on pack lands, and she told me she hasn't fought since she moved here. Guilt ate at me, knowing she loved fighting as Mor'du, but it scared the living daylights out of me to know she did it for so long back home, and no one ever knew. It still pisses me off that Dad had no idea where she was running off to at night. *Didn't he notice the bruises or cuts on her? Shifters heal fast, but not that fast.* Bay must have been seriously neglected and ignored at home for her to make a name for herself like that with *no one* finding out.

I walked into the bunk house that was set up for the enforcers to sleep in and scrunched my nose. This bunkhouse was built back when Ash and Aspen were young, and it was meant to be an extra way for the guys to bond and stay close to one another. They were a team, day and night, and this helped them accept one another as brothers rather than just pack mates. Although sticking a bunch of male shifters together made for some awful smells. *This place reeked!* I thought to myself.

The young wolves were still passed out asleep. Completely dead to the world no matter how loud my boots were. I whipped open the curtains and opened all the windows. This place needed aired out and some of the young pups stirred at the bright light.

"Rise and Shine, meatheads! This place reeks, which means you all need showers!" I shouted, startling some from their bunks. Brody hit his head on the bunk above.

"Ow! God, Bastian... Do you really need to scare us every morning?" he asked, making me grin.

I knelt down to look him in the eye. "Aww... I'm sorry, princess. Didn't get enough beauty rest? Are you a cranky wolf this morning?"

Brody glared at me before shoving off his bed. "Shut up. I just don't like being scared like that!"

I laughed, pushing him backwards. "You better be careful talking to me like that, Brody. I'm still above you, and I can make you pay dearly for your disrespect."

Brody chuckled and playfully pushed me back. My wolf was eager, ready to wrestle and goof off again. Brody wasn't that much younger than I was, but I was ready to show him who was the boss here. I was in my spot for a reason.

"Careful. We had Ash and Aspen as Head Enforcers, Brody. That means we know *very* creative ways to punish the lot of you," my brother Cade chimed in as he strode by. The third triplet, Elijah, was right behind him, carrying colored cloths with him. Lastly my two best friends, Ryder and Johnny, walked behind my brothers completely ready to go for the day.

"Ya know, I think we've been too easy on this group," Elijah stated, kicking the bottom bunk of an enforcer that was seriously moving slow this morning.

"I was thinking the same thing, brother," I said, pacing back and forth at the front.

"Back in our day we were up and at it before the sun came up, and we never smelled this bad!" Ryder exclaimed loudly.

"What are we going to do with them, boss?" Johnny asked, and I grinned mischievously.

"We're going to fix the problem, Johnny. Listen up here, meatheads! I will not tolerate anymore late nights or anyone oversleeping again. You are all enforcers! It's your job to keep the pack safe, but how can you when you're passed out from partying the night before!? That's unacceptable! Like my brother said we've gone *way* too easy with you guys."

"From here on out, you all better be up and showered before the sun rises. Anyone that's late or misses his alarm gets the punishment," Cade continued on.

"That punishment will change depending on who catches you and the mood they're in," Elijah stated firmly, and I noticed all the new recruits began to look concerned amongst themselves.

"Now get in the showers! God, you all reek like rogues! Last one out runs laps alone today!" I shouted, and the group scrambled passed us to the bathrooms in the back.

Cade slammed into my shoulder, grinning like a banshee. "I love my job."

I laughed. "Yeah, it's better being on this end of everything, right?"

"Nah, we had some good days," Elijah chimed in, leaning against one of the bunks.

"You mean *we* had good days," Ryder said, pointing to him and Johnny. "You three were nothing but trouble."

I grinned again, pushing my friend playfully. He laughed and pushed back. Elijah gestured to the door, and the group began to make its way out. We needed fresh air anyways.

"We weren't trouble. We just liked to keep everyone on their toes was all," I countered. "Y'all would have realized that if you came with us once in a while!"

"Oh no! We started becoming guilty by association, so Ryder and I had to avoid you three otherwise we'd suffer the wrath of Ash," Johnny exclaimed before laughing loudly.

"Oh, Ash... We used to make his face turn beat red from anger, remember that?" Cade laughed.

"He was so fun to mess with though. They were good times back then," Elijah answered, and I nodded.

"Yeah, but now they're better. Just wait until you all find your mates. You'll see like Johnny and I have."

"True that! I finally feel complete and way better than these three knuckleheads!" Johnny said as he playfully pushed Ryder. The recruits started to slowly trickle outside now.

"Yeah, yeah. She's out there somewhere. Not all of us are lucky to find them at home like you two," Ryder chimed in.

We turned and stood in a line, our feet spread slightly apart, as we watched the new recruits come out. Habit I guess, but now was the time to turn up the heat. These new ones needed to learn the chain of command and the pack order, so to speak. Now that Patrick was home, our security needed to step it up. They needed to feel the weight of the responsibility they *all* carried on their shoulders now.

"You all will find them, I'm sure. What's Alana up to this morning, Johnny?" I asked without taking my eyes off the new recruits. It was funny to stare them down and watch their wolves squirm under the scrutiny.

"I don't know honestly. She's been acting a little weird lately," my friend replied back, and I could hear the worry in his voice.

I gave him a brief look. "What's going on?"

"I don't know. She doesn't want to leave our cabin or go see her family. She says she feels sick a lot more too."

"That's odd. Bears are about as close to their family as wolves are. Someone upset her?" Elijah asked Johnny.

"I don't think so, but I don't know. She hasn't said anything to me about it if someone did."

"Ah, must be a chick thing," Cade commented, making me laugh.

"A what?" I asked.

"You know like a girl squabble. If she's avoiding the clan then I bet she's fighting with one of the girls there. They don't vent about stuff like that normally," he continued.

"And you know this how?" Ryder asked, raising him eyebrow at him.

"Please, I have experience with girls. Ryder. Besides I live with Baby Girl," he said, shoving Ryder to the side.

"Shanely is the sweetest little thing though. She never gets mad at anyone!" Elijah chimed back in as I chuckled at my brothers.

"Look, I don't see anyone else offering suggestions!"

"Alright, alright, let's just drop it. Maybe today will be better for her,

Johnny? Now let's see who's running laps today," I said as I walked towards the group. I started counting, and I came up with 19.

"Hmm, we're missing one, brothers," I stated, walking back and forth between the line they formed, when suddenly someone came running from the back. He scurried into line, and I smiled wide.

"Benjamin, thanks for joining us today!"

He dropped his head knowingly.

"Laps?" he asked exasperated with himself, and I nodded.

"Laps. Get to it! Someone will find you later tonight."

Benjamin groaned and started running to the lodge to begin his punishment. *He was going to have a long day ahead of him,* I thought to myself. I turned back to the group.

"Just a warning from here on out, running laps will be the *easiest* punishment you all receive. Last one out gets the punishment every morning. Now let's go! We're spending our day by the lake."

"You all have fun today! I've got an errand to run for Cain this morning," Ryder shouted as he jogged away from the group.

The rest of us ran down to the lake not too far from the lodge. It was on the way towards Dead Man's Hollow and running the trails here always reminded me of when I carried Shanely down the mountain. I tried not to think about that day though. It only screwed with my wolf and his temper. We halted the group by the water to start our day of training.

"Today's lesson will be on maintaining your composure when under pressure. Sometimes you won't be the biggest thing out there and running will be your safest option, especially when you're protecting a pack member. You must learn to rely on your wolf's heightened senses to help maintain tactical proficiency and situational awareness. Given time and experience in the field, you will hone a wide variety of skills that play a crucial role in your ability to complete your objectives. The importance of being able to make sound decisions under stress *cannot* be overstated. You may find the consequences of failing to keep a level head nearly impossible to bare," I stated as Caleb came bolting from the woods.

"Sorry I'm late, Bastian!" he shouted as he jogged to the rest of us.

"So he gets to be late?" one of the recruits muttered, and I zeroed in on him.

"Excuse me?"

He paled, trying to shrink back in the line. "Nothing, sir."

"Huh… I could have sworn you were being disrespectful to one of your instructors," I answered.

"That's what I heard, brother," Cade continued.

"Elijah?" I asked.

"I heard it too," he answered.

"Laps, Cody. You get laps today," I commanded, and he groaned. He started turning towards the lodge, when I stopped him.

"Oh no, Cody. You get to swim laps," I said, pointing to the little island in the middle of the big lake.

His eyes widened. "Really? It's freezing in there."

"Questioning, are we? Seems like he needs more, Bastian," Elijah said, but Cody quickly took off to the water.

"No, sir. Laps are good, sir!"

Cody dove into the water as I turned to Caleb. "Good to see you, brother."

He shook my hand, giving me a look. "Wow. Getting tough with them, are we?"

"It's been a long time coming honestly. We've been way too easy with them. We're playing Save the Baby today."

"Ah, Cade was telling about this one. Where do you want me?"

"Applying pressure," I answered, grinning at him. I turned back to the recruits. "Alright everyone take a color!"

They all came up, taking a colored cloth from Elijah before returning to their spot in line. Elijah turned to check on Cody before turning back. He was getting closer to reaching the little island in the center of the lake, and I'm sure was freezing his tail off by now.

"Okay, everyone! Time to play Save the Baby! Listen up because here's how this will go, and I'm only going to explain this once. You each have a baby that you need to keep safe, and these rags will lead you to your dolls. They each have a unique scent on them that will act as your guide to the doll.

Your mission will be to find the doll and bring it back to me safely *without* getting caught. These dolls will record how they're being treated too, so you are officially warned! If you drop your baby or throw it at any point, it will record the damage it takes. Treat it as a real child. Now Johnny and I will stay here on the beach, while Caleb, Elijah, and Cade will be hunting you all. If they catch you or your kid, you will fail and will be joining Cody in the lake."

They all looked past us to Cody, who finally made it to the island in his first lap. They gave each other worried looks before looking back to me.

"Don't worry. You all have been doing well these last few weeks. You guys can easily maneuver past us if you stay focused on the task at hand and to your surroundings," Cade continued, giving the recruits some encouragement.

"And what does it mean to know your surroundings?" Elijah asked.

"It means to use your senses, sir. Trust your wolf," Brody shouted.

"And how do you do that?" Elijah countered.

"Scent first. You will smell them long before you see them," another shouted down the line.

"Then sight. Look, listen, act," another finished.

"Good. They've paid attention, Bastian," my brother said quietly to me.

"We've taught you how to focus and listen. You guys can do this, and remember even if you're spotted it doesn't mean game over. Plans go south sometimes, but don't give up. You might still make it out but know they will not go easy on you today," I said before giving them all a moment to process everything.

I turned to the others. "Alright, go get set up."

Cade saluted me, and I rolled my eyes at him. *Always the goofball.* It didn't take long for them to disappear in the woods, and Johnny and I waited for the sound off. It came loud and clear through the link, and it was time to start.

"Alright, boys. Scent your rag and shift. You have to safely bring me your baby to pass the game," I said, and they all shifted except Brody. He scented his rag in his human form, and I gave Johnny a look. He gave me a small smile before turning back to face the others.

Brody remembered. Scenting is different as a human than as your wolf.

Brody was taking advantage of both forms. He shifted into his dark brown wolf and scented again. The others had taken off already, and he was the last to leave the beach.

"He's improving faster than the others," Johnny finally said, when they were all long gone.

"I've noticed. They're all doing good honestly, but he's shown the biggest improvement."

"He's ready for patrols," Johnny said.

"I think so too. We'll see how today goes, I suppose," I answered, and we stood in silence for awhile. Cody came back to the beach twice before we saw Brody's wolf bolt out of the woods with the baby in his mouth. He was fast, but graceful, and passed off the red baby to me. It was still wrapped in his blanket and looked basically the same as when Cade and I set them out early this morning.

Brody shifted back with a massive grin on his face and entirely covered in mud.

"So... What do I get for winning?" he asked arrogantly, and I laughed.

"You punk. Did anyone spot you?" I asked.

"I don't think so. I was near Elijah, and I managed to get by him but just barely. I got in the mud pit to help cover my scent," he replied, trying to brush some of it off.

Johnny smiled. "Smart man. Elijah's got the best nose, but his hearing isn't as good."

"So what's my prize??"

I snorted. "How about the weekend off?"

"Seriously? No training or anything?"

"You've done well, Brody. You've earned it, and honestly we're talking about putting you on the patrols. We think you're ready for it," I answered as another wolf came out of the woods with Cade hot on his heels.

"Coming in hot!" Johnny cried out as the wolf nearly barreled into us. He tossed the baby into Johnny's arms, who barely caught it, and I glared at the wolf. Cade snapped his jaws at him before taking back off into the woods again.

"Seriously? What part of treat it like a real kid did you not understand?" I asked the recruit.

He shifted back out of breath. "Sorry, sir. It was a last minute decision. I figured a light jostling would be better than getting caught. Cade was chasing me awhile."

I snorted, seeing the kid's point. "Well, good work. You're second today."

He smiled and thanked us before sprawling out by Brody. Suddenly, my phone buzzed in my pocket. I smiled wide, seeing Shanely's name appear on the screen.

"Hey, mate!"

Her voice was heavenly, and my heart ached in my chest. *I missed her badly.*

"Shanely," I said with relief. "God, I've missed your voice."

She giggled at my dramatics. "Bastian, you've only been gone for the morning."

"Too long, let me tell ya. Are you heading to the lodge now?" I asked, hoping to eat lunch with my mate again today.

"Actually, no. I was wondering if you could pick Aerith up from Aunt Cassia this afternoon? They're working at seeing if she can pull on her own wolf or bear, but Aunt Cassia has to work in the clinic around one."

"Sure, I'll grab her. We can head down to the creek to do some fishing. I could use a break honestly. Where are you going then?" I asked. I could hear in the tone of her voice that she was up to something.

"Alana needed to run to town and asked for a girls day. Bay is gone already, so I was hoping to go with her," she replied.

"To town? Are you sure you want to do that? What about your warnings with Patrick?"

Yeah... I didn't like that one bit. With Patrick creeping around, I didn't want her to be alone in town without me.

"I'll be okay, honey. We won't stay too long in town besides Alana could use a friend today," she replied sweetly.

"Shanely, I don't like the idea of you going off pack lands without me, and I'm sure Johnny would say the same thing," I answered as Johnny's ears perked up.

"What would I say?" he asked, stepping closer.

"Are you with Johnny?" she asked.

"Yeah, we're working with the new trainees on tracking under stress. He's assisting me in putting pressure on them. Caleb, Elijah, and Cade are around here somewhere too. Look, why don't you guys just wait until this evening, and Johnny and I will go with you."

"Bastian, I promise we will be okay. I'll keep the link open the whole time and... We're not going alone. Ryder offered to go with us."

"Ryder's escorting you? I really don't like not being there with you, Shanely, but if he's taking you guys out then I suppose," I said, turning to Johnny. He gave me a thumbs up as he was listening in anyways. "Johnny said okay too. Just stay with him at all times, and please be safe you two."

"We will, honey! We're grabbing lunch out, so we'll be back late this afternoon. I have my cell too, and Johnny can reach Alana through the bond as well."

"I can't wait for ours to fully connect, so I can always check in," I told her.

"I know. I'm glad we have the mind-link even if it's only partially there, but it will be nice when it works like everyone else's does. My wolf is stronger just something seems to be stuck. It has to work eventually, right?" she asked me, and I could hear the frustration in her voice. I know this weighed heavily on her, and I felt awful I didn't know how to help her with it.

"I would assume so," I replied, trying to comfort her, but Caleb barreled out of the woods, roaring loudly at two recruits interrupting my mate and I. He moved quickly for being such a big bear, and he soon pinned one of the recruits in the sand.

"Listen honey, I have to go. Stay with Ryder, and don't worry about Aerith. I've got her. I love you."

"I love you too, Bastian. See you soon," she replied before I disconnected the call.

Caleb roared in the pup's face as the other handed me his doll. He shifted and collapsed on the sand out of breath and exhausted.

I laughed. "He wear you out?"

The recruit nodded. "You have no idea. That was way too close."

The other recruit hung his head low as he handed the doll to Johnny and made his way to the water. Johnny grinned at Caleb, who just trotted back into the woods. Cade burst through the trees now, carrying three dolls in his mouth. He was followed by three wolves, who were down right sulking out of the woods. Cade dropped the dolls at my feet and shook out his fur. He was gone again in seconds as the others started their long swim to the island.

"Looks like we still have our work cut out for us," Johnny said with a laugh.

I grinned. "I guess so, brother."

Shanely

I was worried about Bay. She started avoiding me ever since I confronted her about fighting. I felt horrible ripping away something she held dear, and I constantly went back and forth wondering if I did the right thing. So far I managed to avoid Patrick when he came by. It was a small win, but I felt selfish taking it. I know Bay loves doing what she does, but it wasn't safe. Her and I may never see things eye to eye with this, but I wondered if she at least understood where I was coming from. A small part of me couldn't help but feel like I was forcing her away from something she loved because I was too afraid for my own self and family. This whole thing was pushing us apart, and I missed my friend.

I went back and forth over it for hours before deciding that I needed to talk to Bay again. Catching her was the trick though as she was rarely on pack lands. Getting a chance to go look for her had been tricky too. Bastian hired Brody and another enforcer to help take over some of the upcoming jobs the Fenrir brothers had, so he's been a little extra busy showing him the ropes at their shop. Brody thankfully had welding experience already, but there was still some things to go over, I guess. All of it confused me greatly whenever Bastian or his brothers tried to explain it. Right now, I was spending a whole lot of time at home, which don't get me wrong I loved my home, but I was going a little stir crazy in our cabin. And I couldn't find Bay.

Alana called me first thing this morning and wanted to spend the day with me. On the phone she said she needed to pick up something from town and needed my help to go get it. Relief washed over me. I was so game for company! I've been spending way too much time in my own head, and I didn't want to vent to Bastian about everything. He had enough on his plate already. As the two of us spoke a brilliant idea came to me. *Maybe while we were out I might be able to spy on a few areas those fights might be located at. Bay mentioned new owners so maybe they have a better spot for them now.* At this point, I'd do anything to find her again.

The last time Patrick came by he mentioned to Bastian that they hadn't busted anymore fights, which was a relief. I've been terrified they'd catch Bay and cause a whole mess of problems for us, but as Alana continued talking on the line, I wondered if I could catch Bay at the ring. *I'd at least get her to talk to me then*, I thought to myself.

My mind drifted as Alana said her goodbyes. I had spotted Bay going into a club downtown recently, when Bastian took me out for dinner one night, but I didn't think much of it until now. Bay didn't seem like a dancer, and she wasn't with friends when I saw her. I was too lost in Bastian that night to really pay much attention, but now I was going back over everything this last month, trying to figure this out. I could be blowing this out of proportion, but the fights were going on somewhere in town away from the eye of the police. *Maybe the loud dance club was one of the places?* I thought to myself as I got dressed. *It made sense to me. Or maybe I should just drop this?* Things were quiet for the most part, so I should just be happy, but a part of me needed to know for sure if Bay was fighting still. I couldn't shake the feeling she was in trouble and needed help. I hated spying on her like this, but I was terrified she got herself involved in something dangerous. I *had* to help her.

I shook my curly hair out as I slipped my brown sandals on. *It can finish air drying*, I thought to myself. I was too lazy to dry it. I made my way out of my room as Alana's compact car came into view from my new bay windows the boys had put in during the remodel. I smiled to myself. *Perfect timing.* She quickly hopped out and bounded up my steps. I held the door opened for her and gave her a swift hug hello as she came inside.

"I'm so glad you were free today! I really needed to go to town," Alana said as she sat down at the bar stools in the kitchen, "without Johnny."

I raised my eyebrow and grabbed my coffee mug. "So what are we hiding?"

She rolled her eyes and sighed. "Is Bastian here?"

"Nope, just us! Bastian's probably somewhere at the lodge by now, and Aerith is at her class. So c'mon, spill!" I replied as I leaned on my kitchen counter. I sipped on my lukewarm coffee, and she sighed.

"I've been avoiding everyone back in my old clan just in case. It's stressing me out, and I need to just know for sure before someone tells Johnny..."

I nearly dropped my mug. "Wait... Alana, are you pregnant?"

The corners of her mouth rose. "I don't know, I mean I think I am! I can't smell it for myself! And I don't want someone sniffing me out and saying something before I can tell Johnny. I'd like to surprise him *if* I am pregnant. It's not something you can normally do as a bear, but since Johnny is a wolf, I can actually surprise my mate with this!"

I squealed excitedly as I rushed towards her, hugging her tightly as I bellowed, "Alana, I am so happy for you guys! We can totally go to town and find out the old-fashioned human way with a test. You can take it at lunch, and we can figure out what to do before we come back. I honestly would like to make a town trip without Bastian as well."

"Okay, now it's your turn! Why don't you want Bastian there?"

"You cannot tell anyone, promise me?"

"Sure, Shanely. What's going on?"

"Well for one thing I want him to stay with Aerith here. I don't want her in town with us today, and I feel better knowing her dad is here in pack lands with her. But I want to check out a few areas where I think those fighting rings are being held. Bay mentioned a new owner, and I have an idea where the new location might be. I just need to see for myself."

Her eyes grew big. "Why do you want to go there? Bastian and Johnny would never let us go to something like that."

"Because Bay was one of the ones fleeing in that picture Patrick had. She's made some sort of deal and has been fighting as Mor'du again. She said it was safer to continue to fight than back out of her deal, and I don't like her being stuck in a deal with someone dangerous like that. I told her to figure out another way to honor her deal and get out of fighting, but I don't know. My gut is telling me she didn't, and she's been avoiding me ever since. I need to see for myself what's pulling her in, and if I can help her stop."

"Does she really need to stop though? I mean definitely get her out of that deal, but after that does she really need to quit? Wasn't Mor'du like the only good thing she had from her old life?" Alana asked, playing with her hair.

"I've gone back and forth with that too. Her fighting is risky, and my main issue isn't even with the fight itself. What if humans get invited or sneak in somehow? They'd see two people shift! Then the Division would hear about us, and every warning I've ever had would come true. That terrifies me, Alana. More than my guilt of making her quit. Plus, now Patrick's coming around pack lands constantly looking for the ones in that picture, and it's making everything worse. As much as I don't want her to stop doing something she loves... It's a huge risk to her and everyone in the pack and clan. I just don't see another way right now."

Alana nodded as she answered, "I get that too. Agh... You're in a tough spot."

"Tell me about it. So how do we get off pack lands alone? Bastian's been working like crazy lately, and when he's not working he's glued to Aerith and I. While we have more freedom on pack lands, we definitely won't in town now that Patrick is back."

She laughed. "I really don't see us getting off pack lands without an enforcer. There is no way we'd convince them to let us go without one, and if we left without checking in they'd just come find us. So we just need to pick the right one."

I thought about that for a moment as I put my coffee mug in the sink. "Okay... Well Caleb would smell you and your pregnancy right away so he's out. Elijah is really serious, and I think he would tell Bastian where I was heading, so that nixes him and Cade. They notice everything I'd do. We need a wolf that can get distracted enough I can give him the slip for a moment."

"What about Ryder? That's Johnny's twin basically, so my mate would be good with it, and he's an enforcer so Bastian should feel better knowing that too. Plus he's goofy enough that we can get him to just relax and hang out instead of watching us like a hawk. It's a risk, but he might be the best option for us," she replied.

"You might be right," I replied as I grabbed my phone. "Give him a call, and I'll call Bastian. We can take my truck here, so we won't need to go to the lodge and have anymore volunteers to go into town with us."

She nodded and pulled her phone out. "I'll send him a text. I'll let you know when he replies."

I called Bastian, who picked up on the second ring. "Hey, mate!"

"Shanely," Bastian said with relief. "God, I've missed your voice."

I giggled. "Bastian, you've only been gone for the morning."

"Too long, let me tell ya. Are you heading to the lodge now?" he asked.

"Actually no. I was wondering if you could pick Aerith up from Aunt Cassia this afternoon? They're working at seeing if she can pull on her own wolf or bear, but Aunt Cassia has to work in the clinic around one."

"Sure, I'll grab her. We can head down to the creek to do some fishing. I could use a break honestly. Where are you going then?" he asked. *Bastian didn't miss a beat.*

"Alana needed to run to town and asked for a girls day. Bay is gone already, so I was hoping to go with her," I replied.

"To town? Are you sure you want to do that? What about your warnings with Patrick?"

"I'll be okay, honey. We won't stay too long in town. Besides Alana could use a friend today," I replied.

"Shanely, I don't like the idea of you going off pack lands without me, and I'm sure Johnny would say the same thing," he sighed.

"What would I say?" a voice in the background shouted.

"Are you with Johnny?" I asked. Alana was instantly at my side with her ear against the phone now.

"Yeah, we're working with the new trainees on tracking under stress. He's assisting me in putting pressure on them. Caleb, Elijah, and Cade are around here somewhere too. Look, why don't you guys just wait until this evening, and Johnny and I will go with you."

"Bastian, I promise we will be okay. I'll keep the link open the whole time and..." I said as Alana's phone beeped. She quickly showed me the message that Ryder was on his way. I gave her a thumbs up. "We're not going alone. Ryder offered to go with us."

"Ryder's escorting you? I really don't like not being there with you, Shanely, but if he's taking you guys out then I suppose. Johnny said okay too. Just stay with him at all times, and please be safe you two," he replied with a sigh.

"We will, honey! We're grabbing lunch out, so we'll be back late this afternoon. I have my cell too, and Johnny can reach Alana through the bond as well."

"I can't wait for ours to fully connect, so I can always check in," he said.

"I know. I'm glad we have the mind-link even if it's only partially there, but it will be nice when it works like everyone else's does. My wolf is stronger just something seems to be stuck. It has to work eventually, right?" I asked anxiously.

"I would assume, honey." A loud commotion started in the background that sound almost like a roar. Bastian quickly said, "Listen honey, I have to go. Stay with Ryder, and don't worry about Aerith. I've got her. I love you."

"I love you too, Bastian. See you soon," I replied before the call ended.

I gave Alana a small smile and said, "I hate going around him like this."

She nodded. "Me too."

Ryder bounded up on the back porch in his wolf form, startling us both. He barked before running around to the front.

"Well that's our cue," I said as we left my cabin giggling. I grabbed my hoodie last minute to help keep a low-profile once I give Ryder the slip. I felt silly playing detective like this, but if it could help Bay then I'd do it.

Ryder was already hopping in my truck as we headed down the stairs. His smile was infectious. "Hey, girls! Ready to go?"

"Thanks for taking us, Ryder!" I said as Alana hopped into the middle seat followed by me on the end. Ryder started the truck and made his way down my drive.

"So where are we headed today?" he asked, drumming on the steering wheel. He was just like Cade. Always in a good mood or joking about something. He had basketball shorts on with a white tee today, and I wondered if we woke him up with the way his hair looked.

"Umm... Maybe the convenience store first?" Alana asked shyly.

Ryder didn't pay any attention to Alana's nerves and kept drumming on the wheel. "Sounds good!"

The drive to town was pleasant enough, and we all laughed and goofed off with one another like it wasn't a secret mission behind our mate's backs. Ryder was super laid back and so easy to get along with. He just made the ride fun, which is what Alana and I both needed. We were wound up tight with our nerves, but thanks to Ryder's help in distracting us, we were soon pulling into the store's parking lot. We walked inside, and I realized Ryder was going to follow directly behind us the entire time. Alana looked at me, her eyes pleading with mine. *This was my turn to help her dodge him.*

"Ryder, can you give us a minute? I need to buy some personal stuff, and it might be easier on us both if you just waited by the door," I said nonchalantly.

"I'm supposed to stay close. Bastian and Johnny have been blowing up my phone since I got to your cabin," he replied, taking another step forward. *Okay... so I guess I needed to pull out all the stops then*, I thought to myself.

"Ryder, do you really want to be around while I shop for tampons?" I asked blatantly.

His face turned beat red as he stopped dead in his tracks. I cocked my hip to the side, waiting for a reply, all while I tried not to smile. He just looked so flustered, it was hard not to laugh.

He finally muttered, "I'll just go to the door then."

Alana giggled as he left us alone. "I owe you one."

I laughed too. "Don't sweat it. I still need you to help me out later today too."

We walked around the corner to where the pads, tampons, and pregnancy tests were all stacked neatly together. Thankfully, it was in the back corner far away from the door. I grabbed tampons because I might as well stick to my story, and she grabbed a test. We quickly paid for everything at a self-checkout, and she hid the test in her purse. Ryder, who still looked a little red, waited patiently by the door.

"Umm... Are you guys ready then?" he asked, rubbing the back of his head.

I smiled up at him like nothing had even happened, "Yup! We're good! Ready to hit the other stores, Alana?"

She nodded, and we walked down the block, leaving my truck parked in the store's lot. It was actually getting a little warm with this hoodie on, but I wanted it just in case. The place I had seen Bay go into was a new club just off Main Street. I figured I might as well start there, and if I was wrong then maybe I'd stop at the Den and ask around. *Someone had to know where they were. Right?*

As we turned the corner onto Main, I spotted the club on the left. Thankfully, there was another store nearby I thought would work to our advantage. We crossed the street and passed a few shops before I stopped in front of a bra and lingerie store.

I looked to Alana and asked, "Ready?"

She gave me a weird look before breaking out into a big smile. "Yup!"

We pushed into the store as Ryder looked up from his phone. Surprisingly, his face turned an even deeper shade of red than I realized it could get, and I felt a little bad now. *I owed him one big time.*

"Seriously, guys? Here?"

"What? We need to grab a few things," I replied, pretending to be oblivious to his pain.

"Bastian and Johnny are going to kill me," he muttered.

Alana laughed and countered, "Hey, they said it was alright for you to escort us."

"I don't think they had *this* store in mind. *I* didn't have this store or these kind of errands in mind! Otherwise, I would have said no. You can wait for your mates," he replied as he gave us each a pointed look, but I shrugged casually. Ryder sighed, rubbing his face entirely exasperated with the two of us now. "Guys, neither one of your mates will be happy to know this is where I took you shopping."

"Well... We're here now, and it's not like you're going to be seeing us in these outfits anyways. Just sit over here in the chairs, and we can try stuff on. It won't take long, and then we can go eat. Our treat," I replied and dragged Alana through the racks before he could reply. Once we got far enough away I looked back and giggled. There were some older ladies glaring at him while he was so focused on staring at his feet and pretending he wasn't standing next to a display of thongs and panties.

"We seriously need to get him something special for all this," Alana said.

I laughed as I replied, "We definitely owe him, but this place is near the club where I saw Bay go into. I think she went there for a fight. Ryder will never know if I slip out the back. Just keep your phone on, and every so often run out and grab another size of something. He will hear you and think you're grabbing me things to try on."

She nodded. "Go then. I don't know how long he will last in this store before embarrassment makes his wolf flee. Then he's going to come looking for us, and there will be nothing I can do then."

I hugged her and went towards the back. I found the fitting room on the left right across from their employees office. I put my ear to the door and listened in. It seemed quiet in there, so I assumed it was empty. I quickly slipped inside the room and found the door to their side entrance next to a desk. Stealing what I needed, I quickly taped the door so it wouldn't latch behind me. *Now I can sneak back in without anyone noticing,* I thought, feeling rather proud of myself. I quickly bolted out the door and down the back alley.

The club was only a few stores from where we were, but I still didn't want to linger. *Who knew what wolves prowled the town right now?* I smiled at my own joke, pulling the hood over my head tightly as I walked. It wouldn't surprise me if Bastian sent more enforcers to assist in watching over us, and I wanted to make sure no one saw me.

Lots of people were out and about today, and I meandered my way passed a cluster of teenage girls, laughing as they spent their day shopping. A tall gentleman bumped into me then, and I stumbled on my feet.

"Sorry! I didn't see you there," he said as he helped steady me.

"It's fine! Don't..."

I froze as my eyes zeroed in on the person behind him. I blinked as someone in a gray hoodie walked down the sidewalk across the street, turning the corner and disappearing out of sight.

"Ma'am?" the stranger said, and I shook myself from my thoughts.

"Sorry," I stammered as I gave him a smile. "I'm fine though. No harm, no foul."

The man gave me a nod as I looked back to the corner across the street. That hoodie just looked so familiar, but I couldn't place where I had seen it before. Chills ran up my spine, and I forced my anxiety away. *I'm too freaking uptight to be a spy,* I thought to myself as my stomach rolled again. Sighing, I tried to refocus on my mission. I couldn't afford to make a mistake right now, and I was already taking too long as it was.

It took awhile for my eyes to adjust with how dark it was in here. It was empty and clearly not opened yet, but I preferred it this way anyways. I couldn't imagine what it was like at full capacity. It had a bar along the right side wall and some seats surrounding the massive dance floor. In the back were cages, but I did not want to think about what happened in those.

"We're not opened, little lady."

I turned, finding a shorter man behind the bar with a case of clean glasses. He glared at me with his dark onyx eyes, and I scented the air. He was definitely not human, but I also hadn't scented this scent before. I wasn't sure what he was, and that made me feel a little uptight. He was medium-build and bald, wearing a flannel shirt and jeans, and I slowly made my way towards him. There was nothing special about this guy, but he had this shadiness about him that just had my animals on high alert.

"That's okay. I actually had a few questions if you don't mind," I replied, giving him a cheerful smile. He grunted.

"What kind of questions would a shifter like you have in a place like this?"

My eyes widened at his blatant response. *He noticed my scent.*

"Nothing but shifters here. This is an exclusive club for shifters only. We don't allow humans," he replied.

"How do you control it?" I asked.

"It's not hard. Our bouncers sniff them out. We just pretend shifters got the invite and made the list, and we send away the rest," he replied as he began to stock the shelves.

"I just walked in though," I replied, narrowing my eyes.

He looked at me funny. "Like I said, we aren't open. No bouncers are outside, are they? Now what does a mixer want in a place like this?"

My brow rose, but I bit my tongue to keep that sarcastic comment from escaping my lips. "I've heard about the cops busting illegal fights somewhere around town, and I was curious about it. Do you know where it is? I only heard they are in this general location."

He stopped cleaning the glass before giving me a cold stare. "I don't know what you're talking about."

My eyes narrowed. *Oh this shifty man definitely knew what I was talking about*, I thought to myself as I watched him attempt to intimidate me. *The trick was going to be getting him to talk now.* My phone buzzed in my pocket. I was running out of time.

"I think you do. Look, I'm a shifter alright. I'm not part of the awful police force in this town, and I'm *not* here to rat you all out," I replied back.

"You're also a Fenrir and not exactly the kind of shifter we see around here. How do I even know you're trustworthy? Plus like I said there isn't anything to talk about," he replied as he started walking away.

I followed him, my wolf pushing me to be far more courageous than ever before. "Because I know Mor'du."

The man stopped moving, turning around to face me slowly, and this time he studied me hard. His eyes narrowed as he asked, "You know Mor'du?"

"I do. I have a lot of pull with some very powerful shifters. You can tell I'm mixed, which means I'm faster and stronger than the lot of you. Why would I go against my own kind anyways?"

"Mor'du is a legend around here. No one knows who he is though. I can get you *anything* you want for information like that," he said as he leaned over the counter. The gleam in his eyes had my stomach twisting. *This was not what I expected*, I thought to myself.

"Let me make myself clear. I won't be spilling any of Mor'du's secrets today or any day for that matter, but I will ignore the fact that you're digging around Mor'du's identity for the information I want. Otherwise, I'll let Mor'du deal with you the way *he* sees fit."

My wolf inside was beaming. She was so close to the surface, listening to the banter going back and forth. This was the most she'd been awake for months now, and it felt good to have her with me.

He paled at my threat before gritting his teeth. "What do you want to know?"

"Where's the next fight?"

"Here. We have a secret basement that's heavily guarded. Most of the fights take place here now since the new owners got the place," he replied.

"When's the next fight, and how do I get in?" I asked sweetly.

"The fight is tomorrow night at 7. You come into the club and order a Bloody Mary. The bartenders all know the code and will guide you to the fight. You pay the fee up here before you go. It's a *don't ask, don't tell* situation. You don't repeat who you see down there either, and no one will come looking for you," he replied nervously.

"Who are the new owners?" I asked. Another buzz came from my back pocket.

"I'm not supposed to say that," he replied as he shifted on his feet, "and before you threaten me, no I won't tell you. There are others I'm more afraid of than Mor'du."

His reply surprised me. *Who was he afraid of?* My wolf pushed against my skin like she was excited being here, the mischievous little thing. My phone buzzed again.

"One last thing. How many shifters from McCoy's pack and Medvedev clan visit these fights?"

He cocked his head to the side. "You'd be surprise how many different clans, packs, and streaks come in and those are just the big dogs. Then you have all the smaller shifters that don't quite make up such a large group, but we see some from every kind here. Now, I have a question for you, *mixer*. Are you interested in fighting? The boss would be very interested in a mixer fighting for him."

"No. I'm not interested in that, but I will be there tomorrow. You are not to breathe a word of my attending either. Or I *will* send Mor'du after you."

He nodded. "Just promise me that you will come to me if you change your mind. I could use a win, alright?"

I gave him a puzzled look, and he sighed. "You get big rewards if you bring in the best fighters. I already owe some to the boss, so it would square away my debt."

My wolf suddenly pushed a thought in my mind. *His scent. I recognized it now*, I thought to myself, knowing they were shifty creatures that looked out for themselves first generally.

"I'll let you know, fox," I replied.

He gave me a sly grin as I quickly left the club. I ran as fast as I could back to the lingerie store, knowing I took longer than I should have. I snuck in the back door and ripped the tape off. *No one would know I was ever in here*, I thought to myself. Ryder's voice sounded through the door. He was grilling Alana over me, and my eyes widened. I stole a peek outside the door. The dressing room was across the hall from the room I was in, but he was blocking my way out. *I took too long.*

"What is taking her so long, Alana? Is she okay in there?"

She stammered, "Yeah, it just takes time to find the right fit! She's fine, Ryder. Now go sit back down."

He sighed heavily. "Alana, your pulse is racing. What is going on?"

Uh-oh.

I carefully opened the door and met Alana's eye. Her eyes widened briefly before she casually side-stepped to the right. Ryder crossed his arms, waiting for her response. I held my breath, waiting to bolt across and into the dressing room.

"Alana, are you okay?" he asked as he turned ever so slightly. *It was now or never.*

I quietly ran across the hall and behind the curtain. The curtain shifted too far though, and he noticed it moving. I *panicked.* Before I could think anymore I quickly ripped off my shirt and stood there in my sports bra. I had barely turned around just before he ripped the curtain back. I needed him to leave, not get him killed by my mate.

"What in the world was that?!" he shouted.

"Ryder!" I hollered as well, and his face turned beat red. Ryder slammed his hand over his eyes and shut the curtain as fast as he could.

Alana cried out, "Ryder! She's not dressed!"

"I'm so sorry, Shanely! I thought something ran in here..." he stammered, but the poor boy couldn't even finish his sentence.

"It's okay! I'm sorry I took so long! I'm just getting redressed is all," I cried out, putting on my shirt again. I was so glad I decided to wear my sports bra today otherwise I wouldn't have been able to pull this off. Bastian would have killed him if he had seen me in my actual bra. I opened the curtain back up and gave him a sheepish smile.

Ryder's face was still beat red, and I had never seen him so uptight before. "Please... Tell me you guys finally done? I'm really ready to go now."

"Yeah, we're done. Let's go, Alana," I replied as we made our way to the front.

"Aren't you going to buy something?" he asked, turning red all over again. *Crap. I forgot about that.* "Umm... no. Nothing seemed to fit right."

He sighed. "So all that for nothing? Doesn't matter. Let's just go, and for the record I will *not* be coming on your next trip to town. Is that clear?"

We giggled at him. "Sure thing, Ryder. Thanks for taking such great care of us today. Can we treat you to lunch now?" I asked.

Ryder pushed us outside and further away from the store as quickly as he could. He started heading to the Den.

"Yes, you can! I deserve food now," he replied, when Alana tugged on my arm.

Alana looked frantic, and it suddenly dawned on me what she was all bothered about. *The Den was the clan's bar,* I thought to myself. *They'd smell her right away.* It was back to me to redirect for her again. *Good lord, this was all hard to do with an enforcer watching us.*

"Wait! Ryder, can we go to the Diner instead? I'm really craving their milkshakes!" I shouted as I dug in my heels, and he plowed into me.

Ryder's brow rose, but he shrugged his shoulders and gestured to the right. "Sure, I guess. You two are acting really weird today."

I laughed. "It's just a normal Wednesday for me."

Alana laughed, looping her arms in mine. She mouthed a *thank you* when Ryder wasn't looking, and I smiled at her. *She was my partner in crime today.* Ryder followed us as we entered the Diner.

"I have to use the restroom. I'll be right back!" Alana shouted, running off to the back before either one of us could answer.

Ryder sighed before grabbing my arm. "Next time, I'm bringing someone with me. I can't keep up with you two."

I giggled as I let him guide me to our table. I loved this diner. It was so cozy and always had an open table whenever we stopped in. We sat in the back booth and waited for Alana to return before placing our order. She was taking a really long time though, and it was making Ryder nervous. He couldn't stop fidgeting in the booth and looked about ready to go after her, when she finally came out.

"Geez, you alright? It took you forever in there!" he asked.

"Ryder! You don't ask girls about their bathroom trips," I stated, making him red again. *The poor guy,* I thought as he squirmed in his seat. *I'm sure he will never volunteer to watch us again though.*

"I didn't mean... I... uh," he stammered, but Alana saved him.

"I'm fine, Ryder. There was just a line," she replied, and he blew out a deep breath. He rubbed his temples and didn't look back at us.

The waitress came over then, and we gave her our order before I turned my attention to Alana. I widened my eyes, hoping she understood what I wanted to know, and she seemed to understand me just fine. She gave me the biggest smile I had ever seen from her, and I squealed. I hopped across the booth and hugged her tightly. Ryder just gave us a weird look.

"What is going on?" he asked.

I went back to my side, wiping away my tears before he really took notice. "Nothing, I'm just happy to have Alana as my best friend is all."

Ryder looked back and forth between us and shook his head. "You guys are definitely acting weird."

Thankfully, the food arrived fairly quickly and distracted us all. Ryder didn't look up from his plate, and Alana and I couldn't stop grinning while we munched on our meal. *All this sneaking around and evading Ryder left me starving,* I thought as I chuckled to myself. I thoroughly enjoyed my child's order of chicken tenders and fries, and of course I ordered a large chocolate milkshake to keep up with my story. Alana smirked at me when it came, but I just laughed. *This was a cover story I could get down with,* I thought to myself as I took a sip. It was mid-afternoon by the time Ryder drove us back to my cabin.

"I have never been so excited to return to pack lands in my life," he stated, and we laughed. We each gave him a big hug, thanking him for everything today. I honestly had a lot of fun today despite everything.

"We had a lot of fun with you, Ryder," I stated.

He smirked and shook his head. "I like spending my day with you guys too, just next time take your own mates if this is how you plan to spend the day!"

"Sure thing. You are officially off duty, Ryder," I cried out in a mocking tone.

Ryder chuffed. "Alright, tell your own mates you're home. I need a run."

He shifted mid-air and ran into the woods. I had never seen a wolf run so fast away from us, and we giggled again.

I wrapped my arms around Alana. "Congratulations again, Mama Bear!"

"Thank you! I'm so excited to surprise him tonight," she replied. We went inside the cabin and settled in on the couch. Thankfully, no one else was home yet.

"So, what did you find out? You were gone for awhile! It was even starting to make me nervous," she asked.

"I'm almost positive Bay is still fighting, but apparently knowing Mor'du personally goes *a long way* in there. They're definitely afraid of *him*, but I was right though. One of the locations is at that club, and I'm going tomorrow night to find Bay."

"Shanely! You can't go to one of those fights! It's not safe, and Bastian would never let you anyways," she practically shouted.

"I just need to sneak out again," I replied, tugging at strands of my hair.

"And *how* will you do that?" she asked, raising her eyebrow at me.

"Maybe we could have a girls night/baby shower at your place in bear land? Make Johnny stay here with the guys that night. We could sneak..."

"We?! Now I'm going?" she interrupted.

"Well... You can stay in the truck. Be my getaway driver. You're carrying a cub now after all, but I need my friend, Alana. Please? Just drive me there, and I'll sneak in and out," I begged.

"You can't go in that club all alone either!"

"Technically, if I'm right then I won't be alone. Bay will be there. The guy said I'd be surprised as to who shows up to these events too. Makes me wonder who exactly is coming to these fights. Bay may not be the only one putting the pack and clan in danger."

She sighed. "Fine. We do this for Bay. She needs to be safe and have someone in her corner. It feels weird not having her apart of our plans though."

"I know, but I don't know what else to do. The way she made it sound was that she *has* to be there, and she seemed more worried about backing out of her end of the deal than possibly being arrested by Patrick. I need to get her out if I can. You guys are my best friends, and she needs us."

Alana nodded. "Well, I'll head home then. Set up my surprise, and tell Johnny our plans. You get to deal with Bastian though."

She laughed, but I took in a deep breath. *This was getting complicated.* She left me alone with my thoughts, and I decided to try using the mind-link again. After all these years it still wasn't something I remembered all the time. I wasn't sure if it would work honestly. I knew they talked about fishing by the river, but I wasn't sure if I was close enough for it to work.

"*Bastian?*" I asked through the mind link.

"*Hey, baby! Are you home?*" he immediately responded.

I smiled. "*Yeah, we just got home. Alana is on her way home now, and I think we scared Ryder off.*"

I could feel his laughter through our bond. "*Yeah, I need details with that. Johnny and I got a very interesting mind-link a few minutes ago. Something about never doing errands with the girls again?*"

"*Ha! Yeah... We may have went shopping for some very girly items. Lets just leave it at that.*"

He seemed amused. "*As long as he didn't see what you bought, I don't mind.*"

"*Sorry to disappoint but nothing fit right, so I didn't come back with anything. He did walk in on me when I was in the dressing room though.*"

"*He did what?!*"

I laughed hard now, and I know he felt my amusement.

"*It's fine, my love. He thought he saw something and came in to check on me.*"

All he saw was the back of my very motherly sports bra."

He grunted. "Well he's lucky then, but bummer. I was hoping you had something new to show me."

My cheeks heated and I couldn't stop myself from grinning. This man knew how to make me blush, and he wasn't even in the same room!

"Sorry, my love. You'll just have to settle for plain ole me," I teased.

"That's okay. You look better with nothing on anyways," he shot back without missing a beat.

I about jumped out of my skin when I felt his lips graze my cheek.

"Whoa, did you just kiss me?"

"You felt that?"

"Yeah, it was like you were actually here. What did you do?"

"I just thought about kissing your cheek," he replied. "I didn't really do anything."

"Let me try!"

I focused on Bastian and zeroed in on his lips. I imagined myself giving him a real kiss but kept our link opened. I held for a moment before pulling away in my head.

"Whoa, Shanely. That's amazing! I felt your kiss."

"What does this mean? Do other mates have this ability?"

"I've only heard about this in stories. Just another thing to prove how special our bond is."

"I love you, Bastian."

"I love you too. Come find us. We're by the river not far from the lodge. Try using the locator. Maybe it will work this time? I'll see you soon."

I felt him pull away from my mind. I took in a deep breath and tried to focus on our bond. It was more like a cord, when it came to the locator part of it. Our bond had been growing stronger over the years, but until my wolf appears, the final piece wasn't in place. Being this close I could see the faint cord tying us together and slowly started to follow it. I left my cabin and started down the path to the lodge. It took a lot of concentration to keep the locator on, but I was managing.

Suddenly, I heard a twig snap, and I lost the cord. I looked around, but I didn't see anything abnormal. I tried to get a scent, but it all just smelled like woods to me. Not like my senses were fully developed either in my human form but nothing seemed out of the ordinary, so I refocused on Bastian. I lost the locator bond once or twice along the way, but I soon made my way to the river, feeling quite proud of myself.

Aerith and Bastian were sitting by the edge, both with poles in hand. She was kicking her feet above the water with a big smile on her face.

"Mommy!" she cried as she dropped the fishing pole. Bastian lunged to grab her pole before it fell into the water. I picked her up, giving her a big bear hug.

"Hi, baby girl! Having fun with Daddy?"

Bastian walked up to us and kissed me hard. "Hello, my love. Good job with the locator."

I beamed back at him, feeling his pride like it was my own emotion. Aerith continued on, "Daddy and I are fishing! But we haven't caught anything yet."

She looked bummed about that.

"Well maybe I can help," I said as I set her down. I shifted carefully into my pure white grizzly bear. I had gotten better about pulling her through on my own, and it finally felt natural to me.

Aerith shouted with glee and jumped on my snout. She rubbed her face against mine, feeling my soft fur. I chuffed at her, making her slide down to let go. I walked into the water near the small drop in the river. I waited, staying as still as I could. It's amazing how in tune I was with my bear now. It made relying on her instincts and her abilities so much easier. I loved how all my senses were so much better in this form too. I could see, hear, and smell everything *clearly*. Not at all like my human form.

My target swam past, and I dunked my head under the water and snatched a massive fish. Aerith jumped up and down excitedly, while Bastian gave me a proud look as I walked back to them.

I dropped the fish at Aerith's feet, and she squealed as it flopped around. Bastian reached down and grabbed it by it's tail.

"Here, let me deal with this. We can clean it for tonight if you want to eat it, Aerith," he said.

"Yes! It's why we came fishing, right? We don't kill the fish for nothing, right?"

Bastian nodded and tussled her hair. "So you have been listening?"

"I listen to everything, Daddy," she replied as she bounded forward on the path.

He smirked as I shifted back. Water dripped off my body, but it was nice and warm outside. *I'd dry in no time.* Bastian took my hand, and we followed Aerith up the path.

"So I have some news," I said halfway up the path. Bastian raised an eyebrow at me and waited patiently for me to continue.

"You cannot say *anything* because she wants to surprise Johnny tonight, but Alana is with cub," I explained, and Bastian smiled excitedly.

"Really? Good for them! That's great news! Pretty cool she can surprise him too since bears can't really do that."

"Right? That's what we thought too! It's why we went into town today. She wanted to confirm her suspicions to surprise him. She's telling Johnny tonight, but we wanted to do a small celebration for her tomorrow night. Just us girls. It would be at her place on bear land so we'd all be safe."

"You all?"

"Just Alana, Bay, and I. We're inviting her too," I replied, hoping my voice stayed steady while we talked. *God, my anxiety was through the roof though.*

Bastian thought for a moment before answering, "Well I want you to do all the things you want to do. All I'm concerned about is safety, but if you are in the clan's land then you should be fine. Us fellas can hang with Johnny at our cabin."

I breathed a sigh of relief. I didn't expect for this conversation to go this easily. "Thank you! We can see if Aerith wants to spend some time with my dad then. He hasn't seen her this week yet."

"That's a great idea. She loves going to his place, and I can always pick her up on my way to you," he replied. The lodge came into view, and we found a large crowd already formed. It seems like the whole family was here.

"I think the secrets out," I muttered.

Sure enough, Alana was in the middle of the group, with Johnny wrapped around her little waist. Apparently, they didn't make it home or they were so excited they came back.

"I figured they'd take the night for themselves," Bastian said as we entered our circle of family.

"Shanely! Bastian! Come hear the great news!" Uncle Cain shouted.

Uncle Thomas cried out over Cain, "I'm going to be a grandfather!"

I beamed at my two friends and hugged Alana again. "What happened to your surprise?"

She laughed. "Oh, I surprised him alright, but then he hugged me and bolted from our cabin, shouting he was going to be a father to anyone he passed by. I followed him here."

I laughed. "Well congratulations, you two!"

I gave Johnny a hug, and he about picked me up when he did.

"Can you believe it, Shanely? You know if it wasn't for you none of this would have happened!" he cried.

"Congrats, man! We're so happy for you!" Bastian said as they clasped arms together. Aerith put her hands on Alana's belly then, making Alana smile.

"He's going to be a strong bear. I can tell," she said, and everyone froze.

"You mean you guess. Right, baby?" I asked her. "It's a little too soon to tell what gender or animal he will be yet."

"Oh no, I can see it. Can't you see it?"

I looked at Bastian, who looked concerned. I shook my head at Aerith.

She frowned. "I can see him and his bear. It will be a brown grizzly bear but strong."

"An ability?" Bastian asked. I stood up and shrugged.

"She's never done this before. Maybe it's a start of something?" I questioned.

"We'll keep an eye on it, but in the meantime let's celebrate!" Uncle Cain shouted, and we all cheered. Bastian explained our girls night to Johnny, and I gave Alana a thumbs up. Bay walked up then and gave Alana a hug.

"Congrats, girl! I get to be an Auntie again!" she shouted excitedly. Her hands rose above her head, and I zeroed in on a new bruise peeking out. I tried to hide my concern, but now I felt more than ever that I was making the right choice.

"You're coming tomorrow night, right?" Alana asked. I hovered closely, waiting to hear what excuse she'd come up with now.

"Tomorrow night?"

"Yeah, 6:30 at my place. We're celebrating just us girls," Alana replied.

"Oh sweetie, I can't. I have... a date that night. I've canceled twice already. Can I come by later instead? Around 8:30?" she asked, her face falling.

"Sure, we'll still be around celebrating," she replied.

"What about me?"

I turned around to see Octavia standing there with her arms folded. *Crap*, I thought to myself. *She might be a problem.*

"Oh hi, Octavia," I said, with a weak smile.

Well this was just great, I thought to myself. *She's not supposed to be there. How will I be able to do this now?*

"So can I come Alana? I am your actual sister, you know?" she said as she joined our little group.

Alana looked at me when she replied, "Of course. You remember our cousin Shanely, right? And her sister-in-law, Bay."

She looked at the both of us and gave a slow nod. "Yeah, I remember them."

Octavia has never fully warmed up to me over the years. She was really quiet and difficult to get to know, and now I had to figure out how to go to the fight with her around. I had no idea if she'd even keep my secret.

"It's good to see you again, Octavia," I said to her, but she didn't really respond.

She turned to Alana. "I'll see you at your place then, and congratulations. Bye guys."

We waved bye, and Alana gave me an *I'm so sorry!* look. I shrugged, knowing I was just going to have to figure something out now.

We stayed late celebrating with the soon to be parents at the lodge. Aerith had passed out on Cade around 9 pm, so he took her home early. He was up super early every day this week with training, so he needed to crash too.

Bastian was ready for bed around 11, and he dragged me away from everyone at the lodge. I gave Alana once last look before following my mate home.

Shanely

Bastian drove me over to Alana's house the next day, and we were right on time despite my nerves eating away at me. I didn't like fibbing like this, but my mate would never let me go otherwise. And Bay *needed* our help. I love my mate, but if he got wind that Bay was in trouble, he'd storm the club and fight for her freedom. I couldn't risk him either. Not with Patrick lurking around every corner.

I jumped when Bastian opened the truck door, knowing I was lost in my own head again, and let him help me out of his truck.

"Just call me when you're ready to come home, okay? I'll come get you, baby."

"I promise I'll give you a call when I'm ready to come home. I don't think it will be a super late night," I replied as I leaned into him. He hugged me tightly, and I looked over to Alana. Johnny must be giving Alana the same rules too as I could see her playfully rolling her eyes at him.

"I better go, baby," I said before kissing him once more.

Johnny waved goodbye as he passed us and hopped up into the truck. Bastian let me go before getting back into the driver's side. "Be safe," he said, "and have fun you guys."

My mate leaned out the window and swatted my butt as I walked away. I yipped, hearing him laugh as he pulled out of the driveway. We waited until they were long gone and I couldn't hear the diesel anymore before *daring* to speak of my plans.

"Hey! You're the first one here," Alana stated as she met me in the drive. I blew out a deep breath.

"What are we going to do with Octavia? Will she keep our secret?" I asked.

"Well it's no secret she's not the biggest fan of you, but Octavia is loyal once you get to know her. I think she will help us with this," Alana replied.

"Help you with what?"

We jumped as Octavia came bounding around the backside of Alana's place.

"Octavia, you scared me!" Alana stammered.

"Help you with what, Alana?"

With her hands on her hips, she stared down at us. She was not beating around the bush nor letting us change the subject. I sighed, knowing I was going to have to confide in her.

"I need help, Octavia. I think Bay's in trouble, and I need to sneak in somewhere to confirm it," I replied.

She narrowed her eyes. I pursed my lips into a tight line as I waited for her to rat me out.

"Why aren't the fellas here then?" she finally asked. "You all need major security just to go to the bathroom."

I looked at Alana, who gave me a small smile. "Because Bastian wouldn't let me go if I asked. Our mates don't know, and we need to keep it this way."

Her brow rose. I was surprised to see the corners of her mouth rise ever so slightly before answering, "I didn't think you had it in you, Shanely. Always seemed so ready to do exactly what Bastian said."

I frowned. "Bastian can be overprotective, but we've been through a lot. I'm still my own person, even when I do the things he asks for, but I *can't* do this with him. Will you help me?"

Octavia rocked back and forth on her feet. "Alright, but if it's dangerous then Alana shouldn't be there."

"I'm already the getaway driver," she replied, raising her hand proudly.

"Okay, well then let's go," Octavia said as she went to Johnny's truck.

"That went easier than I expected," I muttered.

Alana just shrugged, and we all piled in. Alana drove us into town and parked about a block away from the club. The music was loud enough you could hear it from where we were parked, and I wondered what I was getting myself into.

I pulled my black hoodie on with my hood up. "Ready, Octavia? Or would you rather stay with Alana?"

"I'm with you. Besides if we need, I can mind-link Alana faster than you can call. Wanna telling me what's up though?"

I sighed. "The less you know right now the better. You're about to see it all anyways. Just try to avoid using your name. There are nothing but shifters here, but apparently it's all different kinds. I don't really want everyone to know we're here tonight. They're going to scent me as it is, but I don't want people to know I'm a Fenrir if I can avoid it."

We hopped out of the truck and waved goodbye to Alana. She smiled nervously back at us and locked the door. We walked slowly to the club, and Octavia eyed me curiously when we went straight to the bar. Inside everyone was on their feet either jumping or dancing to the music. Girls filled the cages in the back and danced like no one was watching. Thankfully, they were fully clothed, but the night was still young. *That could change, I suppose.* The music was already incredibly loud, and the strobe lights made me dizzy. *This was definitely not my scene.*

"What can I get ya?" the bartender asked.

"Two bloody marys, please."

He looked me up and down before shaking his head.

"$75."

Whoa. The fees were expensive, I thought to myself. I handed him my card and paid for it. I blinked when I realized my mistake. *God, I shouldn't have use my credit card,* I thought as I gritted my teeth. *What's done is done, I guess.* He gave me my card back then stamped both of our hands. I looked at the red tiger stamp on my hand, and it glistened against my skin. He then pushed us to the back of the club. The bartender pounded on the door and left us to wait.

Octavia gave me a weird look but said nothing. I'm glad she stayed close because suddenly my nerves were going crazy. *I couldn't believe I was actually doing this.* My stomach was in knots as we waited, and I was just glad I wasn't close enough for Bastian to pick up on my emotions. I rolled my shoulders, forcing myself to calm down. *I can do this. I am not helpless,* I thought to myself.

A burly man opened it up, looked at our hands, and gestured us inside. Octavia and I went down the stairs to a very large and very *noisy* room. Suddenly, both my bear and my wolf shot to the surface. It jarred my head having them both standing at attention, and my eyes widened as I took in all these people. All the different shifter scents hit my nose at once, and the room was nearly filled to capacity with people yelling and cheering. In the dead center of the room was a large metal cage, with tall walls and a ceiling. I realized once you were inside, you were locked in. I was blown away as the two of us made our way into the crowd. *I can't believe someone would voluntarily get locked inside that cage just to fight,* I thought as my heart raced inside my chest.

Some in the crowd looked at me weird, scrunching their noses and picking up on my mixer scent. A buzzer sounded, and soon they all cheered excitedly, pushing passed us to see the next fighters coming out. I took a moment to look around, noting every possible exit I could see. Along the back wall behind the cage was a large stage set up for someone important. It was blocked off by ropes and had massive luxurious chairs to sit and watch the fights, but tonight it was completely empty. *Must be for the VIP who isn't here,* I wondered to myself. Looking up, I saw another room above the crowd. A private box with big windows for those inside to watch the cage with ease.

The announcer began shouting the fighters names, and soon two large men stepped into the cage. They each shifted and waited for the bell. All while the crowd roared excitedly. One was an African Lion, while the other was a Bengal Tiger. The bell rang, and they clashed together. The snarls and growls that came from them both were loud and intimidating. I was surprised no one outside could hear them, but then suddenly the blaring music above made sense. I looked at Octavia, whose eyes were wide.

"How did you hear about this place?"

I leaned in to reply, "I think Bay fights here."

"No way! That's pretty impressive," she replied.

"And dangerous," I muttered as the lion collapsed. The tiger roared his victory in the lion's face before leaping from the cage. They had to drag the unconscious lion out of the cage. The sight made me cringe inside slightly. *Did they ever have to do that with Bay?*

"So we're looking for Bay?" she asked.

I nodded. "And making note of anyone else from the clan or pack."

The announcer's voice boomed through the speakers again. I searched everywhere looking for Bay, but I couldn't find her. *She had to be here though!* I thought. My gut was telling me she was here somewhere. Octavia and I watched another two fights come and go, with the crowd going wilder with each one. I pulled my hood down lower, and we pushed closer to the right side.

"Now for the moment you've all be waiting for. The main fight of the night! In the right corner we have the Tiger King's personal pick, Liam Denally!"

The Tiger King.

I froze, hearing his name. My eyes widened as I slowly looked to Octavia. And then it clicked. I looked down at the stamp given to me at the door as the hairs on the back of my neck stood. *Was he here tonight?* I thought as my heart thundered in my chest. *Would I finally get to see the shifter that hunted wolves?* My fear grew, remembering what the mountain lions told me when they tried to take me after I gave birth to Aerith. They insisted the Tiger King would want me because I was a mixer. *Did I just make a major mistake coming here tonight?*

The crowd cheered as a tall man entered the cage. He had full sleeve tattoos with short, almost buzzed, hair. I preferred my mate's tattoos over this guy's. His were all over the place. Just patchwork with random pictures I could barely see from here. Bastian had his clan tag from home along with the McCoy's tag, and he recently added the bear clan to the mix. It ran perfectly down the back of his spine, with tribal marks connecting them all. It was beautifully done, and a twinge of guilt hit me thinking about my mate.

Liam roared riling the crowd once more and forced me to the present. He was scary looking, and with all these different smells I couldn't tell what kind of animal he was. I pulled my hood forward a bit more, when his eyes seemed to find mine. I watched him take a deep breath, and I stepped back into the crowd a bit more. *That can't be about me*, I thought. *Right?*

I may be the only mixer here, but there's *no way* he can scent me out of a crowd like this. *I was being paranoid again,* I told myself. But then I saw him turn to the large windows in the room above us, and I froze. I looked where he did, but I couldn't see anyone through the windows. *Was someone up there though?* I started to pull Octavia further away from his side of the ring, when the announcer startled us both.

"And in the left corner, our undefeated Champion, Mor'du!"

My eyes snapped to the person walking towards the ring. *Bay.* She wore a long robe, almost down to her feet, with a large, heavy hood over her head. You couldn't see anything under that robe, but I knew *exactly* who it was. My temper flared watching her walk towards the ring. *She lied... This ends tonight,* I thought as I crossed my arms. The crowd stepped far away from Mor'du as if they were afraid to get too close when her entourage went by. She had a few guys surrounding her as they made their way to the cage. I had no idea who they were, but they made sure no one touched her.

Bay stepped inside the cage, and the bouncers locked the door behind her. My eyes grew wide, and I dropped my arms. *They didn't lock the other fighters in,* I thought as panic surged through me. *Why would they lock her in?* She had yet to notice us, and I shifted anxiously on my feet. The man shifted first into a large tiger, and I had to admit his animal was impressive. Worry flooded my system when I remembered Bay saying tigers were the only shifters she really needed to watch out for.

The crowd gasped when Bay shifted. Her wolf was abnormally large, and quite a few shifters noticeably hissed. All tigers, I assumed. I guess the hatred wasn't just from the King. I had seen Bay's wolf many times before, but tonight I really noticed her. She was *not* afraid of the tiger in front of her, and it was her confidence I was always envious of. In many ways, I wished I could be more like her.

The bell sounded, and they bolted for each other. They clashed hard, but Bay pushed the tiger against the cage. Liam took a swipe against Bay's side, and she jumped back in pain. I winced, seeing the blood on her side. She seemed to forget her wound quickly as she charged again. Bay cornered him again and again until he was noticeably worn out. There were no breaks or rounds. It was just a fight until a winner was declared.

She eventually grabbed him by the neck and threw him across the ring. He hit the cage hard, and this time he didn't rise. She stalked over to him, waiting for him to move, but he didn't. I held my breath as the announcer rang the bell again. She howled, and the crowd went wild.

"We need to reach her and get out of here," Octavia shouted. I nodded my head as the crowd grew rowdy, bumping into Octavia and I roughly. To my dismay, Bay was already leaving the cage in her wolf form. *How were we supposed to get to her before she went through the doors?* Octavia started tugging me towards the cage's doors, but it was difficult getting through the crowd. As we made our way around the ring, four very large men stood in our path.

"Your presence is being requested."

Shanely

My eyes widened as I took a step back, only to bump into another man behind me. Being this close to him I could catch his scent clearly. Tiger.

"I don't know anyone here, so I highly doubt that. Please excuse me," I said as I grabbed Octavia's hand to drag her around the men, but the big guy blocked me again.

"I said you are being summoned. Now you can follow me or I can throw you over my shoulder just as easy. Take your pick," he replied.

My wolf snarled within me. "You will not touch me," I growled.

"Suit yourself. Darryl grab her friend," he shouted as he threw me over his shoulder. I hollered, but nothing I did mattered. Boy, this tiger was crazy strong, I thought as I squirmed in his arms. He carried me with ease, never once flinching, and simply shifted me on his shoulder when I made any sort of progress. The crowd around us stepped aside and some even laughed at the sight.

"Put me down!" I yelled at the brute carrying me. He ignored me and simply pushed through the crowd towards the side doors. Bay's wolf snapped her head in my direction. I could barely see her as we passed by, but I *know* she saw Octavia and I being carried into the next room.

The man carried me down the hallway away from the ring and then up a set of stairs. We went through another large set of doors before I finally gave up fighting him. This tiger was *not* letting me go.

He suddenly dropped me in a fairly large room, and I landed hard on my butt. When I looked around, I realized this was the private viewing room that we could see from above the ring. Big bay windows lined the room to the ring below, and it must have had some sound proofing because it was fairly quiet up here. Almost like a secret being kept from everyone else.

Octavia landed on the floor next to me. She glared at the man that carried her, but he ignored us both and went to stand guard at the door behind us.

Uh-oh.

"Welcome, welcome, welcome!" a deep voice said from the main chair in the room. It faced away from us, making it hard to get a good look at the guy.

"How do you like my fighting ring, mixer?"

"My name is Shanely Fenrir, not mixer, and whom do I have the pleasure of speaking with?" I asked confidently. *This guy was already pissing me off.*

"Fenrir, you say? I wondered if that was you. You're the first known mixer in quite some time."

Crap, I thought to myself. *Way to go, Shanely.* I just admitted the *one thing* I wanted to keep to myself. Octavia gave me a stern look, and I put my head down.

"And yet I still don't know your name," I finally said, losing some of my spunk.

He laughed. "You're a cocky little thing, aren't you?"

"I just don't appreciate being dragged up here like this is all. I don't even know what we did wrong," I said.

"I do believe my boys asked nicely first," the man muttered as he stood from his chair. My eyes widened.

This man was tall and boy was he *built*. Thick muscles lined his dark shirt, and I held my breath, wondering what trouble I just got myself into. He wore black from head to toe, looking more military than I would have expected. His hood was drawn, but when he dropped it, reddish-orange eyes glared down at me. He ran his hand through his wild and spiky white hair. A design was cut into the side of his hair, but as he stepped closer I realized it was tattoos. He had tattoos on parts of his neck and the sides of his head. I couldn't take my eyes off it. It blended into his messy hair on top. He had one large tattoo on his right arm with some sort of insignia on it. I assumed it was his streak's tag, but I really wasn't sure.

Octavia sucked in a breath, and her eyes were as big as saucers. She looked in awe at him standing in front of us before dropping her gaze to the floor.

"Oh my God, he's gorgeous. I didn't know he'd be gorgeous," Octavia muttered under her breath. I narrowed my eyes.

He smirked at me. "Have you figured it out yet, little mixer? Your friend seems to have."

I shrugged as I replied, "Am I supposed to know who you are?"

Octavia whipped her head to mine, glaring at me. The man who carried me up here grabbed me by my hair, forcing me stand.

"You ought to show some respect," he snarled in my ear. My wolf snapped her jaws angrily.

"Now, now, Finnick. She's technically royalty herself," he said as he stepped forward extending his hand to mine. "My name is Abraham. I'm the Tiger King."

My jaw dropped. *He can't be*, I thought to myself. *He's so young*. "You're the Tiger King?"

"So you have heard of me!"

"Are you kidding? She knows all about you because your stupid bounty hunters chased her and her newborn daughter in Dead Man's Hollow!" Octavia shouted before I could stop her. I gave her a cross look, but it was too late.

He pursed his lips together as his eyes narrowed at me. His cheerful expression was gone when he asked, "You're the one that killed my lions?"

"We warned them to leave us alone. I think that justifies what my mate did to them," I stammered. I tried to justify her slip up, but I didn't like the look forming on his face. The Tiger King was *not* happy to learn who killed his lions.

"Interesting... I've always wondered who did that. I knew it was wolves, and I got a vague scent of a bear, but I never knew which ones. Thank you for clarifying it for me," he said as he walked back to his chair.

Octavia realized her mistake and dropped her head in shame. I reached for her hand and gave it a reassuring squeeze. I let my anger well up inside me now as I turned back to the leader of the Tiger streak.

"Why are you hunting wolves anyways?"

"Be quiet. I need to think for a moment," he replied, and I rolled my eyes.

"By all means... Take your time. It's not like I have anything better to do," I muttered, and he shot me a look. I waited another minute before my temper flared again. "Those lions told me you have a bounty on any wolf head you find. Is that true?"

"Yes, now quiet!" he replied snidely, and rage coursed through my veins. My wolf snarled within me. She was just as angry as I was.

"How could you do that? What in the world happened to you to make you such a monster?!" I bellowed, stomping my foot.

The Tiger King stalked back to me angrily and got in my face. My eyes widened as he towered over me. "I have my reasons, but maybe you should think about the fact that you're a wolf, and I haven't killed you or your bear friend yet. I'm still *mulling* it over, so maybe just appreciate what time you have left by staying quiet!"

My chest heaved as I glared right back at the mad man. Octavia glared at me, I'm sure wishing I would shut up, but I was too angry to be thinking clearly. My animals were pushing against my skin, making any rational thought fly out the window.

"No!" I shouted as I pushed him back. "I don't know what happened to you, and honestly at this point *I don't care* because whatever happened does not give you the right to kill every wolf you meet! Not all wolves are the same, you know?"

The Tiger King stepped back, surprised by my outburst as his guard gripped my arm hard. He studied me intensely, furrowing his brows as I continued to glare. "You're really not afraid of me then?"

"Afraid?! Ha!" I cried out. "The last thing I will ever be is *afraid* of you. I want to leave now! I mean, what's the point of calling us up here? I want nothing to do with you, and you cannot keep us here!"

The Tiger King ignored me and went back to his chair. It was massive, but he flipped it around to face me with ease. He plopped down, throwing his leg over the arm rest as he got comfortable. "I had planned to offer you a job actually. A mixer would bring in a fantastic crowd in my ring, but seeing how your wolf is extremely weak, I have a better idea. Darryl take the girl's phones. Henry send a message to Bastian, please. Tell him to bring his brothers too. Oh, and you... Who do you belong to?"

Octavia glared at him as Darryl yanked our phones out of our back pockets. "I belong to no one."

"No mate? No brothers?"

"My brother is in Russia. It's just me and my sister so no. I don't have anyone you can call," she replied before snapping her mouth shut.

I shot her another look, and she looked frustrated with herself. We both seemed to run our mouths when we were upset. *Surprise, surprise,* I thought. *I had something in common with Octavia.*

"A sister, huh? That can still work. Darryl get this lovely lady's scent here, and then go find the sister. Let's see if she has a mate too," Abraham said coyly.

"What do you want with us? Why do you need our families?" I snapped at him.

He waved his finger at me. "Tsk, tsk, tsk. You are not behaving like a grateful house guest, Shanely. Beside you'll only spoil the surprise, and what fun would that be?"

I was about to blow up on him again, when a knock rattled the door. Abraham nodded his head, and one of the guards opened it. Bay pushed her way inside with bold confidence. She wore that stupid wolf mask again, but this time her hair was completely tucked within the hood.

"Ah yes, Mor'du. Well done on the fight. Liam was positive he could defeat you, but looks like you proved him wrong," Abraham stated.

I narrowed my eyes, watching him eye Bay up and down slowly. It was disgusting, but Bay said nothing in return. I gritted my teeth, expecting her to lash out at him, but she only cocked her hip to one side and waited.

"Oh right... Forgive me, Mor'du. I forgot your payment. I have some guests that distracted me," he said as he snapped his fingers. Two more tigers pushed passed Bay to grab Octavia and I. They dragged us behind the King and into the chairs along the wall. The guards then stood behind us, leaving their hands on our shoulders in warning. I knew the threat they were giving by doing that. Octavia and I were not allowed to leave, and I sat there stewing in my seat. Bay looked at me and then to Octavia, while I glared right back at her. *This was her fault.*

"What are they doing here?" she spoke, dropping her voice so low it was hard to hear her. I wondered if Abraham knew that it was a girl under that mask. I mean he must because despite being long and lean, Bay didn't have the body or stature of a guy. Unless he thought she was just a really tiny man, but I kind of doubted that by the way he looked at her before.

"That's my business," Abraham replied.

Bay snarled. "You know you'll start a war, right?"

He laughed. "Oh, I'm counting on it."

"You need to let them go," she snapped back.

"Or what? See here's the thing, Mor'du. I *own* you. You made a deal with me, and I'm delivering on that, am I not?"

Bay nodded slowly, her hands balling up in fists.

"The deal was you fight for me and only me. You fight when I tell you to, and you stay out of my business. This," he said as he gestured behind him, "is my business. Are we clear?"

She didn't say a word, and suddenly everything made sense. *She owed the Tiger King. That's why she couldn't stop,* I thought to myself as my heart sunk.

"Now you will get some compensation for tonight's fight just like I promised. Step aside, while I deal with this first, and do not say a word. Do we understand?" Abraham asked as his eyes narrowed at her.

Bay nodded and was directed to a corner near us. Bay's massive hoodie and mask covered up most of her features, and she made sure no one touched her as she stepped over to do what she was told. I heard her voice buzzing around in my head as soon as she leaned against the wall.

"What are you doing here?!" she demanded.

"I came to get you!" I shouted right back. *"I knew you were still fighting!"*

"Shanely, I told you I couldn't stop. I told you to leave it alone, but now you've gone and made everything worse!"

"You wouldn't tell me anything, Bay! Not for weeks! You've isolated yourself, and I wanted to make sure you were being safe. I needed to come and make sure you were okay. Little did I know you are working for the Tiger King! He's killing

wolves, Bay."

"I know, Shanely. I have to work for him and up until tonight it was only in the ring! Now... Now I have no idea what he will plan for me. He's smart, Shanely! His whole business is centered around deals. Deals that benefit him primarily. The fact that he hasn't let you go right now means he's plotting something, and I needed time to figure him out."

"Don't you start. He's getting Bastian and your brothers! He's looking for Alana and Johnny too! Everyone's getting pulled into this mess now."

Her eyes glared. "I didn't ask you to lie to your mate and come to an illegal fighting ring. Don't blame this all on me. Mor'du belonged to no one, so no one could be used against me. I knew what I was doing! You blindly followed me here."

My face fell. *She was right*, I thought to myself. *I lied and snuck around Bastian, and now he was in danger. Again.* I looked at me feet and didn't respond to Bay. I just wanted to go home.

"Shanely, I'm sorry," Bay said in a softer tone. "That was out of line. It's my fault for getting involved with him in the first place."

You were right though," I replied, shrugging my shoulders. "You're not the only one to blame. Why did you make a deal with Abraham though?"

"I can't tell you, Shanely."

The doors flew open cutting Bay off. In walked Alana and Darryl. "She wasn't hard to find, Boss. Sitting right outside the club."

Her eyes flew to the three of us as Darryl dragged her to the other opened chair.

"Are you guys okay? Who is this? Why are we here?" Alana's questions were flying off her tongue frantically.

"Shhh! Alana, this mad man in front of us is Abraham. The Tiger King," I said, gesturing my head in his direction, and her eyes grew wide.

Abraham turned around to face me. "You know I can hear you, right?"

I stuck my tongue out in response, and the tiger behind me snatched it. It startled me, and I panicked when he forcefully pulled my head to the side. He started to squeeze my tongue rather hard, and I immediately grabbed his hands to stop him.

"Boss, I think things will be easier if we just cut this one's tongue out," he said nonchalantly. *Like cutting someone's tongue out was a common thing for them!* I thought to myself as my eyes widened. I saw his finger shift slowly, making his nail long and sharp. He drug it across my tongue, and I wanted to hurl.

Abraham just laughed. "Leave her, Finnick. She's quite entertaining though."

He leaned back in his seat, ignoring us now, and I wondered if Finnick would actually listen. The brute finally let me go, and I held my jaw as my tongue throbbed. I wish I had some water to wash down the awful taste in my mouth, but there was no way I was going to ask for anything. Now all I could was wait. Wait for my mate to show up furious over the situation I stumbled into.

Yeah... He was definitely going to be pissed with me.

Bastian

"Thanks for letting me come hang tonight. As much as I hate leaving Alana right now, I really didn't want to be around the girls tonight," Johnny said as we pulled away from his cabin.

I smirked at him. "What are you afraid they will talk about the birth or something?" Silence filled the cab, and I glanced at my friend. Johnny had turned beat red, and my jaw nearly hit the floor. "You're not serious, are you?"

"Oh, c'mon man! That's a whole lot information I really don't need to know."

"You're the *dad*, Johnny. The birthing process shouldn't scare you."

"Alana's so tiny, Bastian. I don't even know how she will be able to do that," he replied, and I could hear the worry in his words. I chuckled, knowing full well what he was feeling.

"Johnny, women have done this since the dawn of time. I mean look at Shanely. She gave birth after being beaten nearly to death in the dead of winter, and she survived. Alana will have Dr. Malin and Cassia with her the whole time too. She's going to do great man," I replied, trying to comfort him. I genuinely felt bad for Johnny. This was all new for him, and I know how it feels to constantly wonder about what *could* happen. It's been four years since Shanely went through all that, and I was only just now starting to let my mate out of my sight.

"I know, and I have faith in her, but I worry. I worry about her delivering, and how I'm going to be a father. I didn't have a father, Bastian. You know that. How am I supposed to raise this kid when I'm barely an adult myself?"

"Yeah well sometimes not knowing your father is a blessing," I muttered, shaking myself from those thoughts. "You just figure it out as it goes. I did with Aerith, so will you with this one."

He sighed as we turned into my drive. "Yeah, I suppose. I don't think I want to watch her deliver though. That part makes me queasy, I'll be honest."

I laughed hard, bringing the truck to a stop. Elijah and Cade were outside already with Cade's Excursion on a jack stand. They were putting on a new tire, and they gave a quick wave hello.

"Yeah that feeling will pass, Johnny. You're going to be smitten with that little one the second he gets here."

"Is that how it felt with Aerith?" he asked me, and I leaned back in my seat, thinking back on the first time I held her.

"Yeah, it was. I know she isn't my blood technically, but when I held her for the first time... She just melted my heart. My wolf claimed her right then and there as one of my own and by God, she looked just like Shanely. Her real Dad with never be anything more than the sperm donor in my opinion."

I opened the door and hopped out of the truck, and Johnny followed suit.

"Seriously though, you are going to be a great dad. That kid's gonna grow up with a massive family just like Aerith. Everyone will be around to help if you guys need it too. We're pack Johnny, but remember you've got this in the bag."

"There's the father to be!" Cade shouted as he and Elijah finished changing out the tire to his truck.

"Hey guys. Need any help?" Johnny asked. He seemed more content than he did on the drive over, and I hoped he wouldn't let his anxiety get the best of him with this. Johnny was going to be an incredible dad despite not having his own father to guide him. He never knew his dad, and he and his mother joined in the McCoy pack back when Johnny was three. I was so happy for him and Alana though because they were going to be great parents.

I left the guys and headed into the house. I dropped my truck keys in the bowl and made my way to the fridge. I grabbed a handful of beers, tossing them into a small cooler that was tucked above the fridge before heading back out. I tossed one to Johnny before handing the other two to my brothers.

I dropped the cooler and drank mine nearly gone before crashing on my porch step.

"The girls doing good?" Elijah asked, and I nodded.

"Safe and sound at Johnny's. Octavia and Bay are supposed to be there sometime tonight too," I replied. I was beat and ready to relax for the night. My girls were both safe and having fun, and I was finally off work. My wolf and bear were itching to run, but I was ready to just stretch out here. I've been gone from home too much lately, and I missed it.

"Good. They need a girls night," Cade commented as he chucked a tool aside and went for the jack.

"Elijah grab that stand, will ya?" he asked, and I watched them slowly lower the truck back down. Elijah raised his hand to me, and I tossed him another beer. It was hard for shifters to feel the affects of alcohol, so we could drink a lot more than most. Not that I really ever did. I didn't like being drunk or dealing with the hangovers that would always come the next day. I usually quit after a few just in case I ever needed to defend my family if something bad happened.

"Well that's one thing done. Next I'll be doing the oil change, but I really don't feel like it tonight," Cade said, collapsing next to me.

"I hear ya. I just want to chill tonight until my girl calls me," I answered back. The fellas and I just hung out on the porch for awhile before Ryder appeared from behind the cabin.

He shifted, bumping into Johnny before swiping his beer from him. "Sup, y'all."

Ryder crashed on the steps next to me, and I playfully pushed him. "So... What's this about you seeing Shanely in her bra?"

Beer shot out from his nose, and his hands rose defensively as he barred his neck to me. "I swear to God, Bastian. That was an accident!"

"You did what?!" Cade growled as Elijah started chuckling.

"Okay... Wait a minute. Let's back up here and state the obvious, alright? I feel like it just needs to be said. I didn't go looking for it! She was taking forever in that freaking store, and I could have sworn I saw something out of the corner of my eye. I thought maybe someone else was in there, but I was wrong, and she ended up yelling at me, and I bolted out of there as quick as I could!"

"Why in the world did they want to shop *there* of all places with you? That's what I want to know," Johnny asked, raising his eyebrow. Ryder was just flustered, running his hand through his blond hair, and I couldn't help but grin.

"I don't know! They didn't say that's where they wanted to go otherwise I would have told them no! They shopped for tampons and bras the whole afternoon, and I have to say it was the worst afternoon I think I've ever had with them."

I suddenly lost it and was laughing hysterically on my porch step. Ryder shoved me in annoyance.

"It's not funny!" he shouted.

"Oh c'mon, it's a little funny," I said, losing it again. We all laughed at our friend, who just looked completely exasperated.

"No, it's not! It was humiliating! These old ladies kept glaring at me the entire time I was in the store like I was some creep," Ryder exclaimed, snatching the beer from my hand. He downed it, and I rolled my eyes. Cade's head suddenly perked up to the drive.

"Big truck's coming, Bastian," he said, and I turned to look. A bright red truck was coming down the drive, and I relaxed.

"It's just Caleb," I replied.

I stood up to stretch my legs now and opened a fresh beer, seeing how Ryder drank my last one. I leaned forward on the railing, waiting for my brother-in-law. It didn't take long for his truck to appear, and the big guy hopped out.

"Hey guys. I ran into Dad, and he mentioned the party was over here tonight. Thanks for the invite," Caleb said sarcastically.

I tossed him a beer. "Sorry, it was super last minute. Shanely wanted to have a baby shower or something with Alana tonight, so Johnny came over here. Ryder just showed up."

He caught the beer and stood in front of us all. The sun was going down, but it was still nice and warm out. I had a few hours to kill before Shanely would want to come home. Honestly, I was ready to go get her now. I missed my mate, but I reminded myself that she needed a night out with the girls. Unless it's a pack meeting, she rarely gets to do stuff like this, so I'm glad I could help make it happen for her. Johnny and Alana's place wasn't directly next to the clan's main lodge, so Patrick shouldn't be able to run into her tonight either. That *seriously* helped my animals relax.

"So... training went well yesterday," Caleb said with a grin.

I smirked. "Yeah more than half made it through, which was more than I expected."

"I caught quite a few as did Caleb and Elijah. They need work, Bastian," Cade chimed in.

"They're improving though, especially Brody. He was fast in the games!" Johnny said, and I nodded.

"Yeah, he was out in under 4 minutes," I spoke up before turning to Elijah. "He used the mud to get passed you."

"Smart. What was his baby's scent?" he asked.

"Uh... He had red, which was one of the harder scents. I think it was pine or something woodsy," Johnny answered.

"Yeah his scent was easier to sneak the doll back, but the trick was finding it in the first place," I chimed in, and Elijah nodded his head.

"That's why the mud worked so well then. The kid smelled like the woods and easier to mask without getting it messy," he said, opening another beer.

"I think he's ready for patrols honestly. It's the next step up," Cade said, and I nodded.

"Johnny and I think so too. Give him more responsibility and get him out of that bunk house. God, that reeked yesterday!" I spoke up, and the fellas laughed.

"Wild animals don't smell that bad!" Ryder said mid-laugh.

We all lost it after that, and man it felt good to just laugh again. It feels like I'm always so busy that I miss out on this kind of fun. I just wish Shanely was here. She'd make the night perfect. My mate could be snuggled up against me under a blanket and hot cocoa with a dash of cinnamon, which was her favorite, and then the night would just be perfect. I was itching to get back to her, but the fellas and I all stayed put on the porch for the next hour, drinking beers and talking about the recruit's next step.

Suddenly, Cade's head shot up, and he leaned forward.

"Bastian, are you expecting anyone else tonight?" he asked, and I leaned forward now.

I strained my eyes to see, but it was really dark, and all I could make out were bright headlights.

"No, I'm not," I replied, standing up. The others followed suit, and we waited to see who was coming onto my land. It was getting late, and no one in my pack had called out or said anything through the link. *Who could it be?* I wondered, and then I thought of Shanely. I checked my phone, but there were no missed calls or anything. I wished my bond was complete with her, so I could check on her right now.

"Johnny link the girls. Check on them," I commanded, switching into my Alpha role without realizing it.

"Already on it," he replied as his eyes glossed over.

A big black SUV came to a slow stop, and my animals started going berserk. *Something wasn't right.*

Elijah emitted a low growl. "Tiger."

My eyes widened as I looked to my brother. The door opened, and sure enough a tiger shifter stepped out.

"I'm looking for Bastian Fenrir."

I stepped forward. "That's me. What are you doing on my land, tiger?"

He shouldn't be here, I thought to myself. This was extremely close to pack lands and I didn't like it. *Why in the world was he here, and how did he even know where to find me in the first place?*

The tiger stepped forward into the porch light, so we could all see each other a bit better. He was average height with dark hair and had the traditional orange eyes that were a tiger shifter's dead giveaway to their animal.

"You are being requested by the Tiger King. You need to come with me," he replied, folding his arms across his chest.

"Yeah, I don't think so buddy. I want anything to do with the Tiger King,"

I answered him. I stretched my arms out ready to deal with him physically if he wouldn't leave my land peacefully.

He gave me a cocky grin before replying, "You will want to reconsider Bastian Fenrir and you too, Johnny McGee."

Johnny stepped forward next to me as the hairs on the back of my neck stood. My animals were on full alert as worry washed over me.

"Alana won't answer me," he whispered, and alarm bells immediately started going off in my head as I turned to face the tiger again.

"Why should we reconsider, tiger?" I demanded. Nothing prepared me for what he was about to say next.

"Because the Tiger King has your females. Shanely, Alana, and Octavia are in his care tonight, and he requests your presence as well."

Shanely

It wasn't long before I felt him.

Bastian.

His link buzzed around in my head sounding fuzzy. *He must be on his way because it wasn't clear yet,* I thought to myself. I looked to Alana, who was white as a ghost. Johnny must be giving her an earful right now, but I didn't dare ask her about it. *Maybe we could use our links to our advantage and keep the guys from making any sort of deal with the Tiger King?*

"Shanely?!" my mate bellowed through the link.

"Bastian!"

"*Where are you?! Please tell me this tiger is lying and you're still at Alana's!*"

Guilt ate at me. "I'm so sorry, Bastian. This isn't a joke, but please whatever you do don't agree to anything he says! You can't..."

A hard smack came across my face and knocked me out of my chair, interrupting my link.

"Finnick?" Abraham asked.

"I can see it, Boss. She's using her mind-link. Bastian must be close."

Alana paled, shutting down her bond as she sunk further in her chair. Thankfully, Darryl wasn't too concerned about watching her every move. *Lucky me, Finnick was my handler.*

Abraham came over and crouched down beside me. He grabbed my chin gently and forced me to look at him. "Now my little mixer... We can't spoil the surprise, can we?"

"*Shanely!? What happened? Are you there?!*"

Bastian's voice boomed through my head now, and I could feel his panic.

My face swelled and throbbed where Finnick struck me, and I stared into Abraham's eyes, unsure what to do or say now. I was fuming mad, but at this point I wasn't sure who I was more angry with. Myself or the prick who hit me.

"Finnick, no more hitting my house guests, alright? And you..." he said, gripping my chin to ensure my attention. "If you want to stay conscience long enough to know what's about to happen then I suggest you ignore your mate's link for now, alright?"

I gritted my teeth but nodded as he helped me back into my chair with a surprising gentleness about him. Octavia tried to lean closer to me but was yanked back by her own handler. I gave her a nod and rubbed my face. Bastian was non-stop with the link, and I hated to ignore him. It killed me to, but I went ahead and completely closed down our bond.

I glared at Finnick, who simply glared right back. I don't even know how that tiger knew, but *good God* he was strong. Bay wasn't lying when she said she needed to watch tigers in her fights.

We didn't have to wait long before the doors opened again as Henry led Bastian, Cade, Elijah, Caleb, Ryder, and Johnny all into the room. They all looked pissed as they quickly assessed everything. Our boys snarled at Abraham when they saw us sitting behind him. I just wanted to sink further into my seat once my mate found me. Bastian's eyes went straight to my face, and I felt his power hit us in waves. The tiger enforcers looked extremely uncomfortable, but Abraham showed no signs of feeling any pain. He stood up to greet our boys with a mocking bow.

"Welcome Bastian Fenrir and his close associates! Glad you all could make it on such short notice. Before we begin I suggest you rein in your Alpha power, buddy. Otherwise, I'll make the girls wait in the other room with my men unsupervised. We clear?"

I could see Finnick grin from the corner of my eye, and I visibly shuddered. I tried to yank his hand off my shoulder, but he wasn't having it and only gripped it harder.

Bastian painfully pulled back his Alpha power before gritting out, "Who hit her?"

Abraham pointed to Finnick. "A simple misunderstanding is all. As long as you keep your power to yourself, you have my word not one of my tigers will harm the girls tonight. Well anymore."

"A simple *misunderstanding?* Her face is swollen!" Bastian snapped back.

"Finnick... Tell the wolf you're sorry," Abraham commanded with a cocky arrogance.

Finnick snorted before spitting out a half-hearted apology to Bastian. Bastian started moving towards Finnick before Elijah grabbed him. He shook his head no, and Abraham laughed.

"There now that we've settled that, let's talk! The girls will not be harmed here, I promise you," he said clearly amused by the whole evening. I was bewildered with the Tiger King. *How could anyone enjoy something like this?*

"Tonight will be the only night you see them, *tiger*," Cade snarled.

Abraham smiled. "We will see, but for now let's talk! I am a busy guy after all."

"What deal do you have for us?" Bastian demanded.

"Getting right down to it, I see. Don't you want a proper introduction, wolf?" Abraham asked as he feigned being offended.

"I know exactly who you are, Tiger King. Shifters come from all over to make deals with you. These deals are only beneficial to you though, and you use your tiger's abnormal strength to get what you want, and now you've taken my mate. My wife, along with others that I care about and have sworn to protect, which means you must want to make a deal. So out with it. Then I can decide *exactly* how I want to proceed with you," Bastian said confidently, and my eyes widened. *It seems Bastian knew more about the Tiger King than I realized.* I could see his eyes shift back and forth between Abraham and I. He was going to be so mad at me when I told him the truth.

Abraham smirked. "You're a smart wolf, I'll give you that. I don't meet wolves too often that impress me, but you are right. I need some things retrieved, and I don't like doing the dirty work myself. Seeing how you personally killed some of my bounty hunters, I'm in need of new ones. I simply got lucky when the mixer stumbled into my ring tonight. The Fenrir brothers are known for tracking, so here's my deal. You work for me and retrieve everything I need, and I'll keep the girls alive, which is saying something seeing how it's not normally how I handle wolves."

The fellas all snarled at his offer. Their eyes turned gold, while Bastian's went blood red. I watched as the grin and playfulness from the Tiger King's face fell away, and in a flash it was replaced with malice and hatred. His eyes flashed brightly, and he squared up to our wolves.

"I'm warning you. Control your temper. I will not stand for temperamental shifters in my house nor do I have any need for them. If I don't have any *need* of you then I will go back to my normal methods of dealing with wolves, starting with the girls," Abraham said dryly.

Bastian looked ready to explode. I could see he was fighting the need to shift. Instinctively, I went for him ready to calm his wolf. I hated seeing him like this, especially when it was all my fault, but Finnick slammed me back down before I got very far.

"Enough Finnick!" Bay hissed, but it was loud enough for Bastian to recognize. He hadn't even paid any attention to the shadow standing into the corner, but his full attention was there now. He was very well aware, and before I could link him anything, he spoke.

"Bay?"

Bay froze but refused to say anything. She slumped back against the wall, trying to disappear in the shadows again. Bastian turned back to me, and I'm sure saw the fear in my eyes.

Abraham looked puzzled for a moment before replying, "Have you met my Champion before, Bastian? This is Mor'du, my undefeated Champion in the shifter ring."

Bastian's fury exploded then. He was unable to stop it, and he looked ready to kill. Bay was definitely taking some of his wrath as she refused to lift her head to him.

"I warned you, wolf. Finnick, the collar," Abraham shouted.

Before I even knew what was happening, a sleek black collar was clamped around my neck. The second it touched my neck my animals disappeared, and I could not feel my bond with Bastian anymore. My eyes widened, and I was scared out of my mind. *What in the world was this thing?* I thought to myself as I tugged on it. The collar had a very long chain on it, which Finnick threw to Abraham.

"Reign it in, wolf! Your mate will forever be my slave resting at my feet if you don't!" Abraham bellowed, and Bastian barely managed to pull back his wrath. Abraham yanked me forward, and I fell at his feet on the ground.

"Don't hurt her!" Bastian snarled as I tried to get to my feet. Finnick was right behind me though and made sure I stayed on my knees.

"Then take my deal! I'll give all the girls back when the work's been caught up. You killed my lions, so now you get to do their dirty work."

Elijah rested his hand on Bastian's shoulder and gave him a nod.

"Bastian, stop! Don't even think about it," I shouted. "This was all my fault! I stupidly convinced the girls to come here…"

A small bolt of electricity shot through my neck, cutting me off. I yelped in pain, while Abraham smirked.

"Stop it!" Cade shouted, pacing the room before us.

"Why would you come here, Shanely?!" Elijah demanded. His eyes were full of worry, and guilt overwhelmed me. I slowly looked to Bay before dropping my head.

"Yes, Shanely Fenrir. Why *did* you decide to visit my delightful ring? Now I'll admit, you have me curious about that too," Abraham said as he knelt down beside me, gripping my chain tightly.

I struggled to breathe as my eyes went back and forth between Abraham and Bay. I didn't know how to even respond to that question without giving her away. The Tiger King hasn't focused much on Bastian's slip up with Bay's name, and I couldn't be the one to officially out her to him. I came here to get her out of her deal, not make it worse. But Bay was right. *I sure did make a mess of things.* Abraham gently rubbed the side of my arm with his finger waiting for my answer, and Bastian charged forward. Cade and Elijah caught him and forced him back, muttering something I couldn't hear.

Abraham laughed. "Now, now, let's give her a chance to answer."

"I can't say," I whispered.

"You can't say? I'm sorry, but I believe I asked you a question, Shanely. And when I ask a question I expect to get an honest answer. Now I want to know how this golden opportunity landed at my feet," Abraham replied.

I nervously clamped my mouth shut, refusing to answer him, when my handler lost his temper.

"Oh for Pete's sake, Abraham. Just light her up!" Finnick bellowed as he ripped the control from Abraham.

I didn't even have time to register what had happened before pain rippled though my neck. I screamed and fell on the floor, clutching the collar. I couldn't focus on anything or anyone as excruciating pain surged through my body. It burned against my neck and felt like my blood was on fire. My whole body convulsed in pain, and soon my vision blurred. A loud roar sounded behind me, and I recognized who's wolf it was. I had come to recognize everything about Bastian, and I knew he was the one who shifted.

As fast as the pain came, it was gone just as quick. I struggled to catch my breath as chaos ensued around me. I slowly opened my eyes to find everyone in a brawl. Bastian had shifted and was fighting a tiger in front of me. Cade and Ryder shifted as well, and we're going head to head with Abraham's guards. Johnny, Elijah, and Caleb were pushing their way to Alana and Octavia, but fighting in their human form rather than their animal form. Abraham had Finnick by the neck, and he... was... *pissed*.

"Enough!" Abraham bellowed as a gun went off. It was loud, and everyone jerked to a stop. Guns weren't something normally used by shifters, but Abraham had one.

"Everyone that shifted needs to shift back now! My men back off," Abraham demanded, holding the gun and Finnick. I looked at the prick who was on his knees and in obvious pain, but he didn't make a move against his King.

Bastian shifted quickly and ran to my side. No one stopped him as he picked me up. I fell against his shoulder exhausted and overwhelmed. He whispered over and over, "Shh, Shanely. It's okay. It's going to be okay."

Bastian rubbed my head and held me as close. I looked around to the others, and everything was just a mess. Alana and Octavia were on their feet but still being held by Abraham's tigers. More tigers had come in once the fight had started and had pushed our guys back to their corner. I didn't realize Abraham had so many enforcers with him, but we were completely outnumbered. To make matters worse, I didn't even have my animals anymore. They were gone, just like when Derek drugged me, and I was helpless again. I wouldn't be able to use my bear to protect anyone.

The boys feet were like lead as the tigers pushed them back. No one wanted to move any further away from us. My pack was livid, and they all were panting hard from the brief fight. They had marks on them, and Caleb's lip was busted, but the tigers looked haggard as well. Johnny began pushing forward again to Alana, but Elijah grabbed his arm. I could see them silently communicating before Johnny looked all around. We were all in a tough spot and things were really tense.

Abraham put his gun back in its holster and let go of Finnick. He rubbed his neck, surprised by Abraham's lack of reaction. But the Tiger King simply ignored him as he knelt down to my eye level. Bastian gave a low-warning growl, and Abraham wisely kept a little distance this time.

"Are you alright, Shanely?" he asked me.

I nodded my head to him, and he seemed satisfied with my answer. *Why did he even care?* I wondered. *He's the one who zapped me the first time. Why did it matter that Finnick lit me up?* What he did next surprised us all. He stood up, stomped straight back to Finnick, and decked him. He laid him out on the floor before towering over him. I could see his eyes glow from here as he repeatedly hit Finnick's face. Over and over again, until his face was so bloody you couldn't even tell who it was anymore.

The Tiger King finally stopped and started wiping off his bloody knuckles. "Henry remove Finnick from my good graces. Stick him on wall duty until I decide to bring him in. And Finnick?"

Finnick, who was barely able to move his head, looked to his King.

"Don't you ever overstep me again. These girls are my guests, and *I* decide what happens to them. Not you. You will not touch these girls again. Do you understand me? The next time you overstep like that it will be the last thing you ever do."

Finnick coughed and sputtered without answering Abraham. I watched Henry and another tiger pick him up by his arms and dragged him out of the room. Abraham came back to me and Bastian. Bastian tightened his grip on me, refusing to be moved, but surprisingly Abraham did not reach for me. My eyes narrowed at this utterly confusing man, trying to figure him out.

"I am sorry about that, Shanely. I swore to your mate that you would not be harmed tonight, and my enforcer overstepped. It will not happen again, I assure you. You did not deserve that level of pain, and for that you may stay by your mate, while I continue my business with him," he said.

Bastian relaxed and kissed my cheek as Abraham walked over to Alana. Her eyes grew wide again, filling with fear as the Tiger King hovered over her.

"You. Shanely is taking a small break from answering questions right now, but you were found waiting in the car outside the club. Getaway driver, I take it?"

Alana shook her head yes but refused to answer him. Abraham nodded before jerking his head to the guard behind her. The guard clasped a collar around her neck and then around Octavia's. She jerked away from him hard, but it was useless. The collar was already on, and they were both feeling the effects of losing their bears.

Johnny roared, "Don't touch her! She's carrying a cub!"

Abraham pointed to Alana. "Her?"

Johnny began pacing back and forth now. His eyes were filled with fury, and I felt horrible. *Alana wouldn't be in this mess if I hadn't dragged her with me tonight,* I thought to myself. *She and her cub would be safe at home, but instead she's chained up like I am. Johnny will never forgive me.*

Abraham smirked gleefully. "Well this keeps getting better and better. Alright someone better start answering my questions because I have asked nicely more than once. Normally, I don't give shifters a second chance, but you ladies I seem to have developed a soft spot for. But mark my words, I will not ask again! Now one of you answer my question. Why did you come here tonight!?"

"Because of me!"

Abraham whipped around to face Bay. "Mor'du? They came for you?"

She whipped her hood off and removed her mask. Her soft black curls bounced around her face as she stared Abraham down. She sucked in a breath ever so subtly before finding her voice again.

"Yes, I'm apart of their pack. Bastian, Cade, and Elijah are my brothers. Shanely found out about me fighting and came tonight to find a way to get me to stop. Please stop hurting them, Abraham. They didn't even know I worked for you."

Abraham froze, his entire body tense as he stared at her. He always seemed to be in control of his emotions, but I think seeing who Mor'du really was unsettled him. His eyes went up and down Bay slowly like he was in disbelief at the truth before him. I looked to Bastian, but he just glared at his sister. I don't think he even saw what I was seeing, and honestly I wasn't even sure what I saw. Abraham regained his composure before addressing her in his typical cocky tone.

"So Mor'du is a girl? I suspected, but it's nice to see it confirmed. I remember the Fenrir brothers having a sister. What was her name again?"

"Bay, sir," Darryl answered.

Bastian rested his head against mine.

"You came for her?" he whispered.

I nodded, but Abraham continued on before I could respond.

"Bay," he said lost in thought before quickly snapping out of it. "Bay, Bay, Bay. Well this changes some things, but not everything. You still owe me, but I am quite happy you dropped this opportunity at my feet."

"What does she owe?" Elijah demanded.

Abraham turned to Bay, who looked at her feet in shame. "Makes sense she didn't tell you about our deal. Did you even know she was Mor'du?"

"We recently found out," Cade snarled.

"Whatever deal she made, let us take the payment. Let her go free with the rest of the girls," Ryder snapped back.

All the boys seemed in agreement with that, and I gripped Bastian's shirt harder.

"I'm so sorry, Bastian. I lied to you and caused all this," I said, my voice raspy.

"Shh... Shanely. None of this is your fault. It's Bay's," he replied before

Abraham interrupted us again.

"My apologies, but it doesn't work that way. You see... Bay here brings in the most money to the ring. I am honoring my end of the bargain, so I need her to stay with me," he replied as his eyes shot to Bay's.

"What deal? What could you have possibly needed from him, Bay?!" Cade spat out angrily.

"Why, Derek's head, of course. You know how difficult it is to catch a worthless shifter, who's hiding in a powerful pack across the seas? I should have it done soon, but then again Bay never specified *when* I needed to deliver my end of the bargain. I guess it's my decision when to take that shifter's head and end our deal."

Abraham sat back in his chair, kicking his leg over the side as he rested his hands behind his head. All eyes shot to Bay's, who wouldn't look up.

"Bay, why would you do that? What about you're own connections?" I asked. My throat hurt, and it was sore enough that my voice was barely a whisper.

Bay looked at me with a sad expression as she said, "My connections bailed on me the moment I didn't return with my father. When they heard whose pack the target was in, they refused to even try. I didn't have many to begin with in the first place, but I gave you my word Shanely, and I'd honor that. I hate it's taken me this long in the first place. Derek needs to die for what he did, and the fact that our father welcomed him into his pack with open arms pisses me off even more. It's disgusting, Shanely. I came to the rings to let off some steam, and I discovered who ran them. As long as I fight... Our deal holds."

"For how long then?" Cade asked, his eyes fixed on Abraham.

"That wasn't put in the contract when I signed. I was so blinded by my rage that I didn't even think about the details. I assumed I'd stop when Derek's head was brought to me. I made a mistake." Bay's voice shook with emotion. She was on the verge of crying, and I just couldn't let her take all the blame like that. If you follow the threads, it all leads back to me. If I had just told Bastian what was going on, we wouldn't be here. If I had never come to Diablo, no one would be in this mess.

"Alright new deal, Tiger King," Bastian said firmly. "We track what you need, and then when we're done you let the girls go, and I mean all the girls, including Bay. But you make one list, and once the list is done then our deal is done. We part ways for good then. You stay out of my pack, and we will stay away from your streak. Deal?"

Abraham thought about it for a moment, and then looked to Bay before answering, "One other condition. We're allowed to communicate with one another without war."

What? I thought to myself puzzled by his reaction. I gave him a funny look, but he just stared back with a blank expression. *Why would he want to stay in contact with us especially since we were wolves? He hates our kind.*

"Why would you want that?" Cade asked, reading my mind.

Abraham shrugged. "You are the first wolves I haven't wanted to kill. You're not shady, and you all seem to actually care about your own. I find it interesting, and we may be in need of each other in the future. I'd like to keep the door opened after this deal. I'll be losing a lot of money letting Bay out of her end of the deal early, but I do need these shifters found. The Fenrir brothers have a reputation at being the best trackers in the shifter community, and I may never get another chance to twist your arm into working for me. Besides, having the shifter world know you all work for the Tiger King, even temporarily, is worth the money I'd lose in the end. However... I also need Bay to agree to never fight for another ring or sponsor. If she fights, she belongs to me *only*, and I will come after everyone in this room if I discover her betrayal. Otherwise, no deal to all of it, and I keep the girls as collateral for killing my bounty hunters. Do you accept, Bay?"

She nodded solemnly. "I will only fight for you, Tiger King."

He smirked before turning to Bastian. "Do you accept the new terms then?"

Bastian looked to me then over to his brothers. They gave him a stiff nod before he glared back at Abraham.

"Deal."

Abraham clasped his still bloody hands excitedly. "Perfect! Alright boys, let's give the wolves 5 minutes with their girls before we escort them out."

We all turned to the Tiger King in shock. I clung to Bastian, who snarled.

"Escort them out? You're not taking them!" Caleb bellowed as the boys all growled towards the King.

"You didn't stipulate where they would stay while the job was getting done. I'd like to keep an eye on them and make sure you boys stay in line and actually do your job."

"Bastian! What about Aerith?! I can't leave her... Not with Patrick around now. She can't be alone with him!" I stammered as my eyes widened. *What had I done?!*

"Patrick? Aerith? Who might these people be, honey?" Abraham asked curiously. I ignored his pet name.

"Aerith is my daughter. I can't be away from her while they complete the deal. Bastian is good for his word, okay? He will do what you ask, but Patrick's a horrible human, and I don't trust my daughter to be without me or her dad. Patrick's the cop that's been sniffing around your fights, and he's..." I look to Bastian as I was unsure how to answer the rest of that question. *The less he knows the better,* I thought to myself. "Just please let me return. Send your tigers to our lands if you want to watch us, but I *need* to go back home."

"The deal's been made, little wolf, but I am not such a cruel man to separate a mother from her child. Your daughter will stay with you in my castle, while your mate completes his job," Abraham replied like it was the easiest solution in the world.

My eyes widened. "She's four. This will be scary for her, and she won't understand Abraham."

"Well... She can stay alone on pack lands without you, if you prefer? This is the last time I will offer though, so choose wisely. I can promise you, no human or tiger, will harm her while you are guests in my house. Even someone as wicked as myself does not approve of harming children, no matter their shifter animal."

I looked to Bastian, and he seemed almost distraught. He looked back at me and rested his head against mine as tears fell down my face. *God, I was so stupid!* To think I could sneak into a place like this without repercussions, and now my whole family was in danger. My mate belonged to the Tiger King now, and it was all *my fault.*

"Baby, it's going to be okay. The boys and I will finish the job fast, and soon you all will be home again. We've gotten through a lot worse, and we can do this too. You can handle this and keep our daughter safe, I know it."

I kissed him hard, and I could feel his hands gripping my hair. He was worried, but he had faith. More than what I had at the moment, and I replied, "I'll have her stay with me then."

"It will be done. You all have until she gets here. Bastian send one in your party to grab Aerith and bring her here," Abraham stated firmly before standing. He made his way to the door before stopping to add, "Oh, and Bastian? They better hurry."

"Ryder go get my daughter, please," Bastian asked, throwing him the keys to his truck.

Ryder caught them one handed and bolted from the door. Bastian helped me up and tried to remove the collar from my neck.

"I wouldn't touch that if I were you," Darryl stated.

Bastian glared at him. "Must they wear these collars the whole time?"

"That's not for me to decide, but you boys need to be able to shift or this whole thing will take even longer. The inside of the collar has obsidian mixed with wolf's bane. It forces your animal to go dormant for a few days if it gets on your skin. The girls won't be allowed to shift in the castle, but it's Abraham's choice how long they wear the collars for," he replied.

Bastian was seething mad, so I hugged him closer to me and whispered, "It's okay, Bastian. As ruthless as Abraham seems, he also seems to honor his word. We'll be okay until you come to get us."

He nodded but glared at Darryl again. "Any of our girls gets so much as a scratch on them, and you can tell your King he's a dead man. Got it?!"

Darryl eyed him carefully. "Your women won't be harmed."

Bastian hugged me tightly as I looked around the room. Johnny had refused to let Alana go, and I could see she was crying softly in the back of the room. Caleb was hugging Octavia, who was taking everything surprisingly well, while Bay stood alone in the corner. Elijah slowly made his way to her as Cade came to me.

"Baby Girl! We can't leave you alone for a second, can we?" he said as he buried me in his arms despite Bastian's protests.

"Cade, I can't breathe!" I muttered, and he released me with a smirk on his face before it fell.

Cade cupped the sides of my face, looking at the welt that had formed from Finnick. He could see the red ring on my neck from the shocks of the collar too. He glared at Bastian. "We do this fast, brother. I don't like knowing our girls are here chained up like dogs."

Bastian gave him a pointed look. "You think I wanted to go slow? I want the list tonight so we can start."

Elijah came over next and hugged me. I sighed, feeling a weight lifted off my shoulders then. *These three boys were my rock,* I thought to myself. *They were my whole world, and I knew I could count on them. Always.* My anxiety started to melt away, having my family so close to me.

"Shanely, why didn't you tell us what was going on?" Elijah asked patiently. He inspected my face like Cade had before glaring at Darryl, who was simply watching the whole interaction.

"I wanted to be wrong. I asked Bay about it and told her to quit, but I couldn't shake this feeling that she was involved in something way over her head. If I was wrong then the plan was to just come home and leave it alone, but if she was here fighting then I was going to figure out a way to get her out. Bay was right though. I jumped in blindly, and I made it all worse for everyone. I'm so sorry you guys for lying and sneaking around. I made the mistake that cost everyone everything tonight," I replied as tears filled my eyes.

I tried desperately to keep them back because I hated crying in front of everyone. The boys seemed to soften at my words, but it didn't ease my guilt. The rest of our group came over except Bay. She stayed in her corner, and my heart broke for her. Before I could call her over, Caleb hugged me. Johnny rustled my hair without letting Alana go, and I gave him a weak smile. He seemed to be okay with me although I was sure he'd never let me hang out with Alana alone again.

"I put everyone in danger, and I'm sorry for dragging you all in this," I said, leaning back against Bastian.

"No... I did."

We all turned to look at Bay. She shuffled on her feet. "I made a deal with the Tiger King in the first place. I thought I could keep this from you all and handle it myself, but I should of known how the pack operates. Now you're all in a horrible situation because of me. I'm sorry I dragged you into this world, and I'm sorry I wasn't smarter when I made this deal in the first place."

Bastian looked towards her, and even though I could feel his frustration his voice was kind with her. "Bay, you did what you thought was right for the pack and for my family. I'm not happy with our situation, but you didn't intentionally throw my family into the path of the Tiger King. You tried to avenge my wife, and I will always be grateful for that, but all you girls listen up because this apparently *needs* to be said out loud. Stop running off to try and fix problems without letting us know about it. We do everything together, and it is our job to protect each and every one of you. We can't do that if we don't know what's going on."

The girls all nodded solemnly, but I frowned. "But we never work actually together. You all just keep us hidden away and never let us do anything on our own. If you don't want us running off then you need to accept that we are capable and more than willing to help out when stuff like this comes up. Alana and I only did this ourselves because we knew you all would get upset that we had even *considered* coming here. Sitting back while you guys go out to fix our problems is hard on us too."

"It's our job to protect you though, " Bastian replied, giving me a pointed look.

"We have those same instincts about you guys too. If we agree to be completely honest then you need to agree to let us in and help," I replied, placing my hands on my hip.

"I agree with Shanely. Up until the Tiger King, we were honestly doing a pretty good job figuring out how to get into this place," Alana said as she stood next to me. Johnny looked stressed the moment she left his arms.

"We would of been just fine too if the Tiger King hadn't found us tonight. It was just unfortunate timing really, but we can fight too! I get why Bay fights here. It's exhilarating just watching," Octavia mentioned, joining our little line.

Bastian gave her a look. "That's not making me feel any better."

"I'm not saying we fight in the ring, but we *can* fight, and we should be a part of the planning. We'd have way more numbers if the girls were more involved too. Plus Shanely's a mixer, which means she's technically stronger than the lot of you," Octavia defended.

"She doesn't have her wolf yet," Bastian hissed quietly.

"Until then she's not running on full power," Elijah chimed in.

"Plus she always seems to be the target around here. No offense, Baby Girl. What happened tonight only happened because you guys were running off with a poorly planned scheme," Cade chimed in.

"Look tonight didn't go as planned, we get that. All we're saying is we want to be apart of things. We want to protect our family too. I can't tell you how frustrating it is always being the one needing saving," I replied, crossing my arms.

"Whether you mean for it or not you are a magnet for trouble, Shanely. The idea of you, or frankly anyone of you, running off alone like this goes against my wolf's instincts," Cade said matter of factly, while the fellas nodded in agreement.

"Baby steps, okay? Just don't immediately shut us down is all we're asking for. You guys can trust us too," I said as Bastian pulled me back in. His nose went to the crook of my neck like he always did when he was stressed.

"You guys are gonna have to trust us now anyways. We're stuck here," Octavia chimed in, and the fellas looked to their feet.

"Baby steps," my mate finally whispered, kissing my forehead.

I smiled up at him and snuggled in close. I eyed Darryl out of the corner of my eye again, who was pretending to be oblivious. I got a weird feeling the Tiger King was watching our interaction somehow, and I noticed cameras throughout the room. He seemed extremely curious with my pack, but I didn't know why.

"This isn't right, Bastian. We're not indebted to Abraham like he's acting. Those lions pursued us despite the many warnings I gave them. They were idiots anyways, and I can't imagine it seriously made a difference to the Tiger King," Cade said stubbornly kicking at the floor.

"Abraham has Bay because of their deal, and he's not letting the girls go now. They came into his place, and now they have these collars on. It needs a key to remove, see? What are we going to do to get them out without starting a vicious fight and someone being harmed in the process? This is the only path that ensure the girls stay alive and don't get hurt," Bastian said.

"At least he wasn't lying. He was being honest when he said we wouldn't be harmed while staying with him," Octavia threw in. It helped us some, but the path ahead was still difficult and albeit scary.

Heavy footsteps came from the other side of the door in the back. Abraham entered the room freshened up from his *dealings* with Finnick.

"The fights are done for the night, so we need to be moving girls soon. Here's the first list," Abraham said as he handed Bastian a piece of paper.

"First list? I said one," Bastian replied angrily.

Abraham smirked. "It is all one list, but I'm not giving you all the names at once. If you lose it then everyone would know who's been marked, and I won't have that. So you get 3 at a time. There are 12 names in total that those lions were supposed to find."

Bastian growled but snatched the paper anyways. He looked at the names and then back to Abraham.

"What did these shifters do?" he asked.

"My business. Your job is to bring them to me. My territory is south of town, so don't bring them here unless you catch them here already and be smart about it. I don't need that cop sniffing around anymore than he already is. Otherwise, I'll have to dispose of him, which can be messy business."

"Get in line, Tiger King," Cade said snidely.

Abraham raised his eyebrow towards our group. "What is the story between you all?"

"We don't like or trust him, but that's our business. Heads up though, he's the son of the Division's Head for our area. Be careful what you do around him," Bastian snapped back.

"The Head's son? Interesting," Abraham said quietly.

"He's not," I snapped back.

Abraham's eyes snapped to mine, but the door opened before he could questioned me further.

"Mommy? Daddy?" Aerith's tiny voice silenced everyone.

I rushed to take her from Ryder, saying a small thank you to him. He gave us a small nod and joined Johnny and Alana. Bastian wrapped his arms around us both.

"Where are we? Uncle Ryder woke me up, and we drove so fast!" she exclaimed. My poor baby was still in her pj's, with her hair in a mess of curls.

"Your Aunt and Uncle have been briefly informed as well as Daniel. We need to fill them in on the rest," Ryder said to Bastian, who nodded in reply.

"Time's up everyone. We need to leave, girls," Abraham said as he headed to the back door.

Bastian squeezed us harder before grabbing my chin. "You stay safe. Stay together, and I will come back to you."

He kissed me hard, leaving me breathless before switching to Aerith. "Listen to Mama, sweetie. Do as your told, and I'll see you soon."

Aerith eyes widened before her little lip began to pucker. My heart broke when she started to cry. "Daddy... Don't leave us."

Cade swore, and Elijah looked heart broken too. Everyone else just glared back at Abraham, who's face had hardened.

"I'd never leave you, baby girl. I'll come find you soon. Daddy just needs to finish a job, and it's safer for you to stay with our new friend Abraham."

She looked at the Tiger King, who gave her a small smile. He looked uncomfortable, which was a new look for him, but didn't speak thankfully. The last thing I needed was him running his mouth and making things worse for Aerith. Everyone quickly hugged us all before being forced to let go.

Darryl came behind Bay and clamped a collar on her. She jerked away from him, but he yanked her back on the chain. I didn't expect her to get a collar since she's fighting still for Abraham. I had hoped she'd keep her wolf, and we wouldn't be totally human and helpless going into the castle, but I guess that wasn't going to be the case. Bastian and his brothers growled at Darryl, but he ignored them and just pulled her along.

"Gently, Darryl. We don't need to scare the kid any further," Abraham said as they passed by. I blinked in surprise. *He could flip a switch from being sweet to ruthless so fast it was making my head spin.*

Darryl picked up the rest of our chains and headed to the door, making us girls back away. Aerith cried harder, and it looked like the guys were about to snap.

"I love you," I whispered, knowing Bastian could hear me.

Bastian disappeared from my view before he could reply. My heart broke when the giant metal door slammed shut, and we were all forced down a dimly lit hallway.

"This one is mine, Darryl," Abraham said as he pulled one of the chains from Darryl's hands. Darryl simply started walking down the corridor with the rest of us. It was then I realized Abraham chose Bay's chain. She eyed him funny and made sure to stay as far away from him as she could.

They stayed a few steps back from us as we headed up the stairs to the back alley. Darryl led us to a large black SUV, where we all piled in. Abraham sat up front, while Darryl drove. The rest of the tiger guards hopped into the vehicle behind us, and we took off in the opposite direction of pack lands.

My heart hurt, and it felt like it broke entirely when we heard the howls. Bay shrunk further in her seat in the back, while Alana rubbed her chest and stared out the window.

Aerith snuggled into my chest, and I just rubbed her back as we drove further from my mate and family. It was a little bit of a drive to get to the Tiger King's castle, and I had no idea what to expect when we got there.

Bastian

Watching my mate and child get escorted from the underground club's private room was excruciating. Johnny was beside himself. Finding out his mate is carrying a cub only to lose her the next day to a mad tiger was more than his wolf could take. I didn't blame him because I was feeling the same way.

I was pissed at Bay, and honestly some at Shanely too. That girl was a magnet for trouble, and yet again she slipped through my fingers. Cade and Elijah were angry as well, while Caleb was just freaking out. We *all* knew the reputation of the Tiger King, but no one had ever actually met the guy. We made sure our paths didn't cross, but leave it to the girls to stumble into a psychopath's house.

"Who's on the list?" Ryder asked.

"Never heard of them before. It at least tells us what kind of shifter they are though. We have two foxes and a black bear."

"Doesn't sound too hard. We need to head back and fill Cain in, and Caleb you need to give Thomas a call too. Then we can get started on this list. The faster we do this, the faster we get the girls back," Cade said optimistically.

I nodded my head, and we all retreated back to my truck. When we stepped outside, multiple officers were standing off to the side of the nightclub. They eyed me as we passed by.

Just great, I thought to myself. *I really don't have time to deal with these guys too.*

Thankfully they let us pass without a word, and we didn't see Patrick anywhere. Which was good because I don't think I'd be able to hold either of my animals back right now. I shoved my hands in my pocket and led the group further away from the cops. It wasn't long before we saw my truck, and that's when Johnny lost control of his wolf and howled loudly. He sounded in agony and looked already in mid-shift. *He wasn't going to make the drive home,* I thought to myself. I threw the keys to Elijah and pushed Johnny forward.

"Come on. You and I are running back."

He nodded but said nothing. *Not like he really could at this point anyway.* I slapped the back of the truck and watched it drive off towards pack lands. Ryder parked closer to the back roads so slipping into the dark of the woods was easy. I pushed Johnny away from the road a bit before we fully shifted. We both howled again, hating we were going in the opposite way of our family, but the faster we made it home, the faster I could get this done. Just thinking about our new *boss* was pushing me into a rage. He knew *exactly* who Shanely was and used her to pull me and my brothers into his mess. I wanted nothing more than to tear him apart, but with those collar on the girls there was nothing I could do, and that *killed* me inside.

My cabin came into view in no time. Our run wasn't nearly long enough, and I could see the truck was just pulling in as we ran up. I could smell my Alpha and his mate along with bear shifters, indicating that Thomas and Daniel were here as well.

Good. I needed all the help I could get, I thought to myself. Walking inside was almost too much though. I could scent Shanely everywhere, and Aerith's stuffed bear was lying by the door. *She must have dropped it when Ryder picked her up.*

"What happened, Bastian?" Cain demanded before we all were even inside. I slowly reached down to grab her bear and held it a moment before answering.

"The short version? The Tiger King has the girls. Bay made some kind of deal with him awhile ago to get Derek killed for what he did to Shanely, thus pulling my mate into the mix when she went to the illegal fighting ring to try and find Bay to undo her deal. Abraham somehow found out I killed his lions and seized the girls," I replied as I collapsed on the chair.

"He put collars on them all," Elijah growled out.

"Collars?!" Daniel asked furiously.

I nodded. "It has obsidian and wolf's bane in it, keeping their animals dormant. They can't shift or use the mind-link."

"That sounds like what Derek used on Shanely," Cassia mentioned.

"If it is I don't know how he got it. Abraham doesn't like wolves, so I doubt he'd deal with them," I replied.

"Why did he make a deal with you then and not just try to kill you guys?" Cain asked.

"He's unpredictable, Alpha, but he seemed amused by Shanely and *very* interested in Bay. He learned she was Mor'du tonight," Cade chimed in.

"God, I really thought we were done with trouble like this," Cain said, rubbing his eyes. *Me too.*

"Abraham allowed Aerith to stay with her mother though. Even swore no harm will come to them, and Octavia confirmed the truth. It was odd coming from him," Elijah said.

"Yeah, he even beat the snot out of one of his tigers for harming Shanely," Cade chimed in.

"Is Shanely okay?" Cassia asked.

I nodded slowly. "She's alright, but without her shifter abilities she will heal slowly. She's going to be hurting for awhile from tonight."

"Did he put a collar on Aerith?" Daniel asked, his eyes turning to our shifter gold.

I shook my head. "No, not to my knowledge. Aerith isn't a shifter to him. She scents like a human, still plus she's four and not a threat."

Daniel and the rest of the group noticeably sighed with relief. *The thought of Shanely in a collar was bad enough. I couldn't even begin thinking about Aerith being in one.* I don't think I'd be able to rein in my wolf or my bear if I saw my toddler in a collar.

"At least she's safe from Patrick. He might forget about her if she's gone," Cassia said as we all mulled over what happened. I dragged my hands across my face, sickened to be in this kind of situation yet again. That prick Patrick had suddenly become the least of my worries and *that* was saying something.

"What are you supposed to do then? I assume you made a deal for them?" Thomas asked.

"Complete the lion's jobs. They had 12 marks to bring in, and now we get to do it," I replied, handing him the piece of paper. Thomas read it then passed it to Daniel. It went around the room.

"Recognize anyone?" I asked.

"The bear, Jesse, is a known gambler. He has run up debts in more than one town and doesn't blend well in a clan. I bet he owes the King a lot of money," Thomas stated.

"The others I don't recognize, but it must be because they went back on a deal," Cain said, giving the note back to me.

"The other two are foxes, we know that much. Abraham didn't give us any information past that," Cade chimed in.

"So the Tiger King has a name," Daniel muttered to himself.

I nodded. "He's young too. Like near our age and as ruthless as we all heard. He seemed to honestly enjoy tonight."

"I've always stayed away from the south. Between the streak and the Blackwood pack, it was just safer to stay near our own lands, especially with the new crowd of smaller shifter kinds coming around lately. When we heard his name after finding Shanely all those years ago I prayed we'd never cross paths," Cain said solemnly.

"Apparently, he's buying up some places in town. He's the new club owner," Johnny finally spoke. I stole a look at my friend. He looked as stricken as I felt. It was an incredible pain to be separated from your mate and child, and he barely got a night with his newly pregnant mate.

"Great. We own most of the places in town, but it's been growing. South side is newer, and there has been investors buying up some of the strip. I didn't recognize the names and didn't think much of it honestly," Cain replied.

"His streak seems to be expanding their territory. Will this become a bigger problem, Cain?" Thomas asked.

"I don't know," Cain replied quietly, and his mate squeezed his hand.

"It was odd, but the other part of the deal was that he wanted to keep peaceful communications open between us. He said we were the first wolves that intrigued him, and we may need each other in the future. He didn't want to 100 percent cut ties after this. Abraham may not be a problem like we all are thinking," Elijah countered.

Cain rubbed his eyes. "This is all a lot to take in. How he expects us to just become friends after this is baffling."

"For now, we need to focus on this list. The faster we find them then the faster I get my family back. Where do we start?" I asked.

"I have something that belongs to the bear. You can use it to track him. You'll need to check around town for the other two," Thomas added.

"Great. Caleb take Johnny and Ryder and grab whatever Thomas has to track the bear. The other two are foxes, so my brothers and I will take care of them. Let's move," I said as we all stood up to leave.

"Wait... You all need to sleep. It's extremely late, and you'll be no good to anyone on such low energy," Cassia stated, blocking our pathway to my front door.

"I can't sleep now, Cassia. Not when my family is with that animal!" I cried.

"Bastian, you cannot run yourself ragged with this! You need to be smart about it. Shanely will be okay, but she will need you to get her out of this. You won't get anywhere if you boys don't take care of yourselves and be at your best."

I dropped my shoulders in defeat. "Cassia... I don't think I can sleep without her."

"I'll help with that. Come lay down."

She guided me to the couch and laid her hand on my head.

"You'll start in the morning," she said before I felt her pulling at me and everything went black.

Shanely

We pulled into an honest to God *castle* deep in the woods. It was so secluded, I don't think most people even knew it was back here. We had passed through a stone wall miles before we even got close to the castle. I could see shifters patrolling the top of the walls as we drove through. Abraham said nothing as we pulled inside the inner wall before the vehicles came to a stop.

"Get them settled in their rooms for the night. I'll see you all in the morning."

With that Abraham left us. Darryl and Henry carried our chains as we went further into the castle. It was decorated in lots of gold and red colors. They had banners hanging from the ceiling with their insignia brightly colored on it. A gold tiger inside a golden circle. *Simple yet pretty*, I thought to myself.

We went up the massive set of stairs and then to the left. Down the hall was a tall spiral staircase. We followed the tigers all the way to the top of the tower. I groaned as I climbed the steps carrying Aerith. *Why are there always stairs?* I wondered as I huffed and puffed my way to the top. A single door was at the top, and Henry opened it. Inside was a gorgeous room. Three beds lined the back wall, and a small desk sat on the right. Still the same color scheme as the rest of this place but with a pretty ivory cream color throughout. There were windows on all sides, and if it wasn't so dark I'm sure it would have a gorgeous view of the forest below.

"See you in the morning, girls," Darryl said and slammed the door behind him.

We all looked at each other and then back to the room.

"We best get some sleep," I said as I laid a now sleeping Aerith on one of the beds. She had passed out on the drive over here. The beds were large enough for more than one person, so everyone quickly found a spot. Nobody was really in the mood to talk anymore anyways.

I curled up around Aerith and tried to find a spot that was comfortable with these stupid collars and chains on. My neck ached as it was, but surprisingly it wasn't long before I passed out too.

* * *

Morning came too quickly, and the sun was bright in our room. I looked around, and the only other person awake was Bay. She was sitting on the window seat, looking out to Abraham's land below. I quietly snuck away from Aerith and joined Bay. The view was as incredible as I thought it would be, with nothing but trees and hills for miles. *No wonder the Tiger King chose this spot.*

"Hey," I said.

"Hey," she replied. She seemed defeated already, and I wasn't sure how to fix this really. *Nothing works better than an apology,* I thought to myself.

"Look Bay... We both made mistakes last night. We both chose the wrong path *trying* to do the right thing for our family. We all love you, Bay, and I'm not mad at you. Thank you for trying to take care of Derek too, but please from now on don't give up your life for mine, okay? I'd rather Derek live than see you stuck in a deal with the Tiger King."

She wiped away a tear that fell and then hugged me hard. "I'm so sorry, Shanely. I feel like everything I do is wrong. Ever since I left my Dad's pack, I've done nothing but screw up! I made a promise I couldn't keep, and it kills me."

"Oh Bay, that isn't true! You've put us all first. You've done nothing but your best for us, and you are one of my best friends. We'll get past this. Our boys are fantastic at tracking. They'll get through the list quickly, and we'll all go home forgetting all about the Tiger King," I replied.

Bay nodded and wiped her tears away. She seemed sad, and I wondered what was going on in her head. Bay was a pretty private person, and I wasn't sure if she would open up to me. *I had to try at least,* I thought to myself.

"Tell me though. What's going on with you and Abraham? He seems almost... smitten," I said quietly, nervous to hear her answer.

She shrugged. "He normally doesn't meet with me personally. Last night was the first time I ever saw him in person. I don't know Shanely, but there's something odd with him."

"Other than what we've seen?" I snorted, but she gave me a look, and I sighed. "Maybe he was just shocked his best fighter was a woman? I don't know, Bay. How did you make a deal with him if you never met him prior to last night?"

"I made it through Henry. He saw me fight and wanted to know if I'd fight for the King. I countered with the deal, and he signed the papers for Abraham right then and there. That was nearly 15 fights ago."

"15?! Good lord! Were you hurt in any of them?" I asked in a hushed tone. Octavia stirred in her sleep, and I quickly lowered my voice. Bay was talking, and I was nervous she'd stop if everyone woke up.

"Some, but I managed to see Dr. Malin for some of the bigger wounds. I just blamed it on over training or a fall," she replied.

Someone banged on the door before abruptly opening it. Henry appeared in the door frame, startling everyone awake. I glared at him.

"Everyone wake up. You've been requested to join the King for breakfast," he boomed, frightening Aerith.

She ran to me, and I shot Henry a frustrated look. He rubbed the back of his head, frowning slightly. I wondered how much interaction he's had with children. *My money was on not a lot.*

"Can we at least use the restroom?" Alana asked, rubbing her eyes.

He jerked his head to the far wall on his right, where there was a door. I was so tired last night that I didn't even notice it before. We all quickly used the restroom before Henry led us back down the stairs. This place was a maze, but maybe that was the point of putting us in the tower? Keep us confused so we can't leave. Eventually, we made it to a dining hall of sorts. My eyes narrowed on the room. The room was simple in design with a long massive wooden table in the center. There was nothing really fancy about this room, and maybe because we were in a castle I just... I don't know expected more? It was still nice and clean at least.

Abraham stood at the end of the massive table and motioned us forward. He wore new clothes this morning, and it was odd to see him look like a normal guy. He wore dark jeans and a simple white shirt with messy hair. Nothing as broody looking as what he wore last night.

"Come in, ladies. Take a seat!" he said loudly. "Shanely, please sit at my right, and Bay at my left."

We looked at each other before taking our seats. I put Aerith in the seat next to mine. She dangled her legs as she looked around at everything. Aerith was small in the chair, but was big enough to eat without needing a booster seat. *At least she was occupying herself and didn't seem too distraught*, I thought to myself.

Abraham sat last and motioned for the food to come out. He sure put on a show with the amount of food in front of us. Pancakes, eggs, sausages, and bacon! *Oh, the bacon smelled incredible!* There was enough food to feed the whole castle, I was sure of it, and I wondered how many were apart of his group or whatever they called themselves.

Aerith's eyes grew wide as she hopped up and grabbed a sausage right off the platter before I could stop her. I panicked, but she just looked back at me thrilled with the food. She started to dance a bit in her seat as she stuffed her mouth full bite after bite. I wasn't sure if we were allowed to eat yet, especially before Abraham. I stole a quick glance towards him, worried for his temper, but he seemed amused by her too and broke the silence with his booming laugh.

"Well, dig in everyone. Follow the wee one's lead," he stated as he filled his plate. I soon filled Aerith's plate and then mine. We ate the delicious breakfast in complete silence. No one spoke. This breakfast wasn't something we were expecting to receive here. I honestly didn't know what to expect, but this wasn't it.

"How did you like your room?" Abraham finally asked the group.

The girls all looked towards me, so I answered for them. "It's great really.

Thank you for the comfortable room and for breakfast."

"You're welcome," he replied with a wink. "I may have a deal with your lads, ladies, but it doesn't mean I want your stay here to be bad."

The conversation ended then, and I mulled over his words. *I couldn't figure Abraham out. He was harsh and brutal in moments, yet he could be really kind.* He puzzled me, and I found myself watching him as we ate breakfast. Whether he realized I was studying him or not, I didn't know. He never let on, and I sat there, trying to figure this man out.

Abraham stood after finishing his plate. "Ladies, it has been a pleasure, but if you don't mind I need to steal Shanely away. One of you will watch her child, will you not?"

Aerith looked at him unamused by this large man. "My name is Aerith."

He leaned down on the table, smirking at her. "Is that so?"

She nodded. "Yup! And when my Daddy comes back he's going to kick your butt for taking us from him."

My eyes widened, and I placed my hand on her arm whispering, "Aerith, hush."

I didn't know what to expect from the Tiger King, but his loud laugh was not one of them. It surprised us all, and the girls kept looking to me for direction. *Little did they realize I was totally bluffing and had no idea what to do or say around the Tiger King.*

"She has your spunk, I'll give her that. Aerith, when your Dad completes his job I'll take you home myself. Deal?"

She looked at him cautiously. "Fine. I guess."

"Aerith go with your Aunt Bay, okay? I'll be just a minute. Be good please," I quickly told her before placing her in Bay's arms.

"This way, Shanely," Abraham said as he gestured to the door on our left. I looked back one last time before I followed him through the door. We walked in comfortable silence before he opened another door at the far end. He led me to his throne room before sitting down in his massive gold chair. I stayed at the bottom of the steps because I had no idea where I was supposed to go. Looking around, I could see a variety of animal heads covering the tall wall behind his throne. I tried very hard not to think of them as shifters.

"You must think of me as bizarre, don't you?" he asked as he rested his hand under his chin.

"Unpredictable would be the word I would have picked," I replied, shifting on my feet. *What in the world did he want from me? To chit chat?*

Abraham smiled at me. "It's actually you, Shanely. You're the unpredictable one. I don't think I have ever met a true mixer before, and I am certain I have never met wolves like you all."

"I don't know what wolves you met before, but I am exactly like the rest of my pack. We take care of each other," I replied confidently.

"I've noticed. It's more of an actual caring for one another versus the pack as the whole."

I was puzzled now. "Okay, I have to know. What packs have you run into?"

His eyes filled with hatred now, almost blackening when I asked the question. He leaned back in his chair, and his playful amused nature fell. "My streak had the unfortunate run in with a pack a little east of here when I was a child. They killed my parents and most of us tigers. They wanted our land, and they took it for a long while. Once I grew strong enough, I took it back and slaughtered the ones I could get my hands on. It's why I have my bounty on wolves. I assumed the less wolves in this world the better, but then I met my champion, which brought me to you."

My shoulders fell. "I truly am sorry, Abraham. We don't stand for things like that. I cannot believe other shifters treated you this way."

He shrugged. "They wanted to live on my land so badly I made sure they never left."

Abraham pointed behind him, and my stomach threaten to toss everything I had just ate. *I was right earlier*, I thought. *These were shifter heads on his wall.* I looked down at him horrified, and he just watched my reaction.

"You seem saddened by this?"

"While I agree with you dealing with them, knowing they sit on the wall behind you is a little disturbing is all."

He seemed to accept my answer and leaned forward answering, "It gave me an amazing reputation, and my streak remains safe. The deals are what keep us going."

"Why are you telling me all this? I am technically a prisoner after all," I replied.

He seemed puzzled by my question and narrowed his eyes, lost in thought. "I honestly don't know. I really don't talk to many about this, but you seem different. I thought it might be nice for you to get to know the real me. Well... For all of you to know the real me."

"You mean me or Bay?"

He stiffened, and a small smirk crept up my face. *Yeah... I was right about that too.*

"Shanely, be careful where you tread. Don't mistake my kindness as weakness. You are a guest in my house, but things can change just as quickly," he said coldly. His warning was crystal clear, but I shrugged, not really caring anymore.

"I'm not in the mood for head games. If you are trying to... I don't know... be friends with us, then you cannot be mad at the questions we ask. If you don't want to answer all you have to do is say so. Friends don't threaten one another," I said dryly as I turned away from him.

The Tiger King surprisingly let me leave and never once came after me. I got lost once or twice finding our room again, but thankfully didn't see another soul. Last thing I needed was to run into a tiger like Finnick and try to convince them I wasn't trying to escape. Aerith jumped in my arms, when I came into the room, dragging that stupid chain behind me.

"What did he want?" Alana asked curiously.

Bay seemed to perk up when I came in too, and Octavia left the window sill to join us.

"He told me the gist of why he hates wolves. It's not a pretty story that's for sure," I replied, sitting down on the bed.

"The fighters in the ring talk about him a lot backstage. He built this empire from nothing it sounds like," Bay chimed in.

I nodded. "He seems intrigued by our pack. We are the first wolves he's dealt with that genuinely look out for one another. Sounds like the pack east of here was quick to throw out a fellow wolf for the good of the pack."

"Oh, he must be talking about the Blackwood Pack. They are ruthless!"

Alana said as she shivered.

"Oh, right! We never even traveled south of town because of them. That rule was made back when we were kids though! What did they do to Abraham?" Octavia asked.

I laid Aerith's head against my chest as I gestured a knife across my neck. Alana gasped.

"His parents didn't make it. They wanted the tiger's land here, and they occupied it for awhile before Abraham took it back," I replied.

"Whoa, I'm impressed. Maybe we have the wrong impression of him?" Octavia asked.

I shrugged. "I can't get a read on him. He's super laid back and almost sweet at times, but then it's like he remembers who he's supposed to be and turns ruthless, especially when he makes those deals. But then there's this whole other side to him. I just can't figure him out, and the back and forth is giving me a headache. One thing's for sure, I do not want to have him as an enemy."

"What do you mean?" Bay asked nervously.

"Well for starters all the wolves he, uh... took care of from Blackwood, are still here. They're on the wall like trophies."

Their eyes grew wide.

"Whoa," Octavia said, rubbing the goosebumps on her arms.

I nodded. "We will need to be careful here, girls, but for now we're okay. Hopefully, our boys are too."

Bastian

I awoke, finding Cade's face over mine.

"Bastian get up. We got a lead on one of the foxes."

I shot up. "How?"

"Elijah woke up about an hour ago. One of the names looked familiar, so he did some research. One of the foxes worked at the Alpha's mill a few years back. We have an old address to check out at least. We're ready if you are."

"Dude, let's go!"

I rubbed my face, trying to wake myself up, before running my hand through my hair. We bolted to my truck, and I followed the GPS to the location just out of town. Thankfully it wasn't super far, but I wanted to do this quickly and quietly. Last thing we needed was to alert the local police that we were arresting people behind their backs. It was a 30 minute drive, and no one spoke the whole way. The only thing talking was Cade's stomach, but for once my brother never complained about it.

We pulled up slowly, and from the outside the house looked abandoned. The yard was overgrown and was as neglected as the rest of the place. It had a funny smell to the place too like it was full of trash inside. It always baffled me how people could stand to live like this. It was dark, but we were searching this place inside and out before moving on. I had nothing but a name to these foxes, and I was finding them even if it killed me.

"Elijah take the back. Cade stay in the truck, and I'll go in the front," I said quietly. "We do this quietly. Foxes have exceptional hearing."

They nodded to me, and we all got in position. It was extremely dark in the house, but thanks to my ability I could still see the room inside. It looked trashed like it was a druggie's house or something. I tried the handle quietly, but it was locked. I quickly thought about my options. Noise was a factor here no matter what, but snapping the door handle would be quieter than breaking a window. As quietly as I could manage, I broke the door handle.

"*This better be our guy otherwise I'm breaking and entering,*" I mind-linked my brothers.

"*It's got to be him. It smells like a fox,*" Elijah said back.

"*Focus, guys. I can hear movement coming from your left, Bastian,*" Cade chimed in.

I slowly entered the house, listening carefully as I took each step. It was hard to hear anything past my own pounding heart though. I carefully stepped over the trash that littered the place, which was hard to do as it covered the floor everywhere. *God... It reeked worse than the bunkhouse,* I thought as I covered my nose. Suddenly, my phone rang and someone bolted from the left room out to the kitchen door in the back. I cursed under my breath and ran after him.

"*Elijah! He's running your way!*"

I heard a loud crash as I ran through the house. Outside, Elijah had the man pinned on the ground, with his knee in his back. The metal trash cans were knocked over next to them, adding only more trash to this dump, and I stomped over towards them. Elijah had his neck in a death grip, and his eyes were solid gold. *Got to hand it to my brother. He was ruthless when he wanted to be.*

"State your name!" Elijah yelled.

I pulled out the paper Abraham gave me. Three names were listed.

1. Aaron Brockwell
2. John Drake
3. Jesse Jacobson

"We're looking for a Jesse Jacobson. Sorry for the intrusion, but if you simply tell us your name then we can go on with our day," I said nonchalantly. Elijah looked at me weird but said nothing.

"Roll with it," I said to him.

The man squirmed around, but Elijah held him firm. He pushed him further into the concrete, and the man yelled.

"Ow, okay! Look you have the wrong guy, I swear! I'm not Jesse! My name is Aaron, alright! Just check my wallet if you don't believe me! Please!"

I grabbed his wallet and pulled out his ID. Sure enough, it said Aaron Brockwell. *Way to go, Elijah.*

"Well what do you know, he's telling the truth," I replied as the man let out a huge breath of relief. "Unfortunately for you, I'm also looking for an Aaron Brockwell. Take him, Elijah. The Tiger King is waiting."

Elijah swiftly hit the man, knocking him unconscious before Aaron could scream. I handcuffed him from behind, and we hauled him up. *Why my Alpha had handcuffs I didn't know nor did I want to ask.* We quickly hauled Aaron up and to the truck before the neighbors came out. *They must be used to the chaos around here because no one even peeked out the windows.* We threw him in the back seat, and I crossed off his name on my list.

"*I'm coming, baby.*"

I sent the link, even though I knew it wouldn't reach her. This was a win, and I was going to take it.

"So next time, maybe we should silence our cell phones before we attempt to arrest someone," Cade jested with a laugh, and I glared at him. I pulled out my phone, frowning when I realized it was already silent. I reached into the other pocket, and it was Shanely's phone that rang. I rolled my eyes. *A scam call nearly ruined this mission.*

"Let's just get going," I commanded, earning yet another annoying laugh from my brother.

Cade drove us back to pack lands to drop this fool off, while we figured out where the next mark was. I was jittery still from the whole ordeal, but feeling rather good after this morning. We had one mark down, and it was within an hour of starting. At this rate we'd have Shanely in a matter of a few days, but I knew better than to bank on that. Something was bound to come up, slowing everything down, but for now we were on a roll, and I was grateful.

Thankfully, the tool in our backseat never woke on the drive back. *Elijah must have really decked him,* I chuckled to myself. Cain and Cassia were surprised to see me and my brothers, driving up to the lodge at 7 in the morning with our first mark already. Cain helped me load the guy into one of the pack's cells for the time being, while we worked the next. I learned when I became the Head Enforcer here at pack lands that we even had cells. They were made for shifters, and apparently every pack was required to have some installed just in case. It was an order from the World Council long ago, but Cain said ours almost never gets used. *Still freaked me out being down here though.*

My phone buzzed in my pocket as I walked up the stairs, and I saw Caleb's name appear on the screen.

Caleb said, "Hey, man. We got the bear's clothing from my Uncle. Apparently, he left it at one of our clan member's place when he stayed here not long ago."

"Lovely. We're going to catch this guy because of his one-night stand," I replied back into the phone as Cassia filled my plate with eggs and bacon. I looked at my plate, and my stomach churned. Food was the last thing on my mind, but I begrudgingly started eating after Cassia glared at me.

"Looks like. Johnny shifted awhile ago and has refused to shift back. He's not doing too well, brother."

I sighed. "I know the feeling. Keep him moving. Don't let him sit and stew on it. He'll go feral before we even find this guy."

"Got it. We're heading out now. Last time Anna saw him, he was high-tailing it into the woods away from town. I'll stay in touch as we go though."

"Perfect. We got one mark in the cell now, so we're looking for our last fox. We should be done around the same time then," I replied, pushing my plate away. It was still fairly full, but I couldn't eat anymore. I felt sick.

"Seriously? Good lord, you guys are good."

"Pure luck honestly, and a huge thanks to Elijah's big brain. He recognized the name after all, and it led us straight to him. Next one's gonna be harder though. No one knows him," I countered.

Caleb blew out a deep breath. "Well this will at least calm Johnny some.

Maybe get him to shift back? We'll leave now, and I'll call you later."

The line disconnected, and I was seriously grateful Shanely was a mixer. Her family owned the rest of the land around here, and we were able to cover so much more territory because of them. I thanked Cassia and headed back to my truck. *Best place to start was in town, I suppose.*

It took another two *agonizing* days to find the other guy. A lot of questioning shifters around town before someone had finally spilled the secret to where that dumb fox was holed up. He apparently scorned enough women in town that they were more than happy to let us know where he was once we found their friend group. That fox was in the next town over, and it took an hour just to reach the ratty motel he was staying in. He was shifty, like a fox is normally, but we managed to take him fairly easily once we found him. He begged us to let him go, and that he'd take care of his debt. To trust him and believe that he would make it right, but this fox didn't realize he was standing in my way of getting my wife and family back. He was coming with us *regardless* of the lies he was spilling.

Jesse Jacobson, the bear, was deep in the mountains. It was taking Caleb longer to track him, but they were closing in. Should have him in a day or two, but I couldn't wait. I needed to see Shanely and get the next set of names. I *needed* my girls. It had already been a few days as it was, and I don't think I could go another night without seeing them. My brothers were game to go on ahead, and we loaded everyone up. Cassia went ahead and used her ability to knock them both out, making it easier to drive them through town without problems. I thanked her and hopped in Cade's Excursion. Cade flew across town towards Abraham's place, while Elijah sat in the back with the two we caught.

First thing I notice when we arrived was how big this place was. Two retaining walls, and I could smell a truck load of tigers. The most I had ever seen together in one place. I didn't realize Tiger streaks got this large. Normally, they were loaners or stayed in small groups but this streak was *massive*, and it alarmed me that they were so close to pack lands. Elijah gave me a look that told me he was thinking the same thing. *Cain needed to know this.*

We pulled up to the front, hauling out our load, who was thankfully starting to come to, when Darryl stopped us. He said the King was finishing up with some deals and needed us to wait.

I rolled my eyes, and started desperately searching for Shanely. I couldn't really get her scent from where we were, and I was angsty. *We brought two on the list in three days,* I thought to myself. *He better let me see my wife.*

Shanely

We spent the next couple of days in our rooms with not much to do. Darryl or Henry were the only tigers we saw, and we only saw them when they brought us our food. Abraham didn't have meals with us like our first morning here, and we were all bored out of our minds. On the 3rd day, however, Henry and Darryl came in with two large dress bags. They threw them at me and Bay. I gave her an odd look, but she looked just as confused as I was.

"Abraham needs you to work tonight. Put these on, and let's go," Darryl said.

"Work? That wasn't part of the deal," I countered.

Henry pointed to Bay. "She's still under contract until the list is done. Unless you want her to go alone, that is?"

Jerk. He knew how to hit me where it hurts, and I glared at him while entering the restroom with Bay. I unzipped the bag, and my eyes went wide.

"Umm... What?" I said, looking at Bay. *Boy, these outfits were... skimpy,* I thought to myself. *What could Abraham possible need us for while wearing these?* I scrunched up my nose in frustration. This was not going to end well.

In each of our bags was a red halter bra looking thing, that had jewels hanging from the bottom, and a long matching skirt with slits that went up our thighs, revealing a whole lot of leg. There was also a bag of make-up at the bottom. It looked like some kind of Arabian princess costume for slutty girls. I raised my eyebrow at Bay, but she shrugged. Clearly, she was as confused as I was.

"I've never had to do this before," she muttered.

We both changed into our new *uniforms* before grabbing the make-up bag.

Henry pounded on the door, yelling at us to hurry up, but I rolled my eyes. I had no intention of rushing anything just to appease them. It was bad enough we were stuck here, but this was over the top. I was tempted to tell them to stuff it, but Bay looked so defeated already that I couldn't let her go alone. It wasn't fair, and even though I'm sure she felt she deserved to go alone, I would never let her. It was honestly my fault we were all here in this current situation anyways. Abraham may have never known about Mor'du's true identity if I hadn't forced everyone into my genius plan.

We helped each other with the make-up, which I was grateful for because I honestly didn't wear a lot of make-up. I wore the basics, but Bay was better at applying it, and she always looked gorgeous. I barely recognized myself in the mirror when we had finally finished up. I just shook my hair out of the ponytail, and Bay did the same. Her tight bouncy curls looked way better than my waves, but I had to admit I looked pretty amazing. Darryl's jaw dropped when we came out of the restroom, and he loudly snapped it shut.

"Let's go," he gritted through his teeth as he grabbed our chains.

Alana and Octavia gave us a funny look, but I shrugged my shoulders.

"Please watch Aerith for me?" I asked, and Alana gave me a thumbs up.

I smiled as Darryl pulled on my chain. I rolled my eyes. "I'm coming, I'm coming!"

We followed their lead all the way to the throne room Abraham took me the other morning. I tried to cover my stomach as much as possible with my arms. You could see the scar across my legs with each step, and the ones on my arm were visible as well. While I had normally never been embarrassed by them before, I was tonight. I was uncomfortable with everyone seeing not only so much of me, but also the scars on my body that were traumatic moments for me. *I didn't want to share that with the tigers here.*

Bay was confident as usual. Taking her normal long strides and not caring how much skin she showed. *I don't know how she did it,* I thought as I watched her. *Back in the room I could see her fear and anxiety, but now her face was cool, calm, and collected.* It was like a wall went up and nothing phased her. I had always envied her bravery, and maybe tonight was the night I tried to copy her. I dropped my arms to my side like her and walked with my head held high. *Never let them see you break, right?* Never thought it would be in this kind of situation though.

Darryl opened the large doors, revealing the Tiger King sitting on his throne. All the candles were lit in the room, including the fireplace, which filled the room with warmth. It just gave the heads on the wall extra large shadows, and I tried not to look at them. Abraham had a tight black suit on, and his white hair was styled nicely. He went all out for whatever was happening tonight. He eyed us up and down as Henry and Darryl walked us further into the room. Well, *correction.* He eyed Bay up and down. I watched as he barely took a breath, refusing to blink as Bay and I got closer to him. He noticed me smirking before he sat up and forced himself to look away. I smiled slightly, but it quickly fell away. I had no plans to piss him off tonight while wearing this.

"Get the big chains, Darryl," he replied calmly.

Darryl handed my chain off to Henry, who placed me directly to Abraham's right, while Bay went to his left.

"Sit," Henry demanded.

I carefully sat on the step below Abraham's chair, trying not to expose myself anymore than I already was. I felt Henry remove the chain on my collar, which was a nice break from the stupid thing. Suddenly, my neck was yanked backwards from the weight of the new chain. A much heavier chain was now attached to the collar, making me actually miss the first one. Henry moved it around to the side, which helped me balance the stupid thing before guiding it up the middle and giving the end to Abraham. The same was done to Bay.

"Is this necessary?" I asked, making Abraham laugh.

"The McCoy's and Fenrir's have made a good name for themselves. Just like me, you all are known throughout the shifter community, and I plan to take advantage of that. I have some deals to make tonight so having you two by my side will help with a lot actually. Now absolutely no speaking at all tonight. Your job is to sit here quietly and look pretty or I will separate all of you. And I do mean *everyone*, Shanely."

Abraham gave me a firm look before looking ahead. *Aerith. She'd spend*

God knows how long alone if we opened our mouths tonight, I thought as panic surged through my chest. *She'd be terrified to wake up all alone!* I looked to Bay, my eyes pleading with her, and she gave me a silent nod before staring out straight ahead again. She understood the threat.

Henry came up behind me and pushed me into Abraham's leg.

"Lean on your King."

I glared at him and tried to push away, when Henry's boot pushed right back.

"I don't believe he's *my* King actually," I snapped back.

"He is until your mate completes the deal. That is *if* he can," Henry hissed back before pushing me against Abraham again.

"Come now, Shanely. I don't bite, I promise," Abraham said, pulling on my chain. I gave in and leaned against the man's knee. My cheeks heated, thinking of Bastian. *What a freaking show this was?!* My wolf snapped her jaws angrily inside my head. She hated being this close to another male that was not our mate.

Bay seemed entirely unaffected though, and I didn't know how she did it. She just sat there, refusing to look back at our captor, while her arm rested against his knee. I tried to get her attention, but she was glued to whatever she was staring at in front of her. *Something was going on with her too.* Suddenly, the doors opened and multiple shifters entered the room.

We had a long night of dealings with non-wolves. Abraham seemed to love having us by his side, especially when they scented me. Everyone in our town knew Bastian Fenrir's girl was the first mixer in years yet for some reason here she was at Abraham's side. They put two and two together and caved to *whatever* Abraham wanted. Bastian Fenrir was somehow in Abraham's back pocket, and they didn't want the largest wolf pack chasing after them either.

It put Abraham in a great mood.

Towards the end of the evening, Darryl entered from the other room and walked up the steps to his King. He whispered something in Abraham's ear, and the Tiger King looked downright giddy before he started laughing hysterically. He waved Darryl away before turning back to us.

"Last one for the night, girls. You're doing splendidly!" Abraham praised us. I just rolled my eyes at him. I was just ready to go to bed.

The doors opened again, and I got a scent that relaxed me to my bones. Bastian. But my face fell, when I realized what Bastian was about to walk into. I glared at Abraham, who gave me a mischievous smile before winking at me. *That wicked man!*

Bastian, Cade, and Elijah entered with two shifters handcuffed behind them. Their eyes immediately went to us, and I could feel their tempers flare from here. Bastian's eyes were glowing red now, and I knew my mate. He was beyond pissed right now and shame stained my cheeks. I covered my stomach with my arms, feeling mortified as the Fenrir brothers stalked towards us. *I finally get to see my mate and this is what happens?!* I thought angrily. *Abraham was a jerk! He must have known my mate was coming somehow and set this up just to piss my mate off.*

The Tiger King smiled wickedly at my mate, who looked ready to shift, he was so angry. I couldn't help it. I leaned forward to rush towards Bastian, when Abraham snapped my chain. The heavy chain made me stumble, and it didn't take long for Abraham to grip the back of my neck and pull me in close.

"I know the mate bond is strong, so I will forgive that one, but I wont forgive it again," he whispered before leaning back in his chair. I gritted my teeth before slumping back to my spot on the steps.

"What do we have here?" Abraham asked, his joy returning.

Bastian stood there shaking. He didn't answer, didn't do anything but glare in my direction.

"Here are two from the first list," Cade said, stepping forward. "Ryder, Johnny, and Caleb are tracking the third deep in the mountain. They will be here within the day, I'm sure."

He passed the frightened men off to Henry and Darryl, who pushed them out of the room to God knows where. I didn't want to find out.

"We want the next list," Elijah demanded.

"I'm impressed. You have done way more than the mountain lions could have in a fraction of the time," Abraham stated as he started to play with Bay's hair. He dropped my chain and ran his fingers through my hair as well.

Rage filled my chest, and I glared back at Abraham, whose eyes were fixated ahead. Bastian snarled viciously.

"Careful, wolf. These girls are in good hands as long as you control yourself and hold up your end," Abraham stated.

"Nowhere in the deal said you had permission to touch them like that. That's still my mate, and you're pushing your luck by aggravating my wolf. Now remove your hand!" Bastian shouted as he paced the floor. *He was mere feet from me...*

I was relieved he kept quiet about his bear though. That was the last thing we needed Abraham to know that Bastian was a mixer too. Everyone assumed he smelled like a mixer because he was my mate, and I wanted to keep it that way.

Abraham laughed. "You're right, wolf. I'll stop playing with Shanely's hair, even though it's just so soft."

"And now Bay's," Elijah stated firmly.

"The way I see it, she's not mated, so I'm really not pushing the sacred mate bond. I think I'll keep it here," the Tiger King replied.

I shook my head, feeling awful for Bay. She didn't move, didn't flinch, when Abraham gave her curls a small tug.

"Bay, push him away. He knows this isn't part of the deal!" Cade shouted.

Bay opened her mouth, but slammed it shut, remembering his threat. She shook her head and looked down, and I exhaled the breath I'd been holding.

"Shanely baby, look at me," Bastian pleaded. My eyes went to him. *God, I missed my mate,* I thought to myself. His eyes softened, pleading with me, but I couldn't say anything! Not without putting Aerith in danger.

"Are you okay? Are you being hurt at all?"

Abraham grabbed my collar again, pulling me close once more. He whispered in my ear, "No mind-link either. I think the collar is strong enough in your system to block it out, but just in case... I want radio silence."

I glared at him and pulled away slightly. I looked back at Bastian, hoping he could read what I was thinking in my eyes.

Bastian glared at Abraham. "Why won't my wife speak to me?"

"Because she's working tonight. She's not allowed to speak," Abraham stated as he leaned back, seemingly bored with the conversation now.

"Working? That was never part of the deal!" he bellowed.

"It was never *not* part of the deal either. They are staying in my house. I'm feeding them all and protecting them. It's the least they can do honestly," Abraham replied.

Bastian roared, and Abraham snarled right back. Their roars echoed in the room, and I held my breath, afraid what the Tiger King would do to my mate.

"I said watch it, wolf. The girls are none of your business *until* that list is complete. You can pick up the next 3 names on your way out. Now excuse me, I have other business to attend to. Come on, ladies."

Abraham pulled our chains, forcing us to stand quickly. Bastian looked horrified as he eyed me up and down slowly. Panic filled the brother's eyes at the sight of our full attire. I felt nothing but shame as they simply stared at us. Abraham arrogantly pulled us along, passing the boys without a care in the world. I squeezed Bastian's hand quickly when we passed by. His touch warmed me and melted stress that had been sitting on my chest away, but it was instantly back the moment I let go. I nearly stumbled from the heaviness and loss I felt from leaving my mate. I couldn't *breathe* and felt Bastian's eyes on me as we left the room.Abraham led us upstairs to our room and thanked us for our services tonight. He left without another word, and I stormed inside. I ran to the bathroom bawling. All three girls sat by me, while I wallowed in sorrow and shame.

Bay explained briefly what had happened tonight, and they were so angry for me. Alana wrapped her arm around me, and I just collapsed against her. They didn't realize how much comfort they gave me. Even Octavia and I were becoming a lot closer since coming here, and she looked genuinely concerned for me. *These girls were my best friends,* I thought to myself. *And I was grateful to have them here with me.*

Alana helped remove my makeup, while Octavia brought me a pair of pajamas that one of the tigers brought us while we were gone. They helped me get into bed after I calmed down, and I was soon snuggled up to my daughter, who was passed out asleep with her mouth wide open just like Cade. It made me smile even just briefly before I too fell into a deep sleep.

Bastian

We were finally ushered forward, and Darryl led us through the castle. The two foxes were pale, and I seriously hoped they wouldn't get sick on us. Although I really didn't know their fate, so maybe they had good reason to be scared. They did try to double cross a ruthless tiger after all. Darryl took us to a large set of doors, and as soon as they opened, I scented her.

Shanely.

My eyes found her in no time, but my jaw about dropped to the ground when they did. There she was in the smallest outfit I had ever seen her wear. My heart began to race just looking at her. She was *beautiful.* God I missed her, but like a cold shower, my stupid brain finally made the connection of where she was and who she was leaning on.

I couldn't help it.

I growled at him. *His promise that my wife wouldn't be harmed was just a fat lie,* I thought angrily to myself. My animals went berserk inside my head, pushing against my skin wanting out so they could shred this arrogant man themselves. Shanely could see my loss of control and lunged forward.

Abraham snapped her chain, causing her to fall back towards him again. I saw red, when he grabbed her by the back of her neck before whispering something to her. She froze and settled back down on his leg without a fight. My eyes widened in disbelief. *This wasn't like Shanely,* I thought as panic surged through me. *What was he threatening her with?!*

I couldn't think straight. I couldn't *see* straight. My wolf and bear were at the surface, fighting to show themselves first, and I was struggling to hold in whatever power I had in me. It was taking all of my focus not to release the

Alpha power I now had because of mating Shanely. All the while Abraham seemed to be having the time of his life.

"What do we have here," Abraham asked. I know he was addressing me, but if I spoke now I wasn't sure what I'd say or *if* I'd keep control. Cade could see my struggle and took over. I was grateful to my brother. I was shaking uncontrollably, but my eyes were glued to Shanely. She gave me a sad look, and it was all I could do not to snatch her away, and then beat the snot out of this prick.

"Here are two from the first list. Ryder, Johnny, and Caleb are tracking the third deep in the mountain. They will be here within the day, I'm sure."

The marks were handed off never to be seen again. I'd pity them if Shanely didn't steal all my focus. I looked towards Bay, and she seemed remarkable calm despite everything.

"We want the next list," Elijah demanded.

"I'm impressed. You have done way more than the mountain lions could in a fraction of the time," Abraham stated as he started to play with Bay's hair. I watched him slowly move to Shanely's hair, wrapping her strands around his fingers. I snarled viciously towards the Tiger King.

"Careful, wolf. These girls are in good hands as long as you control yourself and hold up your end," Abraham stated.

"Nowhere in the deal said you had permission to touch them like that. That's still my mate, and you're pushing your luck by aggravating my wolf. Now remove your hand!"

I started pacing back and forth. I needed to do something otherwise I'd lose control, and whichever animal pulled through first was going to end Abraham once and for all.

Abraham laughed. "You're right, wolf. I'll stop playing with Shanely's hair, even though it's just so soft."

"And now Bay's" Elijah stated firmly.

"The way I see it she's not mated, so I'm really not pushing the sacred mate bond. I think I'll keep it here," he replied.

"Bay, push him away. He knows this isn't part of the deal!" Cade shouted.

Bay opened her mouth but slammed it shut. She just looked at her feet, and I stood there entirely baffled. *What was going on with them?* I wondered.

"Shanely baby, look at me," I pleaded. *Something was wrong with the girls more than with what they were wearing.* Her beautiful green eyes looked at me, and I melted inside. I needed my mate.

"Are you okay? Are you being hurt at all?"

Abraham grabbed her collar and pulled her back. He whispered in her ear again, and her eyes widened. She glared at him as she pulled away and gave me a pleading look. Her eyes softened like they were trying to say a million different things. None of which I knew.

I was pissed at Abraham. "Why won't my wife speak to me?"

"Because she's working tonight. She's not allowed to speak," Abraham stated.

"Working? That was never part of the deal!" I bellowed.

"It was never *not* part of the deal either. They are staying in my house. I'm feeding them all and protecting them. It's the least they can do honestly," Abraham replied.

This time I lost control a bit. My bear roared, and I managed to finally get a reaction from the mad man. Just not the one I wanted.

"I said to watch it, wolf. The girls are *none* of your business until that list is complete. You can pick up the next 3 names on your way out. Now excuse me, I have other business to attend to. Come on, ladies."

Abraham pulled on their chains, forcing them up. *They were leaving!* I thought as panic surged through me. My eyes widened when I got to take in her full attire. Shanely had never worn anything like this before. At least not in public. My body shook as he pulled them past us. All I could do was watch. Watch as my very sexy wife was being dragged away by a chain like an animal!

Does she wear this all the time?

I tried to send her a mind-link, but I got nothing. I was utterly useless as she passed by, and I knew if I moved to grab her I'd only do more harm. She seemed to sense my turmoil and carefully squeezed my hand once before letting me go. All the tension drained from my body, and I briefly felt renewed. But when she let go, all my pain and agony flooded back in me, and it was almost too much to take. I stared at her until she disappeared.

"He will die for this. Mark my words," Elijah stated coldly. Cade was even pacing now, and I felt their emotions through the bond. Everyone was ready to snap.

Henry waltzed back in and handed us a piece of paper before he walked away, leaving us to let ourselves out.

I snarled and stormed out of the castle. I hopped into the driver's seat and nearly broke the truck's window, when I slammed my door shut. Cade and Elijah were quiet as they jumped into the other seats. I stared at the woods in front of me, gripping the steering wheel hard so hard my knuckles turned white. I couldn't take it anymore, and I slammed my hand against the steering wheel. Over and over again until a piece of it finally snapped off.

"What do you need, brother?" Elijah asked quietly, pulling me from my fit of rage.

"My mate! I need my mate, Elijah," I snapped. The cab fell silent, and I leaned my head against the broken steering wheel, trying to calm myself down. I couldn't take my rage out on Abraham, but I knew deep down that Elijah didn't deserve this either. My mind was a muddled mess. The way she looked tonight was too much. All I could think of was her wearing that around all those males. *How many tigers got to see her like that? Was this the first time? And when did she even start working for him?*

"Bastian, reel it in. You're going to end up feral if you don't," Cade said nonchalantly.

I sat up and rolled my eyes. "How do you always know where my head is Cade?"

"Because you aren't the only one thinking those things. We may not feel the possessive mate attraction like you do, but Shanely is still our girl too. It's in our bond so if my mind's thinking those questions then I know yours is too, and it's far worse."

I sighed grateful to my brothers. "I don't know if I'm going to make it through this list. I got to see my wife for a total of five minutes, and she was dressed like *that*. Unable to even speak to me."

Elijah sighed. "I know. She looked horrified to see us tonight. I hope this was the first time the girls had to do something like this."

"What's his thing with Bay too? If it's not Shanely then it's Bay," Cade asked, and I shrugged.

"Maybe because she's Mor'du and our sister? Another way to get under our skin maybe?" I answered and started the truck.

"Yeah, maybe. Let's just focus on the list for now. Who's on it?" Elijah asked, and I handed him the paper.

"Okay so Owen Brehanny, George Davidson, and…" Elijah blinked in surprise, "Nicole Livingston."

I gave him an odd look as we passed through the first gate. "We have to bring in a girl?"

"What is she?" Cade asked, and I could tell my brothers were as nervous about it as I was.

"Whoa… She's a shark," Elijah answered wide-eyed, and I stopped the truck.

"She's a what now?"

"It's what it says! She's a shark. The other one is a gorilla, and then we have another bear," Elijah stated, and I whistled.

"What's a sea shifter doing on land? I thought they preferred to live as their animals mostly and never really stepped foot on land?" I asked as I took my foot off the brake. The truck moved on, and I reluctantly made my way back towards home.

"That's what I thought too. And what's a sea shifter doing all the way out in the Washington mountains?" Cade asked, and Elijah shrugged.

"How are we going to catch her is what I want to know," he muttered, and we all stayed quiet then. I let that question just be for now and pulled out my phone. I quickly pushed a number without taking my eyes off the road.

"Hey man, I was just about to call you! Stroke of good luck, but we got him!" Caleb's voiced boomed excitedly through the speaker.

I smiled proud of my friend's good work. "Nice work, guys. Go ahead and have Cassia pull enough to deliver him to Abraham then, but I need to give you a heads up before you go."

"Yeah?" he asked cautiously, sensing a shift in my tone.

"Make sure to keep Johnny close to you at all times here. I know he won't miss an opportunity to go to the castle nor will he sit in the truck, but you need to make sure he doesn't lose it in there. He *cannot* shift if he goes in."

"Bastian... What happened?" he asked nervously.

I sighed. "Abraham had Shanely and Bay working tonight. They were involved in his dealings, and they weren't allowed to move off his leg or speak to us. He had them in these skanky outfits too, and I don't know if he will make Alana do the same thing when you guys drop off this guy."

"Are you freaking kidding me? That was never part of the deal!"

"That's what we said, but he doesn't care. You need to be very specific with the contract, I guess. He takes it all literally, and Johnny would not be able to handle what we saw tonight. I barely did. Keep him home or make sure he doesn't shift if you take him."

"You got it, Bastian. Did you get another list?" he asked.

"Yeah, we've got another bear on it too. I'm going to take it to your dad or to Daniel and see if we can get more info on him first. The other problem we have is that we have a gorilla and a shark to catch this time around."

"A shark?! What in the world is a shark doing on land? Sea shifters never come out of the water!"

"That's what we thought too, but it's also going to be extra hard because the shark is a woman. We're bringing in a girl this time," I said exasperated with everything now. I was so emotionally drained that I was tempted to have Cassia knock me out again. Shanely's outfit tonight snapped me out of it though, and I was ready to go straight to the Den instead.

"Good lord. I wonder if she broke her agreement or if someone hired Abraham to find her."

That thought killed me. I hated the idea of destroying her freedom if she truly never made a deal with Abraham, and this whole thing just became extremely difficult to stomach.

"I hadn't thought of that. I have no idea though. Abraham didn't tell us anything."

"I guess that's a good thing, I suppose. I don't know how I feel about all this, Bastian," Caleb spoke low, and I knew exactly what he meant.

"I know, and I feel it too, but we need to get our girls out of there. I don't know what else to do, brother," I said quietly, and we were silent for a moment.

"Alright, leave the bear shifter for us. We'll drop Jessie off and meet up with you later tonight. Where you heading?"

"The Den. Someone's bound to know what's up with these two," I answered, turning onto the highway.

"Okay well be careful, and we will see you soon. Don't worry about Johnny. I've got him," Caleb said before the line disconnected, and I tossed my phone in the center console.

"Shanely and Bay are tough, brother. They'll be okay," Elijah said, and I grunted. I know my girl is strong, but there was only so much my animals could handle when it came to her. *How much longer could I hold on knowing she's in a place like that?* I pressed my foot down on the pedal, pushing Cade's truck a bit harder.

"Let's just end this," I said to no one in particular. I was ready to pick my wife up and never see that douche's face again.

Shanely

I awoke this morning completely drained. It had been a few days since I saw my husband while working for Abraham. That night was brutal, and I was still emotionally spent from it and missing my husband something fierce. *Who knew what Bastian's thinking now? Or what he thinks I'm doing here?* Abraham made us keep the outfits, so I have a feeling this will be a reoccurring thing for my mate. That thought killed me. I couldn't shift, and Aerith was here now. She was leverage, whether they'd admit it or not. The Tiger King liked screwing with my mate and pushing his buttons, it seems. It was fun for him, and I just wanted to beat him senseless because of it.

My whole body ached this morning. Not having the bond opened or my mate's touch made things very difficult. Abraham didn't come for me this morning thankfully, but he did send for Bay. I worried about her, but at least she wasn't going in that outfit. I didn't have it in me to be around Abraham right now, and if she was walking out looking like that, then I wouldn't let her go alone. I was still livid for what he did to my mate and I the other night though, and I knew my mouth was bound to make it all worse by snapping at him. I played with Aerith for the morning instead, and Bay didn't returned until lunch with Henry. He left without a word as usual, and Bay wouldn't answer when we asked what he wanted. She just sat back in her corner, looking out the window completely withdrawn from us all.

The next four days went much like this. Abraham would call for Bay for an hour or two first thing in the morning, and she never said much when she returned. Unfortunately, we were forced to help him with his negotiations again. It was the same as before, but thankfully Bastian didn't show this time. Probably the only time in my entire life that I was glad my mate wasn't around. I couldn't bear him seeing us like that again. We weren't allowed to speak, just sit there and look pretty as Abraham would say. Alana and Octavia didn't leave the room much, so they helped me entertain Aerith. It had been over a week since I last saw Bastian, and it was really starting to get to me in every way possible.

This morning started like normal, and I had fully expected it to play out the same as it had been lately but Abraham surprised me when he appeared himself bright and early. He seemed to be in a cheerful mood too, which only infuriated me more.

"Good morning, ladies. I trust you all slept well?"

I groaned, pushing farther into my pillow, and Abraham laughed at me.

"I would like to extend an invitation for you to walk the grounds and meet some in my streak. I thought maybe a change of scenery might be nice."

Alana and Octavia immediately perked up at the offer and rushed to get changed. I, however, was in no rush to spend the day with the man. I slowly sat up and eyed him, but his eyes were on Bay. *Again*. She was doing her best to pretend to be asleep still, but I wasn't sure if he could tell or not.

"Abraham? Can I ask you something about tigers?"

He turned to me and nodded before sitting down on the end of my bed.

"Do tigers have mates? Like wolves and bears do?"

Abraham looked surprised at me but smiled as he said, "We do. All tigers are not allowed to date until they find their life mate."

"How do you find yours then? With wolves, sight is usually enough, while bears need touch."

Much to my surprise, he blushed, and I about laughed at him. He rubbed the back of his head before finally answering me, "Umm... Well we need a specific form of touching. We... uh... need to kiss in order to know. We usually feel a pull towards another, and it's confirmed through a kiss."

"Interesting. Have you found your mate then?" I asked.

"No, I have not. Why are you so interested, Shanely? Curious to see if you have two mates?" he asked, turning the tables on me.

My cheeks turned fire red. "No! Bastian is it for me, but I was curious how it worked for tigers."

Abraham smirked but didn't reply. I decided to press my luck and ask more questions.

"Do tigers allow matings between different shifter kinds?"

Bay stiffened. *Yeah... I hit the nail on the head*, I thought to myself. Abraham stared at me, unsure how to answer, and for once I seemed to fluster him.

"Well... We've never had one before. Tigers usually keep to themselves, although I don't reach out to other streaks or ambushes, so maybe they do, but mates are mates. It's not like you choose honestly. It's chosen for you. Your perfect match, right? So I wouldn't interfere with it, I suppose," he replied as he watched Bay. I don't think he even realized he was doing it. Or that he was just rambling right now. My brow rose slowly.

"Hmm. Who knew the Tiger King could be so romantic?" I asked, smirking at him.

He snapped out of whatever trance he was in to glare at me. His face softened though, and he started to smile.

"Let's just keep that between us, alright?" he whispered.

I shrugged my shoulders. "It's not a bad thing. Makes me like you just a little bit actually."

Abraham chuffed. "I do have a reputation to uphold, you know."

"I don't know. You might have a better one if others could see you have a softer side. All I'm saying," I replied as I swung my legs over the side of the bed. My long scars that covered both legs peeked out through my shorts, and his eyes shot straight to them.

"What happened here? It's difficult to scar a shifter," he asked, his voice a little gruff.

Bay sat up now, her face stoic as she answered for me, "That's the work of Derek, Abraham."

She entered the bathroom, leaving us alone with a sleeping Aerith. He stared at the door for a moment before turning back to me. Abraham looked confused almost.

"The one I was sent to take care of?"

I nodded my head. "He thought I was an abomination because I'm a mixer, so when I was days from giving birth to this little one, he and another bear shifter kidnapped me and shot me full of something... Well something similar to these things," I said as I tugged on the collar before continuing on.

"They took me far away from my home, near Dead Man's Hollow, in the dead of winter. Derek sliced me here to attract animals, and then hung me like six feet off the ground before fleeing. I almost didn't make it."

Abraham's face hardened, and I cocked my head to the side. *Was he upset hearing the story?* He gruffly asked, "What happened after that?"

"Cade and Elijah found me somehow, and I gave birth to her in an abandoned cabin in Dead Man's Hollow. That's when your *employees* found us and wanted to collect the bounty you had on wolves, which is why Bastian was forced to kill them. We warned them many times to leave us alone, but they kept saying I was worth a hefty price with you," I replied coldly, remembering that day very clearly.

Abraham stared at me, eyes filled with what seemed to be rage and maybe even guilt. "I didn't realize all that happened. When we found their bodies I could smell a bear and a wolf on them, but we couldn't figure what happened. I was just pissed that I was down two bounty hunters. I didn't have a bounty on you specifically though. I never knew about you until I saw you by the ring, Shanely."

"You are a confusing tiger, you know? One minute it feels like we could be friends, good friends even, and then the next you do something like the other night with Bastian. I can't figure you out," I said quietly.

The Tiger King snorted. "You're the confusing one. I can't explain it though. I'm drawn to you, Bay, even to this little one here. I've never felt anything like this before. It's almost possessive."

"What about Bastian?" I asked, narrowing my eyes. "Why did you do that to him? He already agreed to the deal, why make it worse?"

He laughed, rubbing the back of his neck sheepishly. "It's a little funny seeing him get all mad."

"You mean you're just messing with him?!"

Abraham laughed harder. "Oh, come on! It's boring being King sometimes. Bastian makes it so easy too! Plus, I've never had trackers like the Fenrir brothers. It seems to be effective keeping that fire lit under them, and you being present during deals adds to the fear. Everyone can smell a mixer, a very strong mixer I might add, and when you're there by my side, it shows that I own you, and they're less likely to double cross me then. In fact, I've had quite a few deliver early since you've been helping me out."

"You don't own me," I said frustratedly.

"I know that, but they don't. It's all about the illusion, sweetheart. I'm just using it to my advantage," he replied as he pushed Aerith's hair away from her face. Surprisingly, it didn't anger me like it should, and I don't think he even realized he did it.

"I'm really not a bad guy, Shanely. I mean, not all the time," he whispered.

"Prove it. Let me and the girls have a night with our fellas. Everyone's been working hard, so give us a night together. I'm getting painfully sore from being away from Bastian for so long, which means he is too. He needs me to relax and take away the pain," I asked as kindly as I could muster. This was the longest I had spoken to the Tiger King where he stayed relaxed and kind almost. *Maybe I was pushing my luck, but I'd do anything for a night with Bastian.*

Abraham thought about it for a minute before asking, "So, you wolves need touch?"

"Wolves are naturally very touchy in general but being away from your mate for an extended time starts to wear on you. You aren't as well rested and soon your muscles hurt. Bastian can't be at his best this way, which means you won't get the ones on the list as quickly as you'd like. He and Johnny work better and faster than the others because they're mated, but soon they will be at their weakest if we can't see them. Please, Abraham?"

Abraham mulled it over as he studied me carefully. Finally. he stood up and answered, "Alright."

The girls left the bathroom while I sat there in shock. I thought I was going to have to beg or annoy him into agreeing. "Alright?" I asked in disbelief. "You're saying yes?!"

"Yes to what?" Alana asked.

"Shanely made a good point. Everyone deserves a break and a reward. Your guys have been the best to ever work for me, so tonight they will stay here with you," he said, and the girls shrieked with happiness.

Bay looked at him surprised, the corners of her mouth rising ever so slightly, and I barely caught the wink he gave her.

Abraham walked over to Bay and whispered something in her ear. Her eyes grew wide, and she turned around quickly, pulling her hair aside. He took a key out and popped the collar right off.

"We're getting the collars off?" Octavia asked excitedly.

"Bay has a fight tonight, so the effects need to wear off for her to be able to shift," Abraham said as he rubbed the spot on her neck where the collar sat. Alana, Octavia, and I looked to one another before turning back to them. He quickly pulled his hand away and stepped back from her. Bay dropped her dark hair and smiled at him.

"I am sorry about the rest of you though. My village here does not trust wolves like I'm beginning too," he said softly, looking at Bay and then to me, "so the collars stay. It's the only way they agreed to let you walk through. Though in time they might come around, but we can lose the chains for today. Just no running, please."

With that, he left us to finish dressing in peace.

"What just happened?" Alana asked as she looked around the room.

I shrugged baffled myself. "I think Abraham's different than we thought. What do you think, Bay?"

She rubbed her neck, staring at the door where he once stood before shrugging. "He is different, I guess. I'm grateful to be rid of that thing though."

"Lucky you," Octavia muttered pulling at hers. "Mine itches something fierce."

We all quickly changed into the new clothes that Darryl sent up to us yesterday and went to meet Abraham downstairs. Aerith was bounding on ahead, and I let her have her fun. I kept Bastian a secret from her though. I couldn't wait to see her face when her daddy showed up. All I wanted was to get through the day and see my mate.

Bastian was in for a huge surprise!

Shanely

Abraham waited patiently for us as we meandered down the stairs. Darryl, Henry, and another tiger I didn't know yet were waiting at the bottom with him as well. The new guy was shorter than Henry with short blond hair, and the one thing I noticed about him was that he was the first tiger I had *ever* seen with piercings. His left eyebrow was pierced as was his lip.

"You all look lovely, ladies," Abraham said, even though his eyes remained glued to Bay's. "You know Darryl and Henry of course, but this is Jake. They will be escorting all of us today."

We all waved hi towards the enforcers, who all seemed a bit more relaxed than we've ever seen them before. It was starting to feel more like a visit rather than a sentence, which was a little bizarre. I wasn't about to argue with the mood change though. I needed my mate and *nothing* was going to ruin our night. That included running my mouth by accident.

Abraham motioned to the guards to start moving, and Darryl and Henry promptly shifted. They were nearly identical in color and utterly massive tigers. I had never been up close to a tiger before, and it was extremely cool to see their sleek orange and black fur. Henry sauntered over and stood near Aerith and I, which was a bit of a shock. His cat easily came up past my hips, and I grinned, looking over to Alana. She giggled, mouthing *So Fluffy* to me, and I couldn't contain my smile. Darryl took up the other side, and Jake stood in the rear, remaining in his human form. Abraham stood next to me also staying in his human form. *Was this formation to protect his streak from us or to protect us from those who still hated us?* That was a sobering thought.

"Mommy, look a tiger!" Aerith shrieked and practically lunged for Henry before I could stop her. He stumbled backwards, looking alarmed as this tiny child practically dove into him.

"Aerith wait! I don't know if Henry..."

Henry promptly laid down and let my daughter snuggle against him. She giggled, wrapping her arms around his neck like he was a stuffed animal for her to play with. Aerith buried her face into his fur and began to pet him behind his ears. He chuffed but remained still, letting her love on him.

"He likes her," Abraham said, with a soft smile as we all watched the interaction.

I looked at him. "Aerith seems pretty smitten too."

"Mommy look! It's a tiger! Can I ride him?"

I laughed at that. "Honey, I don't think Henry will want that."

She looked defeated, and slowly moved her head to his like she'd seen Bastian do to me all the time back home. She put her two little hands on either side of his face, resting her forehead on his. The thought of Bastian pulled at my heart, but I reminded myself that I just needed to get through today. I'd see him really soon.

"Please, Mr. Henry Tiger Sir? Can I?"

Henry nudged her forward a bit ever so gently for being such a big guy. I started to pull her away, when Abraham interrupted me. "He said yes. That's his way of saying yes. Here let me."

Abraham carefully picked Aerith up as Henry stood tall and waited. He set her on his back and said, "Now hold on, okay? It will take some getting used to how he moves."

Aerith nodded gleefully and wrapped her arms around Henry. I watched my daughter ride a tiger as if he were a pony at the state fair. Henry carefully showed her how he moved about, and she giggled beaming ear to ear.

"Thank you both. You have no idea what that meant to her," I said, and Abraham smiled.

"It's our pleasure. She's a delight to watch, and I'd like her experience here to be a good one. She was simply stuck in the middle of everything," Abraham said, and we all followed Henry with Aerith on his back. They led the way out the back entrance, and we walked the trail heading into the woods.

Abraham and I hung back some, while the other girls starting talking to Jake. Darryl took up the position in the rear instead.

"So I'm curious, Shanely, and I hope I'm not being too intrusive, but what happened with Aerith? I can smell Aerith's scent, and it's no shifter. She can't belong to Bastian scenting like that. His wolf is too strong, and honestly he smells a lot more like a mixer now too. My men and I can't figure it out."

I sighed, pushing passed a low branch. "I wasn't raised a shifter, Abraham. When my grandmother left me her cabin in the woods, I found out about myself and my parents. Little did I know when I came here that I was pregnant with her. I fled an abusive ex, and he took advantage of me when he wanted. Bastian just adopted her as his own, and we've tried to keep her somewhat a secret because her biological dad was human."

I slowed my pace even more, putting distance between us and Aerith. Abraham noticed and slowed with me.

"We've been trying to keep her a secret from the Division because of the law but because of Bay's fights, Patrick was forced to return home, and I'm hoping he doesn't ever put two and two together."

Abraham's hands fisted at his side. His voice turned raspy when he replied, "No one should be allowed to hurt you like that and just live. That man deserves death, Shanely. It's the only way to ensure your safety and hers."

"I know, but Peter will never be able to find me here, so we're safe. He has no idea about her anyways. I'm more worried about Patrick right now."

"What is your deal with the human?" he asked as he calmed himself.

"He seemed almost fixated with me at first, but we discovered awhile ago that I'm a seer. Patrick seems to trigger horrible warnings of things to come to all of us. I've avoided him as much as I could, but it's not always possible. I'm afraid he will somehow learn the truth about Aerith and that will give him the excuse to wipe out my pack. So we all wait, and we watch."

"But you work with the bears now? What about your laws?" he asked.

"We've abolished them for our area and put a lot of issues between us in the past. Me being a mixer of half-bear and half-wolf helped bridge the gap. I have family on both sides, so it forced us to deal with problems head on and solve them for everyone's benefit. Just not all shifters are letting go of the old laws, so we just deal with our own. Can't really force the other packs to change," I replied.

Abraham seemed to mull everything over. "And Derek? Your child is what three, and he's still alive."

"Four actually, and it's complicated, Abraham. Besides isn't that why we're here? Because you're supposed to kill him, and for the record I still haven't heard anything about that."

"Well... Like you said it's complicated."

I snorted. "Let me guess. You lied and hadn't even started looking for him."

He gave me sideways glance before replying, "Look, I hadn't exactly heard much about the details of why she wanted him dead, and she never stipulated *when* the mark needed to be completed. I just thought I'd get some extra fights out of her before I actually delivered."

"Of course you did," I said, rolling my eyes. "Can you actually deliver though?"

Abraham arched a brow at me. "Of course, I can. I just need to learn the ins and outs of the Fenrir pack over there, but I'll find out where that snake is lying. Especially now that I know all the details."

"Well even if you don't, it doesn't really change anything."

"You don't seem as invested in his death as your mate or sister," he replied.

I sighed. "They killed Michael within the week for his role in my abduction, but Derek has never returned to the States nor do I think he will after what he did. All I care about is never seeing him again. Either way this ends with him staying out of my life, so I'm not concerned with how I get that result."

We stayed quiet for a little while before a small village came into view, and my eyes widened at what I saw. It felt like we had stepped into a whole different world the minute we entered the clearing. It was *beautiful*! Small wooden huts were built everywhere in this clearing, and a creek ran through the left side. There were quite a few children running around too, and I could hear Aerith's squeal from all the way from the back of our group.

Henry knelt down to let her off, and she ran after the other kids to play.

They didn't seem to mind her one bit, and soon they were all playing tag like they had know each other for years. I always loved how easily she made friends no matter where we were, and after everything that had happened lately, watching her play was the best thing. But when my gaze drifted to the many eyes watching us, anxiety began to roll in my stomach, and I shrunk back some.

Abraham gently guided us along as he showed us everything and introduced us to the streak. They were weary of us but at least pleasant. It was interesting to watch the streak interact with their King. They all seemed to adore Abraham, and he greeted everyone with kindness and care. Not at all the devious, wicked man we all knew him as, but someone entirely new and wonderful.

The streak had many tables set up outside their huts, where they were working on all sorts of tasks. One table was loaded with different spices, which made the whole village smell amazing. Another table was in the process of making some sort of bag that looked really pretty. I wondered what it was for, but the more I looked around, the more I realized they had their own trading system set up between everyone. It was like their own private little market, and everything was handmade and ready to trade. It was incredible!

Around noon, Abraham led us to the creek, and some of the women brought us lunch. They had a variety of cheese and meats with crackers and some fruit. Light and perfect for the sunny and warm day we were having.

Henry and Darryl remained as tigers, but Jake stayed human. He soon had us all laughing hard with his witty remarks, and I forgot for a brief moment our situation. I even forgot about these stupid collars, which surprised me. Jake reminded me so much of Cade, and my heart tugged whenever I thought of my boys. *I can't wait to see them tonight!*

I also noticed how close Abraham sat next to Bay, and occasionally their hands would touch. Bay seemed nervous though, and soon tucked her hands in her lap. When I wasn't laughing with Jake, I was watching those two. I had a strong idea to what was going on, but I kept my suspicions to myself.

As the afternoon went on, I realized I was becoming a bit more comfortable with the Tiger King. Sitting here with us, he didn't seem so scary or bad. Abraham just acted and looked like a normal guy, not the crazy brute that like to torment people when it came to his deals. I raised my eyebrow at him, when he caught me staring, and he just winked at me.

"Mommy, can I go swimming? The other kids are!" Aerith asked. I looked to my left where a lot of the kids were swimming close to the bank. It didn't look too deep, and I wanted her to have fun with the others. Henry and Darryl stayed on the embankment, watching the children play, so I felt better knowing they were there too. They seemed to genuinely care for the kids, so I trusted them. *The whole day was just becoming bizarre,* I thought to myself.

"Sure baby, just don't go past that rock. It looks deeper after that, okay? Stay by the other kids," I replied, but she was racing off before I could even finish.

Abraham chuckled as he turned to Bay. "She's a feisty one and so brave too. It must run in the family."

Bay blushed under his gaze. "She is something else, that's for sure."

Abraham's eye flashed with amusement, and we all started talking about the village. We all felt at home in the woods, which was something everyone had in common with the other. We learned that most of these huts were here when Abraham was a boy. They built some newer ones as the streak grew once he took it back over, but the others had lasted a very long time. He told us that he offered to modernize the huts, and while they took him up on some of the things he suggested, most preferred them to stay somewhat basic and old-fashioned. I thought it was pretty cool honestly that they were staying so close to their roots. We also learned why he called his group a streak or ambush. I never knew that was what a real group of tigers were called. It made sense.

Suddenly, a scream filled the air. The kids were running from the water, and I quickly stood up, looking for my daughter. My heart thundered in my chest as I rushed past the smaller children. I couldn't find Aerith *anywhere*, and my heart seized. *She was there just a moment ago!*

"Aerith!" I shouted as I ran towards the water. Someone faster than me rushed passed, causing me to stumble slightly. My eyes widened. It was

Abraham, and I watched as he dove into the creek. I followed the direction he was heading, and that's when I spotted Aerith in the center of the creek, far past the rock. She looked scared and so tiny in the water. My heart stopped when she went under the water, and my feet were moving towards her. A child dove into me, scared out of her mind, and I quickly hauled her up and out. I desperately needed to get to Aerith though, but another child scrambled up to me, and I helped him out of the bank too.

"Run! Go quickly, children!" I shouted.

Thankfully Abraham was a fast swimmer and made it to Aerith in no time. He dove under the water as I helped the last small child out of the water and appeared with Aerith in his hands. I exhaled deeply, moving further into the creek. *She's alright,* I told myself, trying to calm my racing heart. But then my eyes finally landed on what caused all the panic and screaming in the first place. A very large anaconda swam towards the two, and my heart stopped.

"Abraham behind you!" I screamed, and he jerked his head around, spotting the large snake.

Abraham wasted no time throwing Aerith on his back and swam like mad away from the snake. But he wasn't fast enough. The snake was so much faster in the water than Abraham was, and Henry and Darryl dove in after them. I ran, splashing in the water as I tugged on that freaking collar. It burned against my skin as my anger flared, but I couldn't get it off. *God, this stupid...*

Abraham threw Aerith on Henry's back before the snake pulled him under the water. Henry swam Aerith away, while Darryl searched for Abraham, snarling as he turned in circles. I changed course and swam towards Henry. I watched him and Aerith make it safely to shore moments before I reached the bank again. Henry shifted and hauled me out of the creek, and I pulled Aerith into my arms.

"Oh thank God, you're safe!" I shouted as Henry tugged on my arm.

"We need to get back! It's not safe this close!"

I passed her to Henry, my body shaking from the adrenaline as I got to my feet, and we began to rush back to the others. I took two steps, turning to check on Abraham and Darryl, when I realized neither one of them had resurfaced. I grounded to a halt as something deep inside refused to let me move my feet *any* further.

"Come on, Abraham," I muttered, bouncing on my feet as panic began to take over. "Resurface..."

My chest suddenly burned when no one came out of the water, and I gasped. I hadn't felt this kind of pain since my wolf and bear awoke all those years ago, I thought to myself. My mind was reeling as I struggled to figure out what was going on, but when I focused on that pain, it traveled to my neck and burned beneath the collar. I looked back to the water, and the pain *intensified*.

Abraham finally emerged gasping for air. The snake coiled around his mid-section, and my heart stopped.

Suddenly, like a dam being broke, my bear pushed to the surface. Somehow despite the collar she was coming through, and I relaxed into the shift. The collar snapped off my neck, and I shifted into my beautiful white bear. I roared, feeling strong and free again before charging into the water.

For whatever reason, my bear needed to protect Abraham, who was struggling to break free of the snake's grasp. The snake had wrapped tightly around Abraham's waist, making his movements slow and keeping him from being able to shift. Darryl had reemerged too and clamped down on the snake's belly, trying to get him to loosen his grip, but this was a very strong snake. He wasn't budging. I scented him now that I was in my bear from and snarled again.

He was a shifter.

I went straight for the head and just barely missed as the snake struck my shoulder. I gasped as his fangs clamped down and blood ran down my white fur. I swatted at him, but he still had a death grip on Abraham and me. Soon blood filled the clear blue creek, and Abraham's ragged breath began to scare me half to death. *I had to get him to let go.* I lunged again and managed to bite the snake in the neck. It was difficult fighting him in the water, but I refused to let go and tried shaking him wildly. The snake finally released his grip on Abraham, and the Tiger King took a painful deep breath. Darryl shifted to his human form and grabbed a hold of his King, dragging him further from the snake.

The snake flipped around violently, trying to wrap himself around me now, and my heart thundered in my chest. I couldn't let him do that. I felt it's sleek and slimy body squeeze around my middle, and I nearly gasped at the immense pressure. I had never fought a shifter like this, but if I didn't do something fast, I wouldn't be getting out of this situation. I clamped down on the snake's neck again and clawed it's belly, hoping to just shred the stupid snake. We began to sink below the water as I lost the ability to move my lower legs. We hit the bottom of the creek bed before the snake twisted it's head around, hissing at me before it lunged. My lungs burned in agony as I jerked my head to the side and clamped down on it's head before it could bite me. My vision blurred, but I bit down even harder until I finally heard a snap. The snake instantly fell limp against me. It's tail unwrapped itself from my middle and slowly fell to the bottom. Relief washed over me, and I struggled to reach the surface.

I shot out of the water and slowly made my way to the bank. I heard Bay and Alana shout my name as I carefully made my way to solid ground. I was exhausted, but it was done. When my paws hit solid ground I turned to where the snake lay at the bottom of the creek, and I roared louder than I had ever before. My bear felt proud of her accomplishment, and honestly so did I.

Anger filled my heart when I looked to the crowd that had formed. No one else came to help their King or me for that matter, but I ignored the streak and made my way to Aerith. She lunged for me and wrapped her tiny arms around my head. I was so relieved she was okay. *We all were okay*, I thought to myself.

That moment passed when my vision suddenly blurred. My stomach twisted violently like I was about to loose my lunch. Pain engulfed my body, and I staggered backwards. Aerith dropped her arms. My insides felt like they were rearranging themselves again, yet I hadn't started the shift yet. *What was happening?* I wondered as panic swept over me. I swayed on my feet before finally collapsing on the ground. The pain was excruciating. I had never felt like this after a shift before.

Aerith shouted, "Mommy's hurt!"

Henry quickly picked up my daughter, who looked terrified. The Tiger King wasn't far behind.

"What was going on? What's happening to me?!"

Abraham rushed to my side as I tried to stand again. His chest was completely black and blue. It looked like that snake might have broken ribs.

"Shanely? I... I could..." Abraham started to say, but I groaned loudly, cutting him off. My chest constricted, unable to put air in my lungs, and I couldn't help but let out a whimper.

Abraham pulled himself out of his trance and put his hands on my head. "Shanely, the collar's effects are still within you. I don't understand how you were able to pull your bear out, but it's reacting badly to it now that the danger is gone and the adrenaline is wearing off. You need to shift back now!"

"How? I can't think straight! This hurts so bad!" I answered, already knowing he wouldn't hear me through the link.

Abraham's eyes grew wide again. He shouted, "Think of Bastian! Pull on your mate bond, Shanely! You have it now, and it will help you focus! Come on now. SHIFT!"

My eyes widened. *How did he know what I was struggling with?* The pain surged again, and I tried to do what he said. I tried to just focus on Bastian, and I searched for our bond. It felt wonderful to have it back again, and I pulled on it, remembering all the times we had but in our human form. I was desperately trying to do *anything* to shift back. My bear understood, and I forced what little energy I had to shift. I collapsed in Abraham's arms out of breath and bleeding from my left arm.

"Shh... I've got you, Shanely. You're okay now," Abraham whispered as he rubbed my head. I cried hard from the relief I felt from the pain, and I felt my bear disappear again sadly. *At least that collar was off.*

"Jake run to the wall and ask Finnick how a snake shifter made his way inside?!" Abraham bellowed.

Jake nodded and shifted as he ran into the woods towards the wall.

Abraham turned to our group behind him.

"The first time I bring you girls out, we encounter a snake. Unbelievable! I swear to you Shanely this has never happened before otherwise I would have never risked you guys, especially the kids," he scrambled to explain, but I didn't have the strength to answer him. I was falling into oblivion and would have to be angry with him later for it.

"Lilly, make sure the kids are okay. Everyone else go home for now! I'll have the men do a sweep and make sure it was the only one. Henry, you're in charge of Aerith. Do not let her out of your sight! Darryl, take the rest back to their room and remove their collars now!"

Abraham stood and promptly picked me up. I was so drained. I didn't think I could even stand if I tried. He made his way back to the castle but slowed as he passed the girls. "Are you okay?"

He was looking at Bay I realized, singling her out, and she nodded. "I'm sorry I couldn't shift to help. I was trying, and I... I can't swim. I'm so sorry to you both."

Abraham shook his head firmly. "You trusted me when we came out here with those collars on. I never thought this would have happened, and I'm the one that should be sorry. My wounds will heal, however I don't know what I'd do if you were hurt today. If any of you were hurt," he quickly added before leaving them behind.

I couldn't see Bay's reaction. My eyes were heavy from the shift.

"Close them, Shanely. You'll be safe with me, I promise," he said quietly, and I believed him. The last thing I saw was his sorrowful eyes staring down at me.

Bastian

The hunt was on.

Thomas was helping Caleb and Johnny find Owen Brehanny in the next county over, and they hoped to snag him within a day or two. Owen was a drunk, and he frequented the bars around that town, when Thomas removed him from the clan almost a decade ago. It was a shot in the dark, but Thomas was pretty confident he'd locate the bear. He grew up with him and knew his habits fairly well. I trusted them, and let them figure it out. My brothers and I had a lot harder shifters to track down that needed our full attention. Ryder came with us to help out, but no one knew the shark or the gorilla. I was spinning my wheels, trying to figure out what to do and where to go, when we finally got a lucky break.

We were in the club late one night where Shanely was taken not long ago. The club was loud and obnoxious and the last place I wanted to be, but it pulled so many kinds of shifters in that I couldn't risk not coming here. My brothers and I sat at the bar, watching and scenting *everyone* that walked through the door. Ryder was at another table flirting with a long-legged blonde, hoping to get her to start talking. Between Cade, Elijah, and Ryder, we were sniffing out any information we could get. That was the only thing I refused to do in our search for the marks. I'd leave the flirting to the single guys. I was grasping at straws being here, but I didn't know what else to do. I motioned for the fox behind the counter to get me another beer.

"8.50," he muttered.

I rolled my eyes. "Put it on the Tiger King's tab."

"Excuse me?" he asked, giving me a nasty look, so I decided to slow it down for him.

"I said... Put. It. On. The. Tiger King's. *Tab*. I'm working for him tonight, and this is needed for the job."

"A beer is required for the job?" he asked sarcastically, clearly not amused with my attitude. I could care less.

"Go ahead and call him if you don't believe me. Tell him Bastian Fenrir is working and needs a drink to deal with everything he's putting me through. I am not paying for a thing either," I snapped back as Cade started to chuckle.

"In fact, go ahead and add an order of onion rings to the tab too. I'm starving!" Cade chimed in, making me smile. I gave him a gesture, hoping he'd get a move on already.

The guy looked frustrated and completely unsure of what to do.

"Hang tight," he finally muttered before grabbing the phone from under the counter. He dialed a number, and I chugged on what was left of my drink, while I waited for a new one.

"You're pushing it," Elijah whispered, laughing at me, but I didn't care. I set the beer bottle down as the fox talked to whoever was on the other end.

"Yeah, he said he's working for the Tiger King. No, he said he's not paying for anything tonight. I've tried... Okay hang on." The fox covered the phone and asked, "Dude, what's your name again?"

"Bastian Fenrir. The Tiger King's best tracker apparently," I said, slapping the table as I grinned wide. "And I need another beer, Abraham!"

"Did you hear that? Yeah, yeah... Alright. Here," he said rather gruffly, handing me the phone. I rolled my eyes.

"What?" I snapped into the receiver.

"Seriously, you need free beer and food to find your marks?" Henry's voice came through on the other end.

"Well... I *am* working, and the more sustenance I receive, the faster I work. It's the least he can do since he has my wife and child hostage at the moment," I replied sarcastically. *All right, I might be feeling the effects of the beer now, but at this point it was really hard to care.* I just didn't want to feel her loss anymore, and everything just... hurt.

I heard Henry sigh on the other end. "Dude, lay off the beer, but Abraham doesn't care what you do as long as you get the list done. This isn't a free for all though. Once the list is done, you go back to paying for everything."

"Aww... The Tiger King is such a sweetie!" I said sarcastically before laughing at my own joke.

"Are you drunk?" he asked frustrated.

"Nope! I know my limit, man. Like I said I'm working, and you're wasting my time now."

"Bastian... be careful."

Henry disconnected the call, and I tossed the phone back.

"You heard Henry. Free food and beer!" I nearly shouted, and Elijah nudged my arm.

"Bastian, get a coffee or water now. You're nearing your limit for a night of fun, and we *are* working. We need you," he warned in my ear, but I pushed him away. I was frustrated and missing my mate. My body was sore, and the beer was dulling the pain. He was right though, and I was pissed he even needed to remind me.

Suddenly, a small little thing plastered her body up against my back. I rolled my eyes, in no mood to deal with the flirty, drunk girls that were just looking for a mate in this club.

"Did I hear you say free food?" she whispered cautiously in my ear.

I frowned, turning to face her, and boy was this girl *skinny*. She looked like she hadn't eaten in days, and her eyes were dull in color. I eyed her slowly, trying to decide how best to handle this situation.

"Depends. Do you know anything about a girl name Nicole Livingston or a gorilla named George Davidson?" I asked as I pushed her off me.

Her eyes widened at my abrupt movement before narrowing on me. She replied coyly, "What do you need with Nicole?"

My heart stopped. *She knew Nicole.*

"It's our business but know that we do not wish her harm. I'll make you a deal. You can order anything you want right now. Eat to your heart's content, and then some more to take home for all the information you have on Nicole," I offered the small girl. Her eyes went wide, and it was perfect timing that Cade's order of onion rings came out from the kitchen. The fox slid them to us rolling his eyes before leaving. I grabbed a ring before Cade snatched the basket, and I held it in front of the girl. I swear she was about to drool, and her eyes went back and forth between me and the ring.

"You won't hurt her?" she asked quietly.

Guilt ate me alive, but I needed to save Shanely. I pushed the guilty feeling down deep, and I gave her a reassuring nod. She slowly took the ring, and Elijah moved to the next bar stool.

She wolfed it down in seconds, licking her fingers before sitting down between me and my brother. I passed her a menu and whistled for the fox. He still wasn't happy with me but did nothing except grumble to himself.

"All this will also be on the Tiger King's tab, fox," I told him before turning to her. "What do you want?"

She looked over the menu briefly, and I was impressed when she ordered. She was getting her money's worth in this deal.

"I'll have the burger and fries, with an order of onion rings on the side. A large coke, an order of chicken strips and fries to go, and two slices of cheesecake to go as well."

The fox glared at me but left to go back in the kitchen. The music in this club was loud and annoying, but in this moment I was *thrilled* we decided to stop in here.

"Now about Nicole," I said, tapping the counter. She looked around nervously, tucking her hair behind her ears.

"Look Nicole is very sweet. You have to promise me you won't hurt her," she stammered.

"What's your name?" Elijah asked, and she turned to him.

"Olivia," she said quietly.

"Well... Olivia *the Coyote*," he said. My brother gave her a charming look before winking at her. She lowered her head as a blush crept up her cheeks from his attention. I leaned back in my chair, letting him take over. "We promise we won't hurt her. It is *very* important that we speak with her though."

She fumbled with her hair and leaned back in her seat. "Alright. She's a shifter that lives not far from here. She desperately doesn't want to be found though."

"Why?" I asked before thinking. I cursed myself internally for letting that question slip out. I didn't need to hear the backstory to those I was required to find and bring in. I was setting myself up for a massive amount of guilt, but it was too late. The question was out now.

"She ran away and took something when she left, I guess. That's all I know though, I swear!" she exclaimed as the fox started bringing out her order. She sat up excitedly, her eyes nearly bugging out of her head by the food, and something about that look made my heart hurt. She was eager to eat, but I needed more than what she had given me.

I felt awful for doing this, but I grabbed her chair and scooted her backwards, far away from it all. She looked up at me with those big doe eyes like I just scammed her and was about to take it all away. This wasn't the kind of man I was, but I *needed* an address. Nicole was smart, and I didn't want to spend the next month searching for her in this general area. I don't think this coyote would tell me anything more if I let her eat first.

"I need an address," I commanded, letting her get a full sense of my wolf. She looked back at the counter, then to me. I kept my hand on her seat firmly, while Elijah and Cade stared hard at her. I'm sure we were scaring her more than anything, and I tried really hard not to think about that.

She gave a slow nod, and Elijah leaned over the counter, grabbing the fox's pen and a napkin. The bartender snapped us an aggravated look but wisely said nothing when I glared back at him. I slid her forward again, and she scribbled on the note.

"She may not be home as she travels a lot for her work, but here. Can I *please* eat now?"

I took the napkin and passed it back to Cade. My brothers abruptly stood, and I was ready to get out of this God forsaken club. But something was gnawing at me in the back of my mind, and I had to sort this out. She leaned forward to pick up another ring, when I put my hand on her shoulder, halting her advance. I pushed her back against her chair and leaned into her personal space. Her eyes were wide, and I could hear her heart rate skyrocket as I gave her a firm look. My eyes turn red as my wolf rose to the surface, and the poor girl froze.

"I'm not a bad guy, Olivia, and I will gladly give you another free meal for your help tonight, but let me be clear. If you've double-crossed us tonight and gave us a false address, I *will* find you again. I have your scent, and I *never* forget a mark," I threatened quietly in her ear, inhaling her thick scent of freshly cut grass mixed with smoke. *An odd scent for a coyote, but it didn't matter in the grand scheme of things,* I thought to myself. *I had it, and that's all that mattered to my wolf.*

I let her go, and the poor girl looked petrified. This killed me to know I put that look on her face, but I felt more confident with the address now. *She seemed to be telling the truth,* I thought, and I stood up to leave.

"The tigers weren't lying when they said you guys were the best they had working for them," that fox said, stopping me dead in my tracks, "were they?"

"Thank you, Olivia," I spoke, ignoring the fox altogether. I twirled my hand in the air, signaling Ryder we were leaving. He made his way through the crowd, abandoning the blonde who huffed at him, and I stepped outside into the warm air.

"I think you made her crap her pants, brother. Good lord," Cade said, whistling.

"Well, I needed her scent if she lied to us. She was starving, and it wouldn't surprise me to find out she lied for a free meal. I feel like a puke though."

Elijah clapped the back of my shoulder. "Look, you gave her a free meal for today and tomorrow. It isn't much, but it means a lot to her. See?"

I looked back through the windows, and she was nearly finished with the burger already. She smiled to the fox quietly enjoying her dinner, and it lifted some of the crap I was feeling. *Not all though,* I thought to myself. *I'm sure when she joined our group she expected to give something else in return for the meal, but I'm glad she got to eat at least.* I took the napkin from Cade feeling a bit more sober.

"It's not far from here. How did Abraham never find this chick himself?" I asked sarcastically.

"It sounds like he rarely makes an appearance here. Very few people have actually seen him walk through the club, according to the girls," Ryder said as the door to the club slammed shut. "Our boss is elusive."

We started walking down the street away from the loud club, and I was thrilled to get away from all that. The thin cool air felt good on my skin, and I wish Shanely was here to walk with me. It was a perfect night for a stroll, but I stuffed that thought aside, not needing to fall down the feral rabbit hole as Cade called it.

"What's the point of having all this if you don't enjoy it?" Cade asked as we turned the corner.

"Money probably," I answered. The streets were dark, especially the further we got from town, and I'm sure we were about to scare the living crap out of this girl. It was late and most folks were in bed for the night. I scanned the area, making sure we were alone. Last thing I needed was the police jumping down our throats over this.

"So what exactly is the game plan?" Elijah asked quietly. He and Cade were doing the same thing I was, I realized. We were all scanning the area and double checking no one was following us.

"Not exactly sure here," I answered as we crossed the next street. We started getting into the housing district, and I could see the apartment buildings from here. They were a few more blocks away, but the shark was there.

"Why does this feel more like kidnapping and not bounty hunting?" Ryder asked quietly, and no one responded.

"It's not kidnapping, alright," I finally said, breaking the silence. "Our girls were taken, and once we do this we get them back, simple as that. We just…"

My phone buzzed in my pocket, but I realized it was Shanely's phone again. I still had it since she went with Abraham. Another unknown number showed up, so I answered, "Hello?"

It was quiet on the other end again. I looked at my watch, and it was well past midnight. *Who would be calling my wife at this hour? Who's been calling my wife period?*

"Look, whoever this is you have the wrong number. Stop calling," I said before ending the call.

Cade gave me a funny look, but I brushed him off.

"It's nothing. Alright, she's on the ground floor here in these apartment buildings. Ryder run back and get the truck. Elijah, you have the cuffs?" I asked.

"You want to take her now?" Cade asked, giving me a look.

"You have a better idea? We might lose her if Olivia gets ahold of her before we can come back. Then she'll bounce for good. I don't know why this girl ran, but whatever she did it's catching up to her. Let's get in and get her back to pack lands fast. Ryder go, and hurry up. I don't want any extra eyes on us. Cassia gave us the drug, and it's in the truck. We stick her, and then transfer her to the cells until we catch the gorilla."

Ryder took off, cutting down the first street in the direction where I parked one of the pack's beat up trucks. I didn't want to continue driving my own vehicle to do this job, and Cade said I wasn't allowed to drive his anymore since I broke his steering wheel the last time I drove it. *How shifters and humans did this for a living was beyond me,* I thought as we waited. *I hated every second of being a bounty hunter.* It didn't take long until Ryder was pulling up next to us. He shut the truck off, and I snatched the vial Cassia gave us. It was enough to knock out a horse, so I hoped it would be enough for a shark shifter.

I motioned for my brothers to follow, and everyone knew it was links only from here on out.

"Room 24A," I said to the group.

We turned the corner, and I scanned the area for cameras. Thankfully, there were none, which was probably why the shark chose this apartment in the first place. We made it to her door fairly easily, and Cade listened in. He gave me a thumbs up, and Elijah shifted his finger. He jammed his long claw into the handle, and it clicked within minutes. He gave me a stupid grin, and I rolled my eyes.

"Show off," I muttered.

"Jealousy isn't a good color on you, Bastian," he replied as I pushed the door open.

"We are now breaking and entering, people," I said, feeling like a puke all over again.

We quietly crept through her house, trying desperately not to make a sound. One false move, and she'd scream. One false move, and we were getting arrested. Abraham wouldn't come to our aid then. Her purse was on the counter, and in a last second decision, I grabbed it. I found her wallet inside and pulled out her ID. It said Nicole Livingston clear as day, and I sighed in relief. Elijah gave me a look as I put it back, but I waved him off.

"I needed to make sure it was her. Last thing I need is a real kidnapping charge because we got the wrong girl," I told him, and he nodded.

Cade motioned with his hand to the back room, and I followed him there. I popped the syringe open, ready to stick her before she even woke up. I don't know what I expected, but it sure wasn't *this*. I had never met a sea shifter before, and when we walked inside I noticed she was just an average sized girl with bright red hair. She snored like a freight train though, *good God*. I quietly stepped closer and stuck her with the needle. Her eyes shot open in a panic, but before she could scream, the drug was in her system, and she passed back out. I let out a sigh of relief.

"Alright, let's get her to the truck, guys," I whispered, picking her up and tossing her over my shoulders. Cade led the way since he had the best ears. He stopped us at her door briefly before signaling for us to follow. We made it down the path before Cade halted us again, and we hid in the shadows as someone parked their car near our truck. I swore as we waited. I wasn't sure if I was going to have to run her to pack lands or what. I looked to Elijah, who inhaled deeply.

"Human."

I nodded and turned to Cade, who was staring intently at the car. I couldn't see a thing until those lights turned off. It felt like an eternity, but the car's lights finally turned off, and a guy slowly hopped out. *Must be coming off a late shift because the dude looked dead to the world,* I thought as I shifted her on my shoulder. He slowly made his way into the other door of the apartment complex and never once looked in our direction. I let out a breath I didn't realize I was holding, and we followed Cade to the truck. I laid the girl in the back and hopped in with Ryder. Cade and Elijah sat in the front, and we were quickly pulling out with no one the wiser.

I stared out the window as we made our way to pack lands, unable to look at the girl. Ryder cuffed her hands in case she awoke before we got there, and my stomach twisted. I just felt horrible. I don't know what this girl did to piss off the Tiger King, but this was getting difficult to stomach. It was easier when it was the fellas. You could see they were junkies or drunks and more than likely racked up a major debt, but she seemed different. It was a solemn drive, and I was never more grateful to see the lodge.

I sent Cain a link hopefully waking him up as I grabbed the girl. She wasn't very heavy, but she had long legs, making it awkward to carry her. I threw her over my shoulders again and followed Cade and Elijah to the hidden cells below the lodge. Ryder took the truck back to the garage to refuel and clean.

I laid the girl down on the makeshift bed and locked her inside.

"Now we wait," I muttered, leaning against the wall. My brothers and I slid to the floor, leaning our heads back to rest. It was late, and I was beat. This day just needed to end.

Bastian

I awoke to a groan, and my eyes shot opened. I didn't realize I had passed out by the girl's cell, and when I looked around, I saw my brothers did too. They were stirring awake, and the three of us zeroed in on the girl. Her long red hair fell to her side as she sat up. It didn't take long for the panic to set in her, and guilt hit me hard in the gut again. That is until she opened her mouth.

"Who do you think you are?! LET ME GO!" she snarled, and my brothers and I were on our feet.

"Whoa... Settle down, Nicole. Look, I'm sorry about doing this, but we were hired..."

She lunged aggressively at the cell bars, startling me. Her mouth and teeth shifted, showing her animal's true nature. It looked like she was trying to eat her way through the bars, and I shook my head. Cade whistled, giving us each a look.

"Alright, knock it off. Look, I know you're pissed, but the Tiger King isn't happy with you for some reason. I don't know what you did to piss him off, but he has a bounty on you, and we are required to take you in. It isn't personal, and no one here will harm you," I shouted over her snarls.

She shifted back to her normal appearance, her eyes glaring at us. "I didn't make a deal with that man! I don't owe him anything! Just let me go!"

"Well... You did something to get on his bad side. Think back, Red. Who did you piss off recently?" Elijah spoke up and fear flashed in the girl's eyes.

"There it is. Must be why a sea shifter is living on land. I am curious... What did you take?" I asked, remembering my conversation with Olivia.

Red's eyes widened even more, and her hand instinctively went to her neck. I could see a chain, but the pendant was under her shirt, and there was no way I was looking in there.

"Seems like someone has come to collect the debt through the Tiger King, brother," Cade spoke, cocking his head to the right. Red glared at us, and boy did she have a temper.

She began shouting obscenities at us and clashing against the cell doors. Looking at her, you would have never guessed she was as foul-mouthed as she was. This shark had a bad temper, and good lord we were on her bad side now. We'd need to stay away from her teeth, when we transferred her too, I thought as I watched her thrash around in the cell.

"Let's go, guys," I said, seeing there was no point trying to talk to her anymore. We made our way up the stairs that led inside the lodge. She continued shouting the whole way, and you could still hear her even with the door closed.

"Geez, she's got a set of lungs on her," Cain said, coming around the corner with a cup of coffee in hand.

I groaned, rubbing my face. "You have no idea. I'm so glad we just grabbed her last night. I think if we had waited, we would have been screwed."

Elijah suddenly started scenting the air like crazy and left us standing in the hall. My brows rose, and my brother and I quickly followed him. I grinned when I realized what he was following though. Bacon.

My stomach rumbled, knowing we didn't eat any dinner last night. The only thing I put in my body was liquor. *A whole lot of liquor.*

Cassia was at the stove, cooking a mess of bacon and eggs, with a big plate of biscuits on the counter. She started serving up plates for my brothers and I.

"Ash and Aspen just left and told me to tell you the recruits are doing well, and that they are taking over for the time being until this issue with the Tiger King is resolved."

I groaned again. I had forgotten about their training. *God, I was a mess without Shanely,* I thought angrily. I was their Head but juggling everything here *and* working for Abraham *and* worrying for my mate and child at the same time, it was too much. I couldn't do it all apparently.

"None of that, Bastian. This is how the pack works. Whoever is next in line helps the ones that need it. Ash and Aspen could see where they were needed and just stepped in to help. Just because you didn't delegate it personally, doesn't make you a bad Head," Cain said firmly before kissing Cassia's cheek.

"Well please tell them a big thank you from me. I didn't mean to drop everything. I just haven't been thinking right," I said, taking a bite off the plate she gave me. *God, it was delicious.*

"It's not a problem, Bastian. You've been going through a lot lately. The pack is united in the fact that we want you boys solely working on getting our girls back home safely. We don't want you split between us and them," Cassia said, handing her mate a plate.

"I couldn't have done anything without you all and the pack, that's for sure," I said gratefully. I cleaned my plate quickly, feeling better than I had when my belly was full of liquor. I put my empty plate in the sink and started to wash it, when Cassia hit me.

"Leave it, Bastian. You have another mark to find today. Caleb called early this morning. They're making their way home, and they have Brehanny. He wasn't an issue at all, I guess. They found him plastered outside a bar, and no one batted at eye at them picking him up. They're going to drop him off and crash for awhile. They haven't slept yet, and I guess Johnny is having a hard time sleeping altogether. I'm going to knock him out when they get in."

I dropped my head slightly, knowing the pain Johnny was feeling. Without Shanely and the bond being shut off like this, it affected my body. Everything hurt, like I had spent the whole day prior working out. I was stiff and exhausted all the time, but Johnny was extra uptight because Alana was pregnant too.

"So that's two down, one to go," Cade replied, grabbing seconds. I grinned at him. My brother could eat an elephant and still be hungry.

"Yeah, but this one is a gorilla. I have never even scented one in these parts before," I said, making myself a cup of coffee. I started to reach for my normal french vanilla creamer, but stopped when I saw Shanely's favorite sitting on the counter. Sugar cookie. I grabbed that one instead, and it made me miss my mate even more. I added a pinch of cinnamon to it as well, just how she likes it.

"Well see if Abraham will give you anymore information on him. If it gets results, I don't see why he can't share it," Cain suggested.

I shrugged. "I can ask Henry, but I wouldn't bank on it. Abraham said it was his business the last time I asked."

"He might change his mind in favor of catching him though," Cassia countered, and they had a point. *It was worth a shot.*

"Alright, I'm going to call Henry. You two go shower. You're starting to smell like the recruits," I jested to my brothers and quickly bolted from the room as Cade launched a biscuit at my head. It exploded against the wall, covering the floor in a mess of crumbs. I popped back in, giving him a mischievous grin before taking off outside again. I could hear him yelling at me, but he was cut off by Cassia beginning to chew him out.

"Someone's in trouble," I linked to Cade.

"Screw you, Bastian."

I laughed and pulled out my phone. *Leave it to Cade to make me feel a little bit better.* Henry answered on the second ring.

"What do you want? More beer?"

I laughed. "Nah... It's too early for that, but the free food and beer actually got me results last night. The shark shifter is sitting in my cells right now."

"No kidding. Well Abraham will be happy to hear that. She's been tricky to find."

"Yeah, well she was living right under your noses. Like 5 blocks away from the club," I said arrogantly, and I could hear him bristle over the phone.

"Are you serious?"

"I kid you not. Did you guys ever actually look?"

"No, we don't handle the dirty work. We can't afford to get caught, so we hand that out to specific shifters," Henry snapped back.

"Well, I'm honored to be the one to risk my hide to get them. Oh wait, that's right. I didn't actually apply for this job. Your King twisted my arm and stole my girl to get me to do it," I replied irritatingly.

"I'm sure you didn't call just to piss me off, now did you?" he asked.

"You're right. I don't wish to waste my time talking to you either, but I need more info on this gorilla. No one has heard of him, and I can't get a lead on his scent."

"Oh, so the famous Bastian Fenrir needs help?"

"Seeing as I need something to track yes. Yes, I do. I can't just pull the guy out of thin air. I don't even know what he looks like, douche canoe, so tell me more."

"Careful. I need to ask Abraham, so hang tight," he said and proceeded to put me on hold. I kicked the rocks around the lodge, while I waited for what felt like forever. *Good God, what was Abraham doing that it took this long?*

"Still here, Bastian?"

"Yes, I'm still here. Why'd it take so long? The royal highness in the crapper or something?" I asked sarcastically, and Henry chuckled. The corners of my mouth rose as he quickly began coughing, trying to cover up the fact that *he* thought it was funny. *I don't know why, but that was entertaining,* I thought.

"No. I just decided to make you wait for insulting us tigers. Now back to the point," he replied, making me roll my eyes. He was a tool, but I can't say I wouldn't have done the same thing. "Abraham said that this gorilla came to him for money. He defaulted on his loan, and now needs to pay in full or trade something of equal value. We've reached out to him before, but he has since disappeared, and no one has seen him since. The lions had his address prior, but I doubt he's still there. He's smart and more than likely off grid. His girlfriend lives in the town over to the west, but the lions never saw him stop by or at least that's what they told us. The new bounty hunters Abraham hired prior to you all couldn't find him either. They watched her house on a regular basis for a long while, when they attempted this mark, and he never once showed."

"Why didn't we get this info at the beginning?" I asked, frustrated with this shifter.

"The Tiger King wanted to see what you could do with very little," he replied nonchalantly.

"You mean drag out this deal, so Bay has to continue fighting for him? Yeah, we aren't stupid, Henry," I said irritated with the Tiger King. *I could not wait to be done dealing with them all.*

"Tomato - Tomato."

"God, you're annoying. Alright, I need the address," I said, heading back inside for a pen and paper. Cade and Elijah were gone, but Cain and Cassia were still in the kitchen eating breakfast. I grabbed what I needed as Henry replied.

"Didn't you hear me? He hasn't returned to the house in years, Bastian."

"Yeah, I don't have as much faith in your bounty hunters like you do. I'll check it out myself, thank you very much. I need his scent anyways and more than likely that girl has what I need to find him. I don't think he up and left her, especially if she's his mate. She's probably meeting him somewhere discreet and knew you had people watching the house."

Henry was quiet for a moment, and it was very clear they didn't do this type of work themselves. He finally muttered an address as Elijah walked downstairs. His hair was wet from his shower, and he was drying it with a towel before shaking it out. I smacked him as water hit me, and he just grinned at me.

"Anything else?"

"Nope, at least not yet. He's our last mark, so we'll be seeing you shortly," I replied, leaning back on the counter.

Henry whistled. "Abraham's going to have a hard time letting you all go. You guys live up to your reputation, that's for sure."

"Yeah, well he can kiss my..."

"Bastian!" Cassia scolded me, and I pursed my lips together.

"He's going to have to accept it, Henry. I have to go, but my wife and child better be doing alright," I said in a low tone.

"They're doing well, Bastian. Aerith's a bossy little thing, but other than that everyone is fine. I promise you, they're okay," Henry said quietly, and I was grateful. *He didn't have to tell me anything about them, but I was glad he did.* I smiled at the thought of my four year old bossing around the Tiger King.

"Thank you, Henry. I'll see you soon."

"Did he work with you?" Cain asked, and I nodded. Cassia smacked my arm.

"Ow! What was that for?" I asked, rubbing my arm. *She hits hard like Shanely.*

"You know why, now get to it. Find him, so you can get our girl!" she said, raising her hand to smack me again. I bolted from the room as Cain started chuckling.

"Elijah, get Cade! I'll grab the truck and cuffs," I shouted before she could clobber me again.

Within the next hour, my brothers and I were pulling onto the street where the gorilla's girlfriend lived. Ryder stayed behind to help with Johnny, who was quickly losing it.

"So what's the plan?" Cade asked.

"I'm just going to ask her," I said, pulling into her long driveway.

"What?? If she hasn't given him up already, I doubt she will tell us anything," Cade said, his brows rising.

"I know, which is why you will sneak around the back and see if you can find anything with his scent, while Elijah and I keep her distracted," I said, grinning at my brother.

He did not look happy. "What?! Wait just a minute now, why me??"

"Because you can hear the best, and we can warn you with a whisper. Just do it, please. For Baby Girl?" I said, laying on the guilt trip.

Cade glared at me. "I hate you."

"Duly noted. Now stay here while we go in," I said, hopping out of the truck. I quickly snatched up the notebook that was in the back as a plan formulated in my head. This was a half-cocked plan, but I hoped it would work. I'll admit I was off today, but I just needed this to work long enough we could get his scent. Then I'd be home free. Elijah snickered, catching up to me.

"Thank God it wasn't me," he muttered as I knocked on the door. I gave him a sly grin and could see Cade step out of the truck from of the corner of my eye. He waited somewhat behind it, watching us to know when to make his move.

The door opened and a tall woman stepped out. She had dark skin and very dark, curly hair, but what was really unique were her vivid blue eyes. They were such a contrast to her skin, but they looked very cool. She seemed confident but annoyed we were at her door. The first thing I scented though was ape. She smelled strong of it, but I wasn't for sure if it was because she was a shifter too or she was just recently with George Davidson.

I gave her my most charming smile as I spoke, "Hello, my name is Bastian, and we're from the town council. This is my associate and brother, Elijah. Can we come in for a few minutes? We have a proposal that requires signatures from our neighbors in the area."

She eyed me cautiously before opening the door for us. "I suppose I have a few minutes."

I smiled and stepped inside with Elijah closely behind. Her house was quaint and cozy, and we had stepped right into her kitchenette. She motioned for us to sit at the table before sitting across from us. I looked to Elijah, who was subtly inhaling as much as he could. I knew he'd get a more detailed scent than I would, but from what I could tell, Abraham's bounty hunters sucked because this house reeked of ape.

"So what's the proposal?" she asked, snapping me from my thoughts.

"Go, Cade," I said to my brother.

"Well the town wants to improve road conditions throughout the neighborhood, but it would require buying up some of the land here. Their plan is to add a bypass right here to help with the town's traffic problem," I said as Elijah gave me a slow look.

"You are way too good at lying."

I ignored my brother and continued on, "Would you be interested in the town purchasing part of your land here to put in a bypass?"

She studied us for a long time before responding. It was beginning to make me nervous, and I wondered if she could tell we weren't really from the council.

She finally spoke, "I think it's a little odd that two shifters are here at my house for the city council."

I froze, trying to keep my face from reacting. *Time for Cade to get a move on.*

"*Cade, you better hurry. She's a shifter.*"

I could hear him swear through the link, but I tried to just stay focused on the girl.

"Well, it is against the law to reveal oneself to a human. I could not tell if you were a shifter or had just been around one an awful lot."

I spoke dryly, and I could see her tense slightly at my words.

"I'm a chimpanzee. I'm surprised you couldn't sense that, wolf," she quickly replied, and I could sense her nervousness rising. *She was still in contact with George, that was clear.*

"My apologies. See your scent just seemed different. All I could honestly smell was ape," I replied calmly, letting her stew on that bit of information before continuing, "but then again I'm not real familiar with all the different scents when it comes to primates."

She relaxed somewhat in her seat. "Are you really from the council then?"

I nodded. Lying through my teeth I said, "We are. We don't mean any harm, Miss. Do you approve of the purchase and the bypass getting added?"

"No. I don't want to sell any of my land please. Actually, if you'll excuse me, I'm pretty busy today," she replied, standing up.

"*Cade, time to go,*" I warned through the link.

"*Alright, alright!*"

"Sure, Miss..." I cocked my head to the side, waiting for a name.

She gave me an odd look before understanding. "Charlie Davidson."

Interesting, I thought to myself. "Well, Miss Davidson, I'll submit the forms for your rejection."

I stepped outside, with Elijah but noticed Cade wasn't in the truck yet. I sighed and quickly turned on my heels. *Dang it, Cade.*

"Oh, Miss Davidson?"

She stopped the door just before it shut, and I stepped up on her porch steps, blocking the truck from her view.

"*Get a move on, Cade!*"

"Is there anyone else living here with you? I need it for the forms is all.

Everyone in the house gets a vote," I gave her my best smile, hoping she believed another stupid lie.

"No, it's just me. No one else lives here," she replied and inched the door closer to the frame.

"I'm in the truck now."

Relief washed over me, and I smiled again, giving her a small wave. "Thank you again, and have a good day!"

Elijah and I walked carefully down the path to our truck, knowing full well she was watching. I carefully pulled out of her drive and pulled into the next drive that was a little ways down.

"Did you find anything?" I asked, keeping an eye on her drive. *Charlie was sure jumpy, and I had a gut feeling she was about to bolt.*

"Yup!" Cade cried out, holding a nasty smelling shoe. "I don't think these are hers."

"Good God, Cade! You had to pick the nastiest smelling item in that house?" I asked, swatting the shoe away from my face.

"What? Look at it, dude! It's like a size 20 or something! It has to be his. Elijah, care to take a whiff?"

Elijah covered his nose. "No way am I getting closer to that! I can scent it from here. It's an ape."

Suddenly Charlie's car appeared at the end of her drive, and a sly grin formed on my face. *I was right.*

"We may not even need it, fellas," I said, pointing to her car. "I think she's off to warn our gorilla right now."

She pulled out, heading away from us, and I waited a moment before turning my truck around. Elijah reached down and handed me a hat.

"Here. This might help if she sees us behind her. I don't know how well chimps can see."

He stuck one on his own head, and I followed suit. I turned mine around so it was backwards though. I ditched the jacket I was wearing too. It wasn't the best disguise, but it was better than nothing. We followed her a long ways, and she never once made it seem like she even noticed us. I tried to keep a good distance from her car since I could see her every move even from far away. After a little while of following her, I realized she was heading back towards Diablo.

"Where are you going, monkey?" I whispered to no one in particular.

We were all baffled at her direction, and soon she came up to the state's national park. She waved a card at the main gate and the guard let her though.

"Cade get out. Stay close, but don't lose her," I quickly said, and he bolted from the truck, disappearing into the woods.

I pulled up to the gate, and the second I rolled down my window I smelled another shifter. *Thank the lord shifters were all over this state otherwise this may not have worked out so well.*

"7$ please," the man at the gate asked.

I pulled out $100 from my wallet and offered it to him. "Here keep the change. You scent what I am?"

The young guy slowly nodded, seeming a bit uneasy with the two of us.

"I'm here on Official Shifter business for the McCoy pack. You keep that, and don't breathe a word to anyone that we were here. Not one word or bad things will happen, understand me?"

He nodded, shoving the money into his pocket. "Whatever you are doing, stay away from the main building. It's the only place with cameras, man."

I thanked him before driving forward to catch up to Charlie and Cade.

"Our souls will forever be blackened by this," Elijah muttered, and I groaned, knowing he was right.

"She stopped at the start of trail 3. No one is here, and there is a public restroom just before you get to this trail. Park there, and meet me on foot through the woods. Bring the cuffs and the drugs Cassia gave us," Cade said through the link.

I pulled into where Cade said to go, which was just a small parking lot with a few spaces next to a public restroom. The signs said trail 3 was up further ahead with trail 1 and 2 starting here. Elijah and I looked around briefly, scoping out the area, and there weren't a lot of people out today thankfully. We followed trail 2 a ways before I latched onto my sibling bond with Cade and followed it into the woods and off the trail. Scenting Cade was close, we slowed down and lowered ourselves to the ground in case this girl was out and moving around already. I found my brother with ease, and he was crouched by a large tree that was heavily covered with leaves.

"Where is she?" I whispered to Cade.

He pointed just ahead, and I looked for the girl. I could just barely see her car sitting on top of the hill, and she hadn't moved from it. She just sat there, and I watched her closely.

"What's she doing?" Elijah muttered, and I shrugged. After a few minutes, Charlie quickly got out of her car and started walking down the trail towards us. My brothers and I stilled, careful not to tip her off. I let her get far ahead before we started moving. She followed the trail for quite a ways, and I was curious to know where she was going. The trail was about to turn to the right now, but there was nothing out here. *Where is she going?* I asked myself.

"Any further and she'd be on her way to Dead Man's Hollow," Elijah whispered, and I nodded, recognizing the area. The start of that massive and dangerous mountain was real close to where we were now. *It must be where this ape's been hiding all this time,* I thought to myself, wondering if he was the reason those mountains lions were in those woods all those years ago.

Charlie pulled something from her back pocket and stuck it on the backside of the trail marker. Then she made her way quickly back up the path and disappeared out of sight.

"Settle in, boys. I think we're going to see our ape real soon," I said as I sat down on the ground, trying to get comfortable.

"So you mean I broke into her house and stole his shoe for nothing?" Cade snapped at me as he tossed the large nasty shoe my direction.

I grinned. "Well, we got his scent, didn't we? I just didn't think we'd spook her like that, but it worked out in our favor."

"Do you want me to check the note?" Elijah asked.

"No, not yet. I don't want him to smell wolf on it and be alerted to us. Let's just wait," I replied quietly and scanned the area again.

"Keep your wits about you, boys."

We waited for a few hours for this guy to show. A sound... scent... just *something* to indicate he was here, but so far all we saw was a couple walking their dog. It was late in the afternoon now, and I was getting anxious. *Did that chimp purposely drag us here just to lead us astray?* I wondered to myself, second guessing everything I did today. I wanted to grab this guy and make my way to Abraham's for the next list tonight, but if this guy didn't show soon I'd be stuck waiting another day, and that pissed me off.

My legs burned, but I stayed as still as I could get despite the pain. Cade was sprawled out on the ground, with his eyes closed. I knew he was just listening to everything around us, while Elijah kept his head on a swivel. He kept looking for any signs of the guy, and I'd watch him inhale deeply every so often.

I turned, crouching on my ankles, preferring to stay ready to move just in case I needed to make a mad dash to catch the guy. I didn't want to be caught laying down and waste precious seconds getting myself up, but anger rippled through me. I looked *everywhere,* and I was afraid we were wasting our time here, but where else could he be? *This had to be it,* I thought, praying I didn't just mess up my only shot to nab him.

Cade suddenly shot up from his spot on the ground and put his finger to his mouth. He pointed just to the left of the post, and when I peeked my head over the bushes I could see a very large man walking down the hill. He had olive colored skin with long dark hair and a massive frame. There was a large tattoo that ran up his right arm as well, and I watched him move very carefully down the hill.

Elijah leaned forward ever so slightly, inhaling again. His link pulled me from my thoughts.

"Ape."

This had to be our guy, I thought to myself.

The guy was extremely cautious as he made his way to the trail marker. I handed my brothers each a syringe, so we'd all be prepared to drop him. I quickly grabbed the guy's shoe too before taking off from our spot. He had his back to us briefly as he grabbed the note his girl left, and I was going to use it to my advantage. I didn't know much about primate shifters, and I wondered if they had heightened senses or not. *I guess we'll find out.*

We spread out, trying to encircle him as he read the note. George abruptly scanned the area before shoving the note in his pocket and slowly backing away. He was moving quickly, but I wasn't going to lose him again. *George was coming with us whether he liked it or not.* I stepped out in his path, grinding him to a halt.

"Hello, George," I said simply, and his eyes went wide as he turned to me.

"You the wolf my girl tried to warn me about?" he asked, and I nodded, holding my hands behind my back. I wanted to do this without a fight, but he seemed like he wasn't going to cave easily. *This might be the first fight we will actually end up in,* I thought to myself before I forced myself back in the game.

"She actually led me right to you. I'm sure she'd be mortified to know that though. Charlie really seems to care about you, ya know," I replied back, and he grunted.

"What do you want?" he snarled.

"I don't want anything with you, man, but the Tiger King does. I'm sorry, but you're going to have to come with me," I replied, and he bristled at my words. His face twisted angrily, and he rolled his shoulders. *Yeah... this was not going to be fun,* I thought to myself. George was a big guy. This dude easily towered over me, and I wasn't a small man by any means. *If it came down to a fight, it was not going to be pretty.*

"I've been successfully dodging that prick for years now. I suggest for your safety, you just walk away and pretend you never found me," he snarled.

I tsked at him.

"Sorry man, but you see..." I said as I brought his shoe around to the front, twirling it in my hands, "the Tiger King already knows where your girl lives. He's been... *all over* really. Do you really want him to pay her another visit? Because I know the guy personally, and there's not much he won't do to find his marks. I'm at least kind enough to give you the opportunity to come quietly. I'll throw the shoe out and never mention your girl again, but if you don't come willingly then don't be surprised if the Tiger King takes his wrath out on your girl."

George's eyes widened, turning gold as they twisted into rage. He took a step forward, his hands clenched at his side, when Cade stepped out from his left. My brother whistled whistled saying, "I wouldn't do that if I were you."

George stopped in his tracks, looking at my brother then back to me. His brows furrowed as confliction filled his expression, and I hated using his girl as bait. *I was never going to see her again, but if he thought she was in danger maybe it would work to our advantage,* I thought as I watched him carefully. *I seriously did not want to fight this guy.* I was burnt out already from being away from Shanely for this long.

"You're not like the Tiger King's normal bounty hunters, are you?" he asked, eyeing the two of us carefully.

"No, we are not," Elijah shouted as he jumped out from behind George and jammed the syringe into the guy's arm. George panicked and slammed into Elijah, who flew backwards. I rushed forward, but it was for nothing. The gorilla swayed hard before finally dropping to the ground. I walked over to Elijah, who was groaning in pain.

"Good lord, you can take a hit," I said, chuckling as I helped him up.

He rubbed his chest. "Agh, it's gonna bruise, I can already tell."

"Well, no one asked you to rush in like that! I think threatening the girl was enough to get him to cave," Cade countered.

I laughed as Elijah glared back at him. "Well, I wasn't going to risk it. I'm tired of being a prick to everyone just to get this done. Now I'm injured, so you two get to carry the behemoth up the trail to the truck."

I suddenly stopped laughing and looked at the guy. *This was going to suck.*

"Crap," Cade muttered before grabbing an arm, and I grabbed the other. *Oh. My. Lord. He was heavy.*

"Elijah! Get his legs! He'll wake by the time we get him to the truck!" I hollered, and Elijah rolled his eyes.

"Will he even fit in the truck?!" Cade asked as he struggled up the hill. We slowly made our way up the trail, and I just prayed no one would come down. The hardest part was crossing back over to trail two. There was no path, and we had to go slow in some spots.

"Just be quiet and move!" I barely uttered, and we made the long walk to the truck.

It took awhile, but we made it back without running into anyone. Cade and I threw him in the backseat, and I took a second to catch my breath. I checked George's pulse, and it was steady, so the three of us hopped up front as no one was gonna fit back there with him.

I drove us back to pack lands then and waved goodbye to the man at the gate house. He made sure not to watch our truck leave, which was smart. Now he can't lie.

Cade and Elijah watched the ape carefully with another syringe in hand as we made our way back to pack lands. They were ready to stick him again if he started to wake because I was *not* getting into a brawl in the middle of this truck. Whatever Cassia did was genius though, and he never even stirred. Cain was standing in front of the lodge with Caleb and Ryder when we pulled up. Johnny was there as well, and he looked haggard and broken.

"There you guys are!" Cain hollered. I gave him a grin as I stepped out of the truck, when something hit me hard in my chest. I fell against the truck, breathing rapidly and everyone rushed me.

"Bastian, what's wrong?" Cain asked, holding onto my shoulder. It took me a minute for everything to settle inside me, but the moment I felt Shanely's bond my heart about burst from joy. *It was back. She was back and...* My thoughts ran amuck then. *Why was her bond back all of the sudden?*

"The bond's opened," I muttered before yanking my phone out of my pocket. I called Henry, but it went straight to voicemail. *That's odd,* I thought to myself. *Henry never missed a call.* Fear began to creep in as I dialed again, and it seemed to ring forever. He never took this long to answer his phone, and my animals and I were beginning to panic. Everyone had surrounded me as I waited for Henry to pick up the phone.

"Bastian," Henry said, when he finally answered.

"What happened?" I asked him, sensing an problem already.

"Shanely's okay, but there was a problem today. Abraham has forbid me to say anything more than that, but she doesn't have a collar on anymore."

"I felt our bond open, Henry, but you can't tell me more than that? That's my wife!" I shouted to him.

"I can't. You can take it up with Abraham the next time you see him," he replied calmly to me, and it only angered me more.

"Tonight. I'll be seeing him tonight, Henry," I snapped back.

"You got all the marks?"

"Yes I did, so I'm bringing them in tonight."

Henry sighed. "Bay's fighting tonight, so if you must do it tonight then bring them to the club. He will be there as well, so we will have to make do."

"I want to see my wife. You can tell your King that it is non-negotiable," I demanded, and I heard him sigh.

"Look, I don't know all what Abraham has planned. He hasn't returned since... Why am I even explaining this? Just bring them to the club tonight. Tell the bartender you want a grasshopper, and that will get you in for free. You can discuss the rest with Abraham then, now I have to go," he snapped and disconnected the line.

"What happened?" Cain asked again.

"I don't know, but Shanely got her collar off. I can feel the bond again," I replied, somewhat lost in thought. It felt amazing to feel our connection again, but I couldn't stop the endless horrifying thoughts of what happened today. I know Henry said she was okay, but my wolf was agitated and wanting answers. *What happened? Abraham didn't seem too interested in letting the girls take them off before. Why now, and why her?*

"Johnny, can you feel Alana?" I asked.

He shook his head no. "No, it's missing still."

"Isn't this a good thing though?" Cade asked, confused by my issue with it.

"Henry said something happened. Abraham hasn't released the girls since they got there, and now Shanely is free? Something's up, but I don't know what," I replied before heading around to the other side of the truck to check on the ape. He was still passed out, and Cain walked up behind me.

"Here," he said as he handed me a collar. It looked just like the one Abraham put on the girls.

I gave him an odd look. "What's this?"

"Gifts from the King. It came in earlier this afternoon, while you were gone. He thought you might need some for the shifters you catch. This guy's massive, so I figured we should use it. You all can't carry them into a busy club in cuffs, now can ya?"

I stared at the collar, and my anger boiled. As much as I knew Cain was right, I was just pissed I had to use it. After seeing it on Shanely, I wanted nothing to do with them. Before I could let my emotions control me further, I snapped it on the ape's neck. I went ahead and cuffed him anyways before turning to my Alpha.

"Watch him, will you? Johnny, Ryder? Can you bring the bear? The rest of us, let's grab our shark."

"You need four of you to grab the girl?" Cain asked me, raising an eyebrow at my request.

"You have no idea, Alpha. Cade bring a collar. We're going to need it," I said before trotting to the cells. I walked to Nicole's cell, and she was yanking on the bars, trying to get them to budge. Nicole froze when she saw us.

"I won't go back home. You cannot take me to the Tiger King!"

"Just stop. Nothing you scream at me will change what's going to happen. I don't know who you stole from, and I don't care. Just turn around, and put your hands on your head," I demanded, and she begrudgingly obeyed. I slowly opened her cage, and she flung at me the moment it opened. Her mouth shifted again, and she snapped at my face and throat.

I fell backwards, grunting in pain as we landed hard on the ground. She had partially shifted, and her jaw was snapping wildly mere inches from my face. Cade and Elijah finally pulled her off me, and Cade snapped the collar on. Her face twisted painfully back to her human self, and I watched true fear spread across her face. I felt awful as her eyes widened, and she began to rub her chest aggressively.

"What did you do?!"

"I tried to do this the nice way, but you don't listen. You can't shift right now, and if you don't start behaving then it will only get worse for you, and you may never shift again. You have no idea how ruthless the King is, and he won't tolerate the crap you've tried to pull on us. Now on your feet!"

I yanked her up, pushing her to Caleb. Elijah gave me a questioning look, but I waved him off. I was fine. The crazy chick didn't get me, but my back's probably bruised. We made our way to the truck quickly now that all the fight left her. Nicole was defeated, and I hated doing this. I was ready to get a move on, and it was already starting to get dark.

The other two guys were in the truck already, and I signaled for everyone to load up. We drove in two separate cars and made our way to the club once more. The ape finally woke up, and all three were panicked at losing their animal. I was just ready to pass them off. I was so done with today already. I was not a bounty hunter, and I never wanted to do this job again. We parked somewhat near the entrance to the club, and I turned to look at the three we had to deliver.

"Listen up because I will only say this once. You will *not* fight me. You will walk to your own fate because so help me God you so much as sneeze in the wrong direction, and I will end you. I won't wait to see what the Tiger King wants to do with you because I am done playing his game. I'll end you and deliver the body, telling him you have officially squared your debt away. The Tiger King has my wife and child, and I will not risk them. Understand?"

No one said a word, and I took that as a yes.

"Good. Now as a side note, if you ever want to remove those collars and get your animals back, the Tiger King is the one that has the key. Moving forward you will be uncuffed until we reach the King for appearances only. My entire team is here tonight, and they are just as angry as I am. Now get out, stay silent, and move where I tell you."

I stepped out of the vehicle, taking a deep breath of the warm night air. I was ready to see my wife, and I was going to whether the King wanted it or not.

I pushed the ape and bear closer together as Elijah guided the shark between us. Johnny walked up to my left and nudged me. "My bond with Alana opened up on the drive over here. She doesn't have a collar on either."

I blinked in surprised. "It's a good feeling, isn't it?"

He nodded slowly, lost in thought, or maybe he was just being lost in the comfort that the bond gives us. It made me really curious what the heck happened today for the King to release all the girls. We made our way inside, and I went straight to the bar.

"Everyone wants a grasshopper," I told him, and his eyes widened.

"Sure," he finally said and stamped all of our hands. He guided us to the back door, and we began our descent down the stairs. The noise grated against my nerves, and I could smell an assortment of shifters down here. A familiar one caught my attention, and I jerked my head to the left. Three young pups, who were clearly not supposed to be here, stood near the stairs at the bottom. I snarled, and they paled when they saw me.

"You report to *me* when I get home," I snapped, gripping the back of George's neck and halting the group's advance. "I suggest you go home to your mother *now*."

The smaller kid's wolf whimpered as they stood there wide eyed. Elijah stepped around me.

"Now pups!"

They bolted up the stairs and out the club's door. I gritted my teeth, knowing I'd have to have a conversation with their mother when I returned home. *Freaking pups.*

I shook myself from my thoughts and pushed the group forward. None of them mattered right now. I could scold them later. Only one mattered, and I was seeking her out the moment I passed these tools off. I quickly scanned the room ahead, and nearly did a double take when I found Abraham.

Standing by his side, and dressed nearly *identical* to him was my mate, and by God she took my breath away. She was utterly gorgeous, looking fierce, strong, and confident. Shanely was always beautiful to me, but seeing her in dark clothes with her hood up against her soft pale skin and red hair about brought me to my knees. *This was my mate,* I thought to myself. *She belonged to me...* And that thought almost didn't seem real. Black was her best color, that was for sure, and the way she braided her hair tonight. I don't think I was going to be able to walk away from her now. *Not looking like that.*

"Dang... Baby Girl doesn't look so sweet and innocent tonight," Cade whispered, nudging my arm. He winked at me, and I rolled my eyes.

I turned quickly, so he wouldn't see my reaction, but I knew my brothers knew exactly what I was thinking already. "Shut up, Cade."

I didn't expect to see Shanely here tonight, let alone standing side-by-side to the Tiger King and looking just like him. They looked like they were working together, and as turned on as her outfit got me, I was also insanely confused by her seemingly acceptance of Abraham. They were speaking privately amongst themselves, when our eyes suddenly locked on one another. She looked relieved to see me, and I never took my eyes off her as we made our way to them.

We got about halfway before Shanely made a move towards me, but the Tiger King stopped her. She looked annoyed with him, but the two continued to talk quietly amongst themselves and rage quickly took over. His hand was still on her arm, and that pissed my animals off even more. *I was sick of that man putting his hands my mate, and I didn't care where we were or who was around. I was putting a violent stop to it.*

I stormed through the crowd, shoving the idiots aside who were too dumb to pay attention, but the moment I reached the right side of the cage, it hit me.

A bond with Abraham.

I nearly tripped on my feet as the sibling bond slammed into me, and I stood there wide-eyed and shocked. Elijah and Cade were at my side in seconds as this bond attachment was intense, but I managed to stay on my feet, and I stared directly ahead to my girl and Abraham. His back was turned, and she rubbed his arm affectionately. He seemed to struggle as well, and I stood there dumbfounded until her eyes found mine. She gave me a weak smile, nodding like it confirmed everything, when it explained *nothing*.

"What happened!?" Cade asked worried.

"A sibling bond with Abraham," I whispered quietly to my brothers. They looked shocked, and soon they all started talking at once. I shook my head, unable to answer their questions, when I, myself, had *no freaking idea* as to what was going on.

"Guys, I have no idea, but that was intense. Let's just go and talk to Shanely. We need to get these three delivered anyways because I'm tired of being responsible for them."

I needed my mate now, and I was so ready to get answers to the questions rolling around my head. I had no idea how this could even be possible, but whether Abraham liked it or not... He was going to tell me *everything*.

Shanely

I woke up to a dark and toasty room, feeling far better than I had earlier today. A fire was slowly dying in the fireplace off to the right, and I was laying on the softest bed I have ever been in. It was loaded with fur blankets, and I was snuggled deep in the center of a thousand pillows. I was *cozy*... Until it dawned on me that *this* wasn't my normal room, and I sat up abruptly.

"Be careful. Fighting against the collars like that took a lot out of you. You'll be weak for awhile."

I turned to find Abraham sitting on his desk off to the left of me. He had put his typical dark and broody outfit on, and I knew he was getting ready to conduct business as the Tiger King again. *I wonder where I could find a hoodie like that for Bastian*, I thought to myself.

He smirked. "The women in my village make them. I can send some your way for your mate, if you'd like."

I opened my mouth, but my jaw snapped shut when I realized what just happened. "You can hear my thoughts, can't you?"

Abraham nodded. "All the time now. A bond snapped between us when you shifted in your bear form, and now it's constant. Even when you sleep."

"But how?! How is this possible, Abraham?" I demanded. Panic surged through me as I scrambled to figure out what was going on between us now. *The only way I knew of bonds happening were with mates or within close family members, and we were definitely not mates!*

He looked forlorn. "I don't know, Shanely. You're not my mate, that's clear, but we have this family bond, which means we are closely related."

"But my mother was a wolf, and my dad is a bear! He's home right now and nowhere near anything that even resembles a tiger!" I shouted. I couldn't catch my breath and clutched my head to keep the room from spinning. It had been awhile since I had a panic attack, and if I couldn't get my breathing under control, I was going to pass out.

"Shh... Shanely, breathe! We won't figure this out without a clear head," Abraham pointed out as he sat next to me. He rubbed my back like Bastian always did, helping me to slow my breathing.

"Is your mother back in your lands with your Dad?" he asked.

I shook my head. "No. She apparently ran away when she discovered she was pregnant with me, at least from what we've gathered. I grew up in the foster system, and I was told I had no family at all. When my grandmother died, she left me her cabin and I discovered all this and met my father. He said he never felt her die, but the bond just disappeared entirely, and he never knew what happened to her. This makes no sense, Abraham. You had parents though? You said they died when you were little. How old are you anyways?"

"I turned 21 a few months ago," he answered, mulling over the information. *That would put us like a year apart.*

"You're young to be King," I muttered.

He snorted. "Shanely, from what I *was told* both my parents were tigers, and they did die. They died when I was four. How is this possible?"

"I don't know. My mother was mated. She wouldn't have just gone off with someone else."

"My father wouldn't have taken advantage of her, if that's what you're saying!?"

"No, I'm not accusing him of anything, but my father has never left his lands unless it was to return to the main clan in Russia! So that leaves us sharing a mother somehow. Do you have pictures of your parents?"

He nodded and moved across the room to a picture frame on the fireplace. He handed it to me, and I studied it. *They were a cute couple,* I thought to myself. Laughing and seemingly happy together, but I didn't recognize them at all.

"Abraham... Is there a chance they're not your real parents?"

His eyes filled with pain as he dragged them to mine. "I don't know, Shanely. I'm as lost as you. This explains why I've been drawn to you and Aerith. My tiger knew you were important, but I just couldn't figure out why. It's partly why I insisted you stay here while your mate completed the job. If we're siblings, then this means I'm a mixer too."

"Half-wolf. How do you feel about that?" I asked.

"Somewhat guilty. I slaughtered a lot of my own kind and never knew," he replied as his brows furrowed.

"Do you think it was why the pack came after you guys? Maybe they knew about you? Octavia and Alana both said that pack was ruthless."

I was grasping at straws, and I knew there was a chance we'd never know the truth, but I was just lost. I needed clarity because this was too much. But then my bear pushed her feelings through to me, and I sighed. *Now I know why I needed to save him*, I thought to myself.

Abraham shrugged. "I honestly don't know. There's an old tiger here deep in the woods. He was one of the few survivors of that attack. Tomorrow, we can see if he has any answers. Another thing I really want to know though is why don't I smell like a mixer? I scent solely as a tiger, and I've never felt a wolf."

Now it was my turn to shrug. "I don't know. I was told sometimes the child simply picks one side and doesn't always get both."

He shot me a mischievous grin. "You saying you're more special than I am?"

Abraham playfully shoved my shoulder, and I winced and smacked him back.

"Oh sorry! I forgot about the bite. The effects of the collar should wear off soon, and you will heal," he said as he rubbed the back of his head.

"It's okay. Bastian might be able to help me with it tonight," I replied.

"Speaking of Bastian, I don't feel right about the deal anymore. I never would have made it if I had known," he said sheepishly.

"You shouldn't have forced it in the first place."

"How was I to know I had a half-sister that's a mixer?"

"Why make deals anyways? It's just a lot of headaches, and you make a ton of enemies that way."

He shrugged. "I took back these lands when I was 17. I was extremely angry all the time, and my streak needed essentials like food and medicine. Our family trade was gone with those who died in the fight, so I started trading. It just sort of spiraled and became what it is today. It was two-fold though. I get what they need, and I instill fear wherever I go. Keeps shifters away."

"Except for today. That snake seemed like it was heading straight for the kids, but settled for us," I stated.

"I know. Shifters who hurt children do not deserve to stay alive, and I am grateful for what you did for me and the little ones," he replied as he squeezed my hand. "How did you shift anyways? Those collars are strong, and no one has ever broken one before."

"I don't know. My father said the trigger for my bear is protection towards others. It was how I managed to reach her in the first place when someone attacked Bastian. I felt the pull for Aerith and you. It forced her out, I guess," I replied.

Abraham nodded, and we sat quietly for a moment.

"I'm dealing with how the snake got in, and I've sent Henry and Darryl to your room just in case. They are not to leave their side, while we are gone tonight. Jake will be coming with us with two others I trust completely. We should go if we are to make Bay's fight," he said as he stood up, reaching for a bag on the desk.

"Are you going to keep Bay fighting? After everything? I know you have a connection to her too," I asked.

"I talked to Bay earlier when she came to check on you. She wants to fight, and I won't take it away, but I have released her from her deal. I think the connection is just because of you though, Shanely."

I stood, crossing my arms. "That's crap, and you know it."

Abraham raised his brows at me, and his Kingly voice came back out when he said, "Shanely, there's nothing…"

"Oh no, none of that crap. You can't get away with that voice now. If we are to be family then you have to act like one. Now you and I both know that pull is something deeper than this. Why are you so afraid?"

"Because Shanely!" he bellowed loudly. "My whole life my streak and I have hated wolves. Now I'm just supposed to say, *Hey, my sister is part wolf, and I might be mated to a wolf as well?*"

Abraham paced his room then, and my shoulders fell. He finally stopped and turned to me. "I worry about the both of you. I don't know how everyone will take this."

I snorted. "Probably about as well as my pack did. Some will hate it, and some will learn to love and accept it."

"Yeah, and you nearly died by a pack member," he said, with a pointed look.

"But I didn't, and now I'm happy with my mate and my whole family. We've become like one large family, the bears and the wolves. It isn't fair to push you aside because you're a tiger, and it's not fair to you and Bay to always be incomplete and alone because of what others might think."

Abraham stayed silent and leaned against the desk. "Shanely... I'm afraid."

I walked over to him and put my arm around him. "Start small. Bastian will know immediately when we get close if the connection hasn't already happened. Pick your closest friends to tell first and start there. I think you should confirm everything with Bay though. She's quiet and private, but I can see her being drawn to you too."

He perked up at that. "You think so?"

"I do actually. I've been watching the two of you since we've met."

Abraham smiled. "She's impossible to read."

"That's a Fenrir thing, but you'll figure it out quickly, I'm sure."

He sighed. "Alright, let me mull everything over. Here, go change." He handed me a black bag. I opened it and beamed at what I saw.

"Really? Nothing slutty this time?"

"God, no! Now that I know you're my sister I'm done rattling Bastian's cage. It's weird enough now, plus you were fierce today. I felt like you should be fierce now."

I ran to his bathroom, giddy to put on my new outfit. Black military cargo pants and one of his hoodies. It was sleeveless and low cut in the front, showing off some of my cleavage. It had strings to tie the front together, which I did, making it a bit more modest. The hood was black and dark. It completely covered my eyes, when I wore it up, and I smiled as I looked in the mirror. *This outfit was amazing,* I thought to myself. *Just like the characters in one of my favorite fantasy books.* I quickly braided the left side of my hair into three tight braids, giving myself a viking warrior look.

I looked in the bag after dressing and noticed there was a smaller bag at the bottom with makeup and silver hair clips inside. Just small rings really, and I put them throughout my braid. I added dark eyeliner to my eyes, and then used the eye shadow to create a smokey eye look like Bay showed me. Since my hair was pulled to the one side, I decided to add my pack's markings to the side of my eye. Then the bear clan's mark and finally Abraham's mark below it. I had family in all three now, and I wanted to show that tonight.

I had to admit I looked hot! I thought as I spun around to get a full view. I felt confident and like Abraham had mentioned before, fierce. I left the bathroom, and Abraham's eye went straight to my markings I made. He touched them gently, looking surprised.

"I'm not afraid to say I'm related to a tiger, Abraham."

Abraham smirked and lowered his hand. "Bastian's going to kill me. I was trying to go for fierce and intimidating not..."

I laughed, waving him off. "Please, I make everything look good!"

He rolled his eyes and pushed me out of the room. Bay and Jake were waiting for us downstairs, and Abraham sucked in a breath when he saw Bay.

"Stop fighting it. You'll only make it worse for yourself," I whispered.

He huffed at me but said nothing. Jake eyed me up and down, a sly grin forming on his face, and Abraham smacked him upside the head. Jake rubbed the back of his head then.

"What was that for?" he asked.

"Stop looking at her like that!" Abraham said gruffly, and Bay narrowed her eyes. Then she noticed my markings.

"Shanely, what are you doing? Bastian will be here tonight. What's he going to think about those?" she asked, pulling me aside.

I laughed. "Oh, he will know exactly what it means, don't worry."

She frowned. "What's going on, Shanely? You broke your collar to save him, which should have been impossible," she said, pointing to Abraham. The man hovered nearby, pretending not to be listening to every word. I nearly rolled my eyes.

"You can't have two mates, so why are you acting like it? I mean you've been in his bedroom all afternoon, and this is how you come out looking?" she snapped. My smile fell.

"Bay, I'm not acting like that. You know my bear comes forward when I need to protect..."

"People you care about. Yeah, I know. Look, whatever is going on between you, I don't want to know," she said clearly pissed with me.

"Bay, I think you have the wrong idea," I tried to reason, but she crossed her arms, glaring at me.

"Just don't break my brother's heart, Shanely. Somehow weird things happen to you, but my brother shouldn't be dragged through the mud right along with it."

My jaw dropped. *How could she think I'd do anything like that to Bastian?* My wolf snapped her jaws angrily, and I stepped towards Bay. "What exactly is that supposed to mean?"

She rolled her eyes. "You are the answer to more than one prophecy. You *constantly* find yourself in trouble, and shifters from all over are drawn to you. You're special, and my brother has had his hands full, trying to keep up with you. You overshadow him despite his own amazing abilities and now this..." she said, motioning to me and Abraham. "He doesn't deserve to be dropped for the next model. I don't even know how it would be possible, but if any shifter could have their pick of a mate, it would be you. Just leave me alone, Shanely."

Bay stalked off to the truck, leaving me speechless. Rage consumed me as I watched my sister-in-law storm away. *How could she think I'd ever treat Bastian that way?* I know I've made mistakes and ended up needing rescued, but I'd *never* purposely try to harm my mate, nor would I ever want to push him aside. Bastian is an *amazing* shifter, and his reputation is known among our race. That was something I had nothing to do with. That was all him, and I was honored to be his mate, not the other way around. The fact she thought

I cared so little about Bastian that I'd just drop him for another rattled me and my animals. I know this was just her wolf talking, but it was hard to get my own wolf to calm down and not chase after her. She was jealous and feeling possessive of Abraham, but still her words cut right through me. *Who else felt like I overshadowed my own mate?*

Abraham cleared his throat beside me. "Are you okay?"

I sighed. "Well, my good mood has officially been destroyed."

"Why didn't you just tell her?"

"She's angry because of our bond. She will figure out who you are to me when the bond snaps in place for Bastian. If I say anything now, I'll just be speaking to her wolf, who won't believe me anyways."

He nodded and guided me to the truck. Bay was already in the furthest seat in the back, staring out the window. I hopped in the middle bench, while Abraham took the passenger side, letting his enforcer drive. Another vehicle full of tigers followed behind us, and we made the very awkward and quiet ride to the club. Instead of pulling in the front like I expected him to do, the truck took us into the back alley towards the door there. I stared at the door, remembering leaving this way not too long ago. Crazy how much had changed already.

"Perks of owning the club. We get to sneak in the back and skip the lines of shifters waiting to get in," he said as he winked at us.

I rolled my eyes and smiled back at his playfulness, making Bay nearly snarl at us. Abraham hesitated for a moment before silently leaving the SUV and the two of us. I ignored Bay. She was in a foul mood, and I had no desire to deal with her temperamental wolf right now. She was so far from the truth, and instead of just asking me what happened, she threw accusations at me. *She can stew and find out on her own then,* I thought to myself.

We walked into the dimly lit hallway and followed Jake down the stairs until he stopped at the doors to the main room, instead of going back to the private box where I first met Abraham.

"We're going to be public tonight. The crowds need to see my face every once in awhile, and since I have you with me Shanely, I'd like that to be tonight. Everyone needs to see *we* are on the same side," Abraham told the two of us in the hallway privately. I looked through the window of the door and could see the ring was already full of shifters ready for the fights.

Bay snorted. "I think they'll get the idea since you dressed her up to look exactly like you, Tiger King."

"Bay... I thought we moved past the title."

He seemed almost hurt by Bay's words, but she was still wound tight.

"Look, I need to go get ready for tonight. Can I go?"

Abraham quietly nodded his head, and she bolted with her mask on and hood up. Another tiger quickly took off after her, which left Abraham and I to stand there exasperated. He sighed before turning back to me. "Remember you are fierce, Shanely, and you're here with the Tiger King. Help me intimidate the crowd because all eyes will be on us now. United front."

I nodded. "United front. I rather like being at your side instead of beneath you."

He smirked back at me before giving me a pointed look. "You are my sister, which makes you royalty with the tiger streak now. You will never be owned like that again. Other than by your mate of course, but I rather not get into that. Now, let's move."

I grinned as Jake opened the door, and we let Abraham's enforcers through first to help push back the crowds. Abraham was stoic as he entered the room, and everyone stopped to gape at him. His confidence radiated off him, and I was in awe how he and Bay managed to do it. I was a nervous wreck, but I quickly chased after my brother. I walked next to Abraham as we made our way to the roped off stage near the back. The crowd was enamored with my brother, scenting the two of us as we passed by, and I tried my best to copy him. *Please don't trip. Please. Don't. Trip.* I held my head high like Abraham as we moved freely through the crowd. The longer I pretended, the more confident and empowered I felt. This was a good feeling, and I couldn't help but smile.

Jake removed the rope, which opened the stairs for me and my brother to step up into the private VIP box. It was still weird to call him *my brother*, but I shook those thoughts away and stood center stage next to him. Family was family, even if he was a jerk at first.

All eyes were on us just like he said they'd be, and I tried to pretend I didn't care or even notice. Abraham leaned down and whispered something to one of the enforcers, who then proceeded to create a line directly in front of the stage with the entire entourage Abraham brought with us. The crowd continued to stare, but soon music started playing again, and everyone began to relax and have a good time waiting for the first fight.

"Not so bad, right?" my brother whispered as we stood watching over everything.

"Yeah, it's a lot easier without the collar and chains," I smirked back. He rolled his eyes, making me laugh hard. "Oh c'mon, Abraham! You know I'll be teasing you for a long time over all this!"

"I figured," he snorted before groaning. "Agh, I can't imagine what your mate will say. Thinking back to this week makes me cringe. I'm never going to hear the end of this, will I?"

I chuckled. "I don't think so. Just wait till he gets here."

"Looks like I won't have to wait for long," he replied as he gestured to the main doors. I felt the bond pull on my heart, and I was instantly relieved when my mate came through the doors across the room. Bastian made his way down with all of the fellas tonight. They had two guys and a small woman between them all. None of them were cuffed, and I wasn't sure how they were keeping them in line in such a public place, but I was thrilled they were here. *God, Bastian looked amazing.* Dark blue jeans with his favorite black t-shirt. My mate had a gift for rolling out of bed looking like a Greek God, and I bit my lower lip watching him stalk towards me.

Bastian's eyes immediately went to mine, and he began pushing his way through the crowd faster. A trickle of his anxiety came through the bond, and my feet were moving without hesitation, but Abraham stopped me. My eyes flashed gold briefly, when he gave me a stern look.

"Remember we stay here. He will come to you," he said.

"Why does it matter? He's right there!" I asked, pushing past him again. My brother grabbed my arm and twirled me around, blocking the stairs once more.

"Because like you said I have many enemies. *Everyone's* watching us tonight. I don't spend many fights down here. I'm elusive for a reason, and we need them to know that we still hold all the power here. We can't give them a reason to be close to us. I rather be safe than sorry, sis."

I nodded begrudgingly and watched Bastian force his way through the crowd harshly. His eyes were on Abraham's hand on my arm. I didn't think how our interaction must look to Bastian right now, but he was no longer being kind as he pushed people aside. Bastian was coming after Abraham, and it was not going to be pretty. The crowd soon got the hint and let the Fenrir brothers through with ease.

Suddenly, Abraham gasped and held his chest. He quickly turned around, and his worried eyes found mine. It was clear he had never felt a bond form before, and it had finally snapped in place between him and my mate. I stood near Abraham, helping conceal him, while he gained his composure, but my eyes went straight to Bastian.

Bastian stumbled before coming to a full stop. His eyes found mine, and it was like everything clicked in place. Cade was at his side in seconds, but Bastian's eyes never left mine. He looked bewildered and so confused. I gave him a small nod before Cade pulled his attention away. I could see them conversing, and Elijah ran his hand through his hair.

"So that's what it feels like?" Abraham muttered, and I laughed.

"It's easier if you ever feel it again. The first time is just a little more forceful. I'm not sure if you want everyone else to know though. It will change things for you, Abraham," I replied as he turned back to face my mate.

"We stay quiet for now. We can discuss how to proceed when we are back home."

Caleb gripped the back of whoever he was holding and pushed him forward to the Fenrir brothers. They were all talking before Bastian gestured to us. They started moving quickly again. Jake unlocked the rope gate, and Bastian was the first up the steps. Abraham wisely stepped aside, and I ran to Bastian.

God, he felt so good. I clung to him as he wrapped his arms around my waist, burying his nose in the crook of my neck. The pain in my muscles left me entirely, and I finally relaxed. I ran my hands through his hair and ignored everyone else in the room as he held onto me tightly.

"You smell like him," he growled before running his hands all over me. I smiled, letting him re-scent me to appease his wolf. I leaned in and kissed his cheek.

"Bastian, it's fine. You know why now."

He nodded but continued running his hands over my body anyways. His wolf was front and center, and I let him go. "Shanely, how is this possible?" he asked quietly. "And what happened to your arm?"

I looked down, forgetting about the wound still healing. Now that the collar's effects were gone my shifter healing had taken over, but it still left a mark.

"We don't know, Bastian, but we discovered it when I shifted to fight an anaconda shifter that broke through the wall. That's where I got this from."

Bastian's eyes grew wide, but I stopped him before all the questions I knew he'd ask started. "Everyone's okay, I promise, and we can explain it all in greater detail but not with so many shifters present. Abraham says he knows someone that might know what's happening between us, and we're going to see him tomorrow," I replied.

"I'm coming with," he demanded, and I noticed he wasn't looking at me anymore but glaring back at Abraham.

Abraham simply stuck his hand out. "Wouldn't have it any other way. We will discuss all the details in private tonight when you stay at the castle."

Bastian raised his eyebrow at him. "We're allowed to stay now?"

Abraham nodded. "That was the plan before we discovered all this. Shanely showed me that everyone was working hard and deserved a break."

Bastian studied him a moment before nodding back. "I see you removed her collar."

Abraham's nervous laugh filled the empty space between us, and he rubbed the back of his head. "Actually, I did not. She broke it to save me and Aerith, but I removed the other collars before we came here."

He looked over to Johnny then. Johnny looked relieved and simply nodded back to him.

"Come everyone. Sit! You are honored guests of the Tiger King tonight!"

Abraham practically shouted, making me jump. He winked at me then, and I realized we had a lot of shifters looking at us again.

"Shanely on my right, please," Abraham requested as he took the largest chair. I sat next to him and motioned to the chair next to me for Bastian to sit, but he just stood in front of me.

"This isn't going to work," he muttered.

I took a deep breath, hoping not to fight him about this. It seemed I needed to explain what Abraham told me about being united for tonight in front of all these shifters. *How to do that without letting everyone here know was the trick.* "Bastian please…"

He picked me up before I could say anything more and sat me down on his lap. "Much better."

I laughed as Abraham gave us a weird look before smiling himself.

"So you're not mad?" I asked.

He shook his head. "No. As soon as the bond snapped in place my wolf became docile. I mean, he still thinks he's a dickhead, but my wolf isn't threatened anymore."

"I heard that," Abraham muttered before chuckling to himself. "Though I deserve it."

"Yeah, you deserve a whole lot after what you pulled last time," Bastian replied, wrapping his arms around my waist and nestling back in the side of my neck.

"You look incredible by the way," he whispered as he started gently kissing my neck. I moaned softly at the sensation of his lips on my neck, enjoying every second of it.

"Get it together, guys. You're making us all uncomfortable," Abraham whispered before shifting further away.

I laughed as I looked around the group with us. "I can't help I've missed my mate."

Bastian smiled mischievously. "I've missed you too, and I want to know how this all came about. Every detail, Shanely."

I nodded. "Later, when we can get some privacy. No one in his streak knows yet, and it might be a problem."

Bastian nodded before he started playing with my hair. He pulled me in close. "I do hope you still have that costume you wore last time I saw you. We will need it tonight."

I blushed, burying my face in his neck while he laughed. Abraham shifted uncomfortably in his seat.

"God, I don't want to know any of this," he muttered quietly.

"Hey, you started it when you made her wear that in front of me," Bastian shot back. "Which by the way was a *low blow*."

Abraham seemed exasperated now, his face turning a whole new shade of red. "That was *before* I knew she was my sister. I only did it to piss you off."

"Well, you succeeded! I still want to pummel you despite being family now."

Before the banter could continue the announcer's voice came up over the microphone. He did a great job exciting the crowd, and I noticed many female shifters smiling and waving at all of the fellas sitting up here with me. I rolled my eyes, but I really couldn't blame them. I'd be looking too if I were them.

A few bold male even tried to smile at me, despite me sitting on my mate's lap. They were met with snarls and growls from all the guys at the same time, and I actually felt a little bad when they all looked ready to crap themselves. They moved deeper into the crowd after that, and no one dared looked my way again. My boys decided to stand behind me now to ensure it. Cade took the seat next to me and Bastian, while Elijah stood directly behind us. I squeezed Cade's hand when he gave me one of his devilish smiles.

"Only you, Shanely," he whispered before kissing my cheek. I giggled and just shrugged. There really wasn't anything I could say to even dispute that.

We went through two fights before the grand finale, which was Bay's fight. It wasn't very entertaining, but the crowd seemed to love it. I ended up spending most of my time trying to count how many shifters were actually here, so I could try to figure out what Abraham even made in a night. Anything to avoid looking at the ring. I really hated to watch any of it, but when the announcer began talking about the final fight, I remembered Bay was still mad at me.

I leaned in to whisper to my mate. "By the way, Bay has it in her head that

Abraham and I are something of an item."

His eyes shot to mine before glaring at Abraham. "And why would she think that? Doesn't she know?"

"Oh, don't even go there. No one but us knows right now. I was going to tell her earlier, but she snapped at me and doesn't want to listen to anything I have to say right now. We had an issue today with the snake, and I was unconscious for awhile in Abraham's room. It's put her wolf on edge when I came out smelling and looking like him. I only smelled like him because I was passed out in his bed, nothing more."

"Wait, back up a minute! What *exactly* happened to you with this anaconda? And why would her wolf even care?!" he demanded, but Bay's fighter entered the arena, and the crowd roared loudly, making it hard to speak to one another. My eyes widened when as Nikolai Falin walked through the crowd. He was at least 7 feet tall, standing well over a foot above the crowd, and I abruptly turned to my brother.

"Abraham, he's a beast! *He's* fighting Mor'du??" I asked, my voice turning to a near shrill sound.

Abraham winced. "This fight was planned a long time ago before I knew about Mor'du. I cannot change it, Shanely. Bay will come through. She always does."

The announcer finally called out Mor'du, and I sat up further on Bastian's lap, trying to see past everyone. She entered the fight like she normally did, and Abraham didn't take his eyes off of hers. She seemed so much smaller than everyone else though and fear trickled in. *Please don't let anything happen to her.*

Bay entered the ring but instead of the normal hype she always does, she just stared over to us. Without warning, she threw her head back and revealed her face. The crowd gasped, and the other fighter stopped jumping. Bay paid no mind to the others around her and threw her robe off to the side. Everyone was silent for a moment, and Abraham gripped his chair tightly.

"What is she doing?" Cade shouted.

"I don't know. She was supposed to remain a secret," Bastian said completely distracted now.

I looked at Abraham, who's face had hardened with rage. The other fighter looked angry for a moment as he spoke to his handler.

"It's my fault," I whispered, but the crowd drowned out my voice.

The crowd went wild to finally know who Mor'du was. Some looked angry, I assume because she was a girl, but I was terrified. *What had she done?*

The bell rang, and they both shifted. Bay wasn't fighting like she normally did though. She was full of rage tonight, and it showed in her sloppy form. Guilt rattled me as I gripped the armrest tightly.

The bear she fought played a fantastic defense and struck her when she left herself opened. I winced as she stumbled away. *It was like she didn't care!* I could smell the blood from here, and Abraham looked ready to snap as he gripped his chair tightly. The crowd cheered *every time* she was struck.

"Bay snap out of it! Focus on your opponent!" I shouted, climbing down from Bastian's lap. I reached the ropes on the edge of our box, and Bastian was right behind me.

She wasn't listening though, whether on purpose or not, I didn't know, but it was pisses off me and my wolf. Finally the bear smacked her down hard, and she struggled to get up. I put my hands in my hair as I bounced on my feet.

"This is all your freaking fault!" Bastian bellowed as panic filled my heart. *Oh God... Bay was going to lose tonight.*

The bear struck again, slamming her body against the metal cage. Abraham shot out of his seat now. "Bay, get up! End this now! Please... For me, just *get* up."

She looked our way briefly and slowly stood on her paws. She was shaky, but she was standing at least, and I exhaled deeply. The bear chuffed at her, annoyed that this was his fight tonight. He turned to the crowd and roared.

"Bay, it's not what you think! Please focus! I promise, I'll explain everything! Just win this first!" I shouted at the top of my lungs. Bastian clung to me, while we watched our sister struggle.

Bay seemed to be lost in thought for a moment as her opponent slowly turned back to her. Barring his teeth, he lunged, but Bay swiftly side-stepped him. My eyes widened when she did it again. *Oh, thank God*, I thought as my shoulders shook. *This was Bay.*

Bay started back on defense, and the bear stomped his paws on the ground angrily. He roared again, advancing on her again and again, trying to get his advantage back. But she *never* let him have it. She picked up her feet, spinning the bear in circles as he tried to catch her. The stench of blood filled the air and fear rippled through me. *Was this coming from Bay or her opponent?* Bay finally leapt onto the bear's back and clamped down on his shoulder. He jolted, slamming his body into the cage to throw her off, while she shook her head. He took a swipe at her, but she held on until we all heard the sickening crunch. He roared in pain as she leapt off him and dove for his back leg. She pulled. The cage shook violently as he fell on his stomach, and I held my breath as she drug him across the ring. He roared again, when she twisted violently and snapped his leg. The sound he made sickened me. *This was not something I could ever do,* I realized. Even my animals didn't like watching the fight go on, and I gripped my mate fiercely.

Bay slowly made her way to his head, growling and barring her teeth as blood dripped off her snout. The bear remained still. No one in the crowd moved. No one made a sound as we watched the two in the ring. Then he did something unexpected. Nikolai Falin exposed his neck to Bay. The bell dinged, and the crowd roared. I nearly collapsed in relief against my mate. A collective sigh came from the group behind me before thunderous applause sounded. The corners of my mouth rose as I shook my head. *What a night...*

Bastian cheered so loudly, it rattled my ears, and I couldn't stop my grin from spreading. *Thank the lord Bay's alright,* I thought as I turned to my brother. My smile fell. Abraham stood *rigid* watching Bay shift back. I blinked when I turned back to her. She swayed a bit on her feet and looked worse than I realized. Her arm was badly sprained, and she was covered in marks and bruises, not to mention the blood from the slice she got in the beginning of the fight. I covered my mouth with my hand, gasping at what I saw. *She didn't look steady on her feet,* I thought. *She didn't look alright.*

Abraham suddenly vaulted over the rope, startling everyone, and the crowd parted for him as he pushed his way through. Jake and another tiger took off after him, but he moved fast for a big guy. Abraham just plowed through the crowd, while we stood there with wide-eyes.

"What's he doing?" Elijah asked.

Suddenly, it clicked. "Oh my God! Here, Abraham!? Really?"

I couldn't take my eyes off my new brother. I shook my head in disbelief as he ripped the cage's door off it's hinges and went straight to Bay. She froze, narrowing her eyes as he stalked towards her. Then he grabbed her waist, yanked her close, and kissed her.

The crowd *silenced*. Even Jake came to a sudden stop as everyone stood there gaping at them. A heartbeat passed before the crowd suddenly lost it. The shifters closest to the cage began shaking it excitedly, and my eyes widened. Just like that me, Bastian, Cade, and Elijah all grabbed our chests. The bond formed, and I was *right*.

Bay's eyes grew wide as the two parted, looking too shocked to say anything to him as he cupped the sides of her face, whispering softly to her. The cage rattled again as a female shifter bolted up the stairs towards them. Then another, and Jake barely caught the second girl and hauled her back. Abraham pulled Bay behind him as the crowd began pushing their way towards them, camera phones in hand or items for Bay and Abraham to sign. I had no idea how *popular* the two were in the shifter community, but panic flashed across Abraham's face as the excitement in the room grew louder. His enforcers moved to control the crowd, with Jake barely keeping shifters out of the cage.

"Boys, it's time to move! Get them out of the ring and *out* of this crowd. Let's go," I shouted loudly. We rushed to the stairs, but Bastian blocked me at the top. I barred my teeth, earning a glare right back, and he wouldn't let me go any further. I had to watch from the sidelines again, but I let my frustration go as Abraham covered his arms around Bay and pushed his way through the small path made for them. I held my breath until they finally made it back to us, and I bolted down the steps, slamming into Bay.

"This way," Jake shouted as he led us out a different way. We all followed him quickly, bolting up the stairs and through the outer doors.

"You couldn't wait until we got home?!" I asked Abraham, laughing the second we stepped out into fresh air.

He grinned mischievously. "You told me to quit fighting it, so I did."

"I didn't mean in the middle of the crowded ring!" I snapped back as I hugged him. "Congratulations by the way."

"Wait, you knew?" Bay demanded, tugging my arm to face her.

I nodded as I hugged her too. "I knew before he did, I think."

"But how, Shanely?"

"Because he's my brother, Bay." Her eyes grew wide.

"He's your what!?" Jake asked, grinding to a halt next to me. *Whoops*, I thought to myself. *I had forgotten his enforcers were still with us.*

"We found out today," I said to the group. "But Bay? There is nothing going on between us. Not like that. I would never hurt Bastian like that nor could I ever even *think* about leaving him. He's my soulmate just like Abraham is yours. You get it now, right? You *feel* it."

She nodded before lowering her head in shame. "Shanely, I said some horrible things to you and I..."

I waved her off. "Don't worry about it. Let's just get back, so we can discuss all this together. We really shouldn't talk about it here in the open."

Before I could even take a step I smelled the vile, thick stench of cheap cologne and froze. *Only one person scented like this...* Patrick.

Abraham raised a brow as my boys struggled to keep their wolves in check. Bastian instinctively pulled me behind him.

"Abraham, you need to clear out the ring now," Bastian demanded.

Patrick and another man in a dark Pacers hoodie walked across the street. My eyes narrowed on the two, watching them closely, but they didn't seem to be working tonight. Patrick was in regular clothes, and the two looked like they were making their way to the Den on the other street.

"Who is that?" Abraham asked, motioning to the prick I couldn't stand.

"Patrick. Tell whoever is running the ring tonight to clear out in batches and to pay attention. We don't want to tip them off," Bastian said before pushing me to the truck. I obeyed, wanting to get far away from him as possible. My wolf was on high-alert and extra snarly at the moment, making it hard to focus on anything.

Two tigers came out the back door with the guys Bastian and his brothers had found, and I tried not to look at them when they passed by. They threw them in the other truck and drove off, going a different way than we had come. I watched Abraham make a phone call before getting into the other truck with Bay.

We split up between Abraham and Cade's SUV and made our way to the castle once more. I had missed my family so much, and it was wonderful to finally be together again. Cade drove, and I snuggled right up to Bastian, not giving him an inch of space.

I felt bad for Johnny though, noticing how fast his knee bounced in the back seat. He grew more and more anxious the closer we got to Abraham's place. We made our way back to the castle fairly quickly, but it was still weird to be relieved to be back here.

Henry and Darryl were already at the doors waiting to greet us. *Abraham must have called ahead,* I thought to myself as everyone hopped out of the vehicles.

"Let's head upstairs to the den. It's late, but I'll have Alana and Octavia sent for," Abraham said before giving orders to Henry and Darryl. They both nodded as Abraham turned back to us.

"Henry has volunteered to stay with Aerith for now while we all talk. I don't want her alone tonight," Abraham explained, and I gave Henry a smile as he shifted and made his way upstairs. Darryl wasn't far behind, heading to get the girls, and Johnny took off after them. *I guess he wasn't waiting anymore.*

"And you're okay with that?" Bastian whispered as he gestured to Henry, who disappeared from sight.

I nodded. "Henry helped save her life today. He seems to have taken a shine to her and vice versa. They've become buddies now, and I trust him. She will be thrilled to see you tomorrow though."

Bastian gave me a kiss. "I've missed both my girls, but right now, I want some answers, among other things."

His eyes flashed gold, and I gave him a bashful smile. I pulled him along, following the group inside. *Funny how different I feel about this place now,* I thought to myself. *It seemed more like another home instead of our prison.*

Abraham led us to his den, and we all took seats. I collapsed in the chair, feeling more exhausted than I realized. Much like Abraham's bedroom, this room was cozy and warm. A large fireplace lay along the back wall, and Abraham went straight to it to light it for everyone. The room had a few older looking couches here as well and lots of books to choose from. On the far right wall, two large windows sat side by side, reminding me of Cain's office back home.

Bastian hauled me out of my seat and placed me on his lap. I grinned wide before settling against him. We took the single seat off to the side, while everyone else got comfortable. Darryl came through the door shortly after, with Octavia right on his heels. Johnny carried Alana in and did the same thing Bastian did by placing Alana on his lap in the other large chair off in the corner. They seemed lost in each other, and I left them in peace for now. Octavia gave everyone hugs before cozying up to Ryder and Caleb. We were *finally* all together.

"So what's this about another brother?" Caleb asked. "I thought I was your brother."

"Hey, we are too!" Cade exclaimed as Elijah nodded in agreement.

I laughed. "I have a great deal of brothers, it seems. Honestly, Abraham and I aren't sure how this is even possible. We had an incident today, which led us to make the discovery."

"What happened?" Cade asked, leaning forward in his seat.

"We're still trying to find out how it even happened in the first place. Since I've reclaimed this streak, we have never had a breach in our walls until today. A very large anaconda shifter somehow got through the first time I take the girls through my land. It went after the children playing in the creek," Abraham answered solemnly.

"Aerith was in the creek," I added, and Bastian tensed.

"It all just happened so fast, but Abraham dove in to save Aerith. Between him and Henry, they pulled her to safety in time, but that snake had Abraham in a dead lock under the water. It scared me half to death, and I didn't understand why. Well... until now," Bay said as she kissed Abraham's hand.

He gently pulled her close as he lifted his shirt. It was still a nasty shade of blue, and Elijah swore.

"I bit the snake, but he was large. It wasn't enough. I wasn't enough to break him," Darryl chimed in solemnly. Pity filled my heart as I watched him drop his head, knowing the guilt and shame he felt right now.

"And that's when *your* wife," Abraham said, pointing to Bastian, "broke the collar that kept her animal dormant. She *broke it* and shifted in front of my whole streak. She saved me and killed the anaconda. It's why the mark is on her arm. The snake got her briefly first."

Bastian turned me around to look at my arm closer. The scars were still there, but it had healed nicely. His eyes widened like I amazed him or something. I blushed, burying my head in his neck.

"That's because you do amaze me," Bastian said softly. *"All the time."*

The corners of my mouth rose slightly. *I had missed hearing his voice in my head.*

"You heard her voice, didn't you? When she shifted?" Caleb asked as Abraham nodded. "It happened with me too. We share a father."

"It would appear we share a mother then. Somehow. Unless it is your father? Did your Dad ever *see* a tiger?" Abraham snorted.

Caleb laughed. "I doubt it! He was pretty much a shell of a man until Shanely returned. Shanely's mom was his mate."

"Well, test it out. Can you mind-link one another?" Bay asked.

"We don't have a sibling bond," Caleb pointed out.

"Humor me," Bay quipped back.

Abraham shrugged before shifting into his large cat form. Much like his hair, he was an all white Bengal tiger. *Aerith will squeal when she sees him,* I thought to myself. Bay playfully scratched behind his ears, and he rubbed up against her legs in approval. Caleb sighed before standing up, scratching his head as he looked around the room.

"Uh... I'm a bit large, guys," Caleb stammered. We laughed and scooted the couch farther away from him. He shifted into his grizzly, and the two of them just stared at one another. They shifted back.

"Nothing," Caleb said.

"We must share a mother then, Shanely," Abraham stated as he took his place next to the fireplace with Bay.

"Well any brother of Shanely's is a brother of mine. I already have wolf brothers, might as well have a tiger too," Caleb said, extending his hand with a laugh. Abraham smiled and shook it firmly.

"Who knew I'd have a mixer for a sister, a wolf for a mate, and a bear as a brother," Abraham said, with a laugh.

That got us all laughing. *It felt like something I would say.* As I looked around at our little group, I realized we were kind of forming our own little pack. Right here. My technical Alpha wasn't even here right now. Just my inner circle. We were figuring out this problem on our own, and no one even thought anything of it. That *pleased* my wolf, and I couldn't help but grin wider. Suddenly, something snapped in me, and I sucked in a deep breath. My chest burned again, and the sensation seemed to pulse in a steady rhythm before slowly subsiding. Everyone looked at me.

"You okay?" Bastian asked as he began to look me over.

"Yeah, I think so. I don't know something just took my breath away. It's probably nothing," I replied as I rubbed my chest. I gave everyone a smile, hoping they'd just move past it. We were in a good mood, and I didn't want to bring us down by tossing in whatever just happened.

Bastian frowned but let it go. I knew we'd talk about it later though. Bastian *never* forgot anything that had to do with me.

"So do you know how the snake got in?" Elijah asked.

Abraham shook his head and answered, "No. I called for Finnick since he's the senior guard out there, but he says he never saw a snake. I don't see how no one saw him though. He was quite large."

"He looked like he was heading straight for the children, " I pointed out.

Abraham replied angrily, "Or maybe just one."

My eyes shot to his. "You don't think someone sent him after Aerith, do you?"

"I have never had this happen before. *Ever.* The first day I let you all out, and we have an anaconda? We were all right there too. If this was an assassination attempt then he completely went in the other direction! He didn't even go after me until I got in Aerith's way, and my guys are good. They don't miss something as big as a snake!"

"Well, bring them to me," Octavia casually mentioned as she messed with her nails.

"Wait, why?"

"Because I can sniff out lies. It smells horrible, and I can taste intentions too. It's one of my special abilities," she said so nonchalantly. I shook my head grinning.

"Wait... You all have abilities?" Darryl asked.

"The wolves get them more often but some bears do too. I have no idea with other shifters though," Johnny replied, finally gracing us with his presence. Alana blushed, her lips were bright red and swollen from kissing her mate.

"Well, I can tell you right now tigers do not get *any* abilities," Darryl said frustratedly.

"But maybe you will Abraham? You are half-wolf," I said, winking at him.

He blew out a loud breath. "Okay then... Tomorrow Octavia, you will help me find our rat."

"Then the three of us will meet with that tiger, correct?" Bastian asked.

"You mean four of us?" Bay countered.

I rolled my eyes. "Of course, you can come."

"It sounds like a game plan. I say we crash and start fresh in the morning," Elijah said.

Everyone went in different directions after that. Abraham graciously led us all to private guest rooms down the hall where the den was at. Octavia got her own room too, so she wouldn't have to bunk with anyone else. As we parted ways for the night I noticed Abraham had a death grip on Bay's hand. He pulled her close and whispered something in her ear before she blushed. They disappeared behind his door.

"Come on, you," Bastian said behind me. "I've been away from you for too long."

He started kissing me before he even pulled me into our room.

Shanely

Someone shrieked.

Bastian and I bolted from bed as did everyone else. Everyone stumbled out of their room with me and Bastian, but we quickly ground to a halt. Henry was chasing Aerith around the castle in his tiger form. They ran down the stairs into the foyer, and Aerith twisted at the last second. Henry slid on the tile past her. She giggled hard, clutching her stomach as he revved up before taking off again.

Bastian chuckled softly, pulling me close as we watched the two play. My heart settled within me, and I laid my head against Bastian's bare chest, listening to his heart beat. I didn't say a word when he turned the both of us to lean against the wall, covering the tattoos on his back from the others. I always thought he should show them off, but he was private with them, and I never wanted to push him about it. It was his artwork to show off or not, but I loved that he had each pack and clan's tag etched into his skin.

The beautiful paw print with a wolf inside for the Fenrir pack. Even though the pack became dark and awful now, it was still where he came from, and that made it special to me. The McCoy's tag was in the middle, which was a wolf howling to the moon in the center of these dark swirls. It was simple yet unique, and I loved the bear's clan tag underneath. It was an outline of a grizzly with the mountains etched in the center of the bear. Each and every tag was connected with a tribal mark, and I just thought it was outstanding. I'd been thinking an awful lot about getting the same look on my back to match my mate. I wanted each and every mark to show how proud I was to have the family that I did. I glanced over to Abraham, who was lost in his own world looking at Bay and decided that when I did get my tattoo, I'd add his streak's insignia as well.

"*I was thinking the same thing.*"

Bastian's voice startled me through the link, and I smiled. He had been listening to my internal ramble the whole time and was grinning wickedly at me. He winked before turning back to Aerith and Henry, relaxing slightly against the wall and letting some of his tattoo be exposed to the others. I smiled, leaning further into him, determined to follow through with my plan.

My eye caught Johnny rubbing Alana's belly with a twinkle in his eye. I grinned, seeing the picture he was thinking in my head. One day their kid would be here too, and he'd get to play with his son like Aerith and Henry were. Our kids could play together as they got older, and my heart swelled just thinking about it. Our family was changing constantly, but it was becoming *bigger* not smaller. My children were going to have the life I always wanted, and I couldn't contain the smile on my face.

Bastian suddenly swatted my butt before stepping back in the shadows. I smirked, already knowing where this was going and stepped back giving him room. He shifted, and my eyes widened. *I swear his wolf got bigger*, I thought as he stalked by. The top of his head was almost to my shoulders. I know I wasn't a tall person by any means, but this was *crazy* for a wolf. *No wonder humans made up stories of werewolves.*

Alana and Octavia must have been thinking the same thing, when they noticed Bastian's dark wolf coming out of the shadows. They gave him a wide birth, and Bastian moved slow, like he was in the middle of the hunt before he howled. It echoed throughout the castle, and Aerith and Henry froze.

Abraham watched my mate closely, and I think he realized how much he truly underestimated Bastian. He looked to me and gave a low whistle. I smirked, knowing he was immediately regretting pissing his wolf off earlier.

Aerith quickly scanned the room, recognizing her Dad's howl as we hid in the shadows by the grand stairs. She beamed from ear to ear, pulling Henry towards the curtains hanging on the massive windows. I gently scratched my mate behind his ears, watching my child trying to hide a large tiger.

"Henry come on!" her small voice pleaded. "We have to hurry!"

Henry chuffed but went along as Aerith hid them behind the curtain. Bastian howled again. I stepped aside to let him go. I *loved* watching them play hide and seek.

Bastian looked at me and winked at me. My eyes widened before my head tipped back, and I laughed. *His wolf actually winked at me!* Bastian bolted into the room, and we all poked our heads out to watch. There was nowhere for Aerith to hide besides the curtain, but she stayed quiet and still. *She had been taking her lessons very seriously,* I thought as I stifled a giggle. My poor baby didn't realize her feet stuck out like a sore thumb under those large red curtains, but I had to give it to Henry. He played right along with her, and it was comical to see the large tiger tucked behind the curtain.

Bastian sniffed around, letting Aerith have her fun, and I could hear her giggle quietly. She braved a quick peek towards her dad before ducking back inside and shushing Henry. Bastian barked and jumped to the opposite curtains, sniffing around, when Aerith decided to making a break for it. Refusing to leave a man behind, she pulled Henry towards the stairs as quietly as she could, when Bastian yipped at her.

She bolted to the stairs then, leaving Henry in the dust before Bastian cut her off. He yipped again, and she squealed, jumping on him in defeat.

"Daddy! You found me!"

He barked again as she clung to him, and he laid down, rolling over to his back. The two immediately started wrestling like I'd seen them do a thousand times back home, and somehow that turned into a game of tag. Henry shifted back into his human form and joined us in the corner.

"Thank you, Henry," I said as he got closer. "You go above and beyond for her. I can't thank you enough."

He shrugged, a faint tint of red filling his cheeks. "I heard enough last night. If that's our King's niece, then we protect her the same as we would for him. Besides, she's a doll. It's hard to tell her no."

I laughed in agreement as we watched the two of them continue to play in the main foyer.

"Alright it's my turn, Baby Girl," Cade said, passing me. I didn't realize how much I missed hearing that nickname.

Cade shifted into his smokey gray wolf and ran in to join the fun. *Cade's wolf had grown as well*, I thought as I studied my brother-in-law, which was *odd*. Not quite the same as Bastian, but still a noticeable difference. Aerith squealed again, running right up and tagging Cade right on the nose.

"You're it, Uncle Cade!" she shouted, taking off to hide behind Bastian. My mate began acting as a defensive line between her and Cade. He moved swiftly and helped her stay just out of Cade's reach.

"Well, I guess her favorite uncle should be apart of the game too," Elijah mentioned mid-shift. *His wolf was bigger too! What was going on with the brothers?* I wondered. I gave Bay a look, but she just shrugged.

"Excuse me?" Caleb chuffed. "I'll have you know that *I'm* her favorite uncle."

He shifted too, and Aerith's eyes went wide when he charged forward. Us girls giggled at the sight before us. *It was a good thing Abraham's front entrance was so grand because there were a lot of big animals running around now.*

"That's because she hadn't met me yet," Abraham countered, and my brows rose. A blush formed on his face. "Well not like this."

I laughed as he joined in on the fun. Ryder winked at me.

"C'mon, Johnny," he said, smacking his shoulder. "We better get in on this game with our niece too!"

I beamed over at him. They weren't blood uncles to her but treated her no different than Cade, Caleb, and Elijah. Johnny playfully pushed Ryder as he bolted past, shifting into his sandy brown wolf with Ryder right behind him.

I looked over to the girls. "Thank the lord, this entrance is massive! We can't all fit in here."

They laughed, but it was true. We had one bear, one tiger, and *five* wolves all playing a version of tag that Aerith was inventing on the spot. She was constantly tagging someone and was perpetually *it* the entire time, but no one seemed to mind. Everyone seemed to miss her, and I leaned against the wall, content to watch from her. *She was surrounded by her family, and that was how it should be,* I thought to myself. *Something I wish I had growing up.*

My smile fell as my mother came to mind. I looked over to Abraham. *There was so much I didn't know about her, and now this. What happened to her?* I wondered to myself. My father was her mate, and it was physically impossible to want to be with another once the imprinting started. *She didn't just move on and find another, so what happened to her?* My heart sank then. *What if she didn't have a choice? What if something horrific happened to her?*

Bastian stopped playing to look at me. My wolf noticed the second his eyes found me and pulled my attention towards him.

"Shanely, please don't stress. Whatever happened, just try to focus on the good that came from it. Like Abraham. You wouldn't trade Aerith for anything, right?"

I shook my head, understanding his point. I wouldn't give Aerith up for anything, but she came from a dark time in my life. I sighed then.

"See? There's no point stressing about the past. We have no idea what happened yet, but no matter what we find, just remember to look at the family you have right now. Focus on that and not the bad."

"I love you, Bastian," I said softly, "you know that right?"

He gave a wolfy grin as he sat down, chaos ensuing around him.

"I do," he answered, "but I love hearing you say it anyways."

Suddenly, Aerith pounced on him and howled. The room stilled. *That sounded just like a real wolf,* I thought as I bolted to her. Bastian and his brothers were already sniffing her, trying to check if they could pick up on a wolf within her, but she just giggled, pushing their snouts away.

"She smells the same, Shanely. I don't sense a wolf, but that was so clear," Bastian said, looking back at me.

"Aerith honey, do you feel anything different with you?" I asked.

She laughed as Elijah continued sniffing her with his nose. "That tickles! What do you mean, Mommy?"

"Like maybe your own wolf? It would feel like she's connected to you here," I said, pointing to where her heart was. "You know one like Daddy's wolf or Mommy's bear."

"I don't know. Can we eat now? I'm hungry, Mommy," she asked, crossing her legs and smiling up at me.

"Either she's gotten insanely good at mimicking or we just heard her wolf for the first time," Elijah stated, smiling excitedly.

"We'll let Alpha Cain know today, while you guys meet with that tiger. We'll see what he thinks," Ryder said as we all studied her for a few moments.

"C'mon, everyone. Let's eat! We've got a big day ahead of us," Abraham said, leading us back to the hallway by the stairs. We all quickly changed into our regular clothes for the day, and Abraham led us to the kitchen in the back.

We ate a quick breakfast this time instead of the massive spread like on our first day, and then Abraham and Bastian headed to the front. Aerith bolted to them, reaching for Bastian, who picked her up and kissed her cheek. She still had a doughnut in her hand, which she happily munched on for the announcements.

"Alright, we all have a very full day ahead of us. First things first is dealing with those on the wall. They've all been brought back to the castle for Octavia to read. Once that's accomplished, the four of us," Abraham said, pointing to Bay, Bastian, and then myself, "will be heading to John's place in the woods. It's pretty secluded, so it will be a small hike there. Henry, you are assigned to Aerith at all times."

"As well as Cade. Not that I doubt Henry, but I take care of my own too. I want a wolf with her, so I can communicate quickly just in case," Bastian stated firmly.

Abraham nodded. "The more with her the better. On the off chance I was right, it will take more than one to deal with another shifter assassin, especially another snake."

Bastian nodded in agreement, and my heart filled with pride. I thought I'd have to work hard at getting everyone to get along, but it was like this whole ordeal didn't even happen. Everyone just accepted Abraham and his tigers without hate or malice *despite* our very rocky start. I know the bond seriously helped Bastian out, and Cade and Elijah by extension, but everyone else never said another word about it. I think the whole gang was just happy to be back together again honestly, and we just moved on to the next problem. *Which again was because of me.*

Bastian slowly turned to give me a look, letting me know he heard my internal monologue. I blushed and shoved a strawberry in my mouth. *I needed to remember to keep some things to myself.*

"On the safe side, Aerith should stay here at the castle. We won't be long, and she will be safer behind these walls," I chimed in, still blushing profusely, and both men nodded.

"Okay, which means while we're gone the rest of you all have free rein of the place," Abraham mentioned.

"Actually, Johnny go ahead and take Alana home. Her dad wants to see her, and I'm sure have words with you, Abraham," Bastian said with a sly grin.

Abraham just dropped his head and grimaced.

"Take her home and get her comfortable. She's only pregnant for so long so enjoy it. Ryder head back to the Alpha and fill him in on everything, and see what he can make of Aerith too. Caleb and Elijah, check in on Patrick and his team. I want to know if he's been back to pack lands at any point during this whole adventure. See if he's asked about Shanely or Aerith as well, and guys... Be discreet."

The two both nodded before fist-bumping each other. *Crazy how different everything is now.*

"Okay... Everyone knows where they should be then?" Abraham asked, and the group nodded.

"Then let's get started. I'll see you all later minus Johnny and Alana," Bastian finished.

The group split up then, and I hugged Alana goodbye.

"Thank you," I whispered to her. Our eyes glistened as we pulled away, and she gently rubbed my shoulder.

"Anytime you need a partner in crime, I'm here," she replied, and Johnny gave a low growl. She rolled her eyes. "Oh, you stop that. I'm always here for you, Shanely."

I smiled. Johnny hugged me then, and I wiped my cheek as they made their way out the door. It was silly getting this worked up because we'd be coming home soon, and it wasn't like it was goodbye forever, but she was my partner in crime. *It felt weird that she was going home early.*

Bastian passed Aerith over to Cade, and both brothers gave me a kiss goodbye before following Henry out of the kitchen. That left the six of us. Abraham led us to the throne room, except this time I noticed a few changes. The biggest change was a chair had been placed directly next to his.

He led Bay to the opened chair, and she looked surprised. "For me?"

"Of course. My Queen deserves her own place at my side," he replied, kissing her forehead.

She blushed as she sat down. "Technically, I've always been at your side since I've been here."

Abraham made a face. "Yeah, no one is going to see you like that ever again. My Queen doesn't stay at my feet."

She laughed. "Oh really? Well, will I need to wear those special outfits still? Because I can go change real quick before we get started, if you'd like?"

"Oh, yeah! I mean this is official business after all, Abraham. I can get dressed too," I chimed in, and Bay snorted from laughing. I took a step towards the door, pushing the joke even further.

"You will not!" Bastian exclaimed, yanking me back towards him. Poor Abraham just shrunk further in his seat. His face turned a bright red, and he covered his face.

"Can we just not talk about that?" he mumbled. The corners of Bastian's mouth rose.

"Why not? It was bold and intimidating and showed what a *united* front we were. Wasn't that what you told us?" I asked, wiggling my eyebrows, and Bay nodded her head. She stood from her chair too, when Abraham quickly caught her hand and yanked her back to her seat.

"No one will *ever* see you in that outfit every again, Bay. No one but me. And Shanely?" he said, turning around to glare at me. "Shut up."

I stuck my tongue back at him, placing my hands on my hips, when I realized something. "Hey wait..." I said, frowning. "Where's my fancy chair, Abraham?"

"You are my advisor. Advisors stand behind me," he replied, laughing as I punched his arm.

"Whatever, punk," I replied, and Bastian rolled his eyes.

"We'll be fine back here, love. Octavia up front," Bastian commanded. She took a seat in front of Abraham on the steps to his chair.

"Darryl, please bring in the first batch," Abraham said, and within minutes the doors opened. 10 tiger shifters came in at a time. Abraham asked them all the same questions. All while I watched.

"Did you see the snake shifter sneak onto streak lands?"

"No."

"Did you try to kill the mixer's child?

"No."

Did you see anything suspicious?"

"No."

"Do you approve of the new changes I am making with the wolves?"

"Yes."

"Would you approve of a wolf queen?"

That question caused them to stumble, but they all answered together again.

"Yes."

Octavia sniffed each shifter, studying them each with such scrutiny. They eyed her funny, not understanding what she was doing, but she ignored the weird looks as she walked in the front and then behind them. *This was the first time I really got to see her work*, I thought to myself. *I was in recovery the last time.*

Bastian squeezed my hand, listening to my thoughts again. *He's becoming more in tune with me*, I realized. *I need to remember that if I ever needed to keep a secret from him.* He swatted my butt, and I jumped. Bastian just shook his head, grinning at me before pulling me back towards him again. I couldn't contain my grin as I watched Octavia work. She patted the chests of 7 tigers.

"These 7 are completely free to go. No malice or lies."

The men in line turned to her, their eyes widening in understanding. This wasn't just a standard disciplinary hearing. Darryl blocked their way out.

"You will return to your post at the wall. You will not speak a word of this to anyone until I give the command, otherwise you will be banished from the streak and forced to leave immediately," Abraham commanded. All seven crossed their right hand on their chest before leaving and shutting the door behind them.

Octavia continued, "These last three did not lie about seeing the snake or trying to kill Aerith, but they do not approve of the changes nor do they like the idea of a wolf queen."

Bay flinched slightly before becoming stoic again. *That must have hurt,* I thought. *I knew full well what it felt like.*

Abraham continued to glare at the three in front of him. "Victor, Paul, and Frank," he finally said. "Honestly, this is not surprising. You never seemed too thrilled with my ascension to the throne anyways."

He walked towards them, and the tigers remained quiet and still. I held my mate's hand, watching my brother deal with his streak.

"Well let me explain a few things. You see that beautiful wolf sitting up there?" he asked confidently. Bay blushed under the scrutiny, causing Abraham to smile. They nodded slowly.

"*She* is my mate. I found her last night at the fight club."

Their eyes grew wide, but no one dared speak.

"Do you recognize her by chance?"

They shook their heads no.

"I wasn't sure. I assumed with the rotations you all would recognize her from the ring, but then again even I didn't realize it at first so I suppose not. That, my fellow tigers, is Mor'du. The undefeated Champion of our shifter rings. She is perfect in every way, and absolutely capable of shredding you three to pieces should you step out of line."

The one on the end swallowed hard as they all eyed her. *Clearly, they knew the name Mor'du.*

"That being said, she is also completely capable to protect our lands. She's fair, but fierce. Kind, but ruthless. I think she's the perfect Queen for our streak and that fate has given me the best possible choice for a mate. But the real question is, *do you?* Are you willing to go against our sacred life mates because of a history that has nothing to do with her?"

Their eyes shot to Abraham's. *Man, my brother could be scary when he wanted to be*, I thought to myself. Bastian looked proud of Abraham's defense of Bay. He would protect her well and love her dearly. It was crazy that my new brother was younger than I was and running this large streak all on his own. *Well, I guess he wasn't alone anymore.*

"We won't go against her or you, my King," the one on the right said.

"We didn't mean to offend you, sir."

"We'll stand by you both," the last replied.

Abraham looked to Octavia. She nodded her approval, and he turned back to them.

"You walk a fine line. We have always run this streak together, but I will not stand for any disrespect towards these wolves or against my life mate. You will spread the word about the changes you've seen this morning, but you will not mention Octavia to anyone. Return to your posts."

They left quickly and quietly, while Abraham returned to his chair. Before anyone could speak, Bay leaned over and kissed him hard. The two stayed locked together long enough that I began to wonder if they would come up for air.

Bastian cleared his throat and knocked his boot against Abraham's chair, interrupting them.

They gently pulled apart, and Bay rested her head against his. Her smile grew wide before the doors opened up again, bringing in the next set of enforcers. It took an hour to get through the majority of guards on both the outer and inner walls. I did not realize Abraham had so many tigers under his care. Abraham wanted to clear everyone before leaving the castle grounds today, but the longer I watched, the more I think he needed to see how his men felt about Bay for himself. We haven't spoken a word about our sibling bond yet, and I was waiting until he was ready to tell his streak.

It was definitely spreading throughout the castle that the King had found a mate. Most seemed okay with the change, and some weren't sure about it, but had no intentions of going against Abraham or Bay. Finally, the last set of tigers came through. This time it was only five, but Finnick was among them. My lip curled in disgust. I did not like that man one bit, remembering what he did to me. Apparently, Bastian was thinking the same thing because he snarled at him.

Abraham asked the same questions like before and nothing had changed until Octavia threw up. She heaved in a flower pot that was off to the side, and I rushed over to check on her.

"It's bad, Shanely," she muttered, trying to get her bearings.

"What do you mean?" I asked.

"The malice in this room. The hate... It's disgusting. My stomach can't handle it," she muttered, trying not to throw up again. I took my sweatshirt off and gave it to her. I had nothing else to give her to block the smell, and she gave me an appreciated look before covering her nose and mouth. She turned back to Abraham, who looked distraught. Bastian made his way down the stairs, sensing a problem.

"Shanely, you need to get them to answer more questions. Dig deeper into this," Octavia forced out before covering her nose back up.

I looked to Abraham, who waited patiently, and then back to her. She nodded again, and I sighed.

"Abraham, can I?" I asked, gesturing to his men, and he nodded and stepped aside.

Bastian stayed right on my heels as I made my way before the last group of tigers. "Alright boys, just a few more questions, and then we'll be done."

"Is this really necessary?" Finnick asked annoyed.

"It is," Abraham said bluntly. "Go ahead, Shanely."

"Abraham asked if you sent the snake to kill the mixer child, but did you send it to kill me instead?" I asked.

"No," they all replied in unison. Octavia briefly lifted her nose out of my sweatshirt before slamming it back over. I kept going.

"Do you like the fact that Abraham's mate is a wolf?"

"Yes."

"Are you aware that your King is a mixer?"

Abraham's eyes widened as he turned to me, questioning what I was doing. But I had a feeling where we were going.

"You lie. Our King scents like a tiger and nothing more," Finnick snarled before glaring back at Abraham.

"Did you realize that mixers can sometimes take after only one parent and not both? Only shifters that have dual animals will scent like a mixer." I waited for a response, but no one said a word. Finnick's eyes narrowed as he looked to the floor.

"Did anyone of you know that your Tiger King is actually my half-brother? Making him a mixer and half-wolf."

Finnick glared as us saying, "That's not possible."

"Oh, but it is Finnick," Abraham answered for me.

"Do you wish for Abraham to stay King of this streak, knowing he's a mixer?"

The five tigers stayed silent, processing what we just told them.

They finally answered together, "Yes."

Octavia shook as she stepped forward. "This one let the snake in."

She pointed right at Finnick.

"That's absurd!" he shouted. "She's lying, my King!"

"I'm not lying! He let him in, and these four are in on it! They targeted Shanely primarily, but also Aerith. They've never cared for you as King, and it infuriates them to find out you're actually a mixer, Abraham. That new piece of information is just the final nail in the coffin that you need to go, and I don't see them *ever* accepting Bay. Finnick is oozing out envy, and I think he wants your throne."

My eyes widened as Octavia blurted all that out before rushing back towards the pot and throwing up again. Bay was at her side, helping hold her hair and looking to me in horror. *This was bad.*

The tigers all began talking at once, and Bastian pulled me further away from them. Finnick was quiet though. He just glared ahead at me and then Octavia, refusing to say a word. I looked to Abraham, feeling utterly useless right now. I knew how he felt, and it sucked.

Abraham was quiet and calm surprisingly. He showed no emotion unlike Bastian, who was seething mad. He had already begun pacing back and forth in front of me, I'm sure trying to decide which one to kill first.

"Finnick, is this true? Did you try to kill my sister and niece?" Abraham asked, silencing the group again.

Finnick looked at Abraham, then to us, before stopping at Octavia last.

"I don't know what she is, but you have to understand she's lying," Finnick stated plainly.

Octavia, looking greener than ever, just shook her head and walked over to Abraham.

"Here... See for yourself."

She extended her hand, and Abraham accepted. He sucked in a breath before covering his mouth and nose. He turned *green*, and he forcefully let go of her hand. I had never seen this before and didn't know Octavia could share her power. Abraham took a few deep breaths, shaking himself from whatever scent Octavia was picking up on and turned to Finnick.

"Did you realize that bears and wolves are given special abilities? I did not until my new friend offered up her services to figure out who betrayed me," Abe said firmly.

Finnick shifted nervously on his feet, and I gritted my teeth. *We could all smell his fear now.*

"She can smell lies and taste intentions, and let me tell you what's coming off of all of you is absolutely disgusting," Abraham said, rubbing his face as he stepped closer to Finnick.

"So why, Finnick? I thought we were friends, were we not?"

Finnick's hands clenched at his side as he glared at my brother. "After what the wolves did to us, *why* would you just accept them in with open arms? We don't hire wolves, and we certainly don't allow them on our lands. This is a tiger streak! And now we find out you're not even a full-blooded tiger! You don't deserve to lead, Abraham, but that's been apparent to us for some time. The snake was just supposed to take care of the problem with the mixer and her kid, who you and I both know *shouldn't* be here. It wasn't going to harm any tigers here. She shouldn't exist and by law should be disposed of! I was doing my job, just like you should have done that night in the ring when we first scented her!"

Bastian stopped pacing. Guilt reared its ugly head as I watched the two argue. *I was right,* I thought. *This was about me.*

Abraham slowly nodded his head then. "You're right, Finnick," he said softly, and my eyes widened. "I should have done this the night we scented her."

Suddenly, Abraham reached forward and snapped Finnick's neck. His body crumbled to the ground instantly, and everyone backed far away. My brother roared, his tiger pulling through his voice as he stormed after the ones desperate to run.

"I don't like killing my kind, but this will *not* be accepted. You tried to kill a child! A CHILD!"

Abraham's voice boomed throughout the castle, shaking the walls as he towered over his enforcers.

"I am the Tiger King! But you four are no longer apart of my streak! I banish every last one of you," he commanded. That familiar Alpha charge filling the air. The tigers clutched their chests in agony as their bond was destroyed.

"You will spend the rest of your lives alone in the castle's dungeon. You forfeited every right you had when you decided to go against my family. It's this or death by my hands. I'll let you choose," he stated, waiting for their response.

They all gritted out prison, and Abraham motioned for the other guards to take them away.

"I want collars on every one of them! They will *never* feel their tigers again," Abraham demanded before he went straight to Bay and wrapped his arms around her tightly. Bastian and I walked up to them as Finnick's body was dragged away. Right along with the four shifters heading to their fates.

"Abraham..."

He suddenly engulfed me in a hug.

"I'm so sorry, Shanely. I promised you all that you would be safe here, and I had no idea he'd do something like that," Abraham said, his voice breaking ever so slightly.

"Abraham, you eliminated the threat for my family. I know what you did wasn't easy on you either, but thank you," Bastian said, extending his hand.

Abraham shook his hand before looking back to where Finnick once stood. "He was a friend."

"I am sorry, Abraham," I whispered, hugging him again.

He nodded. "I knew we'd have some issues, but not like this."

"It will get better, Abe. We lost nearly half when we merged with the bear clan," Bastian countered.

Abraham dropped his head. "My father used to call me Abe."

I smiled. "I like it. C'mon Abey, let's just get out of this room."

He smirked. "Abey?"

"Yeah, I get nicknames all the time. It's your turn for one."

Abey chuckled softly, and I grabbed Bastian's hand, pulling him through the side door. We all quietly made our way outside, and Octavia finally gave me back my sweatshirt. She looked a little less green at least. We made it outside, and I sighed heavily. *I needed this,* I thought as a warm breeze fluttered my hair.

"I don't know about you all, but I could use a run," Abraham said as he shifted to his tiger. I smiled and tried to pull out my wolf. She seemed locked still, and I rolled my eyes, pulling out my white bear instead. Bastian and Bay shifted as well, but Bastian chose his bear this time. I loved that he matched me.

We slowed our run once we arrived at the village, and everyone still looked a little uneasy as we passed through. The children ran to their mothers, and a few of the men shifted to their tiger form and began pacing back and forth.

Abraham approached them as the three of us stayed back, giving everyone their space. They seem to be discussing us, so we waited for Abe to give us the all clear. Suddenly, a thought occurred to me. *I had never seen a female tiger.*

"Abey? Why aren't there female tigers?"

He trotted back over to us before responding.

"*Females don't get their tiger unless they've found their mate. We have a few female tigers in the streak right now, but we're mostly composed of males and kids. Not a whole lot of females.*"

"*I see many children here,*" I countered. "*Why do you not have many females?*"

"*We lost most of our women to Blackwood, and we get many male loners that travel through the lands. They find us, and they just decide to stay. It's a rule though that you must wait for your mate to marry, and our women won't even feel their tiger until they've found them. It unlocks all at once for tigers, which leads most to living as a human unless they grew up with shifters. Some of the younger men here were survivors from the attack like I was. We sort of banded together when we had to flee, and since I came to the throne I've been accepting kids we find in need of help. There are some families here as well, with kids of their own though too. We tend to have many twins and triplets, which add to their numbers."*

I was saddened by that. *Many here were orphans.*

"They have new families here, and we make sure they are all safe and happy. Tigers tend to have mostly male children, so females are kind of rare, which makes finding your mate even harder."

I watched as Bastian and Bay laid on their stomachs, trying to interact with the kids around them. They seemed curious about us and many of the adults kept looking back to Abraham and then me.

"They seem to trust you, Abey."

He chuffed.

"Not all apparently."

I sighed, letting my brother stew in silence. It didn't take long for the kids to make their way to Bastian and Bay, and I smiled watching them play. They let the kids pet their heads, and Bay barked playfully before rolling over to her back. She looked back at the kids, with her tongue hanging out of her mouth, making them giggle at what she was doing. The adults watching seemed to relax some. *Baby steps, I guess.*

"We should continue on, Shanely. It's a small hike in the woods from here," Abey said, and I nodded.

Abraham made his way to Bay. He nudged her in the side gently before turning back towards the trail. Bastian shifted into his wolf, and the kids all gasped excitedly.

"Show off," I teased him.

He wagged his tail, lolling his tongue at me before strutting by. I made my way over and could still hear the kids talking to the adults about how cool it was that he had two animals. Jealousy filled my chest.

"Your day is coming, my love," Bastian said to me. *"Won't be much longer before you can go back and forth too."*

I sighed, wondering if that day would ever come. I've known about shifters for four years now, and she still seemed locked away. It was depressing that I couldn't make it work. I didn't understand what I was doing wrong. Bastian always seemed to help me, but it was just to a point. I stayed silent as we walked through the woods. Bastian just remained quietly at my side, letting me stew in peace.

Abraham shifted back in front of a small hut that nearly blended in with the woods around it. If you weren't paying attention, you might actually miss it.

"This is it," Abraham said, motioning us to the door. He knocked as we all waited patiently at the bottom steps.

We heard movement behind the door, which opened to reveal an older man wearing a flannel shirt and jeans. His hair was white, and his eyes matched Abraham's. He wasn't a large man, but he looked strong for his age.

"How ya doing, John?" Abe asked.

John smiled before suddenly noticing me standing at his stoop. He stepped back in shock like he had seen a ghost or something. My brow rose slightly, when he scared the living daylights out of me by rushing towards me. I jumped when he hugged me tightly, and I stood there rigid as could be, trying to figure out what was going on.

"I prayed this day would come! Is it really you, Shanely?"

Shanely

My eyes grew wide as I pulled back from him. "You know who I am?"

"Well, I haven't seen you since you were... What a year old maybe, but I'd never forget those eyes! My oh my, you look *just* like your mother. Come in, come in, all of you!"

I felt like the air had been ripped from my lungs as the older man led us inside his home, and we all piled in on his couch. It was a small room but cozy and comfortable. It had a fire pit in the center of the room with the couch off to one side and a lounge chair on the other. No electronics that I could see. It was very primitive and simple. *Yet, I didn't recognize any of it.* A sadness washed over me, and I turned to take in the rest of the room instead.

I remembered Abraham said most turned down the offer to upgrade their homes, choosing to stick closer to their roots. *This shifter was definitely one of those people,* I thought as I looked around. The kitchen was on the other side of the room, which was mostly just a basin and a counter top, but there was some electricity here because he had a refrigerator and a small air conditioning unit running. Furs of different animals filled the room, and everything smelled of some sort of spice. I couldn't quite put my finger on it though.

"*Smells like mint,*" Bastian voice entered my head.

I smiled softly. "*Get out of my head, you.*"

He smirked. "*Never.*"

"So you finally found her?" John said, breaking the silence.

"I did, John, but it was purely by accident, let me tell you. Why didn't you tell me about her?" Abraham asked.

"I was sworn to secrecy. I promised your parents I would never say anything. It was the only way to ensure your safety and hers," John replied.

"John... I need answers. I'm lost, and I know Shanely deserves them too. Are my parents not my real parents?" Abraham asked cautiously. I felt for him because his whole world was unraveling. Everything he knew as truth were lies, and it wasn't easy to hear. *Even if it was done with the best of intentions.*

John looked saddened now. "No Abe, they are not. They adopted you when you were very young. They had a still born around the same time that you were born, so everyone just assumed you were theirs. Your real mother, Mercedes, lived here with me on streak lands for a short while, and I kept her hidden from the streak. Only your parents knew she was here."

"My mother came here?" I sat up, desperate for answers.

He nodded. "Abe's adoptive father and I found Mercedes unconscious in the woods one day, with you in a basket. This was before the outer walls were built, mind you, but she was just a mess. Bloody and beaten, but the baby seemed alright. You were so tiny, Shanely. I'll never forget carrying you home that day. Your smile..." John smiled fondly at the memory, but then it fell, and I clung to my mate. "When Mercedes came to, all she could remember was getting stalked by a large white tiger. She thought he was hunting her to kill her but was very wrong when he managed to catch her."

Abraham looked forlorn, while my world spun. *My mother...* I couldn't even find the right words to say. I shook my head, not sure I could even hear anymore. Abe reached over and held my hand as John continued on.

"That tiger hunted her into the back section of our territory. She said she wouldn't shift and leave you, so it didn't take long for him to catch her. The way she always looked over her shoulder made me wonder if she was checking for more than the tiger who attacked her, but she never told us what she was doing in our land. She had caught his scent though, and swore she'd never forget it. With the help of your parents Abe, we carefully brought something from each of the males in our streak at the time, but she never recognized them. The only thing we could figure is that she crossed paths with a loner. Abe's parents thought it would be best if Mercedes stayed with me for the time being. We kept her a secret, making sure she could recover, and that you'd stay safe. Do you know why she was in this area and not with her pack?"

"We think it was because of me, John. My mother's mate was a bear shifter, and her father would have never approved. It was kept secret from everyone. When I found my real father a few years ago, he said the day she disappeared their mate bond just went away. It didn't break like when one dies, but it was just *gone*. He smelled her blood on her father later on that day. Alpha wolves have the ability to see pregnancy from the very beginning you see and..." I hesitated for a moment, but Bastian held my other hand. *I didn't know if I could say the rest.*

"What we think happened was that her dad found out she was pregnant," Bastian answered for me. "He was brutal, so we suspect he found out about Shanely somehow and banished her mother. Shanely was attacked some years back and was injected with something similar to make our bond and her animals dormant. Much like the collars you have, Abraham. I *think* Mercedes's dad gave her the injection or maybe a collar to make her invisible essentially. We believe she fled to keep her dad from killing Shanely."

Abraham looked distraught, gripping the sides of his head as he said, "I will never forgive myself for putting a collar on you two."

Bay leaned against his arm saying, "Abe, those were different times. You didn't know anything about us nor did we trust one another yet."

I squeezed his hand in reassurance before turning back to John. "Did you ever see a weird black necklace around her? Or anything to indicate she couldn't shift?"

"She always wore a black bracelet. I just assumed it was special or something because she never wanted to take it off. That would make more sense that she couldn't shift the night the tiger found her. I always wondered why she didn't try to fight it or carry you in her mouth as a wolf."

I felt sick to my stomach. *My grandfather banished her from her pack and her mate while she was pregnant, and then took the only thing she had to protect herself away,* I thought as my blood boiled. *It led to Abraham sitting next to me on the couch.*

"So my real mother lived here with you then, John?" Abraham asked, struggling to keep his voice steady.

"Mercedes needed to heal, and her shifter abilities weren't kicking in like they should have. She said she needed to keep moving but would never tell us why. It was unusual to even see a shifter with a baby and no mate around, but I always assumed maybe he died, and I never wanted to ask her about it. She seemed in pain, and I just thought it was because she missed him. Because she took so long to recover she stayed with us longer than she wanted too. We soon discovered she was carrying another, and that's when things got complicated."

Bastian wrapped his arm around my waist, and I held my breath, knowing it was about to get a lot worse.

"We started having issues with the wolf pack in the east. They wanted our land and had the numbers to do some major damage. I always assumed your mother came from their pack, but I kept her secret from everyone regardless. Your adoptive mother, Maggie, was carrying a tiger cub as well, and I think the stress of Blackwood affected her young. It was a very long 4 months for them both. Maggie and Mercedes gave birth about a week apart from one another. Mercedes gave birth to you right here in this hut, Abraham, and right away we could smell you were a tiger. There was no indication you were a mixer, and as panicked as Mercedes was about the whole situation, she was relieved you didn't smell like Shanely did. Maggie and Arthur had a still born about a week later."

I bit my lower lip, struggling to keep my emotions at bay. *How awful?* I thought, feeling terrible for what Maggie and Arthur endured. *No one should ever experience losing a child...*

"Mercedes was as distraught as Maggie was," John went on, slumping in his chair as the memories flashed by. "One night she started rambling that it wasn't safe to be anywhere near her, and that it was bad enough to be carrying Shanely around, let alone Abraham. She was terrified what would happen if someone else found her with two kids that didn't smell like a wolf. She was afraid someone would discover you both were mixers. It was truly an awful conversation, and I've never felt so sad and useless in my entire life. We didn't know what to do honestly, and the streak was becoming more and more hateful towards wolves because of Blackwood. The next morning she was gone, and she had taken you with her, Shanely."

"And Abe?" Bay asked.

John sighed. "For Abraham's safety, she gave him up. She left a note next to his cot, asking if Maggie would raise him as her own. No one would know the difference since Abe never smelled like a wolf. She left me a letter to deliver, but that was it. I never saw her again. I delivered you to Maggie and Arthur along with the note, and they pretended you were the child they lost. They kept the name Mercedes gave you to honor the gift she gave to them. Then Blackwood did what they did a few years later, and you know the rest, Abe."

We sat back speechless, processing everything John just said. *My mother went through way more than we ever realized*, I thought as my brain felt a muddled mess. My father needs to know everything, but I had no idea how he'd feel about Abraham. *This wasn't fair...* Angry blazed inside, and my wolf snarled in agreement. I was just pissed. Absolutely livid over everything, and it just felt so overwhelming.

"She left me?" Abraham muttered quietly.

"She left me with humans, Abraham. I grew up in the foster system. At least you got to stay among your kind," I spat sarcastically.

Abey's eyes narrowed to mine, and I knew I messed up. "Like *that* was any better. I watched my parents die at an early age at the hands of wolves."

I winced. "I'm sorry, Abey. I'm angry, but I shouldn't have taken it out on you."

His eyes softened. "It's okay. We were both abandoned in different ways."

John leaned forward as his brow furrowed. "No. Don't you get it? She *saved* you. The both of you. Don't you ever hate that women for leaving you behind or with humans. She was troubled and scared for you both, and I believe she did everything she could to keep you both safe."

My lips pursed together in a tight line, knowing I deserved every bit of John's scolding. I felt pretty dumb at the moment. I was being selfish about what I missed out on, when I really didn't stop to think about what she gave up. I made my way back to my family, whereas she never did.

"John? You said she left a letter for you to deliver?" Bay asked.

He nodded. "It was addressed to someone named Willow. I dropped it off at the post office after I took Abraham to Maggie. It was the least I could do for her."

"Willow McCoy was Shanely's grandmother. That was Mercedes's mom," Bastian added.

"Maybe that's how your grandmother knew to leave you the cabin? Mercedes must have given her information about you," Bay chimed in.

"McCoy, you say. I remember the Alpha back then. He wasn't a nice, man. I wish I knew more, kiddo," he muttered, lost in thought.

Bastian rubbed my neck, and I sighed. I shuddered, thinking about where I'd be if John had never delivered the letter. I had way more knowledge than I did before, and I never felt more lost or emotional than I did right now. All the answers in the world still wouldn't bring her back, and that was what I really wanted. All my mother went through because my grandfather couldn't see past his prejudice and hate.

"How did my grandfather get that bracelet? My pack didn't even know of the drug I got when I was attacked. I highly doubt they had a stack of bracelets or collars somewhere," I finally spoke.

"Where did you get your collars from Abe?" Bastian asked.

He shifted a bit, seemingly uncomfortable with the question. "My grandparents had figured out a way to subdue shifters with the help of my father when he was young. My parents had tried to replicate the collars, and it was meant to be used against the Blackwood pack, but we were attacked before they ever made enough of a supply. It's partially why they died. My father had touched the stuff accidentally and was blocked from his shifting abilities. When I took the castle back, I found their private room. I've made them for my own use until a few years ago. We don't sell them often, but they bring in a lot of money for my streak, and we needed it at the time. I don't just sell them to just anyone though. It's only allowed to go to very few shifters, and even then I make collars not bracelets or drugs."

"Unless someone was able to replicate it? Either way, my grandfather had one," I chimed in.

"It's something we need to look into. Makes me wonder what truly happened to your mother then," Bastian said.

I turned to him. "You think she's still alive?"

"Well, we really don't know, do we? If she never got the bracelet off then maybe she's just been living as a human all this time. Just something to think about," Bastian commented as he rubbed my shoulder.

Abraham and I looked at each other. *What if our Mom was still alive? What if we could find her and bring her home?* Hope filled my heart, and I gave my brother a soft smile.

"Tell me about yourself, Shanely," John said, interrupting my thoughts. "I've always wondered about you over the years. I can still smell a mixer within you."

"I'm a wolf and bear shifter" I answered. "I can shift into my bear, but my wolf seems locked for now. We haven't figured out why yet. She's there, we both can feel her, but not enough to summon her. My dad said my protective instincts unlocked my bear, but we have no idea what's needed for my wolf. It's made our bond somewhat incomplete. I also have a four year old back at Abey's castle named Aerith."

"Wow," John said, smacking the armrest of his chair. "If it's alright with you I'd love to meet her! What's her animal?"

"I'd love that, and actually…" I said with a sigh, "she doesn't have one."

"Doesn't have one? A daughter of a strong wolf and a mixer would have an animal to shift into," John replied in disbelief.

I looked to Bastian, and he gave me a small nod. "Bastian isn't Aerith's biological father," I replied. "I fled an abusive relationship with her biological father, and he was a human. We keep seeing traits of a wolf, but so far no one can scent anything or even sense a shifter in her."

John rubbed his chin thinking. "I didn't mean to bring up a sore subject. I'm sorry that happened to you, but I wouldn't worry about her just yet. It might just be her human side blocking all that."

"What do you mean?" Bastian asked, leaning forward.

"I've been around a long time, boy. There were stories of shifters mating with humans. Their touch snapped the bond in place, and that was that. Their children had the potential to be either shifter or human. Always one or the other, but if they were shifters then their human side masked them completely. Aerith may just be undetectable."

I leaned against Bastian, unsure how much more information I could process right now.

"I thought that was against the law," I asked.

"It is *now*, but it wasn't always. The humans that mated with a shifter just kept their secret, but when the vast majority of humans found out about us, and the Division was created, the law came about making it a dangerous thing. It was extremely rare, so it quickly became forgotten as everyone separated," John replied as he stretched in his chair.

"How do you know about it then? Those wars were so long ago," Bay questioned.

"It happened in my family. The information has been passed along from parent to child to help preserve our family's history. I have books dating very far back that shows my family line. I've just never shared them with anyone."

"So Aerith is basically what? A shield?" I asked.

"Essentially, although shields mean something different when it comes to your abilities. Her human side covers her entirely, and you will never know what she is. She won't be detectable with the pack bonds when she officially joins either."

"So she could have a wolf or bear, Shanely," Bastian said to me, and I nodded. I was in information overload now, and I didn't know how to feel about everything we've learned today.

"We appreciate you talking to us, John. I wish you would have told me sooner though," Abraham said.

"I know, and I wish I could have too. But I swore to both of your mothers that I would never say anything, especially after everything with Blackwood. Then you started your vendetta against them, and I knew without Shanely, you'd never believe me anyways," John replied with a chuckle.

"Yeah, I guess that's true. I never would have believed it if I hadn't heard her voice in my head. I wonder why I never took after any of my mother's side though."

"Not all mixed shifters take both sides. It's usually one or the other. Your biological dad must of been a strong tiger for him to win out against an alpha wolf," John countered.

Abraham nodded, and I stood to hug John. "Thank you for meeting us today, and for saving my mother and I. We wouldn't be here without you, it seems."

"I only wish I could have done more. I'm sorry you grew up alone, child. I wish you could have just stayed here with me, but I'm sure your mother had her reasons," he replied, hugging me harder.

"It's okay. I found my family in the end," I answered, looking back at everyone. Bastian reached for me, and I left John to return to my mate's arms.

"We better get back and explain all this to everyone," Bay said, breaking up the silence.

"Thank you again, John," Abraham said, shaking his hand.

"Anything for my King and Queen," he replied, winking at Bay.

She blushed and hugged him. "I think you're my new favorite tiger, John."

"Hey! What about me?" Abraham asked.

"Oh, shush. You know I love you!"

"Alright, let's go, you two," I said, pushing them out the doors. We all waved goodbye before heading back to the castle.

Shanely

Aunt Cassia and Uncle Cain were already at the castle waiting for us along with my father. I ran right to dad, not realizing how much I missed them all. My father and Cain were kind with Abraham, but the tension in the room was thick. Abey hung back somewhat, giving everyone space to reconnect. Bay forcefully pulled him into the group after a little while, but he was stiff as a board the whole time. I couldn't help but chuckle.

Now was the moment of truth though. I had to explain what we found out about our mother, and the longer I looked at my dad, the more I honestly didn't want to say anything at all. *Call me a coward, but he was going to be so hurt with everything we had to tell him,* I thought to myself. *And there was nothing I could do to make it better for him.*

We followed Abraham to the dining room where we could all sit together. He stepped aside and had Darryl tell the cooks to start making something for us to eat. It was getting late in the day, and I was starving. We skipped lunch, spending our afternoon with John, and I barely ate anything this morning. Poor Octavia lost her entire breakfast too, so I knew I wasn't the only one hungry.

Abraham and I stood at the end together and went back and forth retelling the story that John told us. With every word spoken, my father looked more and more distraught. I hated being the one to tell him what happened to her, and Abey had a look of shame on his face.

"She was here then? Another shifter attacked her? She... She had another child!? She had you?" Dad asked, looking downright emotional. I could see the tears in his eyes, and Abraham stiffened next to me.

"She was here for awhile at least. She left with Shanely, leaving me behind," Abraham answered quietly.

"It sounds like she had one of the collars we had on before, but in a bracelet form. It made her unable to shift and muted your bond. She left Abraham in the safety of the streak because he doesn't smell like a mixer. He smells solely of a tiger. We think she was forced to leave the pack," I added.

"Jack," my father snarled.

Cain leaned on the table. "You think her father was the one to make her run?"

"I'd bet my life on it. I always thought he was cruel to Mercedes. When she disappeared, I couldn't scent her anywhere, but our bond was never broken. I've never felt that before. It was like she just disappeared. I bet he found out about the two of us."

"I think our grandfather cuffed her and rendered her invisible to everyone when he discovered she was pregnant with Shanely. I think he drove her away from the pack and threatened to kill her or even you if she ever returned," Abraham chimed in.

"You told me you scented her on Jack. Right before..." Bastian's voice trailed off. We had never told this story to my aunt or uncle before.

My dad eyes flared at Bastian. "I could smell her on him. It smelled like blood. My bear snapped, and I lost control. I never had a chance to even ask him anything."

"You killed Jack, didn't you?" Cain asked.

My father simply nodded, and Cain blew out a deep breath.

"Good lord, that was a massacre," he muttered.

"Good riddance, I'd say," Abraham muttered. My father studied him for a moment, and Abraham shifted nervously on his feet.

"Wouldn't he feel the bond completely snap though if she died then? Does this mean Mercedes is still alive?" Cassia asked, hope in her eyes.

"I don't know. She left me when I was a baby. She never came back to get me either, which makes me feel like something happened to her after she left the tiger's land," I replied.

"Look, I don't think we will ever get the answers we all want or need, but this changes everything. At least for me it does. I want to propose an alliance with your pack and clan. I may not know you all very well right now, but you're Shanely's family, and I'd be honored if you'd be mine too," Abraham said firmly, and I gripped his hand in mine, giving him a knowing smile.

My father stood and walked around the table to him. "Son, any child of my mate's is a child of mine. I would never want to take the place of the father you knew, but I would love to be apart of your life now."

Abraham's eyes widened in surprised, but he shook my dad's hand. "The man who raised me was a good man, and I don't want to forget him, but you are my connection to my mother. You're her mate, and that means something to me. I'd love to get to know you too, sir."

"I hope you know that if I had found your mother all those years ago with the both of you, I would have dragged her back home and raised you both myself. I would have never turned her away over what happened, or you for that matter, Abraham," Dad replied, and the relief in Abraham's eyes was almost too much to bear. I wiped the unshed tears from my eyes before I couldn't stop them.

Bay wrapped her arms around Abey as he replied, "I appreciate that, sir. You would have been my one and only father if you had found us, and I like the idea of getting to know my real Dad now."

Dad pulled Abraham into a hug. "Who knew I'd end up with three children instead of one?"

Caleb chimed in, lightening the mood. "Yeah well... I'm still your favorite, right?"

We laughed hard at that, and it gave my dad and brother a moment to get their composure. I stuck my tongue out to Caleb, watching my family grow once more.

Uncle Cain asked, "Well, I'm sure Bay will want to join your streak and live here then?"

She nodded and then looked to her brothers. "Are you guys going to be okay if I move here?"

Bastian cocked his head to the side. "Bay, you *deserve* to be happy. You're a wolf, so you will still be connected to the pack."

"We will still visit all the time, Bay," Cade chimed in.

"It's not that far of a drive, and we will all be connected in our bonds too," Elijah countered. "We just want you happy."

I hugged Bay hard. "You better keep my brother in line."

She laughed. "Deal, but only if you continue to do the same for mine. We'll be changing things around here and at the club. I want to make sure Patrick doesn't arrest anymore of our people. Between all of us, I think we can work around him and keep you away from him."

"Good. You'll take good care of her?" I asked Abraham.

"With my life sis, although I should probably tell her dad all this too. When will I get to meet him or your mother, Bay?"

"You won't," Bastian answered. "Anything you want to say to him, you can say to the three of us. Bay has no father anymore, and don't ever let that man come near her."

Abraham frowned. "This is a conversation I'd like to have in private before you leave."

Bastian nodded as Cade and Elijah agreed.

"Go. Take care of what you need to. I'll catch up with my dad," I told Bastian. He gave me a kiss as he and his brothers followed Abey into the other room. Bay watched them walk away, and thankfully my aunt walked over to help distract her.

I walked over and hugged my father. "I have missed you, Dad."

"And I you. I was so worried about you being here, especially with Aerith. I wanted nothing more than to throttle the Tiger King. Funny how things work out."

"That is true, although I don't think we will have anymore surprises!" I said with a laugh.

"Oh, I hope not. Not sure how much more I can take," he mumbled under his breath.

"Do you think she's alive, Dad?" I whispered, and his face fell.

"I don't know, kiddo. If that bracelet made her invisible then maybe? But if she died somehow with that in her system, I really don't know if I'd be able to sense it. It just feels like she's missing."

I nodded and leaned against him. Caleb joined us as we talked about my time here with Abraham. I explained the snake shifter we met, and how I managed to break through the collar's effects to get to my bear. Dad said he always figured my abilities would be stronger than most.

"I've always wondered where that medicine Derek gave you came from. Now I know he made a deal with the tigers. They probably have no idea what it was used for," Uncle Cain said, running his hand through his hair.

"Abey said he doesn't sell his collars to just anyone though. Honestly so much gets sold through distributors. Bay and I had to sit in on some of his dealings. The collars are very expensive and sold to specific people for certain tasks, but someone could be taking Abey's collars and recreating them. It's not diluted into a drug nor are there any bracelets. Someone else has to be making them too," I countered.

"But you managed to break it?" Aunt Cassia asked curiously.

I nodded. "I did. I was violently ill afterwards and had to really focus to shift back to my human form, but during my fight I felt great."

"Shanely, at some point we need to discuss a few things. I think it's time you learned some history on wolf shifters," she replied, giving me a solemn look.

"Let's get everyone settled back at home first. We can discuss it all back on pack lands," Cain said as Bastian opened the door. My Fenrir boys seemed nonchalant, but Abey looked downright pissed, which was understandable seeing how he was learning about Liam for the first time.

My uncle and father made their alliance with Abraham an official thing as Aerith came bounding into the room, with Henry right on her tail. He was in his tiger form but shifted quickly when he realized there was an audience. She went right to my dad and wanted up. She talked non-stop about her adventures here with the tigers, when we finally broke it to her that Abraham was her real uncle. She squealed and insisted that it meant she was part tiger too. We just giggled, and let her go. No harm in her believing that if it made her happy, but I think it struck a cord with Abraham and Henry as they looked borderline emotional when she said that.

I hugged my new brother goodbye at the end of everything. I looked between Abey and Caleb, and I smiled. We barely looked anything alike yet we all shared this connection to each other. Even though Caleb and Abraham were only each related to me, they seemed to accept one another as brothers. The three of us belonged to Daniel and Mercedes, and now each other.

Abey kissed my forehead before handing me off to Bastian. I passed Bay as she left her own brothers to go to her mate. I waved goodbye, and let my mate finally take me home.

Shanely

I didn't realize how badly I missed home until we pulled into our drive. Bastian and I spent our nights in our favorite spot once we returned home from Abraham's. He curled up in his wolf form with me on our porch. Aerith ran and played, and we picked up right where we left off. Like nothing ever happened. We spent a week at home just as a family, playing board games and ordering a tremendous amount of pizza. Aerith and I made our famous homemade chocolate chip cookies for the boys, and it just felt good to be home again. But today, everyone was coming over. All to talk to me about things I didn't want to know.

Elijah and Cade were in the kitchen with Aerith making dinner, and I was forced to sit at the table and listen. Apparently, the wolves and the bears both had a prophecy that was kept closely guarded in the clan and pack of a white shifter. White was a rare color in the shifter community, and while the bears have had two White Bears in the past, the wolves have never had a White Wolf before. Now they all think it's one and the same person, me.

"Both prophecies foretell a great change happening," Uncle Thomas said firmly. "The two white bears that came into existence led the clans into war. I don't know how this come about, Shanely, but you will lead us in war. I'm sure of it."

My face fell. *I didn't want to lead a war. I didn't want to lead anyone...*

"For the pack, the white wolf is more so a sign of change in leadership," Cain continued, giving me a sympathetic look. "That wolf is destined to become the Head Alpha over all other wolves."

"Like in the entire world, Shanely," Cassia continued, and I frowned.

"A large Summit would be held immediately after the call of the White Wolf, and everyone would be required to attend. There the White Wolf would ascend to the throne to lead the packs as one."

"We think it's you," Cassia went on. "You already have rare abilities, and with Bastian seeing a white wolf in his dreams, we think when you finally shift, it will be the foretold prophecy coming to light."

"This applies to you as well, Bastian. The mate of the White Wolf would become Alpha as well, and they would lead together," Cain said, and I sighed heavily.

"We didn't want to tell you and add more pressure to your plate. You united the bear clan with the wolf pack, thwarting the possibility of war amongst ourselves and with the Division. It seemed to stop your warnings, but with Patrick returning home, we felt the need to share what we've learned and suspect," Cassia said, giving me a reassuring smile.

"We had hoped to know for sure before we said anything, but no one expected you to take so long to shift into your wolf. We're pretty confident it's you, Shanely. Especially now since you've just made alliances with the strongest tiger streak in our area. Three completely different shifter kinds, all connected together because of you," Cain said confidently.

I stared ahead at the table, unable to really focus in on their words. This was beginning to become a little overwhelming, and my head spun.

"You're breaking all our laws with shifters, and I'm starting to wonder if you'll be breaking the laws we have with the Division too. It would explain your warnings with Patrick," Uncle Thomas countered, "and provide the war I expect to happen from our prophecy."

I don't need to lead a war or be Queen over everyone, I thought to myself. *I just needed my family.* That was enough for me especially after so long of having no one. *They had to be wrong. This prophecy wasn't me, it couldn't be me.*

"Shanely? I know this is a lot to process, but we wouldn't have brought this to your attention if we weren't sure," Aunt Cassie said as she squeezed my hand.

I pulled my hand away and rubbed my face. *This wasn't what I wanted. I didn't ask to be the White Wolf. I just wanted to be me,* I thought as anxiety rolled in my stomach. Suddenly, my phone went off on the counter. Elijah picked it up for me. "It says Unknown. Do you want me to answer?"

"Please."

He answered my phone and stepped into the living room away from us.

"Look, I don't want to rule the wolves, okay? I'm not even a full wolf yet! I can't shift! I would think the White Wolf would be strong enough to shift," I blurted as everything just became too much. I just wanted this to be over.

"It's okay, my love. You don't have to accept anything. If you don't want to be the White Wolf then you don't have to," Bastian replied reassuringly.

"Bastian, she can't just give it up," Cain countered, giving him a pointed look.

"Actually, she can. We don't have to report we found the White Wolf. She can stay a secret within our pack like she's already been."

"I'm sorry, but that's not how this works, guys. The moment Shanely unlocks her wolf and shifts, the *entire* wolf population will sense her power awakening. They may not know where she is or who it is, but they *will* know," Cain said, and my shoulders sank.

Bastian frowned and leaned back in his chair. "Alright, well then the Summit gets called immediately, and after that Shanely decides how to run things. Correct? So if she decides to let the packs stay the same then everyone has to agree, right?" Bastian questioned, crossing his arms.

I turned to my mate, giving him a grateful smile. He was trying so hard to give me what I wanted, but I couldn't help but wonder if I was being selfish. *Would it be for the best for everyone if I didn't become the White Wolf? Or just best for me?*

"Technically, yes. She decides how the packs run, and she takes the seat for the Shifter Council as the Wolf representative, even though it really isn't a thing anymore. If Shanely decides to not change anything then everyone would have to follow her command, but when major issues come up it will go to Shanely and you. There's no going around that. You two will always be the deciding vote there, but no matter what she decides for the world packs, she will have to take control as Alpha of our pack. That isn't negotiable,"

Cain pointed out.

Guilt ate me up inside. My family looked a mix of disappointment and worry, and I felt like I was letting them all down. I set my head down on the table. *I was letting them down...*

"Look nothing has happened yet, but I do want you to think about something, Shanely. If you have a chance to do some actual good for the world of shifters, could you honestly live with yourselves if you walked away? Would you be okay with the problems we live with right now because nothing will change without you? You started something when you merged us with the bear clan and again with the tiger streak. Would you say everyone is happier and better off after the merger or before?" Aunt Cassia asked firmly.

"We're better now," I said quietly, sitting back up. My shoulders sunk as I knew the point she was making.

"I agree with you. Our lives are happier and safer now that we were able to make amends. Don't all shifters deserve the peace we have?"

"Cassia..." I groaned. *She was laying this guilt trip on thick.*

"No, Shanely, you need to hear this. Look, I will support however you decide to handle this White Wolf business, but you need to think about it from all angles. Otherwise, you will have regrets, and you have to be able to live with the decisions you two make. I know this is a lot on your plate, but remember you never have to do anything alone. Your mother would be so proud of you and what you've accomplished already. Just don't decide until you've really thought about everything," she replied as she squeezed my hand again.

"We all love you, kiddo. We're so proud of you and Bastian. We just wanted to give you all the information, and like your aunt said, we will support you guys always," Dad chimed in as Cain and Thomas nodded in agreement.

I gave them all a smile, even though it felt fake. I so appreciated everything they've done, and their words meant the world to me, but the weight of it all was too much. *I barely keep myself out of trouble!* I thought. *How was I going to fix the shifter world?*

Elijah walked back in and handed me my phone. "There was no one there."

I gave him an odd look. "Huh. I've been getting a lot of calls lately, and no one speaks when I answer. I think my phone is messing up or something."

"Have Elijah take a look at it later today, Baby Girl. See if he can figure out what's wrong," Cade said, and I gave him a smile. He threw a pile garlic and onion in the frying pan then, and the smell permeated the room. *Thank the lord, he was making his famous spaghetti.*

"Let's just table this for now. We can figure it all out when the time comes, okay?" Bastian said, and everyone nodded in agreement.

"Well can we help with dinner then? What do you guys have going on?" Cain asked as he walked in the kitchen. He, Cade, and Elijah started talking about trucks then, and I gave Bastian a kiss. He smiled back at me, knowing exactly what I meant by that. *I'd be so lost without this man.*

My dad and I played with Aerith, while the guys finished making the best pot of spaghetti and meatballs I have ever had in my life. It was the one and only dish Cade could make, but he was fantastic at it. He said there was a secret ingredient, but he refused to tell any of us what it was. We ate until it hurt before my family said their goodbyes. I laid Aerith down for bed and rejoined the triplets outside. We all were quiet though, lost in thought of everything we heard today. They tried to be cheerful about it, but I could tell they were all just as worried as I was. I just didn't know which way they were all leaning. *Did they want me to be the White Wolf or were they afraid of it?* Bastian seemed to push for what I wanted, but he never said what he wanted. I mean this was affecting him too. I'd rule alongside him. He'd be Alpha of the wolves as well. *Would he even want something like that?*

We all went to bed early, but I couldn't sleep. My mind raced all night, but around 3 am, I finally passed out.

* * *

A few weeks passed by since our time spent at Abraham's and my conversation with my family. I got a call from Bay a few days ago, and they're doing well. She said she was having a hard time adjusting to their way of life, but it will take time, I suppose. The streak's entire life just got turned upside down, so not everyone was used to having a Wolf Queen. Bay said it was weird being a Queen anyways and felt out of place. The streak just weren't super welcoming yet, but I told Bay to hang in there and start small. Make friends with some of the younger ladies there, and things should start to get better. It's what I did at least, and she thanked me. I ended the call telling them that we'd visit soon and that Aerith was missing her favorite tiger Henry. Abraham said he'd pass that message along.

Elijah checked my phone out, but nothing was wrong with it. I didn't realize Elijah was a wizard with electronics, but he took the whole phone apart and put it back together for me. He was baffled as to why I couldn't hear the other person. Whoever was calling kept it up, and it was getting annoying dealing with all the spam calls. Bastian finally had enough and bought me another phone with an entirely new number. He and his brothers were convinced it was Patrick just trying to harass me, and that thought freaked me out. I hadn't thought about that, but now I couldn't get it out of my mind.

We got word that Patrick and the other officers officially shut down the human fight rings in Diablo. Multiple people were arrested, but thankfully they've never caught wind of the shifter ring. Abraham began taking phones away at the door, ensuring no one would be allowed to post anything about the location. The fight ring bounces between locations now, and the officers have been none the wiser. I was just glad that Patrick wasn't going to be hanging around anymore.

Today was finally Friday, and we were all heading to the street fair tonight. Everyone was going to be there, and Aerith was so looking forward to it. There was no hiding it from her. She saw the posters hanging around Main Street when we came home from Abraham's, and with so many people around, I figured we should be able to blend in fairly well. *Plus, she deserved some fun! We all did really.*

I wore a floral flowy dress and pinned my hair back to stay out of my face. Just simple really. Bastian, however, about brought me to my knees when he put on his ripped work jeans and boots. His blue t-shirt fit snugly against his too perfect body, and it was hard to take my eyes off him. He smirked at me every time he caught me staring, but I couldn't help it. *He was freaking hot!* Bastian swatted my butt as I passed by, causing me to giggle.

"Lookin' good, Mrs. Fenrir!"

I laughed, wrapping my arms around him then. "You don't look too bad yourself, *Mr. Fenrir.*"

"What about me!?" Aerith hollered as I went in to kiss Bastian.

She wore a little yellow sun dress with capri leggings and her dark brown cowboy boots. Her hair was bouncy curly like mine, and she looked absolutely adorable! To top everything off, she wore the biggest smile ever, making the whole outfit perfect.

"You are cute as a button!" Bastian said as he scooped her up.

She giggled. "Daddy!"

"C'mon, my two gorgeous girls! We've got a fair to get to!"

"Don't forget us now!" Cade bellowed as he and Elijah bolted into the room.

They both looked good too, I thought to myself. Elijah wore a blue flannel with his jeans and boots, and Cade was the only one crazy enough to be wearing a hoodie with shorts.

"It's hot, Cade. How can you wear that?" I asked, looping my arms around his extended arm.

He scoffed at me. "It's going to be cold later. You all make fun of me now, but mark my words I'll be all nice and warm, while you freeze during the fireworks."

I just shook my head, and we all headed towards Bastian's black truck. Aerith kept pushing past Elijah and Cade, trying to see past them like she'd be able to see the fair from home. They let her move them all around to see better. Main Street was abuzz with people once we came into town. There was already a band playing in the street's center with people dancing and drinking. Plenty of carnival rides were set up down the street in the big open lot, and to Aerith's joy, bouncy houses we're set up near the Den.

We finally managed to find parking kind of far away, but that was okay. The night was warm, and it felt good to walk. Elijah grabbed Aerith's arms and launched her in the air, causing her to squeal. He threw her on his shoulders with a big grin on his face, and she giggled as she clung to his head. Bastian extended his arm to me, and I immediately grabbed it, while Cade walked on my other side. It didn't take long for Aerith to feel more comfortable being that high on her uncle's shoulders, and soon had let go entirely, trusting him not to drop her.

"Where to first, my girls?" Bastian asked as we made it to Main Street.

"The rides, Daddy! To the rides!" she bellowed loudly, and I giggled.

"Well you heard her, Elijah. To the rides!" Bastian shouted, laughing as we pushed our way through the crowd. We took Aerith to all the rides she could go on before we made our way to the games. My sides hurt from laughing as I watched Cade *attempt* to throw the ring around the bottle. *Who knew that would be so difficult for the big scary wolf?* His arrogant smirk stayed on his face the moment he finally won, and I rolled my eyes. Aerith sure enjoyed the stuffed bear though. *I hadn't had this much fun in a long time,* I thought as I watched my family have fun. A few girls from our pack walked up, begging Cade and Elijah to ride the coaster with them. Elijah had bashfully turned a little red, while Cade ate up the attention, the big goofball. We waved bye as they went on without us.

Bastian laughed. "I am *so* glad I found my perfect mate so I don't have to be in those situations anymore."

I playfully slapped him. "That's all I'm good for then? Just to get you out of uncomfortable situations?"

He gave me a playful smile before his eyes flashed gold. "That's not all you're good at."

My breath caught in my chest, and he grinned, knowing he got to me. *Oh, two can play at this game,* I thought, giving him a seductive smile. "Easy there, Alpha. I don't think you could handle me right now. Maybe later though when we're alone."

Bastian stepped closer, not stopping until he was completely pressed against me. I could feel his breath on my neck as he whispered, "Is that a promise, mate?"

My heart raced, and I grinned wide. "Yes, Daddy."

His hooded eyes looked down at me, widening slightly before he pursed his lips together and stepped back. "Shanely, you...."

Aerith shrieked, pulling us from our moment together. She bolted across the lot shouting, "Fun house! Fun house! Fun house!"

Bastian sighed aggressively as I giggled. "Probably for the best, my love."

"My God, Shanely. You've never called me that before, and now I can't get it out of my head. You just had to be incredibly sexy when I can't do anything about it, didn't you?"

"Ha! Now you know how I feel when you do stuff like that to me, but I promise, it won't be the last time I say it," I whispered.

"Hurry, Mommy!"

Bastian and I caught up to our over-excited little girl. I asked, "You want to do this one?"

She bounced on her feet just like Cade. "Yes, this one! Can I do it myself, Mommy? I'm a big girl now!"

Bastian looked back at the ride. "I don't know, Aerith. You may need help."

"It's made for smaller children. There isn't anything in there she couldn't do herself. You are welcome to still take her, but if you decide to let her go, she will be okay," the carnie said to us with a smile. I looked down at Aerith, who's little lip was jutted out, begging to us to let her go.

"Well, are you sure about this ride? You still haven't gone on..."

I turned only to plow right into Patrick. Beer coated my arm, and he quickly grabbed my arm to steady me.

"Hello there, Shanely! It's nice to finally see you," he replied as I wiped away the liquid. "Sorry about the dress. It looks good on you though."

Great. Now I was going to reek of alcohol, I thought to myself.

Bastian gently pulled me back to his side. "Aerith, go ahead and run in the Fun House, while we talk to..."

She bolted before Bastian had even finished his sentence.

"Hi, Aerith!" Patrick hollered, and Bastian stepped in front to block his view.

"What can we do for you, Officer?"

Patrick shrugged. "Nothing, man. I'm off duty and hanging with a new buddy... Who has disappeared apparently. You know I'm not a bad guy, right? I bet if you gave me a chance we'd even be friends."

Bastian snorted. "You're not exactly a nice guy either, especially with Shanely."

Patrick rolled his eyes. "Oh, don't be dramatic. You know I'd never hurt you, right hun?"

His eyes bore into mine, but I refused to answer. I just wanted him to go away, so I could go back to my peaceful little bubble with my mate.

"You can stop with the pet names, Patrick. You make her uncomfortable. You make *everyone* uncomfortable. I can't believe I actually have to say this out loud again, but Shanely is my wife. Whatever fixation you have with her *needs* to stop," Bastian demanded rather calmly.

My eyes widened in surprise. Bastian was speaking rather civil with Patrick right now. Usually his temper got the better of him or his wolf would loose control, making it harder to keep a shift from happening, but he was cool, calm, and collected today. I looked back to the Fun House and waited patiently for Aerith to pop out of the ride, frowning slightly. I was positive there was no way I could have missed her, but she was taking a long time. *Maybe one of us should have gone?*

"Just because you're married now doesn't mean you'll stay married," Patrick snapped back before chugging his beer. My eyes widened at Patrick's response, knowing this was going south real fast.

"That's it! I've had just about enough..." Bastian snarled, when Cade flew in between them. Elijah was behind me in seconds and pulled me aside.

"Whoa, Bastian... Just let it go. Not here, brother," Cade said quietly, but Bastian shook with anger. I felt his wolf rise to the surface and prayed he kept control.

Patrick just smirked. "As always, it's a pleasure to see you all. I better get back to my group. See you around, Beautiful."

I glared at Patrick but stayed behind Elijah. My eyes went to the exit of the Fun House, and I let out a deep breath. Aerith had finally bounded out the door, but she was holding someone's hand. Someone I didn't recognize and panic rose within me. They jumped off the platform together before he gave her a hug and waved goodbye. I couldn't get a good look at his face, and I let go of Elijah. The man turned slightly as fear gripped my heart. *Who was that guy?* My bear heighten my sight, and I watched him twist around a Dodge Ram hat on his head, but his face was just out of view. I didn't understand why my stomach rolled in anxiety, but I had to move. I had to get to Aerith. Goosebumps trailed my arm as a bad feeling washed over me.

"What's wrong, Shanely? Is it another warning? I can hear your heart race," Bastian questioned, but I didn't answer. My feet were already moving towards Aerith, leaving the boys behind. A large family stumbled into me, and I quickly scurried around them. By the time I got passed them, Aerith was by herself and moving towards us again with a big smile on her face.

"Mommy! That was so much fun. Can I go again?"

"Aerith, who was that man?"

She shrugged. "He's my new friend. He went through the Fun House with me!"

Bastian was right behind me now. "What's going on?"

"Can I go on the Fun House again, Daddy?"

Bastian eyed me. "Shanely, what's wrong?"

I was puzzled. "I don't know, Bastian. She came out with someone I didn't recognize."

"What in the world did Patrick want?" Elijah asked in a hushed voice.

Bastian picked Aerith up and gave her a hug. He scented her quickly before shrugging at me.

"I don't know. He seemed like he just wanted to push Bastian's buttons," I replied a little shakily.

"I can't smell anything but human on her hand," he replied.

"I don't know, Baby Girl. He seemed to me like he was making a claim on you," Cade replied, and Elijah shook his head in agreement.

"Did your friend give you his name?" I asked, more concerned with my daughter at the moment.

"No, he said he was a nice cop and wanted to help me go through. He was funny, Mommy! You'd like him!"

"A cop?" I questioned, giving Bastian a look of alarm.

"Might just be someone from the station. I wouldn't worry, my love. She seems fine."

I looked around still feeling uneasy. I couldn't shake it though. I felt close to a panic attack, but Bastian was right. Aerith was fine. *Maybe it was just another off-duty cop?* I thought to myself. Something didn't seem right though.

"Let's just get something to eat and go back to our pack. I'd like…" Bastian said, when my eyes suddenly rolled to the back of my head, and I dropped to the ground.

Shanely

"I wouldn't try that if I were you."

"What did you do?" I asked, my voice shaking with rage. I wanted to shift and rip him to shreds. I wanted Bastian, and the last thing I wanted to do was cry in front of this vile man. I held tight on my emotions, refusing to give in to them.

"I already told you. War was coming to the pack for awhile now. No one trusts you freaks, but I made a deal with my dad. You'll be safe with me, baby," Patrick said, smiling at me.

My eyes widened as my heart started to thunder in my chest. "Where's my mate and family?!"

I stood up angrily, and he stalked towards me, breaking my confidence just a bit. I was no longer a powerful shifter, but a pregnant human, and he stood way taller than me.

"As I told you last night, you better forget about your so called mate. He isn't coming, Shanely. You belong to me now, and you better start acting like it or I'll never let you see your daughter again. Got it?"

My eyes widened as fear gripped my heart. Patrick smirked, knowing he had won.

"You have Aerith? How?" I said, my voice starting to crack. I took a few deep breaths, trying to get myself to stay calm.

He walked back to the chair, collapsing in it like it was just a regular Tuesday or something. He stretched back, giving me a smile before saying, "I do have her, and it really wasn't that hard, Shanie Baby. I just had to run that shifter off the road, and it was easy to dispose of him and snatch her. You can still keep her, but only if you get it through your head that you will be my wife. That Aerith and this kid here will be mine, and you will never say Bastian's name again. Otherwise, I'll give the kid to the Division to do God knows what with her, seeing how she's half-human."

I slowly sat down on the bed as my reality came crashing down around me. What was I to do? I was human again with this bracelet on, and I couldn't feel my mate bond anymore. I had no idea if Bastian was okay or not, my daughter was in the hands of a psychopath, and I was helpless yet again. Patrick slapped his knees before hopping up on his feet. He yanked out a pair of scissors from his back pocket.

"Now let's take care of a few things, alright? I think you'd look amazing with shorter hair, don't you think? Although, I'm not sure why you changed the color."

I glared at him. "You want to cut my hair? Why?!"

He snarled. "Because Bastian loved your hair long. Now sit still or I'll shave you bald instead."

I snapped back to reality as Elijah held me against his chest. Cade was close to help block anyone from seeing me completely passed out, and Bastian looked almost as haggard as I was. He seemed to be coming out of his trance too and loosened his death grip on Aerith. I took a few deep breaths as Elijah rubbed my back.

"You guys okay?" Elijah asked.

I nodded slowly. I couldn't stop thinking about this new warning as I gently reached up to touch my hair.

"I don't pass out when she has them, but my entire vision is gone, and all I can see is what she's seeing. I can't move or anything," Bastian replied before reaching for me. I buried my face in his chest and gave myself a moment to calm down. My vision blurred with unshed tears, and I forced myself to take deep breath after deep breath.

"Was it bad?" Cade asked quietly.

"She was taken by Patrick, who helped start a war between the Division and shifters. He cut her hair in this one," he replied.

"What in the world for?" Elijah demanded.

"Because I love it long. He told her I wasn't coming back," Bastian said quietly.

"Is Mommy okay?" Aerith asked. Her voice was uneasy, and I forced myself away from Bastian.

"Of course, I am! Mommy just got a little overheated, baby. Maybe we can go get some food and take a break from all the rides. Do you mind if we leave for a bit, Aerith?"

She reached for me, nodding her head yes. I held her close and started making my way to the food stalls. The boys stayed near, and Bastian's hand soon found it's way to my back. I gave him a grateful smile because I needed his touch. It soothed me, and I forced myself not to think about my warnings. Today was supposed to be about fun, and I was sick of everything always getting ruined by problems. My aunt's words hung heavy on my mind as we walked through the fair though. *Maybe if I became the White Wolf I could prevent this war with the Division and by extension keep the problems with Patrick from ever happening?* It was a sobering thought.

I forced everything out of my mind, refusing to let it ruin our night. There was nothing I could do about it anyways, and it wasn't set in stone. I let Aerith choose all the food she wanted to try, and soon Cade and Elijah both had their arms loaded with everything from walking tacos to elephant ears and fried Twinkies. Bastian set Aerith up on his shoulders as we made our way past the Den to where the live music was playing. The afternoon's heat was starting to cool off, and Cade was right. It was getting a little chilly, but I wasn't about to admit that to him. I spotted my family sitting somewhat near the band, and a large crowd had already formed on the dance floor. *It looked like fun,* I thought as we approached. Bastian set Aerith down next to Uncle Cain and pulled me right onto the floor. He knew exactly what I needed, a distraction.

We danced until I couldn't stop laughing as Bastian twirled me repeatedly around the floor. Then my mate spun me around to my father. He bowed and extended his hand out to me, which I readily accepted, and he continued to spin me around the floor. I looked back to my mate, but he was already preoccupied dancing with Aerith. I grinned, watching him teach her the steps. Us girls took turns dancing with all the fellas, and my warning suddenly became the last thing on my mind.

Abraham and Bay finally showed up, fashionably late, with a plethora of enforcers. At least they all looked normal and acted like a group of friends rather than a security force, but I noticed the tigers wore special contacts so no one could see their orange eyes. It was weird, seeing them with normal looking eyes though. I didn't like it.

Abraham showed up all the guys on the floor, when he and Bay started dancing. He flipped her around the floor with ease, and my jaw dropped watching them. *He was an incredible dancer!*

Emma was the only issue I had left to deal with. She was not having a good time, and if looks could kill, I'd be dead already. She thankfully stayed in her little corner with some of the other girls from our pack, but I wish she'd just get over her disdain for me. It was just another complication I didn't need right now.

Caleb led me off the floor back towards our group, when Aerith bounded up to me. "Mommy! I have to go, like bad!"

She squirmed where she stood, and I looked over to the other side of the make-shift dance floor and found port-a-potties in the corner. I held out my hand to her. "Let's go, baby! Caleb, can you tell Bastian we're going right over there?"

He followed to where I was pointing and nodded as he made his way to my husband. Bastian looked to be in a serious conversation with Cain, but that was something I wasn't going to focus on. *At least not anymore tonight.*

We hurried over to the port-a-potties, when she put her hand up stopping me from entering in with her. "I can do it, Mommy!"

I retreated with a smile. "Okay. I'll be here if you need me."

She quickly ran inside and slammed the door closed. I chuckled and rocked back and forth in my boots. *She's had so much independence lately,* I thought to myself, feeling a little saddened by that. I wish she needed me still. A shadow fell upon me, and I turned around to see Emma standing there looking annoyed.

"I'm surprised you're allowed to walk this far alone," Emma snidely commented.

I gave her a weak smile. "It's just to the bathrooms, and I can see everyone.

Can you really blame them though? I mean after everything your father did to me, and the fact that he's still alive puts everyone on edge."

She bristled at my comment. "So you want him dead too?"

"Wouldn't you? I mean doesn't shifter law dictate that justice should be served? Micheal paid the ultimate price, and he was just the middle man."

God, she pissed me off. I don't understand why she ever stayed in this pack. Derek's family followed him to Liam's pack, so why did she stay?

She eyes glowed gold, and she stomped her foot at me. "This whole thing with you is just wrong! You have ruined *everything* for shifters. We aren't meant to mix with others like this! I mean this county fair is crawling with tigers even, and it's not surprising they're here with you. You shouldn't even exist yet here you are mated to an incredibly strong Alpha! I am so sick of hearing about how amazing you are. You are nothing but a whore, not fit to be Alpha Female! Everyone knows Bastian isn't even the father to your kid! All because you couldn't keep your legs closed, he's stuck with a kid that isn't his! You don't deserve him, Shanely, and I wish you would just leave..."

The door creaked open, and Aerith stepped out. "Mommy?"

My eyes widened. I could have just died right there. Aerith's face has fallen, and I watched tears fill her eyes. Suddenly, my animals roared within, and I turned back to the wolf who had finally crossed the line. She took it too far tonight, and I was no longer in the mood to be understanding or kind.

"I want you gone from pack land's *tonight*."

She snarled. "You are not my Alpha! I don't have to listen to you! And the brat needed to know someday... Might as well be today."

Something snapped inside me, and my wolf pushed her way to the front. I understood the struggle the boys always felt holding back a shift, but my wolf *silenced* my bear, snarling as she pulled my Alpha power from my core.

"Emma Ferguson, you are hereby banished from the McCoy pack," I snapped, my power striking her in the chest. "You do not belong with us, and I sever the pack bond with you."

She gasped for air, clutching her chest as the pack bond severed between us. Emma dropped to the floor, looking completely stunned as I picked Aerith up.

"Be gone by the time we get back home, understand?"

I made my way back through the crowds, my wolf growling in my head to go back and chew her out again. I just wanted my mate. I wanted to fix this with my little girl, but I didn't know how. I didn't know if anything would ever be right again.

"There you are!" Bastian cried out as he rushed towards us. "You scared me half to death. We all sensed an Alpha nearby, and I couldn't find you! I wanna leave in case it's a rogue..."

"No need," I said, relaxing the group. "Everyone calm down! It was just me. No rogue came through tonight."

I ignored my family's surprise and set my daughter down on the chair. The look on her face was breaking my heart. I pulled her chin to look at me, and a tear fell down her cheek.

"Mommy... Is he not my Daddy?"

Everyone froze as she pointed to Bastian and devastation filled my mate's face. His eyes searched mine, looking distraught, and my heart broke a little further

"Aerith, why would you ask...." my aunt started to ask, but I interrupted.

"Aerith, this man..." I replied as I pulled Bastian to our level, "this is your Daddy. He took care of you when you were safe in Mommy's tummy, and he's taken care of you ever since then. For every fever, every boo-boo, every misstep, *he's* been there. There is no one else, baby. This is your Dad, I promise you. That women was just trying to ruin our night because she doesn't like Mommy very much."

"I want to go home," she whispered softly, and my shoulders fell.

Bastian opened his arms then and said, "Aerith, come here."

She didn't move at first, but Bastian waited patiently. *God, this just destroyed her whole little world*, I thought as my heart ached.

"Please, baby girl?" Bastian whispered.

She abruptly fell into his arms, and I could hear her soft cries against his shoulder. He gave me a look as he started to rub her back.

"I'm going to talk to Aerith. I'll be back, and you can tell me what happened."

I nodded and watched him take Aerith back on the dance floor. He gently rocked her to the music, whispering something in her ear. My poor baby never lifted her head. She just had her entire world turned upside down. I clenched my fists in anger, wishing I did more to Emma than just banish her.

"What woman was Aerith talking about?" Abraham asked sternly. Everyone looked as visibly angry as was I.

"Emma," I replied as Cade and Elijah groaned.

"What did she say?" Aunt Cassia asked.

"I can't even feel her bond anymore. What in the world happened over there?" Uncle Cain asked, pushing closer to me.

I gritted my teeth. "You won't feel her bond anymore because I banished her from the pack. I sent her to get her things and told her never to return. As for Aerith, Emma was making a number of snide comments about me ruining this pack and Bastian. She said he was now stuck raising a whore's child because I couldn't keep my legs closed. That was the part Aerith overheard."

"Are you kidding me?! God, she was always annoying, but this is a whole new low for her! Why would she do that to Aerith or to Shanely!?" Cade asked, throwing his hands up.

"You're kidding? Emma hates Shanely ever since she mated with Bastian. How in the world did she know about Aerith though?" Elijah countered.

"What I want to know is how did you banish her? You're not Alpha of McCoy pack yet. I can still feel it within me," my uncle asked, and everyone turned to look at me.

"Don't look at me! I have no idea! I was just pissed and pulled from that power I discovered years ago. It seemed to work."

"You are something else, Shanely," Caleb muttered.

Bastian walked back up to us, interrupting the group's conversation. "I think we're ready to go find a spot for the fireworks now."

I turned, my eyes roaming over the two, but Aerith was laying her head on his shoulder, with her arms around his neck. She wouldn't look at me, but she managed to stop crying.

Bastian softened when our eyes met. "She's doing okay, but when I find Emma…"

"You heard?"

He nodded. "Every word. My hearing's gotten better."

Bastian reached for me, and we led the whole group towards the field, where the fireworks were being shown. No one else felt like dancing anymore after that. The field was crowded already as everyone was trying to find the best place to see the show. We laid down our blankets, not caring about finding the perfect spot, and cuddled together ready to watch them start.

Aerith stayed in Bastian's lap and lost her bouncing joy she had earlier today. I didn't know how to heal this wound for her. I didn't know what to do, and the solemn looks on everyone's face told me they thought the same thing. My family got her to smile a few times, but it never stayed, and she refused to leave Bastian's lap.

The sun was long gone, and it started to feel cold out. Cade rolled his eyes at me as I stuck out my tongue, pretending I was fine. He laughed hard even though we could all see goosebumps forming on my arms. Bastian rubbed my arms with his free hand, and I snuggled into him. Cade caved when he saw Aerith shiver, and without missing a beat, he flipped off his hoodie and threw it over her. She was swimming in it but looked so cute curled up on Bastian like that. I leaned against his other shoulder and stayed as close as I possibly could. Elijah laid down on his back behind me and pressed his legs up against me, giving me something to lean against.

"Thanks, Elijah," I said as I settled my weight against his shins.

"Anytime," he responded.

Aerith sat forward when the fireworks started. *I had to give it to the town. They were really spectacular this year.* So many bright colors, and the designs were absolutely amazing, but I couldn't help but watch my daughter. She smiled big during the show, and I let go the breath I'd be holding. I sent my mate a mind-link to check on him, but he didn't have much to say. Sadness trickled in through the bond, and I didn't push him on it. I think it broke his heart that she knows the truth now. He just wants her to see nothing has changed, and he will always love her, but Emma didn't just hurt Aerith tonight. She hurt Bastian too.

Before long, Aerith's head started to drop. Her little eyes started to roll, desperately needing to close but trying to stay awake to continue watching the show. Bastian rubbed her back gently, and soon, she was out like a light. He nudged me then, and I gave him a nod.

"Need us to come home?" Elijah asked, and I gave him a soft smile.

"Nah, stay," I answered. "We'll be good to head home early. Besides, I think we'd upset a few girls if we stole you for the rest of the night."

I grinned as I motioned to the group of girls, smiling at the Fenrir brothers. Cade rolled his eyes. "They're not our mates and family comes first. If you need us to help you get home, we'll go."

I kissed his cheek. "Thank you, but Bastian is scary enough in the daylight, let alone at night. We'll be fine."

We said our goodbyes and left our group to enjoy the show. My body shivered when I felt someone's gaze on me, and I turned to find Patrick watching me. He grinned, and I narrowed my eyes to the man he was talking to. I recognized the gray hoodie and Dodge Ram hat. *The man that came out of the Fun House with Aerith earlier this afternoon was friends with Patrick?* I thought to myself.

Patrick waved, and his friend turned. I couldn't make out his face from the dark shadows that fell from his hood, and the two watched us leave the field. His buddy waved, and my stomach twisted in knots. Frowning, I turned around and gripped Bastian's hand a little harder for comfort. I was glad I remembered to shut our link off. I didn't want to worry my mate for nothing.

He had enough on his plate already.

Shanely

The next week was pretty uneventful. Emma wisely listened to my threat and left pack lands. Caleb told me she's still around town and comes into the Den quite often to complain and drink. I don't know where she's staying but I honestly couldn't care less! Aerith has gotten back to her old self, but she's not quite the same. Instead of being carefree and silly, she seems quiet and reserved in moments. Like she's got to think and process everything now, and I wonder if she's questioning everything in her little mind, wondering if it was somehow a lie or not. Her moods come and go, and I worry for her. Bastian thinks we should just give her some time. Emma rocked her whole world, and he wanted to just show her that nothing has changed. Emma was just a bad lady who said horrible things. I followed his lead, telling myself everyday how lucky I am to have found a mate like Bastian.

Saturday rolled around, and I wanted to get Aerith out of the house. We *needed* to get out of the house. Aerith was just struggling today, and it felt like we had a teenager in the house already. She seemed the most content in the woods, so I thought maybe a change of scenery would help. Bastian had already left early to complete the new trainee's course with Cade and Elijah, and I dug my phone out of my pocket and dialed my mate's number.

"I don't really want you guys going alone," Bastian said over the phone after I told him my idea of picking wild berries.

"We'll be on pack lands far away from people. We should be okay, my love," I countered.

"Yeah, but it's a haul to the patch. You're out of range for the link to work, and it's still the woods. We have regular animals to watch out for as well," he replied back, and I sighed. *I wasn't really thinking of that.*

"Mommy, can we go?" Aerith begged at my feet.

"I've got to do something with her today, Bastian," I whispered. "She's going crazy inside the cabin."

Bastian sighed, when I heard another voice in the background. "Hang on a minute, Shanely."

I could hear him talking to someone, while my four year old bounced on her feet excitedly. Finally, he came back to the phone. "Okay, so I can't make it today, but Brody volunteered to escort you guys. You okay with that?"

"I mean we'd always prefer you, but I'm good with Brody too. He's great with Aerith, and if it gets us out of the house today then I'll take it."

"Thank you, Shanely. I feel better knowing you have an extra wolf with you in case you run into another bear or something. Brody's the best of the new recruits at scenting critters in the woods, so he can help if your senses turn off for some reason."

"No, I get it. I was just thinking we're still on pack lands, so we should be away from Patrick, but I wasn't thinking of the rest. She's just bored with everything and having a hard time today. We're totally okay with going with Brody though," I replied sweetly.

I felt him kiss my cheek through the bond, and I smiled.

"You're getting better at that, ya know?" I said as he laughed.

"I plan to be good enough it's just second nature with us. I want to be able to kiss you anytime I want even if I'm not with you."

"I love you, Bastian," I said to him.

"I love you too. The boys and I are heading into the woods now, but I'll send Brody to the lodge. He will wait for you two there. I can meet up with you guys around noon today, and then I'm all yours. Have fun today, girls."

He disconnected the phone, and I told Aerith the good news. She jumped up and down and bolted to change her clothes again. I giggled, watching her worry about her outfit even though the jeans and t-shirt she wore was perfectly okay to wear in the first place. She settled on her overalls with a different t-shirt and her cowboy boots.

"Ready?" I asked.

"Yup!" Aerith replied as she marched herself to the back door. I smiled, looking down at my own outfit. I wore a simple flannel shirt and tank top with jeans, but if I had a pair of overalls, I would totally go change just to match her today. I slipped my own boots on, and we headed down the trail. It didn't take long for us to make it to the lodge as it was a beautiful day. The sun peeked through gaps in the canopy of trees overhead, and we enjoyed a gorgeous breeze as we walked over to Brody. He was still in his training clothes and playing on his phone when he saw us approach.

Brody hopped off the steps, shoving his phone back in his pocket as he shouted, "One enforcer at your service, my princess!"

He bowed to Aerith, and she giggled. "Brody! I'm not a princess!"

He gasped. "What? That's not what I was told! I have very important instructions to protect a princess today, so it must be you!"

Her eyes went wide, and she looked at me for confirmation. I winked at her, and her grin grew wider. *Oh, Brody could not have come at a better time!* I thought smiling. She grabbed her basket that Brody had set aside for us and hollered, "Well, come on then!"

We laughed, and I grabbed my basket as well. He reached over and grabbed his baseball hat on the railing and put it on backward, and we chased after her.

"Thank you, Brody! You have no idea how much that meant to her and me. She's been off ever since the fair, and I've just been worried about her. You are a great distraction for her today," I exclaimed, nudging him playfully as we walked.

"No problem, Shanely. I heard about what happened that night. No one should ever hurt a child like that, and I, well all of the new enforcers really, have soft spot for her. We'd do anything for a smile."

"Well, she loves you guys! She always wants to go to work with Daddy," I replied as I laughed.

He laughed too. "Yeah, she's a mini Bastian for sure! Keeps us all in line, but she also got me out of training today, so I've gotta give her that!"

"Bastian making ya work for that job, is he?"

"You have no idea," he grunted. "But I'm glad. It makes me a better shifter and hunter. I love knowing I get to protect the pack like this."

"Well, you do an amazing job. All of you guys do," I replied.

Brody playfully bowed at me/ "Thank you, ma'am."

I rolled my eyes before gently pushing him. "Oh, none of this ma'am stuff! I'm barely older than you!"

He laughed back at me, but Aerith interrupted us before he could respond. "Hurry up guys! I'm ready to pick berries!"

We followed her as the path winded around and went slightly down the hill. I internally groaned, thinking we were going to have to go back up this hill on our way back.

"Where exactly does this trail lead too?" I asked.

"I think this is near the border on the right side. If I'm right, and please don't tell your mate I'm guessing here, but I think the main road is somewhere over there," he said, pointing to the right of us. "If you take this trail past the berry patch, it eventually leads you to our main river. If you cross the road there, you will hit the bear's land."

"Oh, is this the same river that everyone goes fishing near the lodge?"

He nodded his head. "Yup! It just goes and goes. No one in the pack really goes down that far though. I think the last time was when everyone was looking for you."

"Ah yeah, that was a fun day, wasn't it? I was clear over on Dead Man's Hollow. Which Bastian still hasn't told me why they call it that."

Brody shrugged. "From what I've heard the Fenrir brothers have gotten into all kinds of mischief growing up. They're older than us, so we never ran in the same group of friends, but the stories about them..." he whistled. "*Everyone* talks about them. Dead Man's Hollow is a steep mountain side, which you are very familiar with I'm sure, but it tends to be full of rouges, loners, or those who have been banished. Most of the time, shifters run there when they need to hide so bounty hunters frequent the area as well. It's usually blocked off in the winter too because of how much snow that side seems to get. The wind is just awful, and they get freak storms year round. It's really dangerous over there."

"And how do you know all that?" I asked curiously.

He smirked. "I told you everyone talks about the Fenrir brother's stories. From what I remember, they got stuck up there one winter. They were goofing off when a small avalanche pushed them into a cave. It took them a few days to get out and back home. Cain was about to send out a search party, when they finally entered the lodge like nothing happened. *Everyone* on pack lands could hear Alpha scolding them that day, but they've been all over that mountain side. I think it's why the three of them took that mountain instead of the others."

"He's never told me any of that! For the love...That man better not ever go back!"

Brody laughed at me. "Bastian isn't one to tell many stories about himself."

I laughed now, shaking my head. "I guess that's true. Most of what I've heard has come from Ryder, Johnny, or Cade honestly."

"Yeah, Ryder's pretty easy going with all of us. The only time we see him get super serious is when we're scenting in the woods. Then it's all work and no play."

"I can imagine after what happened to him when he was a new recruit. How are Cade and Elijah? Are they serious like Bastian or more goofy?"

"Uh... Neither one is as strict as Bastian, but they're all tough in their own ways. Cade tends to laugh and goof off once we get through the drills, but never before, whereas Elijah tends to start drilling us with questions right away. What would we do in this situation kind of thing. They all have an area of expertise, so we tend to bounce through the instructors, but we're almost done with the main course. We will be able to do patrols on our own then. Right now, I'm the only one in the group that is shadowing the patrols, but the next step will be running my own."

"Well, good for you! Do you have anymore training then after that?"

"We can specialize in something if we want to enhance a specific skill. The more training you complete, the better jobs you're allowed to apply for, or this would be the point if we wanted to transfer to the World's Council security. That's a whole different program."

"Huh? So that's just made up of volunteers then?"

We ducked under a fallen branch as he responded, "Yeah, basically. The World Council makes it out like it's a privilege to live and work for them, but it's a glorified title really, and it kind of sucks because you only get to see your family once a year during the Summit."

"Huh. I don't think I'd like that. What's the Summit like? We've skipped the last few ones because of Aerith and me being a mixer and all," I asked him, and he shrugged.

"It can be fun, but you also have everyone always looking over your shoulder. The World Council is strict and harsh in moments. Usually everyone goes to try and find their mate though."

"Mommy! I see the berries!" Aerith shrieked as she ran ahead out of sight. We hurried along the path to catch up to her. He smiled before bolting forward, scooping her up playfully and setting her back on her feet. I smiled and watched them play. *I really liked Brody,* I thought to myself. *He reminded me a lot of Cade, and I hoped he decided to stay with our pack and not leave for the World Council.*

This section of woods was really nice, and I was enjoying exploring the area around here. I really never come down this far except once in a while to pick berries for everyone, but sometimes the other women get to it before I do. Then I miss it all together. It was pretty with the leaves changing colors. It had many rocks to climb up on, and I'm sure you could see a decent chunk of the woods from way up there. *Not that I would ever voluntarily climb up there though,* I thought as I strained my neck to look towards the top. This area was full of berry bushes and fruit trees, which the pack took advantage of every year. A lot of the women here loved to can and make jams and jellies for all of us during the winter. *Hopefully this will be a decent start for them this year.*

Aerith and Brody immediately went to town filling up our baskets, and I walked past the large rock on my left for the other bushes to choose from. *Might as well try to get a variety while we're here,* I thought to myself. It honestly didn't take us long to fill up our baskets, and I realized there was still a lot of fruit to pick. *We need to come out and get more so it doesn't all just rot here.* I looked back to the path then. *It would be a slow walk back home* with our baskets as heavy as they were.

We passed by the large rocks on our right, when Brody turned around to face us. Aerith was already struggling with her basket, and Brody smiled down at her.

"Here, let me carry these. A princess should not carry..."

Suddenly, he shouted in pain, and his body twisted violently before he dropped to the ground. Brody gasped for air and groaned in pain, while Aerith screamed, dropping her basket as someone yanked on her arm. Berries spilled all over the trail as my eyes settled on a man I thought I'd *never* see again.

Peter.

My eyes widened as we stared at one another. He looked different, thinner, and his face was scruffy, even though he never wanted to grow a beard back home. Peter looked deranged as he glared at Brody lying on the ground. My body trembled as I recognized the gray hoodie and Dodge Ram hat. *He was the man with Aerith in the Fun House,* I thought as that night flashed before my eyes. The shadows faded away to reveal his face. My heart stopped. *He was the man Patrick was with.*

They knew one another.

Peter held a small black device and two darts stuck out of Brody's back. *Peter had tazed him,* I realized. Brody slowly tried to stand when Peter put his taser away and pulled out a gun. He aimed it at Brody, my heart stopped when he shot him twice. Aerith's eyes grew wide, and she tried to push his hand off her arm, but he had a death grip on her. Her arm turned colors all while I shook with fear. I couldn't move... couldn't breath as I stared at the man who plagued my nightmares for years. *This couldn't be real,* I thought to myself. But Brody fell on the ground and didn't get up.

"Calm down. He's not dead," Peter snarled, and a sob escaped my lips.

His chest was *moving,* I thought, feeling a wave of relief wash over me. But something was still wrong because Brody didn't get up again.

I glared at Peter. "What did you do to him?!"

"He's fine. Just sleeping off a nasty headache. Surprised to see me, my love? It may have taken me some time, but I found you *just* like I always promised I would."

Peter put his tranq away and pulled out his real gun. I *vividly* remembered that gun. I had seen it a thousand times back when I lived with him. He pointed his gun at me, and I felt like I was reliving my past all over again.

"*This* Shanely, is going to cost you. You have no idea what I've been through nor do you realize the trouble you caused me in finding you. I got suspended because I wouldn't stop looking for you."

All the ways he used to make me feel came flooding back, and I shook slightly, falling right back down to my cowardly ways. My eyes drifted to my daughter, who tugged on her arm. *He had Aerith...* Suddenly, my bear pushed to the surface, and I snarled, "What you've been through? What about what I went through because of you!? Let her go, Peter."

"I saved you, you ungrateful whore!" he bellowed right back. The gun waving in front of me.

"Only to beat me every chance you got! You nearly killed me on more than one occasion, Peter! Why do you think I ran away from you in the first place? It was because I never wanted to see your face again! I HATE YOU!"

My bear was pleased, but I immediately regretted opening my mouth. He gritted his teeth as he turned the gun towards Brody. My breath caught in my throat and panic flashed around my eyes before I could stop it. I took a step towards Brody instinctively, and Peter grinned at me.

"You care for this one, don't you? But he's not the one that's taken what's mine, is he? No... This one isn't Bastian."

He knew about Bastian? Of course, he did, I growled in my head. *He was with Patrick. God, that vile man must have told Peter everything!* I kept my mouth shut, trying to figure out what to do now. *If I shifted, he could shoot anyone of us, and then I may never be able to save my daughter.* I didn't know how to fight against someone with a gun, and I gritted my teeth in anger. *What was I to do? I've never trained for something like this!*

"Listen up, Shanely, because I am only going to say this *once*. You are coming back home with me. I've been in these God forsaken mountains long enough, and I'm ready to go home. If you be a good girl I won't punish you as severely as you deserve, but if you refuse, then I'll shoot this one here and now. Now get over here or I'm leaving with my daughter alone."

My heart stopped. *How? How did he know?*

Peter laughed abruptly, startling me from my thoughts. "I'm not as dumb as you think I am, Shanely. I've been wondering ever since I laid eyes on this little girl. I was planning on grabbing you a long time ago, but then this little one changed everything. I didn't realize how much being a Dad would excite me. I even got to go on a ride with my little girl. Didn't we, sweetie?" he asked, gently shaky Aerith. She cried softly, and he just grinned. "I almost took her after the fun house that night, but I decided to wait. I wanted the whole family back together again after all."

"We are not your family, Peter. You came all this way for nothing," I replied, when it finally dawned on me how stupid I had really been. "It was you, wasn't it? The unknown number calling me. That's been you the whole time?"

He smirked. "I needed to confirm I was on your trail. Then it was simply that I just missed your voice and wanted to hear it again. That is until that stupid *prick* kept answering the phone instead! I can't believe you left me like that, Shanely. You are *my girl.* Mine!"

Peter pulled Aerith towards me, and I scrambled to come up with a plan. I *needed* help. *Maybe I could just stall him long enough for Brody to wake up?* I didn't know what to do, but maybe keeping him talking was the way to go. I couldn't fight him, and he still had Aerith. I didn't know how I was going to get her away from him without hurting her in the process. He seemed more unhinged than usual.

"How did you even find me, Peter?" I stammered, desperate to stall him. Anything to give Brody a chance to come to our rescue. No one else would even notice what was happening until it was too late.

Peter stopped and eyed Brody for a moment before answering. "It took me a bit to find your trail, I'll admit, especially since you ditched your phone. After I searched the city and every lead I had led to a dead end, I finally convinced my friends from the station to put up a missing persons report. You packing your stuff before you ran away made it *very* difficult to get that done, but once I got it, I was able to use more resources from the station to locate you. Your phone records led me right to that lawyer. After some... persuasion, he finally caved to his involvement with you. I've been up here for the last few months, waiting for the perfect moment to take back what was mine to begin with. She..." he said, shaking Aerith's arm, "changed everything though. I was just going to grab you quietly and head back for home to get my suspension lifted, but then you disappeared for a while, and no one knew where you went. That cop around town helped me fill in some of the blanks though. He doesn't seem too thrilled with your husband either, did you realize that?"

Peter chuckled to himself then, and my stomach churned. "That cop gave me what information I needed to know on the whole lot of you, but even he didn't know where you took off to. He was the one who told me you had a daughter. From the first time I saw her, I *knew* that she was mine, and I am *not* happy you kept her from me. Now let's move before this one comes to, otherwise I'll have to shoot him again but with this gun instead."

Tears filled my eyes as I tried to figure out what to do. Brody didn't so much as move a muscle and panic filled my chest. I didn't want to risk Aerith or Brody, but I couldn't see a way out. I never wanted to put my daughter in the path of her real father, and now I needed to figure out a way to get her away. I had to get *her* far, far away.

"I won't go back to Indiana with you Peter, and neither will *my* daughter. You should just go back to that awful town because there is nothing here for you," I said firmly, and his eyes flashed with rage.

"You're such a selfish brat! You used to be grateful for everything I ever did for you, but now you're acting like some rich hussy! I saved you remember?!"

Suddenly, my temper flared, and I took a step towards him. His eyes widened. "Grateful? Grateful for what? For all the times you beat me? All the abuse and emotional damage you gave me? I don't belong to you, Peter! You may have given me a roof over my head, but it *wasn't* a home. You are a monster, and I don't ever want you near me or my kid. This is your last chance to walk away with your life. You have no idea what you're even dealing with."

Peter's face twisted in rage, and he stalked towards me. "I said we're leaving. As in *all* of us, right now. Unless you want me to just shoot you and take my daughter. I bet I could find a more grateful whore to take your place and be her mother because I'll be honest, Shanely, ever since I found *her*, I've realized I want to be a Dad more than I need you."

Bile rose in my throat, and I tried to steady my breathing. *It wasn't working... I wasn't scaring him into leaving,* I thought as my fear and anxiety grew. All the hurt and damage he caused me flashed before my eyes, and now the man I tried so hard to escape from has my daughter in his hands. *I'm not enough to save her,* I thought, and my wolf shrunk beneath my skin. *I needed Bastian, but all she had here was me.* Peter was always unpredictable, but now he seemed even more unglued. I looked down to my daughter and made my decision.

"Please let me carry her though," I said softly. "She's frightened."

Peter studied me for a moment before that vile smile appeared on his lips. "That's a good girl. You always were smart, Shanely, but let me spell it out for you in case you don't seem to fully get the situation you're in. You so much as take one step in the wrong direction, I will shoot you and take her instead. I want to be a Dad more than I need you. Do you understand? *You* can be replaced, and I won't hesitate to leave you at the first sign of trouble. Now that I have her, I'm not letting go, and even if you manage to survive the bullet, you will never see her again. Understand?"

Tears threatened to fall as I nodded my head. I extended my arms out for Aerith, but he yanked her back.

"I need to hear it out loud, Shanely. Who do you belong to?"

"You," I gritted through my teeth.

"And who is Aerith's father?"

I glared at him through unshed tears. "You are."

"Will you be a good girl and do as you're told?"

"Yes, Peter. I won't ever run away again, now please let me have our daughter."

He seemed satisfied with my answer and let Aerith go. Her arm was bruised already, and I quickly scooped her up. I inhaled her scent and let out a huge sigh of relief. She bawled on my shoulder, but before I could take a step,

Peter yanked on my arm, hauling me against his chest.

Peter kissed my cheek, and his lips felt like acid against my skin. My bear snapped her jaws angrily, but my wolf just stayed quiet. I didn't understand why she would leave me like this, and a single tear rolled down my cheek.

Peter leaned in to whisper, "It seems I've been forced out of the last few years of my daughter's life, so it's time for me to try and make up for lost time. *You* have also been a little slut by opening those pretty little legs to others, and I plan to remind you exactly who you belong to when we get back home."

I nearly gagged as he started to drag us through the woods and away from Brody. I stole one last glance at him, but he still wasn't moving. I don't think he's going to wake up in time to help us, but I prayed he'd be okay at least and that nothing else would find him in this state. Aerith clung to my neck and buried her face in my shoulder away from Peter.

"You know I've been picturing everything I'd do to you when I finally found you again. Most of my ideas weren't very pleasant, I'll be honest. I've been angry for a long time with you, Shanely, but now that we're together again, I'm willing to forgive most of it," he said before glaring at me. "But you better be a good girl from here on out and give me *exactly* what I want. Otherwise, I'll make sure you pay for everything you've done to me."

I glared at him. *God, I was going to be sick and Aerith was listening to all of this.* She was stuck in the middle now, with a gun pointed at her back. I knew I was too far away, but I tried anyways.

"Bastian!?? Bastian!!!!"

Silence.

Rage boiled my blood. If my freaking wolf was here, our link would work. *God, Peter found me.* I insisted to everyone that he would never be able to find me yet here he was. I kept everyone from going after him, and now we were paying the price. I felt so dumb as he dragged me through the woods. I looked down to Peter's gun and memories from my past flooded my brain. The gun was stuck in Aerith's side and tears clouded my vision. I quickly blinked them away. *There must be something I could do,* I thought as I scrambled to think straight. I had to do something because I didn't know if Bastian would find us in time, and I could not go back with him.

I refused to return back to Indiana with this man.

Peter moved quickly through the woods, to the point I was having a hard time keeping up with him. He looked over his shoulder constantly, and I wondered what Patrick told him about us. But then another question came to mind. *What exactly did Patrick know?*

"My truck's not far. We're going to head back to my hotel, where we can catch up," he said as he winked at me before his eyes darkened. "That Bastian won't ever find you two again."

"You mean my husband? I'd think twice about this plan of yours. You have no idea who you're up against, and he *will* find us. He always finds us, and you'd be white as a ghost if you saw the last guy that tried to hurt me. You've been marked for death, Peter. Your days are officially numbered."

Peter gripped my arm so tightly that I gasped. I tried to pull back, and it only forced him to squeeze even harder. Blood trickled down my arm from where his nail dug into my skin. Suddenly, a plan formed in my head.

"I suggest you forget about that man. Do you hear me, Shanely? Keep running that mouth of yours, keep pissing me off, and see how fast I disappear with my daughter. Unless you want me to carry her the rest the way, I suggest you say nothing except yes sir! We clear?"

I nearly flinched, when he raised his hand, pointing his gun at me. I took a deep breath, knowing I was going to have to piss him off greatly for him to do what I needed. *He just needed to lose it just enough to hit me*, I thought. *Just enough to make me bleed.* I blinked, remembering Bay. *I needed to fake it, and it was now or never.*

"Wow... You really are dumber than I remember. What's your plan anyways? Kidnap us and then lock us away in your house and never let us leave? You're *not* my husband, nor are you her father. Bastian won't stop until he finds us, and I promise you will regret this when he does."

That did it. He raised his hand, hitting me hard with his gun, and I dropped to the ground with Aerith. Blood gushed from my head, and Aerith scrambled to her feet. Peter yanked her up, and she screamed. My vision blurred as I wiped away the blood from my head, spreading it on the grass below. *It would be enough for Bastian to scent,* I thought to myself.

"I warned you, Shanely. Now get up. Get up and move or I'll walk away with her right now! This is the *last* time I'm gonna tell you," he snapped at me.

I shakily made my way to my feet. The blow to the head made it extremely difficult to focus, and I blinked rapidly, trying to clear my vision.

"Give me back my daughter," I asked as calmly as I could. Blood continued to spill down my face and off my hand, and I let it flow freely, but I knew it wouldn't last long. My shifter abilities were kicking in.

"*Our* daughter. She's my blood too, Shanely," he snarled at me. His wild eyes glared at me, and he held the gun in front of me. I looked at Aerith, who still reached for me, and my heart broke. *Enough is enough... I won't risk her.*

"Our daughter. You win, Peter," I said solemnly. "She's your daughter too."

Peter studied me a moment before caving and passing Aerith over again. She clung to my neck, and I could barely breathe under her death grip.

"Now let's move," he said before grabbing my arm again/ "And quit pissing me off. I'm sick of correcting you."

I felt the gun against my back now, and I moved forward without a word. *Maybe I had stalled enough that Bastian could find us?* I thought, knowing that was wishful thinking. The road wasn't far and a small blue truck was parked on the side. *Bastian wouldn't make it in time...*

Peter drug me over a fallen log, scraping my legs as we went, and I was grateful he had moved the gun off Aerith. It jammed in my side, and I winced in pain.

Aerith continued to quietly cry on my shoulder, and all I wanted to do was rub her back like Bastian always did, but I could barely hold her as it was. Peter had a death grip on my arm, and I couldn't barely keep her upright as we moved swiftly through the forest.

"C'mon, we're almost there! I need out of these freaking woods. I am sick to death of all these hillbilly people and bugs. I cannot wait to get us home."

Suddenly, I heard the song.

"My mother told me someday I would buy
  Galleys with long oars
  Sail to distant shores"

Uncle Cain slowly walked around the large tree directly in front of us, forcing us to skid to a stop. My eyes widened. *How did he managed to get in front of us without even me seeing him?* I thought to myself, but my Uncle was Alpha for a reason. Peter swore as he tucked me closer now. He moved the gun to my head and glared ahead, but my uncle continued on with his song anyways. He was angry. You could see the rage in his eyes, but his voice stayed steady and calm.

"Stand up on the prow
  Noble barque I steer
  Steady course to the Haven
  Hew many foe-man
  Hew many foe-man."

Slowly more and more enforcers came out from behind the trees, and I let out the breath I'd been holding. Peter's eyes widened at the sight of so many in front of us. My pack was everywhere, and they were all singing the song with Uncle Cain. Just over and over again. Never anything more than the song, and it was freaking Peter out. He had no idea the mess he landed himself in, but he was quickly figuring out that this wasn't going to go the way he hoped.

Peter turned as my pack circled around us, trying to take it all in and watch his back at the same time. *It was useless though,* I thought. *There was nowhere for him to go.*

I desperately searched for my mate as the entire team of new enforcers stepped out, looking livid. Brody appeared in the mix as well, and the look he gave me was hard to stomach. I knew he blamed himself for losing us, but I was just relieved to see him alive.

Peter continued twisting us around, trying to see everyone all at once. The pack hadn't even done anything yet, but he was coming unglued. Suddenly, Bastian shoved his way forward. His eyes were blood red, and Cade and Elijah were right behind him, snarling at Peter.

A sense of calm washed over me then, and our eyes met. *He was here,* I thought to myself. *My mate was here, and Peter was about to see how scary he could be.* Bastian looked relieved to have found us, but it quickly turned into something feral when he looked back at Peter.

"Bastian!" I cried out, but Peter pushed the gun against my head harder.

"Back off, everyone! I'm leaving with *my girls*, and no one will stop me!" Peter shouted.

They ignored him and continued singing. Everyone except my boys. They snarled viciously at Peter.

"My mother told me someday I would buy
　Galleys with long oars
　Sail to distant shores
　Stand up on the prow
　Noble barque I steer
　Steady course to the Haven
　Hew many foe-man
　Hew many foe-man."

The chant grew louder as Bastian paced back and forth in front of us. He was furious, and Peter glared right back at him. *He was such an idiot,* I thought smirking. *Peter had made a very critical mistake trying to take us.*

Bastian shook with anger as he stepped forward and shouted, "You took something that belongs to me! I suggest you let her go because either way you are not walking past these wolves alive. So what will it be? A quick death or a slow one like you deserve?"

Peter gripped my arm tighter and put the gun against my side now.

"So, here's the famous Bastian! Nah man... I'm taking back what was mine in the first place. Did you think you could just step in my shoes, and I wouldn't come after you? I'm leaving with my girl and my kid! I'll let one of your many enemies deal with you instead. Now move!"

I whispered to Aerith, while Peter was distracted with Bastian. "Run to your Daddy. Okay? Don't look back, just keep moving forward!"

I felt awful, but I threw her as far as I could one handed. She scrambled to her feet and like the good girl she was, she bolted. She never looked back and pride filled my chest.

Peter screamed as he lunged, but Bastian scooped Aerith up in his arms, holding her tight as he looked at me. Peter yanked me back close to him, with the gun firmly against my head. The familiar feeling of the cold steel against my skin scared the living daylights out of me, but this time I was surprisingly okay with it. *I saved my daughter, and that was all I could hope for in this moment.*

"*I love you, Bastian,*" I said through our link. "*Whatever happens... Please know that I love you.*"

Bastian gave me a feral look and slowly passed Aerith to Cade. Peter screamed louder and twisted my arm to the point I felt like he was about to break it. He was always somewhat unpredictable, but I had never seen him like this.

"Just go everyone!" I shouted. "He is my mistake. I don't want anyone hurt."

The pack's eyes flashed gold, but I gave them a firm look in return. *Peter would lose, but how many would die in this process?*

The chant continued, and Peter hollered trying to break the circle, but the pack wouldn't let him. They kept a safe distance from us, waiting for the go ahead. The fact there was a gun to my head kept everyone at bay.

Peter shouted, "I'm not leaving here without what's mine! Now hand over my daughter!"

He tapped the gun against my head, and I winced as his eyes frantically searched for a way out. The trauma I had worked so hard to get through was rearing it's ugly head, but Peter was my mistake. I took a deep breath. *No one should have to deal with him, especially like this. I needed to be the only one to risk their life to end such an awful man. I just needed to be brave.*

"Shanely, tell them to back off! Tell them what I'll do if they don't!" Peter bellowed.

One by one, the pack started to shake. Cain raised his voice louder, continuing the song as they each shifted in front of Peter.

Peter's eyes grew wide. "What in the world? WHAT ARE YOU FREAKS?!"

I watched in awe as the shifted. I finally understood what my uncle told me all those years ago. *Their wolves answered the call.* My uncle, Bastian, and Cade were the only ones who fought the shift and stood in their human forms. I looked to Cade, and I could see the pain he felt by refusing to let his wolf out. He held onto Aerith tightly, and I smiled, knowing she'd be safe.

The gun left my head multiple times like Peter didn't know where to aim his gun at. Me or the wolves before us. We all could smell his fear, and the song continued on. Even my own wolf rose to the surface, and my chest burned, listening to the words repeat over and over again. I focused within, feeling her power build and remembering who I truly was. I wasn't the same girl as before. I was *a mixer*, half-bear and half-wolf. I was strong and brave, and my thoughts drifted back to what I did at Abraham's. I thought of Derek and the pain I endured from him. I *survived* him. I always survived, and it wasn't due to luck. I had an inner strength that I never paid much attention to before, but it was something to be proud of. For the first time in my life, I felt free of the hold Peter had on me.

I slowly looked to Peter, noticing how small he seemed all of the sudden. I don't know why he had such a hold on me, when he was just a powerless human. *He was weak, but I was not.* I looked back to my mate, and his eyes were forward, not showing an ounce of fear. I was mated to *him*. I was his equal, and I didn't need rescuing from this man. *Why it took me this long to let go of the old me, I will never understand.* My eyes shifted gold, and I inhaled deeply, focusing on my rage and hatred and felt my wolf rise to the surface.

"I asked you a question, Peter! Do you want a slow, agonizing death? Or will you be smart and let my mate go?" Bastian bellowed.

Peter shoved the gun back against my head, glaring at my mate, and Bastian's eyes flashed again.

Bastian bellowed, "Wrong choice."

My mate shifted.

The white that covered his paws now crawled up his legs, and he was nearly double what everyone else's wolves were. Seeing him amidst his pack felt new. His canines were large, and he showed them all as he snarled viciously at Peter. His ears were back as he stalked towards us. Cain looked at Bastian, concerned momentarily before focusing back on me.

Peter's eyes went wide as he screamed, "You all are freaks! I'm..."

He stopped talking, like he finally believed Bastian. Peter wasn't getting out of this. His entire focus was on the sight in front of him. He didn't once look at me like I was a threat. My eyes remained gold, but no one noticed. *It was fine,* I thought. *I wasn't normally a violent person, but today would be different. Today, I would save myself.*

"I warned you, Peter. You never listen to me," I told him, my voice no longer shaking with fear.

Peter slowly turned to me, looking horrified when he noticed my gold eyes. My wolf surged forward, and I slowly started to shift into my wolf. I wanted him to realize his life was about to expire *by my hand.* Not by my mate's or anyone else's. He would *never* be able to harm me or my family again because I was going to finally get the justice I deserved. I was going to make it happen, and it felt amazing. I didn't look around to see if my mate realized my decision or not. I didn't wait for permission. I never broke eye contact with Peter, and he staggered away from me. I had made sure Aerith was taken care of and that she was safe. Now it was time to show her that her mother was just as strong as her dad.

As my body began to twist and break, Peter looked more and more horrified. He was genuinely afraid of me, and for the first time in my life, I wasn't afraid of him. My wolf howled within and feeling her finally emerge felt incredible.

Suddenly, a loud sound startled me. It stopped my shift, snapping me back into my human body, and I felt my eyes return to their normal green state.

Time slowed as my body seemed unable to process what just happened. The pain started to burn inside me, and I looked down to find blood soaking my shirt. I stumbled where I stood, unable to hold myself up anymore.

Peter shot me.

He shot... *me.*

Bastian

"I warned, you Peter. You never listen to me," Shanely said, her voice unwavering and strong.

Pride filled my chest as I saw such conviction coming from my girl. It had been a long road to recovery for her but looking at her now, she seemed different. Suddenly, her body shook slightly, and my eyes widened. *She was shifting,* I thought to myself. Peter's face twisted in fear, and then the most sickening sound split the air.

The gun went off, and Shanely *stumbled.*

"You're a monster," Peter shouted, and she collapsed on the ground.

My heart stopped. Silence filled the woods, and we all stood there frozen in disbelief. I walked into this situation feeling confident I'd reach him before he'd hurt my girl. He was one skinny human against me and my whole pack. I knew he wasn't getting out of this, but I never thought he'd shoot her.

I never thought she'd get hurt...

Aerith's scream rippled through the air as I felt our bond nearly snap in two. Agony filled my chest as I clung to our bond. I couldn't do anything as it faded away from me. *Shanely was fading away from me.* My wolf snapped his jaws, pulling me out of my grief, and I looked for Peter. The coward was running towards the road back to his truck. Shifters were not allowed to harm humans, but in this moment I didn't care.

I was going to kill him.

I started moving before grinding to a halt. *If I went after him that would mean leaving Shanely. I had to decide which way I was going to go. After him or to her?*

I howled, snapping everyone out of their trance.

"Cade! Elijah! Find him now!"

Cade passed Aerith off to her uncle before my brother's took off in Peter's direction and the majority of wolves followed. I bolted towards Shanely and shifted back as I slid into her, my eyes widening when I saw her wound. Shanely was losing too much blood, and her breathing was already labored.

"Cain, what do we do!? What do we do!?" I frantically asked. My hands were covered in her blood as I pressed on the wound to slow down her bleeding. There was too much blood though, and our bond was nearly gone. *This can't be happening! I can't lose her!*

"Cain!" I bellowed as he stared at his niece, lost in thought.

I heard a man's scream off in the distance, and I knew my brothers had caught up with the monster.

"Make him suffer," I commanded.

I sent to the pack, and I could hear the howls in response. Suddenly, Cassia started singing the wolves' song behind me. I gave her an irritated look, but her eyes were solid gold. I didn't understand what was happening, but I didn't have time to question. I didn't have time to do *anything*.

All the female wolves were singing now. I could still hear the snarls off in the distance as well as that prick's screams. Cain started speaking, but his words went right over my head. My own animals were pushing against me too hard, but my wolf was relentless. He was painfully trying to shift but gripped me. *If I let him out then I'd never get control again*, I thought as anxiety rippled through me. *I needed to be here for her!* I needed to help her but I felt useless. Her chest was barely moving, and Cain suddenly grabbed me and shook me hard.

"Bastian, listen to your wolf! He answers the call of our song, you know that! Stop fighting it, and let him take control. *Help* her! You need to help pull out her wolf now and force her transformation. Force her to shift!" Cain shouted as he shook my shoulders again.

Without hesitating, I trusted Cain's command and let my wolf take over. The girls sang it differently than we had moments ago. It wasn't intimidating but rather heavenly as if their voices were angelic. The rhythm hit my wolf differently, and I felt a charge swirling through the air around Shanely and I. Cain was right. My wolf knew what to do, and I could taste the shifter venom on my fangs. I gave him full control. *Anything to save her.*

He bit her right over the wound. For as panicked and feral as he was feeling at the moment, my wolf was surprisingly gentle with her. Just enough to break the skin and put the venom inside her. I prayed this forced her wolf out. She had one, and we needed her to shift, so she could heal herself before it was too late, and I lost her forever. *Her abilities were too weak without her wolf, and where he shot her...*

Pain filled my heart as I looked away from her wound. My wolf bit her again, this time over our mate mark and then again, just in case. He released his tight grip on the controls, and I stepped back as co-pilot. I pulled back away from Shanely before howling long and sorrowful.

Cade and Elijah rushed back to the group, looking frantic between the two of us. I waited for what seemed like an eternity. They kept singing as the males howled in their wolf form. I waited and watched Shanely. She was still bleeding, and I couldn't see any indication that the venom had worked.

"Come on, my love. Shift!"

She took in one last haggard breath, and her chest fell. It didn't rise again, and I felt utterly empty inside. Where her presence and light once were inside me was gone. Nothing but agony and darkness filled the place where she used to be. My pack stopped singing, and the woods fell silent. No one moved. The only sounds you could hear were the sounds of muffled cries around us. I gently nudged her with my snout. *She can't be gone! This isn't real,* I thought to myself. *This isn't happening!*

"Shanely?" I bellowed.

"Shanely?!"

I looked to my brothers, and they looked back to me broken-hearted. Cade ran his hands through his hair with tears in his eyes, while Elijah rubbed his chest frantically. He looked at me and shook his head no. *He couldn't feel her bond either.*

I snapped my jaw, showing my teeth before roaring loudly.

She WILL not leave me! I shouted inside my head. I felt full of rage, and I pulled my venom again, biting her thigh. Then her arm. I bit her repeatedly over her whole body before I howled in pain. My daughter cried behind me, and I knew I needed to go to her, but I couldn't tear my eyes away from my mate.

I failed her… I couldn't keep her safe. I was arrogant and foolish. Ready to take my time with the man that abused her for so long. I thought I had it under control, and because of it… He killed her.

I howled again in agony, and my sanity started to break. I was losing control of my animals, and soon I wouldn't be able to recognize my own pack anymore. My vision grew dark around me. *I can't live without my mate,* I thought in agony. *I should have never let her leave without me this morning! I should have just went with her instead of working.*

Suddenly, my vision cleared abruptly, and something burned inside my chest. My wolf whined in pain. *Was this how it felt when your mate dies? When the bond dies?* The pain intensified, and I started to waver on my paws, unable to stand on solid ground. My breathing started to labor, and I shook my head.

"Bastian?" Cain asked.

I howled again, but this time it was because of my own *physical* pain. I didn't understand it why I felt so sick all of the sudden. Everything just *hurt*, and I shook on all fours. *Something was seriously wrong with,* I thought to myself, but honestly I welcomed the pain. *Maybe this was how I could follow her?* I didn't want to live in this world without my mate. I shook my head violently, and the pain increased.

I couldn't take it anymore and collapsed next to my mate's body. My vision went completely dark despite being conscious. My brothers shook me, and everyone began talking at once.

"Bastian, what happened?!" Elijah bellowed in my head. I couldn't answer him though. I just laid there in agony.

The pack sounded panicked, and I didn't blame them. *For all they knew, I was dying too.* I was ready to let go, when a small face filled my mind. Aerith. As badly as I wanted to go with my mate in death, I couldn't leave our baby girl. *I needed to stay alive for her. She shouldn't end up all alone because I let my own pain and suffering guide me to give up.* If I didn't have Aerith, I would have welcomed death, but right now I needed to stand up.

I tried to move my legs, but they wouldn't work. The pain grew worse. Whatever was happening rippled through my body like it was *alive*, pulsing through my veins like a strong current, and a power began to flow into me. Suddenly, my vision cleared, and I saw my family hovering over me. The world around me was bright and colorful. It was better than it had ever been before, and I could see *everything* in great detail. More than that, I could see colors swarming myself and the pack. It was unlike anything I have ever seen in my life, and I couldn't take my eyes off it.

I looked to Shanely, and her wound glowed. My eyes widened as the glow spread throughout her whole body, and everyone backed away from us. *They could see it too,* I thought as I lifted my head slightly. My head jerked to my tail, and I realized I was glowing too! *What in the world was this?!*

I tried to stand again, but my body was too weak. Suddenly, I felt another shift in power. I looked to my Alpha as his eyes widened. The power he had from being our Alpha was being pulled away from him. He clutched his chest as this red color left him. It drained from him and poured right into us. As the power filled us, I felt stronger, faster, and more vicious than I had ever before. *Is this what Cain has always felt as Alpha?*

Cain's face was in complete shock as everything left him and went into me and Shanely. Both my wolf and my bear were empowered, and I stood strong on my paws again. That's when I heard a sickening crunch.

Shanely's body started snapping and cracking violently. I cringed, watching her body slowly twist and shift around, but it was hard to watch. *She was shifting, but it wasn't instantaneous as our shifts normally are.* Her eyes were still closed, but I prayed. I prayed right there to let her wake up and come back to me.

"Shanely. Please hear my voice! Wake up, baby."

She glowed brighter, and I covered my eyes as she shifted fully into her White Wolf. Everyone around the two of us was forced to the ground. I realized we were emitting a strong Alpha power, stronger than Cain's ever was. I tried to pull it back, but it was painful, so I let the transformation complete itself. It pulsed as if it were alive before finally stopping altogether.

I felt different. Complete and strong. Our mate bond was complete, and it glowed so brightly between us. I could sense everything about her. Her wolf was as large as mine almost. I would stand taller, but not by much. Her wolf was beautiful, and I stood frozen in disbelief.

Shanely's wolf was finally here, and I slowly took a step to her, when an odd sensation hit me square in the chest. A steady *thump-thump* matched my own heart beat, and I smiled. The two heart beats fell in sync with one another, bringing peace and comfort to my whole body. Even my wolf and bear were relaxed by the sensation, and I knew *exactly* what it meant. I couldn't believe it. We were fated mates, which was rare for shifters. Her heart beat was just as strong as mine, and she was breathing. Shanely was *alive*, and I nearly collapsed in relief. I nudged her gently with my nose, needing her to wake.

"Shanely? Come back to me, my love."

Shanely

Everything was cold and dark.

Like I fell into an abyss of nothing with no way out. I was utterly alone, and that scared me half to death. *Am I dying?* I thought to myself. *Is this what it feels like before everything just stops and my life finally ends?* My heart hurt, knowing I was never going to see Bastian again. Aerith would grow up without a mother, just like I did. *I didn't do enough. I should have done everything differently, and maybe this wouldn't have been my outcome.* My past had finally caught up to me, and *this* was the result of all my poor decisions.

Suddenly, a warm feeling burst from my core. It forcefully pushed it's way through my veins as something deep inside came alive. My wolf emerged, and I felt my bear return again. This powerful feeling shook everything inside me, and I felt my body begin to crack and twist. *I was shifting,* I realized as my eyes widened. *How though?* A massive power suddenly slammed into me, startling me, and I felt like I stumbled in this abyss. It was so strong, and it just *kept* coming. My wolf seemed to understand and accept it, so I let her take control as she pushed forward. The power grew and grew until suddenly *everything* stopped.

I didn't know how, but I could feel wind on my fur. I could hear everything in the woods now. All the birds flying in the air. The deer running off in the distance, to the littlest bugs moving in the dirt. It was overwhelming yet exhilarating. *I had shifted into my wolf.*

Something nudge against me, and I whimpered softly. I put my paw over my nose in irritation.

Another nudge.

I slowly peeked open an eye and saw white paws. My heart sunk. *I was the White Wolf,* I thought to myself. *There was no denying it now.*

I lifted my head slowly to look around. Most of my pack was here, and Aerith eyed me cautiously from my aunt's arms. Everyone else looked overjoyed. A snout nudged me, and I turned to find Bastian. My Bastian. He looked different in the eyes of my wolf, but he was absolutely magnificent. His eyes were a solid mix of gold and red, while his fur was a beautiful mix of black and white. He was no longer smokey gray like before, and I didn't know how to take his new look. Bastian slowly approached me.

"Shanely?"

Bastian's voice entered my head, and my heart swelled at the sound. I slowly stood on my new paws before leaping into him. I embraced him, nuzzling myself as close as I could get against my mate.

"Bastian! My wolf... She's here!"

"Oh, thank God," he said, his voice shaking. "You're alive."

Memories flooded my head of what happened, and I stilled. "How Bastian? How am I alive?"

"*I had to help trigger your shift, my love. Shanely, I'm so sorry! I got here as quick as I could. As soon as Brody's link came through, we all left to find you, but I nearly lost you again. I was ready to kill him slowly, but I never thought he'd actually shoot you. I am so sorry, my love. I should have killed him more quickly.*"

I gently nudged him. "*I'm okay, Bastian. Peter was my mistake, and I should have never thought I'd be able to hide away from him. If I had found my confidence sooner, none of this would have happened. Where is Peter though?*"

"Cade and Elijah made sure he would never come back to hurt you. He's gone for good."

"Mommy?"

I turned to the tiny voice on my right. She was on the ground now, standing next to my aunt. I slowly approached her before laying down completely. Her face was red from crying, and she had leaves in her hair from when I dropped her.

"*Aerith! You were such a brave girl. Mommy is so proud of you.*"

She smiled and jumped into me. She clung to my neck, burying her face in my neck. "Mommy! I wasn't brave! I was scared."

"You were brave, baby. You did exactly what I told you to do, even though you were afraid."

Bastian walked up behind us laying down next to Aerith. He leaned in nearly covering her entirely in his fur.

"My daughter is strong and brave just like her mama," he said through the link, and Aerith smiled big.

"Wait... Aerith can you hear them?" Cain asked.

She nodded. "Mommy and Daddy are talking. Can't you hear them?"

He shook his head no. "Not in this form. It's not normal for you to hear them like this. Another reason you are so special, I guess."

I looked back at him and tilted my head to the right. My uncle looked different too. That's when I realized his Alpha power was different. It was greatly diminished, and he no longer seemed as strong as he was before. I felt my own Alpha power deep within me then. It was like a never ending well, and I huffed out a deep breath. *This would take some getting used to,* I thought to myself. My wolf pushed for control then, and my eyes widened when she pulled on our pack bonds. Except it wasn't just our pack bonds anymore. Thousands of wolf shifters were connected to me. Their cords pulled me to all parts of the world, and *that* frightened me.

Cain smirked as he knelt down to our level. "Shanely, you and Bastian are the fated Alpha's. The two prophesied to rule not just our pack, but *all* wolves in the entire world. Every Alpha on this planet just felt your power emerge, and it's time to take your rightful place on the throne."

I stepped backwards, scurrying away from everyone

"What? Cain, I'm not meant to rule this pack let alone the whole world of wolf shifters!"

His eyes widened. "I take that back. I can hear her too."

"You can hear her?" Aunt Cassia asked.

He nodded. "She must have the ability to use the link whenever she wants to, but Shanely... *this* is what you were born to do. You are our White Wolf!"

Everyone shifted now and howled. They all laid down in front of us as if accepting their new King and Queen, and I looked at Bastian. *What was I* going to do? I wasn't ready for this.

"Go," Cain commanded. "You two need to claim one another as wolves. Complete your bond, and we will take care of Aerith and deal with the body. Go... Run with your wolf, Shanely. Come back when you are ready."

Bastian nudged me before turning to the woods away from the lodge. I licked Aerith's face as she giggled before Cade and Elijah sandwiched her between them. They each rested their heads against mine, and I was relieved they were alright.

"I'm so glad you're okay, Shanely. Don't worry, we won't leave Aerith's side," Elijah said, and I nudged my head against him.

"I promise you that man will never bother you again, Baby Girl."

"I can't thank you two enough," I replied. "You guys are my best friends. I hope you know that."

They pushed their heads against mine once more before Bastian began nudging me away.

"Shanely, I can only hold my wolf back for so long. He has waited a long time for this."

I turned back to Bastian, cocking my head to the side. I looked back at my pack one last time before I took off without warning. I was *fast*, so much faster than my bear, and I loved every second of being my wolf. The wind whipped through my white fur as Bastian and I ran between the trees and over the small creek. I was lost in pure bliss finally feeling my wolf. She was smart and cunning. *No one* was coming to harm my family. *Never again.*

I ran through the brush, when I realized I was alone. I slammed the brakes as my paws dug into the ground. *Where was Bastian? I didn't hear anything happen while we were running through the woods, but why would he leave me like that?* The woods weren't silent by any means, but Bastian was silent as a mouse. I had no idea where he went. I sniffed the air, trying to pick up his scent when I realized how dumb I was being.

I pulled on our mate bond, and the ribbons shot out, connecting right to him.

"Cheater."

The bond disappeared, and I gulped, realizing what was happening.

"I didn't know you could do that!"

I could feel him smirking through the mind-link.

"There's a lot you will be learning, I suppose, but for now you don't need to know where I am. Just know that I'm coming."

Then he closed the link entirely.

Cautiously, I stepped backwards, listening for any indication he was near. I had no way to steal a peek at where he might be either, and I had to rely solely on my wolf's abilities. My wolf tugged for control, and we bolted left. We ran as fast as we could, and I could feel his presence getting closer behind us. I squealed in delight, when he darted into sight. I jumped to the right, changing courses entirely, and I heard him skid to a stop before redirecting as well. I was fast, but Bastian was slightly faster, and he soon pounced on me. We tumbled to the ground, and he rolled on top of me. I squirmed, trying to get away, to give him more of a chase than this, when he bit down on my shoulder abruptly. I gasped and felt a final pull towards him.

Slowly, I started to feel a steady thump against my chest. It stayed in rhythm with my own heartbeat, and I realized it was Bastian's heart. He let go before licking the wound.

"I can feel you, Bastian. I can feel your heart."

He nuzzled his snout against my neck as I stayed very still. Afraid if I moved, I'd lose this feeling forever.

"I can feel yours too. I have ever since we pulled your wolf out. It's amazing. You're amazing Shanely."

"Will this ever go away?" I asked.

He pulled back from me, tilting his head to the side.

"You don't like it?"

If I could roll my eyes right now...

"No, I love it. I was afraid I was going to lose it."

He laid down next to me, resting his head against me.

"Good. And no, it stays from what I've been told. Very special mates get this ability. They're called fated mates."

"I've heard you guys say that before. I just thought it was another term for mates," I answered.

"It is, but it's just a rare form of mates. So rare that it became more like a story than an actual thing. Unique shifters have unique bonds, and their mates are usually fated. They have special abilities most mates don't have, like the ability to touch without being present. The heartbeat is the first and most obvious sign."

"Wait, you knew we were fated mates back then? We've been able to kiss one another through the bond for awhile now."

"Well, I wasn't for sure. The heartbeat is the actual confirmation, but it must have been all backwards because our mate bond wasn't fully connected."

I thought about what he said. Fated mates. Alpha Female. The White Wolf and Bear. *I was many different things, it seemed.* Now my uncle was throwing another thing at me. I wasn't even sure I wanted to be Alpha of the pack right now, let alone to the entire shifter community of wolves. Then I thought about Peter, and I stood up abruptly. Bastian stepped to the side.

"He shot me."

Rage consumed my mind, wishing I had the chance to give him the justice he deserved. It was surprising how quickly my emotions changed. I frowned then. I didn't like the temper my wolf had.

"It's okay, Shanely. Your emotions will be heightened for the first few weeks after the first shift. Wolves are just that way, plus it should of been you. He hurt you, babe, and I wish you could have been the one to end him."

"Every time I end up the victim, and they either get away entirely or I'm too weak to do anything about it. Michael was killed before I even left the recovery room, and I have no idea where Derek is. It seems like Bay and Abraham haven't been able to reach him, and now this. I'm sick of being this way, Bastian."

"You were never weak, Shanely, and today it seemed you finally realized it. I know you did everything you could to protect Aerith and Brody, and watching how brave you were today was amazing. I am so proud of you, and I am proud that you are my fated mate. I'm the one who made the mistake. I was the arrogant today, when I assumed he was weak even with the gun. I expected him to shoot me, not you. I was ready to take the bullet, and then end him but... He shot you instead."

"It took me way too long to realize what I can do and who I really am. It's hard not to see myself the way I've always been, but I promise you I won't need rescuing again. I want to train with the enforcers, Bastian. I want to be able to eliminate the threat before you all even find out about it."

When I finally finished ranting, I turned to him. He was sitting on his back legs just watching me pace back and forth, cocking his head to the side.

"What?"

"You know how sexy you are when you're all fired up?"

"Bastian... I'm serious though."

"Oh, I know you are. I know you are fully capable of defending yourself, but as your fated mate, I will always make sure you're safe. That's my job, and one I don't take lightly. I will always take care of you and our children. Now my wolf has waited a very long time, so I seriously suggest you run, my love."

"Run?"

"I'm trying to be a gentleman here, but my wolf is about to take over. Run. I'm giving you a 20 second head start."

"You know... I still haven't marked you in this form either."

Bastian's eye flash gold as I backed away slowly. *Oh... He was definitely excited about that*, I thought to myself. His wolf emitted a low growl as his eyes glowed brighter.

"Shanely..."

I bolted before he could say anymore.

Series Order

Shifter series
Shifter Awakened
Shifter Prophecy
Shifter Deliverance
Shifter Sacrifice

Nightlocke series
Realm of Darkness
Island of Horrors

Enjoy a sneak peek into Bay and Abraham's life
in these two incredible bonus chapters!

Bonus Chapter

Henry opened the door for Bay to step inside. My heart fluttered as her hips swayed with every step towards me. My eyes seemed stuck on her near perfect lips and her oceanic eyes, but I quickly shook myself from those thoughts, flashing her a smile as she stepped onto the mat.

"Welcome Mor'du!" I said in my typically charming voice. The one I used to tipped deals in my favor without someone realizing. I cleared my throat nervously as her brow rose. I gestured to the room then. "I thought since you work for me, and have nothing better to do at the moment, we could train."

Silence. Bay said nothing as she quietly assessed my offer to help her train. For the first time in my life, I felt awkward. My tiger squirmed under her intense gaze, and I shuffled over to the weights. I had to do something with all this nervous energy, but the old me came to the front when I couldn't take it anymore.

"Let's go, Fenrir," I said gruffly. Her eyes flashed, and she quickly moved to the set of weights. I immediately regretted the words the second they flew out of my mouth, but there was no taking them back now.

Henry stayed quietly by the door, guarding me from the tiny woman across from me. I gave him a long look.

"Don't you have other tasks to do today?"

Henry blinked.

"Go on," I commanded. "What's the worst that can happen?"

He slowly dragged his eyes to mine. *Finally a reaction,* I thought.

"She's your champion, sir. And a wolf at that. It would go against the oath I took when I became one of your enforcers. I will not leave you."

I gritted my teeth as I turned away from him. *Henry wouldn't leave,* I told myself. *Not without explaining why I wanted to be alone with Bay.* He was one of my oldest friends, but I wasn't ready to have that conversation with him. Not yet. Not when I didn't know myself.

A clattering sound startled me, and I turned to find Bay putting away her weights. I frowned when she went to the next machine without me. *This wasn't exactly how I thought it would go. Then again; what exactly did I want to happen?*

I set down the dumb bells I was awkwardly holding and walked over to her. She was perfectly content to ignore me the entire time, but I was determined to get to know this girl. When the guys first explained the deal they made in my behalf, I was skeptical. Then I saw him, or rather *her*, fight. I was blown away. Mor'du was a beast, and the money just started pouring in. I had to stretch the deal. It's all in the details with the deals I make, and Mor'du figured out pretty quickly that I had time to deliver my end. But as I watch Bay drop the bar to her chest and push it up effortlessly, I felt a little bad.

I had no idea who was beneath the hood until that night she came into my personal box above the ring. Henry or Daryl always paid her before, but she sauntered up the stairs, her hips swaying with every step, and challenged me for those girls.

I shook myself from those thoughts and stood behind her. *Focusing on the past wouldn't help me win this girl over,* I thought anxiously. I was already at a disadvantage with the sort of man I had become. Now all *this* lie between us. Her eyes narrowed on me as I approached.

"What do you want?" she asked coldly.

I pursed my lips together. *That was a loaded question.* "I'm spotting you."

She scoffed and put the bar on the rack. "I don't need a spotter."

Bay rose from the machine and went to the row of treadmills I had along the back wall. I followed.

"Everyone needs a spotter," I challenged as she hopped on the machine. Bay began to casually jog in place, and the breath caught in my chest as I watched her body move. *God, she was beautiful.* Her high cheek bones and tight curly hair... I had never seen anyone look like her before. That rosebud scent filled my nostrils, and it was all I could do to tame the beast within. My tiger wanted out. He wanted *her*.

"Not me," she said, between breaths. I got on the machine next to her and started in on a lite jog. She frowned. "Don't you have other things to do than... well this?"

My tiger bristled, but I quickly shoved him aside. "Nah, I've got nothing today, and I thought it would be nice to have a buddy during my work outs. I'm usually alone."

Bay frowned further. "I'm not your buddy."

Silence filled the air, and I tried to focus on my feet instead of the heavy pressure sitting on my chest. I didn't really know where to go from here, but I wanted to get to know her. God, the word *mate* had been muttering about in my mind since I scented her that first night. *But figuring the answer to that question required... Nope. Not going there.*

"Why are you usually alone?" she asked, startling me.

"Uh..." I stammered as I got control of my feet again. "It's not easy being King, I suppose. I handle things a certain way to keep my streak safe, but it's off putting to some, and the rest still look at me like I'm untouchable royalty. No matter what I try to tell them."

Bay's eyes narrowed as that little mind of hers spun its wheels. I don't know why I admitted so much, but it was like my mouth had a mind of its own when it came to this girl. I just wanted to share everything with her.

Hating the awkward silence that filled between us, I upped the speed on the treadmill. My lite jog turned into a decent run, and I was beginning to feel my shirt soak itself. Bay narrowed her eyes before pushing the button on her machine too.

A soft grin formed as I noticed she went just a little faster than I did. *Competitive little thing,* I thought to myself.

I pushed the button again, my feet moving quicker than I liked on one of these things, and sure enough, Bay joined me. The two of us were sprinting like mad men on these deathtraps, trying our hardest to one up the other. My chest heaved as I struggled to put air in my lungs, and I bravely stole a glance towards her.

Sweat beaded at her brow, but Bay's breathing was even and controlled.

Unlike mine. I swore under my breath and made my feet move faster. But Bay *kept* going.

My feet were quickly getting tangled up, and I swore loudly as I slammed my hand on the emergency stop. My face was beat red, and my shirt stuck to me in all the wrong places, but nothing felt worse than the fact that she beat me. She beat me and then some as her legs continued to run, while mine slowed down. The machine finally died, and I was able to give my jello legs a rest.

Bay stopped her machine, hopping off like that was nothing, and grabbing a towel from the shelf. *Just to add insult to injury...*

"Are we done here?" she asked quietly, and I scoffed. *Good lord, this girl's a freaking beast,* I thought to myself. I nodded my head, unable to even speak let alone breathe right now. I tried to casually lean against the treadmill in a small attempt to salvage some dignity, but the corners of Bay's mouth rose slightly. *She knew,* I thought to myself. *Of course, she knew I was dying inside. She was a freaking cunning wolf.*

Bay dried herself off and tossed the rag in the near empty barrel. She started for the door but stopped. I cocked my head to the side as she turned.

"It sucks being alone, doesn't it?"

I frowned, not liking where her mind went just now. Before I could say anything, Bay turned and left, following Darryl out the door.

I stood there dumbfounded as I watched the door continue to swing on the hinges. Henry made his way over to me. When that infuriating judgmental brow rose, I stormed over to the shelves and grabbed a towel.

"Don't start," I said, hearing him chuckle behind me.

"I wasn't saying anything," he said, with a sly grin. I rolled my eyes.

"Sure, you weren't," I said, drying myself off. "What's on the agenda today?"

"Oh, not too much," Henry replied. "You have a few deals getting delivered this afternoon, and then we have the enforcer meeting this evening. Did you even notice when Darryl walked in?"

My cheeks heated, and I promptly turned away from my oldest friend. "What does Finnick want to talk about?"

I ignored the blatant stare from him as I cleaned the machines Bay and I used. My tiger bristled, while I schooled my face to look nonchalant.

"A status report," Henry finally said, and I gave a slow nod. I made my way towards the door, when Henry said something that startled me. "You know I would not judge you if Bay is your mate."

My anxiety rose as I turned to him. *Thinking it was one thing. Saying it out loud was another.* Sighing, I rubbed the back of my head.

"I don't know what she is," I replied honestly.

Henry's eyes narrowed. "Is that because of your pull towards the bossy one?"

I snorted, shaking my head as I shoved open the door. "There's no pull there either, and she has a mate and child, Henry."

He chased after me. "You softened with her," he said, and I stilled. He gave me a pointed look saying, "We all saw it, Abe. You're handling things differently than you ever would have with these girls."

My mouth opened to protest, but he held his hand firm, silencing the lies we both knew were coming.

"Twisting the deal to use the Fenrir triplets, that makes sense," he goes on as he stepped closer, "offering your home for those girls..." he clicked his tongue in annoyance, "a stretch, but I can somewhat understand. Extending it for the child, however, *that* I didn't see coming. You even waited for them to fetch her! Then breakfast, the excessive hovering and buying them crap so they actually *enjoy* their time here..."

Henry tossed his hands in the air as I gave him a blank stare. *He had me,* I thought angrily. *He knew it. I knew it. Everyone in this castle apparently knew it.*

Henry sighed as he shook his head once more. "You and I both know the old you would have offered them a cell instead of the tower. You would have left them to figure out what to do with the kid too. Both those options light a fire under the Fenrirs like no other, and the jobs would have gotten done the same! They're wolves, Abraham. You have a bounty on them as we speak! Beau just delivered a head *this morning,* yet you do something like this?"

Anger rose within me, and I stormed down the hall. I had managed to put that bloody head behind me, and he had to bring it up again. It didn't give me the relief it used to when a wolf shifter was caught. I just felt sick when I had to pay him for it. I pulled the bounty from him right after, but I have dozens under my employ. *What would Bay think if she knew?*

Henry grabbed my arm. "I am talking to you!"

My anger rose with my power, and I gritted my teeth to keep it from leaking through. *Not to him. Anyone but him.*

"What do you want me to say?!" I snapped, yanking my arm away.

"I want you to tell me the truth!" he hollered, and I blinked. *Henry almost never yelled*, I thought to myself. His nostrils flared, and he quickly rubbed his face. "We've been friends for years, Abe. We *lost* our home together. We lost our family, our friends, everything in a blink of an eye. I stood at your side through all the bloodshed and stupid crap we dealt with, and never once did I have to question what was on your mind. And then this girl shows up..."

I shut my eyes, tilting my head to the ceiling as I tried to even find the words. Henry was right. He was more my brother than friend really. *If I couldn't talk to him; who could I talk to?*

"I don't know how to explain it," I said softly. My head looked in either direction of the hall before settling on Henry. "My tiger wants her, Henry."

"Bay?" he asked, lowering his own tone. "Or Shanely."

"In a weird way, both. With Bay, it's possessive," I said, leaning against the wall. "I keep thinking she's my mate, but the only way to find out is to..."

"Kiss her," he finished, sighing hard. "That's gonna go over well."

I gave a slow nod. My lips pursed together as I tried to think of a solution, but I couldn't.

"And Shanely?" Henry asked, pulling me from my thoughts.

I shrugged. "I don't know. My tiger feels protective of her and the kid. Like he knows them somehow and just decided they're important."

He frowned, but at least didn't chastised me for any of it. I gave him a pleading look then.

"Please do not say a word," I begged. "Darryl's fine, but no one else. Not until I figure this out."

Henry rolled his eyes. "Like I talk to anyone other than you anyways."

The corners of my mouth rose slightly. "True."

We walked in silence towards the throne room, and I had to admit, a weight seemed to lift from my chest. It felt good confiding in someone.

"Thank you by the way," I said as we passed the kitchen. Voices and the cluttering of pots and pans sounded through the door as I gave my friend a genuine grin. "You gonna be alright if my mate's a wolf?"

He shrugged. "I'll get used to it."

I spat out a laugh as we turned the corner. A familiar scent filled my nose, and I knew which deal was here already. *Why those sharks even bothered to leave the water before the deadline was a mystery to me.* I just hated that my home would smell like saltwater for days now.

"What would I do without you, friend?"

Henry gave a small smile in response before opening the doors to the throne room. "Let's never find out, shall we?"

Bonus Chapter

I sauntered down the steps from my room, butterflies filling my entire core as I made my way to the throne room. Darryl was on his way to fetch the girls again, and God I would be lying if I wasn't eager to see Bay in that outfit again. It rattled Bastian seeing his mate like that, and the anger on his face, knowing there was nothing he could do to stop it was just icing on the cake. I've *never* seen bounty hunters like the Fenrirs before. It grated on me that Bastian knew my reputation and worked the deal in his favor though. The expiration date was coming to an end.

But not my deal with Bay. I was going to hold onto that deal with a death grip. At least until I figured out how to reach her. She has yet to really acknowledge me since that first morning in the gym. But she continued to exercise with me every morning so that was something.

I rolled my sleeves up on my arms, sitting down on the gargantuan seat made for a king. *Made for my father*, I said to myself. Something gripped my heart as the memory of my father came to mind. My tiger bristled, pushing another thought my way.

Made for you.

I leaned my chin on my hand as I waited for the girls. Henry opened the door and took a stand behind me.

"Any issues I need to be aware of?" I asked.

"Standard night tonight, sir," Henry answered. "We have a few deals getting delivered as well as two appointments for new deals."

A small smirk appeared on my lips. "Excellent."

"Any reason why the girls are attending again tonight?" Henry asked, and the smirk fell away. "Bastian isn't coming."

"It's just for the illusion," I answered. It wasn't a lie honestly. Just not the whole truth.

"Ah," Henry said with a clipped tone. "Bay isn't talking to you during the day, so you're forcing her to attend tonight."

I shot him a glare before rolling my eyes. His smirk said it all.

"Well, what would you do?" I snapped back, more frustrated with myself than anything.

Henry shrugged. "Maybe forcing them to work *like this* isn't the way to go."

The main doors opened, and that rosebud scent filled the air. My whole body relaxed and felt at peace as Bay and Shanely entered the room. Bay held her head high like she always did, but Shanely... She wouldn't look at me.

"Welcome ladies!" I said, smiling as I held out my arms. "Thank you for assisting me once more."

Shanely scoffed, saying nothing as she plopped down at my right side again. My lips pursed together. I wasn't going to make them sit like that again. Not this time. Bay sat on my left, and suddenly it just felt wrong. I didn't want her at my feet. Bay deserved... Well *everything*.

I cleared my throat, and the two looked at me. "Shanely, why don't you stand beside me tonight?"

Her eyes narrowed. "Is this some game I'm not understanding?"

Heat filled my cheeks, and I twisted uncomfortable in my seat. *Get it together*, I told myself. *But good God if her intense stare didn't scare the daylights out of me.*

"No game," I answered. "I just thought you'd rather stand."

Shanely got to her feet in a huff and stood behind the throne. I sighed, not knowing how to fix this with her, and looked to Bay. I patted the cushioned armrest then.

"I got a spot saved for you," I said, flashing her a wicked grin. She frowned slightly, but my tiger zeroed in on a faint sound. Her heart started to race. *She was nervous*, I said to myself, unable to contain the grin that spread across my face. "I won't bite. Promise."

Bay snorted before promptly covering her mouth. Our eyes widened, and I couldn't stop the deep laugh that rumbled from my chest.

BONUS CHAPTER

"Oh, for the love," Shanely muttered as Darryl opened the door once more. I patted the armrest again as two stallion shifters slowly walked forward. Bay gave a small smile and sat down, brushing against ever so slightly.

I turned my attention to the shifters as pure heat filled my veins from that single touch of Bay's soft skin. Her arm rested against mine as she leaned back to get more comfortable on the arm rest. My mind was a jumbled mess, and I don't think she even knew what she's doing to me right now.

"My King," Henry spoke, his tone an icy indignation that I snapped out of my trance. He gave me a pointed look before gesturing to the stallions. "They request an extension."

My eyes narrowed then. These two have been yanking my chain since coming to me two winters ago. They borrowed money and have been taking their sweet time paying me back. They shifted nervously on their feet.

"What is the excuse this time?" I asked, my hand slowly reaching up to play with Bay's hair. I couldn't help it. I couldn't keep my hands to myself, but the corners of my mouth rose when she did nothing to stop it. When her cheeks turned a slight shade of pink, my confidence soared to the point of pure arrogance, and I sunk my fingers further into her dark locks.

"It's just a lot of money, and my family's farm has fallen on hard times, your Majesty," the tall one said. I never remembered their names. It was always easier that way.

"We just need to get through to the end of the season," the other begged, and I rolled my eyes.

"You shouldn't have borrowed so much," I snapped angrily. "Not if you knew it would be a struggle to pay back."

Shanely scoffed behind me, and my face soured. I dropped my hand from Bay's silky soft hair as the two before me began to babble incessantly. I don't know why my tiger wanted the White Wolf's approval, but it was beginning to become a problem. Because now my anger was subsiding and pity was filling the empty space.

"Please, your majesty!" the tall one begged, dropping to the ground. "We promise to pay on time at the end of the season."

My eyes narrowed. They were lying, I could see it clear as day. But something inside was keeping me from punishing them the way I should. *God, these two were making me soft.*

"Shall we take the farm and sell it?" Henry asked through the link.

I bit my lower lip as Bay's gaze drifted my way. She cocked her head to the side, and for the first time in my life, I wanted someone else's opinion.

"What would you do?" I asked her softly, and her eyes widened. She went from me to the stallions, studying the situation carefully. My tiger's pride filled my chest as I waited for her answer.

"They're farmers," she finally replied. "I'd give the extension. The end of season is when they get their money anyways, right? Plus, it's not like they're extremely wealthy to begin with."

A small smile appeared on my lips then. I turned to the shifters then. "You heard her. You've got till the end of the season to pay up."

Relief flooded their faces, and they hugged one another.

"However," I cut in, stilling the both of them, "if you miss your next deadline, the farm is *mine*. Do you agree to the new terms?"

They gave one another weary looks, and my right brow rose. "If that does not please you, then you can give up the farm tonight. I'm feeling lenient for the moment, but that moment can change *quickly*."

Bay narrowed her eyes, and I wondered what I did wrong now. *I took her advice, didn't I?*

"We accept," the tall one said, and I motioned Darryl forward.

"Draw up the paperwork and send them on their way," I commanded, and the three made their way out.

Bay shifted away from me, and I slowly drug my eyes towards her.

"What?" I asked firmly. "I gave the extension."

She scoffed along with Shanely behind me. I turned to give her a look too.

"You gave the extension with heavy strings attached," Shanely said, cocking her hip to the side.

"You should have just let them off the hook," Bay continued. "They don't have a lot of money in their line of work."

Henry's eyes landed on me, and I gritted my teeth. He was mad at me too. Just for other reasons.

"Ladies, this is the third extension I have given," I said, defending myself. A puzzling look appeared as they looked to one another. "I'm not as heartless as I may seem. Normally, I would have taken the farm tonight, but I am giving them one last shot. I gave them *a lot* that my streak needs back."

The two stayed quiet as Darryl walked inside.

"The human is here," he said, and I could feel the girl's heavy gaze on me once more.

I nodded saying, "Let him in."

Darryl disappeared behind the heavy door, and I turned to Bay and Shanely.

"Not one word understand?" I warned. Bay's eyes flashed before that fierce control took over, and she looked forward again. That one look nearly brought me to my knees and guilt ate at me.

"Not like that," I said quickly, hearing heavy boots just outside in the hall. "He's not your typical human, alright? I need you to ignore him *no matter what.*"

I turned to Henry then. "You should have warned me."

His nostrils flared. "I didn't expect the girls tonight. This is not my..." The doors swung open, and Darryl lead the cocky military man inside. I gritted my teeth as I watch his gaze slid from Shanely to Bay. A low warning growl burst forward from my chest, stilling the room. I forced my tiger aside, owning what I had just done instead of allowing embarrassment to form.

"Colonel Alwyn," I said in a firm tone. "I did not expect to see you tonight."

His slimy smile appeared as he placed his hands on his hips. "It was a last minute request, King Macan."

Alwyn's smile shifted to Shanely then. "Well, you're a new addition to this little soiree. What's your name, little lady?"

Shanely's brow rose, but thankfully she said nothing.

"Aww, are we shy?"

"They work for me," I answered plainly. "They will not answer you, nor are they any of your concern. Now, what do you want from me this time?"

Alwyn's eyes narrowed. He straightened that ridiculous tie around his neck saying, "I need 8 guys to run security two weeks from now. I have a shipment coming in, and I cannot afford any disruptions."

I narrowed my eyes. "What sort of shipment?"

He grinned. "That's *my* business. Your men bring a unique set of skills to the table. I have another team doing the actual unloading and delivering, but I need *your* guys to make sure they stay uninterrupted. I don't care how they eliminate issues that arise. Just make sure they do the job."

I studied the Colonel a moment. I could only begin to imagine what was coming in that shipment of his, and I debated having my tigers apart of any of it. *But... The money he brought in was sorely needed*, I thought to myself. Running this streak was expensive, and I shifted in my seat.

"Done," I answered, and he grinned again. "But you will only have my men for one night and one night only. Any police interference, and *you* will be require to get them out. Financially, legally, the whole nine yards, if you catch my drift. This *other* team must understand they cannot breathe a word about what they might see that night. Otherwise, I will be the one coming after them. Do we understand one another?"

"Entirely," the sly man said, and I motioned my enforcer forward. "Well, wait one minute before we sign on the dotted line."

I looked back to the Colonel. "Do you need something else?"

His eyes drifted to Bay. "Is she's on the table?"

I stilled, slowly cocking my head to the side as if I heard him wrong. I felt Bay stiffen as silence filled the air. She held her breath, and that pissed me off.

Like I would ever sell her.

"She is *not* for sale," I growled. My eyes flashed red as my tiger roared within. He was pissed too and wanted out, but I held him back and wrapped my arm around Bay, yanking her to my lap.

Alwyn's face blanched. "My apologies, Abraham. I did not realize she was yours."

"And her sitting on the armrest of my throne told you nothing?" I snapped. My canines enlarging as rage burned through my system.

Alwyn cleared his throat, shifting on his feet like the nervous rat he was. *The fact he was on active duty...*

"Well," he said quietly, "is the other..."

I had enough and stood promptly. "I'll have my men ready the moment you call. You have two weeks to get that shipment in otherwise my men won't go anywhere."

"I'm on a time limit?"

I shrugged. "It's what you said. You have a shipment coming in two weeks and need my men for security. *You* set a specific time, and now I'm following it. However, you will owe me double this time."

Alwyn scoffed. "Double? Why?"

I straightened, rolling my neck as I said, "Because you pissed me off tonight and insulted the women in my care. Now get out before I decide not to assist *at all*."

Colonel Alwyn stared at me a moment before slowly walking out. I turned to Henry. "Cancel the rest."

"You can't," he replied firmly. My anger rose again as he crossed his arms.

"I'm in no mood..."

"It's Frank," he said matter of factly. My temper softened, and I gave a small nod. I will never send that man away, but I was done having these two down here with me.

"Henry, take the girls back to the tower," I said quietly. "They're done tonight."

Bay blinked in surprise. Her beautiful blue eyes looked into mine, and it was all I could do not to lean down and kiss her. My tiger grated against my skin, but I held him back. Now was not the time, and I took a step back.

"I am sorry about the last meeting," I said to the two of them. "I did not know he was coming tonight."

Bay just watched me. I wondered what was going through that gorgeous mind of hers. Shanely wrapped her arms through Bay's and gave me a soft smile.

"Thank you, Abraham," she said as she pulled Bay down the steps. Henry slowly followed after the two as Darryl opened the door. His brow rose, but he said nothing as they passed.

"You ready for Frank?" he asked as I stared at the opened door. I gave him a soft nod, even though it was killing me to stay here and work. My body rippled in pain as I kept my feet grounded on the dais.

"Abraham, my boy!" Frank's deep voice sounded as he walked into the room. I pulled myself from the wolf who captured all my attention to the older man walking my way.

I gave him a genuine smile before clasping my arms around him.

"It's good to see you, Frank!" I said with a half smile. "Tell me, how are things going?"

He shrugged. "Can't complain. I brought my payment."

Frank reached inside his pocket and handed me a check. I sighed. "I wish you'd just let me wipe the debt clean. It's not even a debt to me."

He waved a hand at me. "We're not having this discussion again, my boy. You want to tell me what's bothering you though?"

My brows furrowed, earning a laugh from the old man.

"I've been around you long enough, Abe," he said, grinning. "Who's the lucky girl?"

I scoffed, turning from him and plopping down on the throne. "Who's to say it's any girl? Maybe it's just the absolute nonsense I find myself in every day."

Frank's brow rose. "You are the one who put yourself in this life, and don't for a second think you can lie your way out of this. Besides Henry told me as he escorted two beautiful young ladies up the stairs. Is that really the only clothes you could find them in this big ole castle?"

My cheeks heated. Frank stood before me with a wicked little grin, knowing full well he had me.

"You tattled?!"

"I'm not a man of many words. Someone needs to guide you here, and it can't be me," Henry said through the link. *"Darryl and I agree. You need help, Abe. Because this isn't working."*

I rolled my eyes, and Frank laughed harder.

"Oh, don't yell at them," he said, still grinning. "They mean the best."

I groaned, covering my face with my hands as I slid further into my chair. "Fine. I think one of them is my mate. Happy now?"

I braved a peek as Frank laughed again. "Which one? The red head or dark and kinky?"

I snorted. *Might be the perfect nickname for her*, I thought to myself. I sat up and leaned on my knees. "Dark and kinky. Red-head's taken already."

Frank nodded slowly and crossed his arms. "So what's the big deal?"

I gave him a pointed look. "You and I both know what it takes for my tiger to know for sure, and she hates me."

He shrugged. "So?"

I narrowed my eyes. "So every time I try to get to know this girl, she brushes me off. And I won't just run up to kiss her and hope to God I'm right."

"Well why's she down here dressed like that?" he asked, and heat filled my cheeks once more. "I doubt that girl's interested in these little deals of yours."

I sighed. "Well... no. We're sort of in a deal with each other already."

Frank snorted. "Seriously? Are they both..."

"Yes," I interrupted, "both of them for two different things, alright?"

Frank stared long and hard at me. Long enough to make me squirm in my seat, and I stood to move out of his gaze.

"So you're telling me, the first time you've ever so much as looked at a girl, you decide to show off your *unique* business?" he asked, and my shoulders fell. He shook his head. "Abe, you and I both know you have so much to offer, but this whole tough guy *Kingly* persona you've adopted... It's not the way to win this girl's heart."

I slowly looked back to him. "It's all I know, Frank. I have nothing left."

Frank walked the dais towards me. He placed his calloused hand on my shoulder saying, "You and I both know that's not true. Your father always said you were marked with greatness, and he was right. Show this girl the *real* you. You'd be surprised how far you'll go once you do."

I pursed my lips together as I thought about what he said. My stomach rolled at the thought of even softening this hardened exterior just a little, but Henry's words came to mind.

"*You softened with her. We all saw it, Abe. You're handling things differently than you ever would have with these girls.*"

Frank clasped me on my back, pulling me back to reality. "I have to head home, but it was great to see you again, kiddo. Same time next month?"

My mouth rose to a smile ,and I gave him a nod. "Same time. Unless you're ready to let me cancel the debt?"

Frank waved goodbye as he sauntered down the isle. "Absolutely not! I'll honor my debt until my dying breath, thank you very much!"

I chuckled to myself as the crotchety old man left. I plopped down on my throne again and stared up at the ceiling. *Maybe I could show Bay a different side, and maybe she'll love me flaws and all.* My mother loved my dad despite his flaws. Maybe, *just maybe,* I could find someone to love me *for me.* Bloodshed and all.

The door creaked open again, and Darryl stuck his head in. "Got another, boss. You ready?"

The corners of my mouth rose.

"Yeah," I replied quietly. "Yeah, I am."

About the Author

M. L. White is a Fantasy, Romance writer who is obsessed with wolf shifters and all things fantasy or dragon related. She loves to read and actively seeks out books that suck her in and make her feel like their world is better than reality, so she is determined to spread that same joy to others with her writing. Her books are like movies in your head with characters you can't help but fall in love with.

When M. L. White is not writing, she's chasing after her three children and taking care of her wonderful husband. They're her whole world so she's pretty busy spending as much time with them as possible. You can find her walking the trails with her two dogs or gaming with her husband and son in her free time as well!

You can connect with me on:
- https://www.authormlwhite.com
- https://x.com/Author_MLWhite
- https://www.instagram.com/author_mlwhite
- https://www.tiktok.com/@author_mlwhite

Subscribe to my newsletter:
- https://dashboard.mailerlite.com/forms/1169872/137001126070322601/share

www.ingramcontent.com/pod-product-compliance
Lightning Source LLC
LaVergne TN
LVHW091714070526
838199LV00050B/2393